TITLE   Untied kingdom

UNTIED
KINGDOM

Also by James Lovegrove:

Novels
The Hope
Escardy Gap (co-written with Peter Crowther)
Days
The Foreigners

Novella
How the Other Half Lives

Short Fiction
Imagined Slights

For Children
The Web: Computopia
Wings

UNTIED KINGDOM

James Lovegrove

GOLLANCZ

LONDON

Copyright © James Lovegrove 2003

The right of James Lovegrove to be identified as the
author of this work has been asserted by him in accordance
with the Copyright, Designs and Patents Act 1988.

First published in Great Britain in 2003 by

Gollancz
An imprint of the Orion Publishing Group
Orion House, 5 Upper St Martin's Lane,
London WC2H 9EA

A CIP catalogue record for this book
is available from the British Library

ISBN 0 575 07385 3 (cased)
ISBN 0 575 07386 1 (trade paperback)

Typeset at The Spartan Press Ltd,
Lymington, Hants

Printed in Great Britain by
Clays Ltd, St Ives plc

This book is dedicated to my sisters
Philippa and Kate
(because they'll kill me if it isn't)

CONTENTS

1. DOWNBOURNE

'Sir? Mr Morris?'

'Yes, Clive?'

'Sir, did you hear that?'

'Hear what?'

'I'm sure it was a motor.'

Fen listened, and heard nothing but the arrhythmic tick and buzz of bluebottles throwing themselves against the classroom's only closed window. Six other windows wide open, liberty readily available, yet this particular batch of flies was too stupid, or too lazy, or too intent on suicide, to realise. He continued to listen, making a show of it now, head cocked, hand cupping ear. Nothing.

'Can't hear a thing, Clive,' he said.

'But sir . . .'

'Get on with your reading, Clive.'

The rest of the class, the brief distraction over, bent their heads again, returning their attention to the books in front of them. Clive looked as if he was about to insist that his teacher was wrong, then decided against it and bent his head, too. He was reading a hardback copy of *The Red Badge of Courage* which, as with every book from the school library, was battered and dog-eared and life supported by a few brittle, browned snippets of scotch tape.

Reading hour. The final hour of the school day, when Fen's pupils, crammed to the brim with learning, could relax a little, and so could he. From his table at the head of the classroom he cast an eye over the boys and girls, each of whom was concentrating with an intensity of frown in inverse proportion to his or her age. The room was silent again, or at any rate there were just the background noises that signified all systems normal: the shuffles and snuffles, the dry turn of pages, a cough here, a scratch of an itch there, and of course the bluebottles, still battering their heads against the panes. They had been at it since morning, and had developed a kind of rota, so that whenever one knocked itself insensible and tumbled to the sill, another rose to take its place,

attacking the window in a frenzy until it, too, was stunned – glazed!
– and sank to the sill, unable to continue.

The hush was, to Fen, contented. It spoke to him of work done,
another day finishing, a satisfying sense of things being rolled up
and put away. He glanced at his watch. Ten minutes to go. Leaning
back in his chair, he listened again for the motor Clive had thought
he heard. From outside came the thrum of a blazing hot afternoon,
insects and birds and the ruffle of a breeze through summer-cured
leaves. The one remaining swing in the school playground (the
other had had to be dismantled after its plastic seat developed a
dangerous split) was swaying almost imperceptibly back and forth,
its chains emitting tiny, mouse-like squeaks. A collared dove hooted
the same three notes over and over and over. Far off, the lazy bleat
of sheep.

No motor. Clive had been mistaken. But then the boy was only
eleven. An eleven-year-old born and brought up in a town like
Downbourne had probably heard a motor, what, a dozen times in
his lifetime? If that.

It had just been the flies, that was all. The buzzing of the foolish
kamikaze bluebottles, trapped behind the one window that was
stuck fast in its frame, impossible to open.

The idiot flies.

Class was dismissed punctually at three-thirty. The books were piled up on Fen's table, and then his pupils were out, away, free, gone. Fen realigned desks and wiped the blackboard clean with a rag. Proper chalk was hard to come by, so he was obliged to use the raw stuff, rugged lumps of it harvested from the downland soil. The marks they made were greasy and indistinct, only just legible, but at least (a small compensation) they could be erased with minimal effort. A flip of the rag, and that morning's maths test – basic geometry questions for the younger portion of the class, trigonometry posers for the older – vanished.

When the classroom was tidy, Fen closed all the windows, then stooped to pick up the folded mouse mat that he used to wedge open the door and create a through-draught. He tossed the mouse mat over on to the pile of computer hardware which sat, haphazardly stacked, in one corner of the room. It amused Fen to think how all this equipment – costing several thousand pounds when new, monitors and hard drives and keyboards and peripherals – now lay in a heap, gathering dust, cream-coloured housing going yellow in the sun. It amused him, too, in a mildly astonished way, that his pupils could barely comprehend what these devices were for, what they used to be capable of. In a short space of time, a startlingly short space of time, computers had gone from technological be-all and end-all to hunks of redundant, inoperable junk. To a whole generation, the concept of deriving information and entertainment and a sense of connectedness from them now seemed bizarre, even implausible. Likewise television. Some of the kids, the older ones, thirteen and up, could remember watching broadcasts, back when the electricity worked, back when TV stations transmitted. Some of them could even remember watching programmes that weren't government public-information bulletins or street-riot reportage. For the younger ones, though, the big glass-fronted box that still occupied a corner in most living rooms and lounges was just an inert object, an item of furniture of considerably less practical significance than a table or a bookcase. They had never watched images dance across its screen, never been captivated by its firelight thrall; they had no idea of the reverence in which this defunct household god had once been held.

Fen strode along the corridor that led to the school's main entrance, his footsteps echoing through the empty building. The school was two storeys tall, blocky and utilitarian. Built in the early nineteen-sixties, its facilities were designed for a student body of about two hundred, a staff faculty of about twenty. A decent-sized local school, in other words. So it housed hollowly, like a dried kernel with a few seeds rattling inside it, its one class of seventeen and its solitary teacher.

Emerging into sunshine, Fen squinted, loosened his shirt collar, and set off for home.

Moira glances at the kitchen clock and thinks, he'll just be leaving now.

Within minutes, the walking had brought him out in a sweat. He had been perspiring throughout the day, stickiness accumulating at his armpits and crotch, but this was different; this was good sweat, the sweat of activity, a cooling release, profuse and welcome. Opting for one of the more circuitous routes home, Fen made his way down to the river and followed the towpath, passing first a meadowy football pitch where a few horses were contentedly browsing inside a hazel-fenced enclosure, then the backs of the units of the town's business estate, empty aluminium-sided shells where the only industry now was the web-spinning of spiders and the scavenging scurry of mice. Soon he arrived at a footbridge, a cantilevered arc of concrete and steel whose shadow lay pristine on the river's chocolate-milk surface.

Reginald Bailey was, as ever, stationed at the bridge's midpoint, a human keystone. Bent-backed, the old widower leaned on the railing, clutching his fishing rod and staring down at the float on the end of his line and the tiny ripples that trailed from it in a chevron pattern.

'Any luck?'

Reginald raised a hoary eyebrow. 'Afternoon, schoolteacher. No, not yet.'

'Oh well. Still worth a try, eh?'

Reginald nodded, and for the umpteenth time Fen wondered whether the old fellow knew, as everyone else did, that the river ran rich with heavy metals and other pollutants and had not played host to a living fish in years. He must do. Yet every day, without fail, Reginald trooped down to the footbridge, cast his line into the water and stood for hours, patiently waiting for a bite. Hope? Madness? Maybe a little of both.

Moira fills the kettle from the rainwater butt and lights the hob, thinking her husband ought to have a nice cup of tea waiting for him when he gets home.

Past the bridge lay a small public park that was kept in shape by a group of dedicated volunteers who regularly clipped and sickled its bushes and shrubbery, and also by a troupe of tethered goats which happily discharged the responsibility of keeping the grass trimmed, their work taking the form of overlapping circles that were nibbled to a neatness any bowling-green groundsman would have been proud of. Children often played a game here in which they would tiptoe through the unkempt passages between the circles, daring the goats to butt them. This was not happening today, however, and that was just as well, since the game was not approved of. Fen would have been obliged to tick the participants off, and he didn't like being the teacher outside as well as in the school.

Beyond the park was a patch of waste ground, through which ran a footpath worn by countless shoe soles, meandering among clumps of brambles taller than a man, clusters of stinging nettles that sprang even higher, great airy clouds of cow parsley, purple-taloned profusions of buddleia. Here and there, embedded amid the greenery, could be glimpsed items of domestic detritus: a porcelain lavatory minus its lid, a rusted bicycle wheel, a refrigerator, an anglepoise lamp, a stereo speaker, all so surrounded and inter-penetrated by shoots and stems that to retrieve any of them, should anyone have been overcome by the inexplicable urge to do so, would have entailed a good half-hour's work with machete and secateurs.

Undergrowth rustlings attended Fen's progress through the waste ground, for a colony of feral cats had made this spot their home. They skittered away as he approached. Now and then he glimpsed a pair of eyes glowing amid the plant shadows; more often, a flash of rear paws and tail as a cat darted for deeper cover.

The footpath eventually disgorged him onto Hill Street, which, true to its name, climbed a steep slope, with a staggered parade of terraced Victorian houses on either side. Several of the houses were empty, but it was difficult to tell from appearances alone those that were from those that were not. Front doors stood ajar, window-panes were broken, roof-tiles had slipped, paintwork had peeled,·

guttering sagged on occupied and unoccupied premises alike. All along the kerbside, cars rested on prolapsed tyres, their bodywork rust-riddled, their chrome trim dulled, their windows opaque with dust. They looked as purposeless as people queuing for an event which no one had told them had been cancelled.

To escape the sun, most of the residents of Hill Street were indoors, but, outside one of the better-maintained houses, Fen came across little Holly-Anne Greeley. He said hello, and Holly-Anne solemnly enquired whether he would like to join in her game. She was sitting with dolls spread out in a circle on the pavement in front of her, an assortment of smooth pink plastic humanoids, all of them unclothed and many of them missing at least one limb, in a couple of cases their heads. Tiny twelve-inch amputee women in round-table conversation with decapitated monster babies. Fen shook his head and said no thanks, maybe another time. Holly-Anne sniffed and rubbed her dirt-smudged nose and said OK, never mind.

'Are you looking forward to coming to school?' Fen asked. 'We're looking forward to having you join us.'

Holly-Anne nodded vaguely. Just turned six, she was due to enrol as his pupil in the autumn. Her father, Alan Greeley, was a skilled handyman, able to mend almost anything around the home. He was also a Mr Fix-It when it came to obtaining hard-to-get supplies, and the promise of repairs whenever they were needed at the Morris household, plus a couple of butane cylinders for the stove, had seemed to both him and Fen a fair price in return for a year's worth of education for his daughter.

Inside the house, an infant began to cry.

'That's my little brother,' Holly-Anne explained.

'I know,' said Fen. 'Nathan.'

'He's noisy,' Holly-Anne said, with a very adult sigh.

'Little brothers always are,' said Fen.

Moira goes to the back door and calls into the garden: 'Come on in and get washed. Your father'll be home any time soon.'

At the summit of Hill Street, most of Downbourne came into view. Lichen-speckled roofs spread to the east, south and west, a mile in each direction, shelving away to the town's outskirts. From there the houses continued out along the approach roads, spaced further apart the further from town they were. Five miles away, blurred by the hazy air, lay a ridge of hills, a great rumpled chalk undulation running parallel to the one on which Downbourne rested. It was possible to make out what remained of a figure etched into the distant hillside, the nameless giant who had presided

8

over the valley since pre-Norman times, calmly observing Down-bourne's evolution from peasant collective to market town to Home Counties backwater to whatever it was these days – perhaps a large peasant collective again. All that was left of the figure's white outline were the stumps of its legs. The rest was a deep ragged gouge, courtesy of an International Community fighter pilot who had taken it upon himself to obliterate the giant with an air-to-ground missile, either mistaking it for a legitimate target or, more likely, out of a savage (if strategically unsound) sense of fun.

Fen headed downhill on Monks Avenue, famed as Downbourne's most sought-after address, a sycamore-lined haven of detached des-res gentility. Or at least, it had been, before its residents abandoned it, moving abroad to live in holiday homes or with relatives, or bribing their way to political asylum in Canada and New Zealand, part of the national exodus of the well-heeled. The big houses were now in decay. Their front gardens had welled up, thick and rank, and brimmed over their boundary walls, inter-tangling, uniting. Driveways where people carriers and latest-model saloons had once proudly stood were scribbled over by ivy and bindweed. Where there had been spreads of striped lawn, daisies and summer celandine ran rampant. The sycamores themselves, untrimmed, had grown exultantly profuse, and formed a tunnel over the roadway. Pavements were verges.

The end of Monks Avenue intersected with Harvill Drive, which, if Fen had turned left, would have taken him to the town centre. As he neared the junction he heard the ringing clip-clop of horses' hooves on tarmac. Three horses, he guessed, judging by the pattern and cadence of iron-shod strikes; and sure enough, as he rounded the corner, turning right, he was confronted with a trio of riders coming towards him at a gentle amble.

Two of the three riders were dressed in ordinary outdoor gear – jeans, checked shirts, hiking boots – and looked less than comfort-able on their mounts, clutching the reins too tightly and sitting tense, as if expecting to be unsaddled at any moment (though the horses beneath them seemed placid, nodding creatures, too docile even to think about bucking). They looked like people who would have much preferred to be at desks, signing documents and making phone calls, rather than patrolling through town on horseback. Their names were Henry Mullins and Susannah Vicks, and they were both prominent members of Downbourne's town council.

The third rider, who was perched astride a magnificent dappled-grey steed, cut an altogether more imposing figure. He had a vast,

9

bushy growth of beard and deep-set, piercing blue eyes, and he sat tall in his saddle, head high, shoulders relaxed, arms exerting just enough pressure to keep the reins taut, no more. The most striking thing about him, however – striking even to someone like Fen who was well acquainted with the man – was that he was, from top to toe, green. Not only was his clothing green (green canvas gilet, green shirt, green corduroy trousers, green wellingtons) but his skin was green, too, and every visible strand of his hair, so that from the shoulders up he was more hedge than head. He was an emerald emir, a vision of virescence, startling and majestic, and as he drew alongside Fen he brought his horse to a halt and acknowledged Fen with a brief, stately nod.

'Mr Morris, good afternoon,' he said, while his two colleagues pulled up, with some awkwardness, beside him.

'Afternoon, mayor,' said Fen. 'Lovely day.'

'Mother Nature has once more blessed us,' the Green Man pronounced, with a glance at the cloudless heavens. 'And how are the flower of Downbourne's youth? I take it they have just benefited from another day of learning at the feet of our esteemed pedagogue.'

Fen had become practised at the art of hiding smirks in the Green Man's presence. 'One does what one can.'

'No need to be so modest, Mr Morris. Everybody knows what a fine job you do, training and guiding our young saplings so that they may grow into mighty oaks.'

'Perhaps I'd believe that if more people were prepared to send their children to me.'

The Green Man nodded and sighed. 'Alas, though I wish it were otherwise, not everyone has goods or a skill to offer in exchange for your services, and perhaps not everyone sees the need for a traditional education any more.'

Fen gave a shrug, as if to say he was only too aware of this sad fact. In truth, he would not have been able to cope with more than perhaps a half-dozen extra pupils. A class size greater than twenty would be hard to handle, for above a certain number children achieve a sort of critical mass and become wilful and unruly, beyond the power of a single adult to control. Fen had raised the subject simply so as to demonstrate that he was a good and loyal member of the community, keen to do his bit. That sort of attitude pleased the Green Man, and there was something about the Green Man that made you want to see him pleased.

The Green Man pointed to his two-person entourage. 'We're on our way to see how preparations for the festival are coming along,' he said. 'I expect we shall see you there this evening?' It was only partly a question.

'You shall.'

'And your lovely wife, of course.'

'If she can make it.'

'Excellent.' The Green Man lofted a hand in a farewell salute, then, with a cluck of his tongue, urged his horse into motion. His sidekicks followed suit, albeit with more trouble, yanking on their reins and digging their heels in several times before their horses at last – possibly just because they felt like it – got going.

Fen watched them trot away, this queer little procession of three, then turned and resumed his journey along Harvill Drive.

Water splashing in a bowl; a bit of rubbing to remove a patch of really ingrained dirt; protests as a rogue lock of hair is wetted and smoothed into place; then everyone is clean and smart and ready, and the kettle is just starting to whistle.

Ducking down a narrow cut-through between two houses, Fen walked the length of their back gardens, towering leylandii on one side of him, a half-collapsed slat fence on the other. He crossed a back alley, passed between two more gardens, two more houses, and finally emerged onto Crane Street.

Seven doors down on his right lay his destination, number 12.

He did not deliberately slow his pace as he neared home. All the same he was conscious of his stride shortening, his legs seeming to grow heavier, every step becoming incrementally more difficult to take than its predecessor, until, for the final few yards to his front gate, he was all but trudging. A weary kind of anticipation balled in the pit of his stomach as he undid the latch and swung the gate open. He hated the feeling. More, he hated himself for feeling it.

He went up the path. He grasped the handle of the front door. He turned the handle and pushed the door inwards. He entered.

Silence in the house. A silence heightened by the ticking of the hallway clock, counting out the half-seconds like a time bomb.

He listened hard and discerned a soft snoring coming from upstairs. He crossed the hallway and entered the kitchen. The kettle sat on the hob, stone-cold. He took the plastic washing-up bowl from the sink and went out into the garden to fill it to the depth of an inch from the rainwater butt. Indoors again, he removed his shirt and washed himself, dousing his face and torso with the sun-warmed water, then using a sparing amount of soap – some strongly-scented French brand – to clean his armpits and neck.

He rinsed himself off, went outside and poured the soapy water over his onions. He stood for a while in the garden, relishing the prickling sensation of coolness as his skin dried. Just a few feet away from him a fearless blue tit foraged in his herb bed for grubs. Next door, the neighbour's chickens clucked and flustered in their run.

Back in the house again, Fen heard movement upstairs, a crunch of bedsprings. The act of washing had been his way of informing Moira, quietly, that he was home. Turning over in bed was her way of letting him know she had heard and was awake.

Pulling his shirt back on, he went up to see her.

The bedroom was hot and stuffy, and filled with the rich stench of shit. Moira had used the chamberpot and not emptied it out.

She was lying beneath a single sheet, wearing just a grey T-shirt. Her long auburn hair was clumpy and dishevelled, stray tendrils of it adhering to her forehead. Her face was doughy from sleep. She peered up at Fen, blinking as though he were the source of a bright light. Her voice was a croak:

'What time is it?'

'Gone four.'

'Fuck.'

'How long have you been asleep?'

'How should I know?'

'I only asked.'

'Since midday, maybe.'

'Are you hungry?'

'I don't know.'

'I could make us something to eat.'

'I don't know if I want anything.'

'We've still a couple of eggs left. We should use them. I think they're near their best-by.'

'Don't feel like eggs.'

'OK. Something else then.'

'Look, if you want to eat, go right ahead. I can't be bothered.'

'Well, all right. You have a think about it. I'll be back in a mo.'

Fen picked up the chamberpot, which was draped with a tea towel, and carried it downstairs to the garden. There, carefully and at arm's length, he tipped the contents out over the roots of the runner beans that were growing along the rear wall, then folded the earth over with a trowel, soil over soil. He rinsed out the pot with a trickle of rainwater and took it back upstairs.

Moira was sitting on the edge of the bed, hands on knees, arms straight, collecting her thoughts. Her T-shirt had ridden up around her waist, exposing a delta shape of ginger curls that bushed out over the cleft where her thighs joined. Fen's gaze was reflexively drawn to this, but his interest, once attracted, was more clinical than anything, as though he were a trichologist and the density and texture of Moira's pubic hair conveyed all manner of scientific information. If the sight stirred any sexual excitement in him, it was only the faintest of frissons, a vestigial response to a stimulus that had long since ceased to have any meaningful effect.

He checked himself, averting his eyes. If Moira caught him staring, it might be an excuse to have a go at him. Not that she always needed an excuse.

Setting the chamberpot down next to the bed, he went to open the window.

'Bumped into the Green Man just now,' he said, wrestling with the window's stiff upper sash.

Moira gave a snort.

'What?' he asked, glancing round.

' "The Green Man",' she said. 'His name is Michael Hollingbury. Why not call him that?'

'Because he wants to be known as the Green Man.'

'Is that what you call him to his face?'

'I don't call him anything to his face. Except "mayor".'

'But whenever you talk about him you refer to him as the Green Man.'

'Because that's how he wants to be known.'

The sash finally budged, and fresh air drifted into the room.

'But don't you see,' Moira said, 'it only encourages him.'

'Encourages him?'

'To be a deluded prat. The man is a dairy farmer called Michael Hollingbury who dresses up in green and dyes his skin and hair green with vegetable dye and make-believes that he's some mythical figure from English folklore, just like all those idiots up in Notting-ham who go around saying they're the reincarnations of Robin Hood, and that fellow who thinks he's King Arthur, the one down in Cornwall.'

Nowadays it was known as St Piran's Peninsula, but Fen did not correct her. Moira was clearly not interested in accuracy just at this moment.

'And?' he said.

'Well, they're all just stupid sad-arses and they shouldn't be encouraged!'

He took a deep breath. As pretexts for an argument went, it was not one of Moira's better, or for that matter more original, efforts.

He kept his voice even, remaining reasonable. 'Say what you like, Moira, but they do a lot of good. King Arthur. The Robin Hoods, however many of them there are. That Lob fellow in Oxfordshire. Herne the Hunter over in Kent. Lady Godiva in Coventry. What's-her-name up near Leeds, Queen Mab. Them and all the others. They've kept communities together, given people something to gather around, a rallying point. I admit it's a bit hokey, what they do. The costumes, the folklore aspect of it. A bit daft.'

'A *bit*!'

'But without them, certain areas of this country would be in a lot worse shape than they are. Including Downbourne, probably.'

'Oh yes. Let's let a bunch of nutters lead us. Let's put the posturing loony show-offs in charge.'

Fen gave vent to a rounded, cynical laugh. 'Well, isn't that what we've always done? Anyhow, look – I'm really not in the mood for a fight.'

'You never are,' Moira muttered.

He ignored the comment. Adopting a tone of for-your-information formality, he said, 'I'm going downstairs to make something to eat, then I'm going outside to do a spot of work in the garden, then I'm off to the festival, which you may recall is on this evening. If you wish to join me in any of these activities, you're welcome to do so. If not, that's fine too.'

Judging this a neat line to exit on, he made for the door. But Moira, as was so often the case, had to have the last word.

'You just don't care any more, do you?' she said, not with rancour, but tiredly, dispiritedly.

Fen shrugged. He could have answered back, made some comment such as *perhaps if you gave me a reason to care*, but in the event he merely held his tongue and left the room, easing the door shut behind him.

Hammer in hand, a one-inch nail sticking out from the corner of his mouth, Fen stepped back to inspect the repair. The fruit cage looked secure again. Sometime during the day, birds – blackbirds most likely; they were devious buggers, blackbirds – had unpicked one corner of the nylon net curtain that served as a mesh, tugging it away from the frame to create an opening. He reckoned the gang of thieves could not have numbered more than three, because the blackcurrant and raspberry bushes inside the cage hadn't suffered too severely from their depredations. The raiders had eaten their fill, then flown the scene of the crime, and luckily no other members of their species had taken advantage of the opportunity that they had provided. The damage, he gratefully acknowledged, could have been much worse.

He was proud of the fruit cage. He was proud of all his horticultural structures: the fruit cage, the arrangement of canes that supported the runner beans, the cloches he had created out of old mullioned windows, the piano-wire trellises along which he had trained apple and pear trees, the tunnels he had fabricated from bin-liners and straightened coat-hangers to cover his rows of root vegetables. He had never thought of himself as an especially practical person, and so had been pleased and surprised to discover, when put to it, an aptitude for improvised garden engineering. That wasn't to say that the skills had come easily to him. Each project in the garden was the end-product of a lot of sweat and fuss, a significant amount of trial and error, and a great deal of swearing. Nevertheless he had put these contraptions together himself, with his own hands, with little advice or assistance from anyone else, and, rickety though some of them were, they worked. He had learned the basics of produce-growing, too – crop rotation, not putting onions close to peas, things like that – so that now, through knowledge and constant ministration, he and Moira had fresh food to eat and, in times of abundance, exchange for other goods at the weekly town market. By the standards of others this might be considered a minor achievement, but for Fen it was a triumph.

Satisfied with his repair work, he thrust his hammer handle-first into a loop of his belt, like a knight sheathing his sword after the battle is done, then spat the nail into his hand and pocketed it. As he glanced around the garden, wondering if there was anything else that needed to be fixed, he caught sight of Moira at the back door, watching him. She had pulled on a pair of shorts. Other than that, she was exactly as she had been in the bedroom: puffy-faced, somnolent, dishevelled. How long had she been standing there?

He waved to her jauntily, as though the sniping conversation of forty minutes ago had never taken place. 'Did you see the bowl on the sideboard? Spanish omelette mix. I've used half for myself. You can use the rest, if you want it. Very tasty.'

Moira nodded noncommittally.

'I'm pretty much done here,' he continued. 'I just need to change my shirt, then it's off down to the festival. Maybe you'll come along too? When you've eaten?'

She fixed him with a look of such spite then, such withering contempt, that had he felt more for her than he did – had there remained any love for her in him beyond a hard-baked residue, the indelible patina left behind by a dozen years of coexistence – he would have been crushed. As it was, the look inspired only weariness. Just for a change, it would be nice to receive a kind word from her, an expression of gratitude however token, a brief acknowledgement of the efforts he made on her behalf, the many things he did for her. Was that really too much to expect?

Probably, he thought. These days, probably.

He headed for the door, and Moira stepped back to allow him through.

'Thank you,' he said.

Had Fen known that this was the last time he would see his wife for a long while, might he have said something different? Might he have tried to fix an image in his head of how she looked in the kitchen? Taken a mental snapshot of her, retouching it so that she was not so unsmiling, not so sullen-eyed? Might he have made more of this parting moment, ceremonialised it with all the paraphernalia of taking leave, the speeches, the promises, the drawn-out goodbyes?

Perhaps.

And perhaps, even gifted with foreknowledge of what was to come, Fen would have said and done nothing more than he said and did: 'Thank you', and upstairs to find a fresh shirt, and downstairs again and out through the front door without another word, heading down the path and onto the street and, without a backward glance, starting to walk.

The front door closes and he's gone. All that's left is a faint lingering whiff of his BO from when he washed here earlier.

Maybe you'll come along too? When you've eaten?

Damn him. Damn him and all that I'm-so-thoughtful, I'm-so-fuck-ing-tolerant crap of his. Why can't he just be honest? Why can't he, just for once, come out and say what he really feels? Admit that he can't stand me? He won't even *argue* with me. If he had the guts to argue with me, stand up for himself, at least I'd feel an equal to him. I'd feel like a real person. But oh no, he can't do that. Instead, he's got to humour me. Treat me like a simpleton. A special case.

And it's not strength, being so patient and sensible and under-standing. It's not strength, it's weakness. An aggressive type of weakness. Weakness being used as a weapon.

Hard to believe that I used to like that about him. That I used to find it charming that Fen was so agreeable, so compliant all the time. Always so concerned about me, wanting to be sure I was happy.

Why doesn't he just leave me? At least then he'd be showing some spine.

But of course he couldn't do that, could he? He couldn't let the whole town know that we're a failure. So he insists on keeping the illusion going, letting everyone think it's all fine and wonderful with the Morrises . . . when of course everyone knows the illusion is bogus, everyone knows he's faking, everyone knows we *are* a failure.

Idiot.

Let's have a look in this bowl, then.

Looks like someone's thrown up in it.

I'm not hungry anyway.

But I suppose I shouldn't let it go to waste . . .

And once I smell the omelette frying, I realise I *am* hungry after all, very hungry, and when the omelette's ready I wolf the whole thing down in about three bites and I actually feel a little grateful to Fen.

Maybe I *should* go along to the stupid festival.

No. I don't have the energy to wander around all evening being nice to people, or pretending to be nice, which is what it'll have to be, and which is much harder work.

Then again, it'll be good to get out of the house for a bit. I'm sick of this place. And Fen won't be expecting me to turn up.

Yes, maybe I'll go, just to spite him.

Downbourne, like almost every other small provincial town, hadn't been able to evade the hawk-eyed aim of modern commerce. Back in the early nineteen-eighties it had been winged and bulls-eyed by that traditional two-shot attack, the out-of-town supermarket and the pedestrianised shopping precinct, a both-barrels blasting that few of the local retail businesses had survived. Those which the supermarket, part of a massive conglomerate chain, had failed to annihilate, the shopping precinct had comfortably finished off. The precinct had also had the effect of effacing the centre of town. With its mix-and-match selection of established brand-name outlets, it had rendered a segment of Downbourne's high street effectively anonymous. Standing in the middle of it, you could have been anywhere, in a shopping precinct in any one of countless towns.

That was then. Now was now. The supermarket had long ago closed its doors, rolled away its trolleys and decommissioned its petrol station with the enticing per-litre discount. A few cars, hollow wrecks, still occupied spaces in its car park, as though in anticipation of a grand reopening. Meanwhile, inside the building itself, rats roamed the aisles, hunting for morsels, while pigeons made their nests on the steel ceiling joists and Jackson Pollocked the empty refrigerators and bare shelves with their droppings.

The shopping precinct, likewise, lay abandoned. Gone were the travel bureau, the stationer-cum-newsagent, the fashion boutique, the off-licence, the chemist, the record shop, the electrical-goods store, the choose-from-catalogue emporium. Gone, leaving only empty premises and logo-flagged façades behind.

The precinct, however, had not fallen completely into disuse, since its brick-paved broadway was where Downbourne's residents gathered once a week for market, once a month for town meetings (weather permitting – in town hall if wet), and once a season for festival.

Of the four annual festivals, the summer one was always the best attended, for the obvious reasons – longer evening, warmer weather. Not only townsfolk came but inhabitants of the outlying villages too, trooping in on foot, on horseback or by bicycle to join in the celebrations. What was actually being celebrated remained something of a mystery. Each of the other three festivals was more-or-less related to a specific calendar event: spring to the vernal equinox, autumn to the harvest, winter to Christmas. Summer was problematic, unless you considered the season itself a cause for rejoicing, as many did. Others regarded the lack of clear *raison d'être* for the summer festival as the best *raison d'être* possible, for what better excuse to be frivolous and have a good time than no excuse at all? For many, too, the absence of celestial, agricultural or religious significance was a kind of statement. It symbolised freedom from tradition, from convention, and therefore a rejection of the past and of a culture which, arguably, could be blamed for England's present parlous state.

Such were the rationalisations, but once the drink was flowing and the music was playing and the dancing got under way, people generally forgot why they were at the festival and simply enjoyed being there.

Approaching the precinct from the direction of the war memorial, Fen heard a drumbeat first, then tinkling music to accompany that drumbeat, then the sound of voices. He had joined a loose-knit, slow-going flow of people, all converging on the same destination. With nods and smiles and innocuous friendly comments, they acknowledged one another. Most were carrying bottles, some whole boxfuls of them, along with china mugs, tin cups, plastic beakers. The bottles contained home-brewed beers, wines and spirits – concoctions that Fen knew from experience could be potent in the extreme. There were seldom any identifying labels on them, so if you were not careful you could find yourself drinking a moonshine strong enough to power a moon-rocket, a gin that was a fatal trap to the unwary, a dandelion wine that could blow you away, a near-homicidal cider. More hazardous yet, you could find yourself mixing your drinks and turning your stomach into the vessel for an uncontrolled experiment in organic chemistry. Getting generously sozzled was all part of the fun of the festival, of course, but Fen had reached the age when the costs of inebriation now far outweighed the pleasures. A hangover was no longer something he could laugh off, the way he used to in his twenties. A hangover was a debilitating, head-clenching nightmare that could lay him out flat for an entire day, and consequently a thing to be avoided if at all possible. He promised himself there and then, as he turned a corner onto the high street and the precinct came into view, that this evening he would exercise moderation. He knew, however, that it was a promise he might not necessarily be able to keep. Where alcohol was concerned, circumstances had a way of hijacking good intentions. And given the situation at home, if he *were* to get totally plastered – well, who could blame him?

There were perhaps a hundred and fifty people already in the precinct, milling about beneath the lines of tattered bunting strung between the eaves of the shop buildings. Torches – short shafts of wood with tar-soaked rags wrapped around one end – had been fixed to every lamp-post. Their illumination would not be required for another four hours at least. On a podium of trestle tables sat the band: flautist, trumpeter, violinist, accordionist, and drummer with three-piece kit. They were bashing out a jazzed-up version of 'Widecombe Fair', each instrument taking it in turns to carry the melody while the others improvised.

Fen moved among the revellers. Since it was still early and there were children present, the mood was good-natured rather than, as it was bound to become later, boisterous. A man in a home-made jester's outfit was juggling three beanbags, now four, now five, for the entertainment of a gaggle of under-tens. Another group of children, teenagers, watched from several yards off, vaguely scornful of the junior group's rapt fascination but also not unimpressed by the juggler's feats. Someone was making bespoke origami animals out of old magazine pages, demonstrating each twist and fold to a mixed-age audience who did their best to follow suit, and in a corner well away from the band a husband-and-wife team of puppeteers had set up a stage and, masked by a screen of bedsheets, were manipulating papier-mâché marionettes to tell the story of Beauty and the Beast. Meanwhile, the bottles and drinking vessels that people were bringing were being collected and stowed behind the counter of the erstwhile off-licence for later distribution.

At the far end of the precinct, a bonfire-to-be – a tall, teetering mound of wood, like the ruins of a collapsed cathedral – arose from an area of paving that bore the scorch-marks of numerous previous conflagrations. Good-quality firewood was a precious commodity, so for each festival the bonfire builders scavenged the area for the kinds of combustible material that would not fit or burn cleanly in a living-room hearth: big unwieldy chunks of plywood and chip-board, sections of painted timber, with the odd tractor tyre, chair cushion and foam mattress thrown in for good measure. This generated an impressive blaze but also, invariably, an acrid smoke which, if the wind was unfavourable, had been known to bring the festival to an abrupt, choking halt. Tonight, Fen reckoned, they would be spared that. Such breeze as there was, was blowing along the precinct towards the bonfire. The smoke would carry towards the river, most likely staying well above the rooftops.

'Fen!'

It was Alan Greeley, Holly-Anne's father. He and Fen shook hands, Greeley grinning. He was a short, thickset man with an almost cubic head and an air of unfettered geniality about him that made him impossible to dislike. He used this to his advantage when striking deals. Even though, as a customer of Greeley's, you always suspected he was getting the better end of the bargain, somehow you didn't mind. It seemed somehow right and proper that he should profit at your expense, as if there existed an unofficial surcharge for niceness.

'Holly-Anne says she talked to you today. "The Lesson Man", as she calls you.'

'That's me. She wanted me to play dollies with her.'

'The dullest game on the planet. They just sit there and have long conversations about the most boring shite you can think of. It's an obligation for parents only. No one else should be expected to endure it.'

'At least she's using her imagination. Mind you, kids don't really have a choice these days, do they? It's imagination or nothing. Anyway, I politely declined.'

'Good on you. You should have called in, though.'

'I was a bit tired. Wanted to get home. Andrea here?'

Greeley shook his head. 'Nathan's teething and we thought it better not to bring him out.'

'What about Holly-Anne?'

'Over there.'

Holly-Anne was in the puppeteers' audience, sitting cross-legged and watching the show with open-mouthed concentration.

Greeley cast a quick glance over Fen's shoulder. 'Moira manage to make it?' He phrased the question airily – *just a casual enquiry, nothing meant by it.*

'I don't think she's up to it today.'

'Not well?'

'A bit tired. You know.'

'Ah. Shame.' Greeley leaned closer. 'Listen, Fen . . .'

Fen sensed a sales pitch coming.

'I've just been "down to the coast", if you know what I mean.

Took my cart, did my usual human dray-horse impression, picked up a few nice little items. Toiletry essentials, that sort of thing. I don't suppose you'd be interested in having a look? Priority customer. Ahead of the pack.'

'I might. We are a little low on lavatory paper right now.'

'Been a while since the last International Community leaflet drop, hasn't it?'

Fen laughed. ' "Now is the time for a concerted effort to overthrow the government at Westminster." It's hard to decide if they're really that ignorant about the situation here or they just have a finely developed sense of irony.'

'Still, good absorbency, eh?'

'If only.'

'Well, my cross-Channel chums have provided the answer to your prayers.'

'*Vive* the Dunkirk spirit.'

'Come round and see me tomorrow, and we'll see what we can do for you.'

'Sure. OK.'

'Oh, and I'd recommend the damson gin in the Perrier bottles.'

'Yours, of course.'

'Of course.'

'Thanks.'

'Really, it's very good, even if I do say so myself.'

'I'll give it a try.'

Greeley trotted off to accost someone else – another potential customer, most likely – and Fen wondered with what he could barter for the lavatory paper tomorrow. Garden produce? He knew Greeley was well catered for on that front. Candles? Greeley was not short of them either. What about some AA-size batteries? Fen had been given a boxload of them as part-payment for teaching Bill and Janice Sayer's son Clive (he of this afternoon's imagined motor noise). He wasn't certain that all the batteries still worked – a couple of them had leaked their corrosive ichor – but those that did work were undoubtedly valuable. Many people used small portable radios to find out what was going on in the outside world, and also what was going on in their own country, by tuning into news broadcasts from Wales and Scotland. Those radios needed a power source. A couple of four-packs of batteries in exchange for a roll or two of lavatory paper – that would probably do it.

Now the band was performing some medieval-sounding piece, one of those plodding, repetitive hey-nonny-nonny numbers, which they were giving a reggae treatment, to surprisingly good effect. Parents and children were dancing in front of the podium, fathers jiggling toddlers on their shoulders, mothers and older offspring swaying from side to side, hand-in-hand, or clapping together. Watching this display of familial togetherness, Fen felt a sudden and unexpected pang. It was envy, but also it was an emotion far deeper, something closer to grief. He searched around, the emotion turning outwards, becoming resentful, demanding appeasement. He caught sight of Gilbert Cruikshank, sitting hunched on an upturned plastic milk crate, hands resting on the crook of his white-tipped walking stick, chin lodged on top of his hands.

Ah yes.

To look at him, you would have thought Cruikshank was soaking up the atmosphere, relishing the sounds of music and gaiety as they washed over him, deriving delight from the happiness of others. Anyone who knew him, however, would recognise the sneer in the old man's nutcracker smile, the irony with which he nodded along in time to the music. Misanthropic and all but blind, Cruikshank loathed this sort of occasion. He came, like a spectre at the feast, to jar with his presence. He came to silently mock.

'Mr Cruikshank?'

Cruikshank's head twitched. His cheeks and chin were a battlefield of shaving nicks and small patches of bristle his razor had missed. His nose was large and spongy, as only an old man's can be. 'Who's that? I know you.'

'It's—'

'Don't tell me who it is! It's Morris, isn't it? Our saintly Mr Chips.'

'How are you this evening?'

'My hip aches like hell and I have clouds of grey blobs floating in front of my eyes. Like you give a damn.'

'You seem to be having fun. It's a marvellous occasion, this, isn't it?'

'It's absolute sodding nonsense and you know it.'

'I like to think it brings everyone together. Like that line from Larkin: "something they share/That breaks ancestrally each year—" '

'Don't ruddy quote poetry at me!'

' "—into/Regenerate union." '

'I said don't ruddy quote poetry at me!' Cruikshank stabbed the air with an open hand, the gesture aimed in the general direction of the off-licence. 'Have they started dishing out the booze yet?'

'Not yet.'

'Pity. Otherwise you could have made yourself useful and gone and got me some.'

Now the resentment was riding high in Fen. He couldn't curb himself. His tone became breezier as he shifted up to a more piquant level of baiting.

'D'you know something, Mr Cruikshank?'

'What?'

'It puzzles me. Why you always come to the festivals when you so obviously dislike them.'

'Why not?'

'In fact, it puzzles me why you live in Downbourne at all.'

'What's got into you? What are you jabbering on about?'

'You with your London permit. If I had a London permit, I'd be off up there like a shot. Running water, cars, electricity – all mod cons.'

Cruikshank, who had so far kept his focusless gaze fixed straight ahead, now turned his head in Fen's direction, zeroing in on the sound of his voice.

'London's not all it's cracked up to be, Morris, believe me. They're supposed to have things sorted out there, but that's not true. They don't, not really.'

'Yes. And also, you wouldn't get the free handouts there that you get here.'

'If people want to bring me food, who am I to refuse it? Anyway, who says I have a London permit?'

Fen just chuckled. Cruikshank had left London a little over six years ago when his eyesight began to fail, moving to Downbourne because he had a sister living there. Having had no communication with his sister in a long time, it was only on reaching the town that he learned that she had in fact been dead for a year. However, the difficulties he had experienced on his journey south, and the compassion shown him by the local community, convinced him that he had nothing to lose by staying, so he stayed, although for the first few months he made it clear to anyone who would listen that he could return to London any time he felt like it (perhaps believing that this made his presence in the town somehow the more cherishable). After a while he seemed to realise that this boast, while not hindering his cause, was not helping it either, and so he fell silent on the subject. It was nonetheless reasonable to assume that he was in possession of a London permit – how else could he have left the capital and retain the option of going back?

– and it was an assumption Cruikshank had never explicitly refuted.

'Yes, well,' Cruikshank said, 'one could of course ask *you* a similar question, Morris. Why do *you* persist in living here? I mean, there's nothing to keep you in Downbourne, is there? You could leave any time you wanted.'

'And go where?'

'Anywhere.'

'But I like it here. I've lived here for fifteen years. And there are my pupils. And there's Moira to consider.'

Cruikshank's lips pulled back, revealing an old broken boneyard of teeth. 'Ah yes. Moira. Moira who sits around the house all day doing nothing. Darling Moira who hasn't had a civil word to say to you in ages.'

'Now, hold on a second. I don't see that that's any of your—'

'I wonder when was the last time you and she actually, you know . . .' Cruikshank leered. '*Relations*. I wonder, Morris, when was the last time you actually felt like a properly married man.'

'Mr Cruik—'

'She was *my* wife, I'd damn well assert my conjugal rights. Force her if I had to. Force her to do what a good wife should.'

Fen spun on his heel and stormed off.

'What's the matter, Morris?' Cruikshank called out after him. 'Can't handle a few home truths?'

Red-faced, fuming, Fen strode to the opposite side of the precinct, where he could no longer see Cruikshank.

Well, *that* had worked out nicely, hadn't it?

He had got no more than he deserved, of course. He had provoked Cruikshank, misjudging how far he could push him. And Cruikshank was notorious for his sharp tongue. But still . . .

Bastard.

As if Cruikshank knew anything of how it was with Moira. As if a lonely, crotchety old git like him understood anything about vows and loyalty and patience and hope. Life with Moira would get better, Fen was quite convinced of that. Had to. It was just a matter of time, that was all.

But how long has it been? How many months have you been putting up with her like this? Twelve? Eighteen? Nearly eighteen. For nearly a year and a half you've been making allowances for her. Pitying her. And it's not as if you too weren't affected by what happened eighteen months ago. You deserve pity too.

Fen made a beeline for the former off-licence.

Hazel Watson was laying out cups on the counter. A plumpish woman (she had, before the nation's current state of attrition, been downright fat), Hazel was just good-looking enough and just the right side of middle-aged to make flirting with her a credible proposition, absurd to neither her nor Fen. A few smiles, a couple of well-chosen compliments, and Fen had secured himself a decent-sized dose of Alan Greeley's damson gin. 'Only because it's you, Fen,' Hazel told him, with a conspiratorial, just-this-once wink.

The damson gin had the colour and consistency of blood, and tasted very little of fruit and very much like fire. Fen gulped it down. Heat seared his oesophagus. He visualised a thermal-imaging picture of himself, his body lit up in rainbow colours, with a sinuous, bright white band tracing the path of the gin from his mouth to his stomach.

That was better.

He was considering whether to go back for a second helping when he heard the band launch into 'Greensleeves', the tune that traditionally accompanied the official arrival of the Green Man at the festivities. Craning his neck, he saw the Green Man enter the precinct and proceed towards the podium, greeting people as he went, bestowing nods and smiles on either side. Arriving at the podium, he exhorted everyone to carry on dancing, and joined in himself.

He was not what you might call a natural mover. It was clear from his rictus grin, the inhibitedness of his gesticulations, that he considered dancing to be a necessary indulgence, beneath his dignity. Yet he danced anyway, and the crowd danced with him, taking their cue from him, swaying as he swayed, falling in line like breeze-brushed corn. All at once, where the Green Man was had become the focus of things. All other activities ceased. The children in the precinct couldn't take their eyes off him. The same, Fen noted, was true of most of the adults. As if unable to help themselves, everybody moved towards him, summoned by some tug inside, needing, fascinated. The desire to be close to him and do as he did was all but overwhelming.

The music swelled and accelerated, the band progressing from 'Greensleeves' to 'Green Grow the Rushes' in a transition so smooth it seemed that even they themselves were not aware they had done it. The dancers picked up their pace, and then the Green Man, with his stern jollity, broke into song:

. . . What is your one-oh?
One is one and all alone
And ever more shall be so.

No further prompting was necessary. Dozens of voices joined in at the top of the next verse, and the precinct resounded to the chorusing of the song's countdown lyrics, words that over the course of centuries had lost their meaning but now, in this England, seemed to make an arcane kind of sense again:

. . . Three, three, the rivals,
Two, two, the lily-white boys,
Clothèd all in green-oh,
One is one and all alone
And ever more shall be so.

Fen was among the very few who did not take part, either as dancer or singer. He adopted, instead, a detached stance, happy to observe and ponder. He felt the same affinity for the Green Man as everyone else, the same attraction to him, and yet was distanced enough from the feeling to wonder at its nature. What was it about the Green Man that commanded this attention, this affection? Perhaps it was just that old indefinable, charisma. Michael Hollingbury certainly had it in spades. But Fen wondered, too, whether the allure was not altogether more fundamental; whether, by adopting the guise of a mythic archetype, Hollingbury hadn't also adopted some of that archetype's power. The Green Man, as a concept, had survived for centuries, openly during pagan times, latent during more rational, orthodox eras. Perhaps a male incarnation of Nature was an iconic image preprogrammed into the human software, an evolutionary default setting. That was why people responded to Hollingbury so positively; why, for all his grandiloquence, his pomposity, he commanded loyalty and respect.

Or was that just a load of Jungian bollocks?

'Green Grow the Rushes' rolled to its conclusion, and the Green Man took this as a signal – possibly an excuse – to call a halt to the proceedings and beg in a loud voice for silence. As silence came, in dribs and drabs, he clambered up onto the podium where everyone could see him.

'Friends,' he said, 'fellow townspeople, neighbours, I shall keep this short.'

Predictably, a couple of humourists yelled out, 'Hear hear!'

'In these uneasy times,' the Green Man continued, unabashed, 'there are few certainties and even fewer causes for cheer. This, the Downbourne summer festival, is one. We come together here, as we have for several years now, to roister and revel, and defy misery with our laughter, just as summer, with its warmth, defies winter. The rest of the world has turned its back on this country and treats us with arrogance and contempt. It blockades our ports and punishes us randomly with missiles and bombs. Even our fellow Britons despair of us and despise us, erecting walls and defences to keep us out. Yet we are still England. England endures in us.'

This time the 'Hear hear!' was widespread and heartfelt.

'And here, tonight, in Downbourne, we commemorate that fact. With song and dance and merriment, we show the world that we are not bowed, that our spirits are not broken. We—'

The rest of the speech would forever go unheard, for at that moment a distant rumble echoed through the town, a deep mechanical drone, low at first but rapidly gaining in strength and volume, and a few perplexed murmurs drifted up from the crowd, coalescing into a nervous hubbub. Engines? Yes, engines. Lots of them.

Heads turned this way, that way. It was hard to tell where precisely the sound was coming from. It seemed to be coming from all directions at once.

Then the first of the vans appeared, rolling down the high street towards the precinct.

The van, a white Ford Transit with tinted windows, moved like a cruising predator, certain of itself, unnervingly unhurried. People coming to the festival along the High Street scuttled out of its way, seeking the sanctuary of the kerb, to stand and stare as it rumbled by. To them, and to those in the precinct, the van was an apparition of a kind they had not set eyes on in years, a ghost from the past, a once-familiar sight that had been made, by its abrupt recession from their lives, infinitely strange. Eyes were wide. Fingers pointed. Children pressed themselves against their parents.

Then a second van appeared, trailing in the wake of the first. A little Bedford, also white, also with tinted windows.

Simultaneously, at the other end of the precinct where the bonfire stood, a third white van, a lofty-sided Luton, drove up to the iron bollards that had been put there to enforce the distinction between pedestrian and non-pedestrian territory. A fourth pulled up in swift succession.

And now another white van hove into view on the High Street, and another, and yet another; an entire convoy of them, all makes and models, and more appeared beyond the bollards. In no time both ends of the precinct were blocked off, the vans parking at angles to one another, interleaving, forming an almost impenetrable cordon.

It was only then, as the festival-goers in the precinct realised that the vans had trapped them in a pincer movement, cutting them off from the rest of town, that their murmurs mounted to a clamour and a sense of panic began to swell. Fen saw Gilbert Cruikshank turning his head this way and that, demanding that someone, anyone, tell him what was going on. On the podium, the Green Man appealed for calm. He had to shout to make himself heard.

The white vans sat there, motors idling, windscreens menacingly blank, radiator grilles grinning. No one seemed in any hurry to disembark from them.

Gradually the Green Man's pleas began to take effect. It was either that or the puzzling reluctance of the vans' occupants to emerge that led to voices petering out among the crowd and an anxious quiet prevailing. The vans' engines growled on, the smell of diesel exhaust permeating the precinct, causing a number of people to cover their noses. The Green Man fixed his gaze on the vanguard van, the Transit. He waited. Everyone waited.

At last, the Transit's engine cut out, its driver-side door opened, and a man climbed out onto the road.

He was short and stockily built, and his hair had been shaved to a fine down, a transparent fur cap. He had a lumpen nose, evidently once broken, and eyes that were set deep in their sockets, as though pushed into place by force. He was dressed in a polo shirt, tracksuit bottoms and trainers, all of them adorned with trademark logos, and there were tattoos on his arms and neck, blurry blue statements of oath and fealty. One was a monochrome Union jack. Another, on his right biceps, was simply two words in Gothic script:

𝕶𝕴𝕹𝕲 𝕮𝖀𝕹𝕿

The man stared, hard and contemptuously, at the crowd. Dangling from his right hand, twitching like a pendulum, was a stubby length of two-by-four.

Then another van door opened and another man stepped out. He was almost the twin of the first – same close-cropped hair, similar clothing, tattoos. Slightly taller, slightly leaner, but from a distance the two of them could well have been brothers. From *his* hand hung a stainless steel baseball bat.

And then more such lookalikes were climbing out from all the vans, from their front-seat doors, from their rear doors, from their sliding side doors. The vans rocking and jolting, out filed the men like paratroopers, falling swiftly into position, forming a line across either end of the precinct, a dozen of them, two dozen, three, four. Sportswear was their uniform, close-cropped hair their chosen tonsorial style, tattoos their *de rigueur* body ornament, along with the occasional earstud or signet ring. Though of various sizes and shapes and complexions, they all conformed to a sartorial template, doing their best to resemble one another, or one particular exemplar, as closely as possible. And all of them toted hitting weapons of some kind – if not a length of two-by-four or a baseball bat, then a cricket bat, or a broom handle sawn in half and brandished like a truncheon.

Still more of these men appeared, and the Downbourne residents began drawing together, moving towards the middle of the precinct, putting distance between them and the strangers. It was the instinctive response of the gazelle herd when the lions appear, gathering into a tight knot so that no single individual stands out and makes itself a target. Fen happily became a part of the communal merge. By his estimate, the Downbournians outnumbered the new arrivals three to one, but that made no difference. There were old people and children here, and the new arrivals were true thugs. Professionals in violence. It was written in their physiques, their stares, the stance that each of them adopted: head slightly cocked, feet apart at shoulder-width, muscle-corded arms folded or hanging at their sides with cocky insouciance. Even unarmed, each would have been a match for any three Downbourne adults.

Only the Green Man was not cowed, or if he was, he gave no sign of it. Standing his ground on the podium, he eyed up the opposition, his gaze finally settling on the driver of the Transit, the first of the interlopers to have shown his face.

'You, sir,' he said, pointing to him. 'Whatever you may want here, we do not have it. Please leave.'

The other man took the suggestion on board, seemed actually to consider it, and then smiled, displaying a glint of Gold Tooth. 'You know what?' he said. 'You don't half look a twat.'

There was a churning sound, laughter, from his near-identical cohorts. Shoulders pumped up and down.

The man with the Gold Tooth, pleased that his witticism had been so well received, decided to expand it into a full-blown comedy routine: 'In fact, you look like a fucking human cabbage. Don't he, lads? Was your mum fucked by a cucumber? Was your dad a fucking cucumber? Or was it the Jolly Green Giant? The Jolly Green Giant stuck his jolly green dick up your mum, and you were the result. And what's that lawn doing stuck to your head? Oh yeah, it's not a lawn, it's hair.'

The Green Man bore the invective impassively, while Gold Tooth's colleagues chortled and guffawed their appreciation.

Then, when Gold Tooth had run out of permutations on the theme of greenness, the Green Man said, 'I've asked you to leave. Please do so. We are a poor, peaceful town, holding a small celebration. We have nothing for you, and we don't want any trouble.'

'Ah now, that's a shame, innit,' said Gold Tooth. ''Cause *we* do, don't we, lads?'

There was a lowing cheer of assent.

''Cause what are we?'

As one, the men from the white vans cried, 'British Bulldogs!'

'And who's our boss?'

'King Cunt!'

'And what does he like?'

'Havoc!'

This finely-turned example of strophe and antistrophe was evidently a prearranged cue for the so-called British Bulldogs to attack, for no sooner had they uttered the word 'Havoc!' than they launched themselves at the assembled Downbournians, laying into all and sundry with their weapons. People screamed and ran this way and that, trying to escape. Parents carried children, or crouched around them to protect them. The puppet-show stage was knocked over and collapsed with a splintering of wood and a billow of bedsheet. With practised efficiency the Bulldogs set about their victims, teeth bared in ravenous glee. All at once the world became a milling, buffeting, terrified confusion, and Fen was in the thick of it. He glimpsed a Bulldog coming straight for him and took evasive action, moving left, but this brought him into contact with another Bulldog, who was busy belabouring someone with a baseball bat (the victim was a neighbour of Fen's on Crane Street, Stephen Talbot, or so Fen thought, although he could not tell for sure on account of all the blood). The Bulldog broke off from his task to lash out sideways at Fen with the bat, catching him a glancing blow on the shoulder, and as Fen reeled away he collided with the man in the jester costume, the juggler. Saul Oliver was his name, and he clawed at Fen, trying to shove him out of the way, but then a Bulldog caught Oliver by the collar of his jester's tunic, yanked him backwards and set about him with his fists, punching him again and again in the face, while Fen stumbled off in another direction.

It wasn't all fear and fleeing on the part of the residents of Downbourne. There were small pockets of resistance as here, there, people stood up to the Bulldogs, attempting to fight them as equals. Fen glimpsed Alan Greeley trading punches with a fellow almost twice his size. He saw the flautist from the band, Colleen someone-or-other, pounding the back and shoulders of a Bulldog with her instrument while he, apparently oblivious to her blows, continued to stomp on the shin of one of her fellow band-members, the accordionist, who lay on the ground, writhing. Up on the podium, the Green Man was grappling with the Bulldog with the Gold Tooth, both men holding on to the length of two-by-four, each trying to wrest it from the other's grasp. While Fen looked on, one of the trestle tables beneath them overturned and they went crashing out of sight in a flail of limbs.

For all that, the outcome was inevitable. The British Bulldogs had chosen their moment well. An hour later, and there would have been too many locals present, more than even they would have dared to tackle. With that tactical genius common to all bullies, they had picked a fight they knew they couldn't lose.

Fen, to his astonishment still barely scathed, reeled through the mêlée, all around him blood and thumps and yelps of pain and the shrilling of frightened children. He hunched low, trying not to draw attention to himself. He was no fighter. He had never raised a hand in anger, not even as a kid. He saw fists and feet and weapons inflicting damage, and he cringed inwardly, praying it would not be his turn next.

Then, appearing almost magically in front of him through the throng: an open doorway. The off-licence. He stumbled towards it, obeying some animal imperative, the need for shelter when the storm comes down. There was a back room, he recalled. Somewhere in there he might be able to hide till all this was over.

He made it through the door and as far as the counter, and then heard footsteps behind him and a shout of 'Oi!'

Instinctively, not fully comprehending what he was doing, Fen reached for one of the dozens of bottles stowed behind the counter. He snatched it up and hurled it desperately at the Bulldog behind him. The projectile found its mark, but Fen had made a poor choice of weapon. A glass bottle might have done some harm, might even have knocked the man unconscious, but the one that had come to hand was plastic. It struck the Bulldog on the shoulder, splitting on impact and showering him with a clear yellow liquid, then bouncing off onto the floor and rolling away, leaking.

The Bulldog wiped his face, snarled 'Wanker!' and lunged at Fen.

Within minutes, it was over. Across the precinct the festival-goers sat in defeated clusters. Here and there a body lay sprawled on the brick paving – whether dead or out cold, it was impossible to say. The British Bulldogs, meanwhile, strutted around, clapping one another on the back, sharing jokes, and every so often breaking into a chant, gracing the tune of 'Rule, Britannia' with lyrics of their own:

British Bulldogs!
We're tough, we're brave, we're class
And . . . if . . . you get in our way
We'll kick your arse.

Fen was in one of the clusters. He hunkered miserably down, beset by injuries. His lower lip was a stinging bulge of flesh that tasted of blood when he probed it with his tongue. He could feel his left eye swelling, the lids thickening and tightening. A finger felt broken (although it was probably just badly bruised). The left side of his ribcage throbbed. Each source of pain had a cycle of intensity, increasing and then abating, and the cycles were out of phase, so that the pain became a kind of sonata, an interplay of crescendos and diminuendos that every so often coincided and massed to a gruelling peak. He could only be grateful, for what it was worth, that the Bulldog who had attacked him had elected not to use the cricket bat he was carrying, preferring instead the medium of feet and fists. In the Bulldog's own words, as he had set the bat aside: 'You ain't worth the trouble.'

Worse than the pain, though, and the vague humiliation of being deemed too unthreatening an opponent to merit assault by cricket bat, was the fact that someone whom Fen had never seen before in his life and with whom he had no quarrel had taken it upon himself to hurt him. That, somehow, was the truly awful part. Not the beating itself, but the injustice, the *affront* of it. What had he done

37

to deserve such treatment? By the expressions on the bloodied, bowed faces around him, he could tell others were asking themselves the same question.

The children, thank God, had been spared. Though, like all the adults, they were shiveringly scared, none of them had been attacked, so far as Fen could determine. The British Bulldogs had left them alone. That was something.

Amid the turmoil of his thoughts, Fen remembered Moira. Earlier, on the way here, he had felt guiltily relieved that she wasn't with him. At the last festival she attended, winter the previous year, she had embarrassed him by moping around with a face like thunder, refusing to talk to anyone, then heading home after less than an hour, complaining she was cold. Now, he found he was still relieved that she wasn't with him, but, happily, for a far more charitable reason.

There, Cruikshank, he thought. Isn't that suitably husband-like behaviour, to be glad that your wife is safe and well, even while you yourself are suffering? Isn't that what one would expect of a 'properly married man'?

Of course, that was not exactly the point that Cruikshank had been making. And Fen wasn't, he realised, that much more concerned about Moira's welfare than he was about the welfare of the children here. And it said a lot about the state of his marriage that he had to consider justifying himself, even in his thoughts, to someone like Gilbert Cruikshank.

His various bodily aches and pains came together in throbbing, sickening symphony, then receded again.

He wondered what was happening beyond the precinct. The rest of the town had to have heard the vans, and the people coming to the festival had seen the British Bulldogs close in on the precinct. They must have been able to deduce, from the rumpus, what had gone on subsequently. The question was, what were they going to do about it? Might they get together and launch an attack on the Bulldogs in an effort to liberate their fellow townspeople? Had the Green Man been out there to organise them, then yes, doubtless they might. As it was, Fen thought the likelihood of a rescue attempt a slim one, and even if such a thing did take place, he rated its chances of success as minimal. The Bulldogs had the precinct sealed off. They would be able to hold out with ease against any incursion. They were free to do whatever they liked with the people they were holding captive here.

All at once, through his misery and the ebb and flow of his pain,

Fen became aware of a crackling sound, and then the peppery, pungent smell of woodsmoke. He looked up.

The British Bulldogs had pulled down torches from the lampposts, ignited them using the cigarette lighters from their vans' dashboards, and thrown them onto the bonfire. Separate cores of flame were brightening and glowing, gathering strength, slowly uniting.

Why had they lit the fire? What were they going to do with it? An answer occurred to him.

He didn't like it.

As the flames took hold, reaching up into the guts of the bonfire, seething and raging, two of the British Bulldogs dragged the Green Man in front of their gold-toothed leader.

The outcome of the fight between Gold Tooth and the Green Man was abundantly clear. The Bulldog stood erect, chest out, hands clasped together behind his back sergeant-major style. One sleeve of his T-shirt was slightly torn, but that was it as far as damage went. The Green Man, by contrast, sagged, staring vacantly ahead, his eyes white moons amid the glistening, blood-marbled pulp that had been his face. The two Bulldogs gripped him firmly by the arms, but their task was more one of support than one of restraint. Without them, the Green Man would have been incapable of remaining upright.

Gold Tooth eyed his vanquished opponent for a moment, then reached for the Green Man's shirt collar and wrenched downwards. Buttons tore, and the Green Man's chest and navel were exposed. Below the level of his collarbone, his skin was pallidly, vulnerably white, his chest and belly wisped with unremarkable brown hair.

Gold Tooth nodded as if this was no more than he had expected. He jerked a thumb, and his two cohorts hauled the Green Man off to the bonfire.

The Downbournians, in their huddled groups, watched in dull horror as the two British Bulldogs, grimacing against the heat from the bonfire, held the Green Man out in front of them, offering him a foretaste of his fate. At first the Green Man was too dazed to react, but the heat soon stirred him to his senses. His eyes swirled and found a focus in the flames. His mouth began to move, but no words came out, only a long stringy gobbet of blood that unspooled to the ground. The Bulldogs pushed him closer to the bonfire and held him there for several seconds while patches of his facial hair crinkled and shrivelled. Then, laughing, they pulled him back.

'Want me to put that out?' one of them offered, gesturing at the

Green Man's singed beard and eyebrows, and then at his own crotch. 'Got my fire extinguisher right here.'

There was, in the throat of every Downbournian looking on, a cry of protest, a great painful *NO!*, caught like a fishbone, impossible either to choke out or to swallow down.

The Bulldogs assembled around the bonfire to watch, and a debate sprang up among them as to whether the Green Man should be thrown into the flames head-first or feet-first. Then Gold Tooth said, 'Hold up, fellas. I think he wants to say something.'

A mockingly attentive silence fell.

'Come on, out with it, mate. Your famous last words.'

The Green Man moaned a few mumbled phrases.

'Louder,' said Gold Tooth, grinning. 'Can't hear you.'

The Green Man repeated himself. Fen caught only snatches of what he said. Something about immortality. Being impossible to kill. You could harm him but never destroy him.

Fen would never be able to decide if the Green Man genuinely believed this or if it was just bravado.

Either way, it didn't save him.

Gold Tooth started the countdown.

'Three!' he shouted, and the Green Man was swung backwards.

'Two!' the rest of the Bulldogs joined in, and parents covered their children's eyes, and some of the Downbournians looked away and others wished they could.

'One!' the Bulldogs all yelled together, and the Green Man, groaning, was launched forward and propelled headlong into the bonfire's heart.

He shrieked and writhed for a full minute. After that, he no longer shrieked, and his body continued to move only involuntarily, twisting and squirming as it cooked, contorting with heat and internal pressures, flesh bubbling greasily. The British Bulldogs cheered, faces aglow with the bonfire's radiance, while the air was filled with a horrid barbecue stench that set several Downbournians retching.

On a pyre of denatured wood and man-made products, the Green Man slowly roasted.

Having just seen their mayor burned to death, the captive Downbournians could do nothing other than meekly comply when the British Bulldogs ordered them to get to their feet. With Gold Tooth issuing instructions, the townspeople were separated into three groups, men, women and children. The men were then subdivided into smaller groups and herded off, limping and shuffling, into the surrounding buildings. Fen was pushed, along with five others, into a stockroom at the back of the one-time record shop, a musty, windowless space littered with broken shards of CD case and trodden scraps of old promotional poster.

'Stay in there and keep your traps shut,' one of their escorts told them, and slammed the door, leaving them in total darkness.

For a while the six of them did as advised and kept quiet. There was a clenched, agonised knot in each man's belly. Each was certain that what had been done to the Green Man was going to be done to him too. This stockroom was merely a temporary holding pen, an antechamber to death.

Finally one of them, unable to contain his dread any longer, started whimpering. Somebody else told him to shut up, but this only succeeded in making the whimperer more vocal, not less. He began to babble, uttering imprecations to the Almighty, a patchwork of fragments of half-remembered prayers.

'Please, for heaven's sake, stop,' said Fen, his voice tight and tremulous too. His fat lip had given him a slight lisp. 'They'll come for us first if you don't stop.'

That did succeed in silencing the whimperer, though had he, whoever he was, been thinking more clearly, he would perhaps have spotted the logic-flaw in what Fen had just said, namely that it made little difference whether the British Bulldogs came for them first or last, and indeed postponing the inevitable might well, under the circumstances, be a bad thing.

For the next few minutes the six men did nothing but listen. They heard one another's breathing and, dimly, like a portent of another, more lasting inferno, the crackle and roar of the bonfire.

Finally someone, in the faintest of whispers, said: 'Why?'

'Why what?' said someone else, no more loudly. The second speaker was Henry Mullins, town councillor.

'Why are they here? Why are they doing this to us?'

'Because they can,' said a third hushed voice, which Fen knew to be that of Donald Bailey, retired policeman and elder brother (by a year) of Reginald, the footbridge fisherman.

'Donald,' Fen said, 'it's me, Fen Morris.'

'I know you're here, Fen. There's also Andrew Quinlan, right? And young Kenny Gibbs.'

The latter mumbled an assent, and judging by the direction his voice came from Fen was pretty sure Kenny had been the one whimpering. He felt sorry for him. Kenny, not much older than twenty, had simply been articulating what everyone in the room was feeling.

' "Because they can"?' Fen prompted Donald.

'Because we can't stop them and they know it. Why else do you think they've come all the way down here? Fifty miles' worth of diesel. Hundred, if you bear in mind it's a round-trip. That's a hell of a lot of fuel. But they knew when they got here it'd be worthwhile, because there'd be no opposition to speak of. Up in London, they'd never get away with this sort of thing. The other gangs. There's a kind of truce on. A balance of power. Down here . . .' Fen didn't need to be able to see Bailey to know that he had just shrugged.

'You're sure they're from London?' asked Mullins.

'That accent? That tribal look? Of course they are.'

'But the International Community . . .' This was Kenny talking now, offering up those two words – International Community – which had become, to the English, both a curse and another name for God. 'I thought the whole point of the bombings and the blockades was to keep people like those lot in their place.'

Someone laughed hollowly.

'Unfortunately, Kenny,' Fen said, as kindly as he could in order to compensate for the laughter, 'what the International Community claims it's trying to achieve and what it actually does achieve are two different things.'

'*Very* different things,' Mullins chipped in.

'Fact is,' said Donald, 'I reckon we should count ourselves lucky.'

'Oh yeah? And just how do you come to *that* conclusion?' This

43

comment, scornful and with an edge of hysteria, came from a new source in the room, its sixth occupant. Fen recalled glimpsing, just before the stockroom door was closed, an out-of-towner among them. The man's face was familiar but Fen had no idea of his name.

'Lucky it hasn't happened sooner,' Donald elaborated, patiently. 'We've all heard of London gangs straying beyond the M25, haven't we? It was only a matter of time before one of them got this far. Actually, I'm surprised it took this long.'

'Oh well, that's great,' said the out-of-towner. 'That makes me feel a whole lot better.'

'I'm not saying it to make anyone feel better. I'm saying it as a statement of fact.'

'Perhaps we *should* have been prepared for it,' said Andrew Quinlan.

'The Green Man mentioned something like that to me the other day,' said Mullins. 'He said Downbourne has had it peaceful for so long, there's been so little trouble in this area, that if trouble does come we won't be ready for it and we won't be able to defend ourselves against it.'

'Well, great,' said the out-of-towner. 'That's great. So the Green Man knew this was going to happen.'

'It was just a passing comment. He couldn't have predicted this.'

'Yeah, well. Still. Serves him right what's happened to him, then.'

'Hey!' said Mullins. 'That man was a friend of mine, you know.'

'All right, keep it down, everybody,' urged Donald. Voices had risen somewhat. 'Come on, let's be calm.'

Mullins muttered some comment about respect for the dead, and an unhappy silence prevailed.

Then Fen said, 'I heard a van engine this afternoon. Well, not me. A boy in my class did. It must have been them. The British Bulldogs. Reconnoitring. If they'd come in on the northern road, they could have stopped a mile outside town, on the rise there. Up there they'd have got a good view of everything. They'd have seen the festival preparations, the bonfire, all that.'

'Your point being?' said the out-of-towner.

'Nothing, except . . .' Except he should have believed Clive Sayer. He should have informed the Green Man that a vehicle engine had been heard at the outskirts of town. Would it have made a difference? Perhaps. Then again, perhaps not. 'Well, it might at least explain how they knew we'd be here, a whole lot of us together in one place at one time.'

'But it still doesn't explain why they're doing this,' said Quinlan, who was the one who had raised the question of the Bulldogs' motives in the first place. 'Unless it's just to . . . you know, for kicks.'

'Locusts,' said Donald. 'They're like locusts. Swarm all over a place, stripping it bare.'

'Of what?'

'Food, supplies, things they can't get in London, or can't get easily.'

'That might mean they aren't going to kill us,' said Kenny.

'Possibly,' agreed Donald.

It was only a small *possibly*, a thin fingernail of a likelihood, but all of them, even Kenny and the out-of-towner, drew succour from it. Suddenly the outlook no longer seemed bleak. Suddenly there was a chance, just a chance, that they might survive this after all.

As time passed, that chance appeared to improve. No one came to fetch them for the bonfire. Even more reassuringly, although they heard voices out in the precinct, sometimes shouting, there were no screams or entreaties or other sounds to indicate that a programme of systematic execution was under way. It still didn't seem safe to believe that everything was going to turn out all right, but as the minutes ticked by, the odds against their imminent immolation lengthened and more and more reasons suggested themselves as to why the British Bulldogs might spare everyone's lives. What, besides an arbitrary, bloodthirsty thrill, would the Bulldogs have to gain from slaughtering a couple of hundred people? They had killed the Green Man just to set an example, to demonstrate to the townspeople that they meant business, to intimidate them even further than they were already intimidated. Not only that but, without their leader, the captive Downbournians were less likely to mount a concerted resistance.

So the men's fears, which they could now perceive to have been exaggerated, began to subside. They weren't about to die. They felt this, they hoped it, but they were not sufficiently confident to put it to the test. None of them dared open the door and take a peek outside to see what was going on. The possibility was raised and rejected several times. What, and be spotted by a Bulldog standing guard outside? That, surely, would invite down on their heads the fate they were beginning to believe they were going to evade. And since the door was secured by a Yale catch, the option of peeping through a keyhole was out.

Gradually, one after another, the six men settled down on the floor, each finding an area for himself, fitting his legs in around the others' legs.

There wasn't a chink of light in the stockroom. The darkness was absolute. In the invisible proximity of five others, each of the men waited. Silent. Afraid. Hoping.

In all, the townspeople shut away by the British Bulldogs in the back rooms of the shops spent a little over half an hour as prisoners. To some of them it felt a great deal longer, to others barely a few minutes. Half an hour was what it was, however, and although they didn't realise it, throughout that time they were not, strictly speaking, prisoners at all. No one was standing guard outside their makeshift cells. The doors were not locked. They could have opened them and walked out any time, had they dared. Just as the Bulldogs had intended, fear was their jailer. Fear kept them subdued and in place, while the Bulldogs took what they had come for and departed.

No sooner had the last of the white vans vanished from view than the people who were left in the precinct hurried to liberate those who were interned in the shops, while the people who had been prevented from entering the precinct now came rushing in, demanding to know what had been going on. With the rumble of diesel engines still audible in the air, but dwindling fast, out came the prisoners, blinking in the early-evening light, shielding their eyes against the low sun and the flare of the bonfire. Children ran to fathers. Husbands and wives were reunited, often tearfully.

But some reunions did not take place. People were missing, and the ex-prisoners were soon enlightened as to what had gone on in the precinct during their incarceration.

Only the menfolk had been forced into the shops. The Bulldogs had then gone among the women and children like prospective buyers at a cattle market, grading and evaluating. Selections had been made, and those chosen – all females, all young, all classifiable as attractive – had been manhandled into the vans. Anyone who refused to go or who struggled had been threatened with the bonfire or a further beating. All told, some dozen women had been taken. The oldest was thirty-nine, the youngest fifteen.

The news was met with silence. Then rage.

But the rage was unfocused, diffuse. Mainly it was outrage,

which is rage of the least productive kind. There were protests and expressions of indignation and half-formed plans of action and plenty of impassioned breast-beating. No one, however, had any clear suggestion to make, any clear idea what to do. Somebody proposed chasing after the Bulldogs on horseback. Somebody else pointed out that, even if a horse rider did manage to catch up with the vans, what then? He was just going to ask them to pull over? Another idea mooted was to send a delegation over to Wyndham Heath, the nearest large town, where there was a police station still open and still staffed. But the police station, everyone knew, was of chiefly symbolic significance. Run by volunteers, few of them trained law-enforcement professionals, it was, for the residents of Wyndham Heath and its immediate environs, a comforting reminder of past certainties, but its efficacy in pursuing wrongdoers and punishing their misdemeanours was negligible.

The dispiriting truth, which none of the Downbournians present wanted to acknowledge yet, was that they were helpless. A dozen women had been abducted – wives, mothers, daughters, girlfriends, friends – and, realistically, there was nothing anyone could do about it except wail and agonise and despair.

The bonfire burned on, sending gouts of black smoke up into the air, as a pall of gloom settled over the festival-goers. A few people, those not directly affected by the abductions, started to drift away, heading home to nurse wounds or put children to bed. Others knelt to tend to the victims whom the British Bulldogs had beaten senseless, checking to see how badly they were hurt and attempting to revive them. The rest congregated in knots of three or four and continued arguing, not only about the monstrous offences the Bulldogs had committed but also, now, about whether the whole terrible episode could somehow have been prevented. Here and there, people stood alone or in clutching couples, weeping, desolate.

Fen, surveying the scene, decided there was little to be gained by remaining. He was unable to open his left eye at all now, his bruised finger had swollen to sausage size, and his ribcage was so sore that it hurt to breathe. Time to go home.

He wondered how Moira would react when he showed up, battered and bruised, and told her what he had just been through. Probably with her usual indifference.

But maybe not.

'Oh God, Fen. Those poor women. Poor you! Look at you. Thank heaven it's not worse, that's all I can say. I mean, those men, they could have . . . I don't even want to think about it.'

48

Yes. Maybe this was the catalyst he had been waiting for. The jump-start his marriage needed. Seeing him hurt, learning about the women being abducted – maybe it would startle Moira out of her Slough of Despond. Bring her round like a dash of icy water. It wasn't entirely inconceivable. Maybe that was the good that would come of this episode, the silver lining to this cloud.

As Fen was leaving the precinct, Donald Bailey fell in step beside him.

'See you've had the same idea,' Donald commented. 'Not much point in sticking around.'

Fen nodded.

'How you doing?'

'Been better.'

'Any aspirin at home? Paracetamol? Something like that?'

'I think so. Well out-of-date, but . . .'

'Better than nothing. Of course, an ice pack would do wonders for that eye.'

'An ice pack frozen how?'

They turned off from the high street, heading towards the war memorial. Fen observed that Donald was favouring one leg as he walked. He also saw dried blood, cracked and black, encrusting the rims of the old man's nostrils.

'How bad did they hurt you?'

'Could have been worse. Would have been, if I'd fought back. Maybe I should have, but sod it, I'm sixty-three. Thirty years ago – well, then it would have been a different story. Obviously *you* stood up for yourself.'

'Um . . . yes,' said Fen. Well, he *had* thrown that bottle. He moved swiftly on to another subject. 'So, what do you think's going to happen to them? The women they took?'

'I really don't want to imagine. What really gets me is it's so damn barbarian. So damn Genghis Khan. They come, they kick us around, they steal our womenfolk. I mean, what century is this?'

'Think there's any chance we can get them back?'

'Doubt it. Look at it this way. London's a big place, and even if we did know where these British Bulldogs live, what part of the city they call home, how are we going to get there? No permits, and I don't know about you but I don't fancy my chances trying to get across the M25. You'd have to be mad even to think about it.'

'Perhaps we *should* send someone over to Wyndham Heath.'

'What for? You don't need to be an ex-copper to know there's no law there. There's no law anywhere, at least not "law" in the sense that we used to understand it. There's just people agreeing to pull together and pool their resources and get on, and then there's people like the Bulldogs who come along and take advantage. And until things improve, if they ever do, that's just how it's going to be. I know how you're feeling, Fen. I'm the same. Sickened and angry. They took Frank Fothergill's kid. Did you know that? Zoë. Fifteen. Fifteen years old. That's plain evil. Don't think I wouldn't move heaven and earth to get that child out of their clutches, if I thought I had any chance of succeeding. But I can't. At least, I don't think I can.' Donald sighed. 'Sometimes, you know, I wonder if brother Reg isn't the only sensible one among us. He may be a bit simple, but . . . Go down to the river every day and fish. Don't think about any of it, just let it happen around you. Maybe that's the way to be. Anyhow . . .' He halted and gestured towards a side-street. 'Here's where you and I go our separate ways. See you around.'

Fen continued homewards alone. He was finding walking tricky with only one functioning eye. Distances were hard to judge and he had to concentrate on every step, making sure his feet came down where they were supposed to. Wherever he went, townspeople were out on the streets, gathered in groups. There was distress in their faces, disgust in their voices. Word of events at the precinct was spreading outward through town, like tremors from the epicentre of an earthquake. Beneath a dusk-tinged sky and an early, opalescent moon, Downbourne was assessing and assimilating its misfortune.

On the corner of King Alfred Street and Harvill Drive, Fen had to stop. All at once his legs felt rubbery, boneless, and he was cold all over, shaking uncontrollably. He grabbed a wall to steady himself while the shudders passed through him, beginning at his groin and running up through his chest. He saw the Bulldogs rushing through the precinct, hitting, kicking, beating, bludgeoning, hurting. He saw himself on the off-licence floor, curled up on his side, his ribs getting stamped on. He saw the Green Man being tossed into the bonfire like so much human lumber.

Nausea overcame him. His stomach heaved. He bit back bile. He told himself he would not vomit. It was just shock. Delayed reaction. He would not vomit.

Gradually the shaking subsided, and Fen took a few deep breaths, then looked up. There were people around him, some of them neighbours, faces he knew, faces showing concern. Concern and . . . something else? Something more?

One woman, Beth Allworthy, laid a hand on his shoulder. 'Fen?'

He nodded weakly. 'I'm fine,' he said hoarsely. 'Just need to . . .' He straightened up. 'Need to get home.'

'Fen, please understand,' Beth said, 'there was nothing we could do.'

Fen frowned at her. 'What do you mean?'

'They came this way,' said someone else. 'Those vans.'

'They just climbed out and grabbed her,' said a third person. 'It happened like *that*.' A snap of the fingers. 'There was no time to react.'

Now Fen began to look carefully at the people addressing him, and he recognised the expressions on their faces around him for what they were: not concerned but pitying.

Her.

Grabbed *her*.

'Moira?'

'One of the vans stopped and a couple of men jumped out, Fen,' said Beth. Her hand was still on his shoulder. 'Jumped out, grabbed her, pulled her into the van, drove away. I can still hardly believe it. It happened just a few minutes ago. She put up a fight, but . . .'

It was a joke. Fen swivelled his head, peering from one face to the next. They were having a joke on him, surely. Moira? It hadn't been Moira. Mistaken identity. Moira wouldn't have been here on King Alfred Street because Moira had not been going to the festival. She was at home. It was someone else who had been snatched by the Bulldogs, someone who looked like Moira. Not Moira. It wasn't possible.

Was it?

He pushed Beth aside. He shoved past another woman. Then he was staggering up the slope of Harvill Drive, gaining speed, breaking into a clumsy run.

He lurched along the cut-through.

He lumbered down Crane Street.

He stumbled up the front path.

He tumbled through the front door.

The house was empty. He checked every room. He even checked the back garden. No Moira.

And in the bedroom, the drawers of the chest of drawers were open, each protruding a little further out than the one above, like a staircase to nowhere. There were signs that Moira had put on clothes. A pair of her shoes were missing from the floor of the closet.

He slumped down on the unmade bed, breathing hard. The

sheets smelled of her. Her body, her sweat. Ghosts of her secretions. The pillow still bore the dimpled imprint of her head.

Gone. Taken. Like the women at the precinct.

He couldn't believe it.

He didn't want to believe it.

And at the same time, in a small dark corner of his soul, he not only wanted to believe it but was eager to.

They make me lie down. Among their feet. Feet in trainers. Sweat-smell and perished rubber. White socks. All I see are logos. Logos, flashes, names, imprints, ticks, initials, numerals. The lumpy treads on soles.

They make jokes. They swear and they talk about 'bitches'. A bitch-hunt. That's what this has been, apparently. A bitch-hunt.

I'm too scared to move. There's an ache in my throat. My heart's going nine to the dozen. They're talking about me, but I don't want to hear what they're saying. It's my hair. Something about my hair. That's why they stopped for me. Red hair. 'He' will like it. Whoever 'he' is.

The van sways and bounces, and down here on the floor I feel every blemish in the road surface, every crack and bump and pothole, and there are plenty, and the driver swerves a lot, perhaps to avoid the worst of them, and the shock absorbers creak, and sometimes I hear the sound of other vans up ahead, the rest of our convoy. When was the last time I was in a motor vehicle of any kind?

My heart's hammering, I'm scared beyond belief, but I can still wonder about the fact that I'm travelling in a motor vehicle. Isn't the mind a strange thing?

After a while they let me know that I can sit up if I want to. I think they liked seeing me on the floor. It amused them. Then it got boring. So I sit up, because I'll be more comfortable that way. I press myself against the side of a seat, doing my best to make sure I'm not touching any of them and none of them's touching me. No physical contact. No eye contact either. I want to be small. I want to be insignificant. I stare at my feet. My shoes. Old shoes. Is there any other kind? Simple comfortable sandals. Stitching split on the right one. Upper and sole starting to part company. Dust engrained in the wrinkles in the leather, like pale capillaries.

It's dim in the van. The tinted windows don't let in much light. I'm aware of how we all move together, the men, me, synchronise. Jerking like puppets whenever the van jolts.

If only I hadn't . . .

No. Mustn't think like that. Too late to think like that.

Eight years ago. Early autumn.

That was the last time I was in a motor vehicle.

We had some petrol. We took Fen's battered old Renault down to the coast. Things were starting to get very bad then. The political situation. Deteriorating. I think, deep down, we knew we might not have another chance to do something like this. This might be the last opportunity we had. That sweetened it.

It was a bright, clear, warm day. The sea was every shade of blue imaginable. At least, that's how I remember it. Shades of blue you'd expect in the tropics, but not in the Channel. Cobalt. Turquoise. Peacock. Sapphire. Aquamarine. Purples, too. Lilac. Amethyst. We parked on a clifftop and looked down, and it was like looking down on the contents of a vast jewel-box. God's own treasure chest, opened for our benefit.

We had a picnic on the clifftop, on a blanket. Sandwiches, pie, soup from a thermos flask, cherry tomatoes. Halfway through the meal a magpie appeared and began strutting around us, flexing its wings, fluffing out its feathers, flicking its tail up and down, chattering. Fen waved it away, laughing, but it kept coming back. Then it started making aggressive feints towards us, and we realised it was after our food. We were, it seemed, being mugged by this avian hoodlum, and successfully, because in the end the only way to get the magpie to leave us alone was to throw it chunks of bread crust, which it snatched up and gulped down until eventually, glutted and ap-peased, it flew off.

'I suppose,' Fen said, with a droll smile, 'you could call that "de-manding manna with menaces".' Then, the smile fading, he said, 'That bird is our future, you know.'

'What, one for sorrow?' For a moment I thought he was referring to me and him, and could not see why. 'Fen, is there something you need to tell me?' I added, only half joking.

'Something . . . ? Oh no. No, nothing like that, Moira. I meant the nation's future.' He pointed to the magpie, which had alighted on a clump of gorse a hundred yards away and was cawing and preening triumphantly. 'If everything goes the way it seems to be going, then the country's going to belong to bullies like him. It'll be their time. They're the ones who'll thrive.'

I felt a chill. A presentiment, on that magnificent autumn after-noon, of the depth of the downward spiral into which England was headed. Fen was right. But I didn't want him to be right. 'You don't think that really. Do you? You don't. I mean, it'll all get sorted out, won't it? This is just a dip in our fortunes. We've weathered worse in the past.'

Quickly he said, 'Of course. Of course it is. Of course we have.' Lying for my sake, as people often have to with their loved ones. 'I just like to be the voice of doom. You know that. A professional Eeyore.'

And he took my hand and we kissed.

We were happy then. Even then.

The van lunges into a deeper-than-usual pothole, twice, front left wheel, rear left wheel, and the men all jeer and hoot and call the driver names, and the driver calls them names back and says any of them is welcome to come and take over.

On we roll for a while, and the light inside the van gets dimmer and dimmer, until the men are all silhouettes. They go quiet. Some of them start to snooze, and I think about making a bid for the rear doors. I could scramble over, pull down the handle, hurl myself out . . . but I know someone would grab me before I got there, and even if I managed it I know they'd stop the van and come out after me.

Even more time later, I don't know how much, a long time, we slow down, and then we halt, and then we move forward in fits and starts, and one of the men says to me, 'We've got this all covered, but just to be on the safe side you keep your head down and you *shut up*. Got that? Not a dicky-bird or I break your neck. Understand?'

I nod.

A minute or so later we halt and the driver pulls on the handbrake and winds down his window. A torch beam shines in.

'Permits.'

The driver hands over a sheaf of documents, and something else. A bribe of some sort, I assume, because he says, 'There you go,' meaningfully, and the man with the torch, just as meaningfully, replies, 'Right. Thanks. Well . . .'

The torch beam flashes briefly over the interior of the van.

This is the moment. If I'm going to scream, it should be now.

But a hand clamps on the back of my head, just where my skull meets my vertebrae. The man who told me to shut up or he would break your neck. His fingers exert pressure, enough to tell me that they can clench much harder. Much, much harder if necessary. It's as if he knew what I was thinking.

I'm not sure I want to live, not if my future is these men. But I realise I don't want to die either. Not yet. Not like this.

'That all seems to be in order,' says the man with the torch. 'On your way, then.'

The van moves off, and the hand lets go and pats me on the head. Like I'm a pet. An obedient dog.

And I hear someone say, 'Welcome to London.'

Two days after the raid by the British Bulldogs, a town meeting was convened.

Very few people turned up and not much was resolved. It was agreed that Henry Mullins should act as mayor *pro tem*, until such time as an election could be organised. It was also agreed that a funeral service should be held at St Stephen's Church for Michael Hollingbury (dead, destroyed, Hollingbury was no longer the Green Man, just a man). Other than that, nobody had much to suggest or much to say. The purpose of the meeting was to discuss the Bulldogs' actions and formulate some kind of response, but there was a general reluctance to address the subject. There was a general reluctance even to mention the word 'Bulldogs', or, for that matter, the names of the women they had abducted.

The same was true all over town. While there were those who spoke loudly in favour of following the Bulldogs to London and getting into the capital somehow and locating the abductees somehow and rescuing them somehow, the great majority of Downbournians appeared to have come to the conclusion that it was best simply to forget the whole episode and act as if it had never occurred. The unfeasibility of any rescue attempt – all those *somehows* – was too daunting. Rather than openly admit defeat, however, people admitted nothing. A veil was drawn. The subject of the kidnapped women became taboo. When it cropped up in a conversation, the conversation faltered. If ever it was referred to, it was referred to by a stretch of silence. It was as though a huge alien spacecraft was hovering over town and everyone was acting as if it wasn't there, even though everyone felt its immane presence, the chill of its shadow.

England had suffered greatly since the government's unlucky gamble and the series of escalating crises that had followed as the country, stripped of any last illusions of faith in its leadership, slid inexorably into anarchy. Even in a town like Downbourne, affected only indirectly by all the upheaval, significant adjustments in lifestyle had had to be made. Surrogates for central heating, electric lighting and running water had had to be found, as one by one these basic amenities ceased to function. Luxuries large and small had had to be forgone. Things once taken for granted had now to be treated, if they could be obtained, as treasures. Privation and frugality had become a way of life, and this had led to a sense of resignation which had in turn led, inevitably, to an outward and inner toughening – a thickening of skins, a hardening of hearts. People, sometimes surprising themselves with their own fortitude, had learned to do without, to settle for less, to endure. And the ability to endure often meant the ability to turn a blind eye to unpalatable truths and bear with a shrug situations they knew they could not change. Emotional sensitivity is not a survival trait, and over the past few years Englanders had become, if nothing else, survivors.

So the residents of Downbourne embraced a policy of mute denial, and tried to get on with life as before. It was as if the bulldogs incident was a price that had to be paid for the comparative good fortune the town had up till now enjoyed, a sacrifice that had to be offered up to the gods of balance. The townsfolk, with a few murmurs of dissent, gave up their due.

Physical injuries inflicted by the British Bulldogs were seen to by Nurse Chase. Downbourne's last remaining GP, Dr Whittaker, had died of salmonella poisoning four years previously, after eating a bad tin of corned beef – a physician who had healed many but, when it came to the crunch, proved unable to heal himself. Anne Chase, his surgery nurse, had stepped into the breach to perform what curative works she could with her dwindling stocks of dressings and pharmaceuticals. As she tended to the Bulldogs' victims, she was relieved (and somewhat surprised) to find that nobody had been too severely hurt. The exception to this was Fen's neighbour Stephen Talbot, who had been beaten into a coma. For him, alas, Nurse Chase could do nothing other than advise his family to make him comfortable and pray he recovered consciousness soon. Otherwise, it was just contusions and abrasions and the odd broken bone, all things that were in her power to treat.

As for non-physical injuries, it was left to the individual to handle these as best he or she could. Psychiatry was one of the excrescences of the past which present national circumstances had ruthlessly pruned. There was no therapy any more, no counselling to featherbed the tortured soul, so people either coped with the traumas fate threw at them or caved in; and of course, among the residents of Downbourne – as among all Englanders – coping rather than caving was the norm, so that even in households where a family member, a loved one, had been lost to the Bulldogs, the prevailing mood was one of stoic acceptance. There was anger, certainly. Frustration too. There was sorrow and mourning, for the loss was in many respects a bereavement. But after only two days there was also a sense that life must continue as usual, or at any rate be seen to do so.

12 Crane Street appeared to be a perfect example of this.

Here, one need look no further than the front garden, where, on the afternoon of the day of the town meeting, Fen was out trimming the hedge. There had been no school yesterday – there never was, the day after a festival – and it was the weekend now, so Fen was free to carry out domestic duties. Which he did, just as if nothing had happened. Stripped to the waist, he manoeuvred the shears along the hedge, vertically, horizontally, cutting the little privet leaves and twigs with aggressive precision, going over every patch several times, clipping nature to geometric perfection. The sound of the shear-blades' incisive applause echoed along the street.

It was hot yet again, and Fen's torso was bathed in sweat, which glazed and intensified the colours of the bruise that spread over several square inches of his left flank, making the browns chestnut, the purples aubergine, the yellows buttercup. That contusion was now the most evident, and the most painful, of Fen's injuries. His lip and finger had shrunk back almost to normal size, and his left eye was reddened and puffy but looked like it was afflicted with a bad stye rather than suffering from the after-effects of a right royal shiner.

Frowning with concentration, Fen ministered to the hedge until he was interrupted by the arrival of a visitor.

Alan Greeley, having dared to engage in fisticuffs with one of the British Bulldogs, had paid for his temerity with a broken wrist. His arm, splinted and bandaged by Nurse Chase, hung in a sling, and walking was exquisite torture for him. However carefully he trod, each step jarred the wrist and sent crackles of pain shooting along to the elbow. Nevertheless, having learned of Moira's abduction, he had decided to call on Fen as soon as he felt able to, in order to ascertain how Holly-Anne's 'Lesson Man' was faring.

Greeley was, in his way, as altruistic as the expatriate smugglers who supplied him with the goods that he passed on to his fellow townspeople. What the smugglers brought over from the Continent they brought over at their own expense and, since they were braving the International Community naval blockades, at considerable personal risk. Greeley benefited greatly from these freely donated gifts, but anyone would agree that he earned whatever he gained. He went to a great deal of time, trouble and effort to retrieve the goods from various stashes all along the local coastline. He was, moreover, no stranger to acts of charity, always quick to offer a handout, slow to call in a debt.

So the fact that Fen was a valued customer, and it was therefore pragmatic to display concern for him, was neither here nor there. Greeley's solicitude was genuine enough. He liked Fen.

As Greeley approached, Fen laid aside the shears and ran a thumbnail along each of his eyebrows, scraping away the sweat.

'Nice job,' Greeley commented.

'Hm? Oh, yes. Well. Needed doing.'

'You all right?'

'Yeah. Sure. Yeah.' Fen nodded at Greeley's arm. 'You?'

'Bloody awful,' Greeley replied, and smiled a smile that was half grimace. 'Hey, look.' He was carrying a bag, in which there were several small brown bottles. 'French beer. Fancy some?'

Fen was on the point of refusing, then relented. 'Why not?'

In the back garden, on a small square of patio, the only space that was not given over to produce-growing, Fen set out a pair of deckchairs. Their striped canvas had once been white and dark green. Now those colours were fish-flesh grey and a spearmint-toothpaste shade. The chairs' metal frames were oatmealy with rust.

The two men made themselves comfortable, and Fen uncapped two of the bottles and passed one to Greeley. Each took a sip and winced.

'Disgusting,' said Greeley.

'Could do with being chilled,' Fen agreed.

'You can just hear a Frenchman laughing somewhere, can't you? "Ze Eenglish and zeir warm beer." '

Fen half-smiled and took another sip. Disgusting or not, the beer was welcome. He and Greeley sat and drank in companionable silence for a while, and Fen could not help being struck by how ordinary it was, how classic: two Englishmen sitting in a garden in deckchairs, sharing a beer and a moment of quiet.

'I heard, of course,' said Greeley, not knowing how else to start this conversation. 'About Moira.'

'Of course.'

'I'm really sorry.'

Fen rested the rim of his bottle against his lips. 'Yes.'

'I mean, I know things weren't . . . you know. Between the two of you.'

'No. No, they weren't.'

'And feel free to tell me if this isn't any of my business.'

'It wasn't really a secret, I suppose.'

'But if I've overstepped the mark . . .'

'No. No.'

'But Christ, you must be . . . Well, shit, if it was Andrea they'd taken, I'd . . .' Greeley shook his head. 'Frankly I don't know what I'd do.'

'She wasn't meant to be at the festival,' Fen said, after a moment's pause. 'Well, she wasn't *at* it, was she? Wasn't meant to be heading there. I don't know why she went. She didn't seem to have any intention of going. She must have changed her mind.'

'Or she heard the vans. Came out to investigate.'

'Possibly. I've thought about it and thought about it. Why did she go out? But in the end it doesn't make much difference, does it? They got her, that's the thing. She was walking by, and they pulled over and climbed out and got her.'

'And no one tried to stop them.'

Fen shrugged. 'Not that surprising, really. Is it?'

'Maybe not.' Greeley gave his damaged arm a gingerly pat. 'If they had, I doubt they'd have come off any better than I did.'

'What are people saying?'

'About Moira?'

'Generally? About all this?'

'I've not been out and about much, but the feeling I get is no one really wants to talk about it.'

'Yeah. Me too.'

'The Green Man – Hollingbury – would have done something.'

'You think so?'

'Don't you? Organised everyone. Had a plan. Told us what to do.'

'Probably.'

'Without him, we're a bit of a lame duck.'

'I'd say a headless chicken.'

Greeley laughed. 'Damn schoolteachers. Always correcting you.'

'It's my job.'

'Yeah, it is,' Greeley said. 'Again, stop me if I'm overstepping the mark here, Fen, but does it bother you at all?'

'Bother me?'

'That they took her.'

'Of course it does. Why? Does it look like it doesn't?'

Greeley studied him, and saw in his posture – hunched forwards in the deckchair, elbows on thighs, the stringy muscles of his arms taut, the joints of his spine standing out like the ridges of a rolltop desk – certainty. In his face, too: in his fixed-focus eyes, in the deep vertical crevices which, pilgrim-style, scored his cheeks. Unmistakable, unshakeable certainty.

'No,' he concluded. 'In fact, it looks to me like you've very definitely made up your mind about something.'

Fen nodded. 'At first I wondered if I had a choice. It seemed – I'll admit this to you, Alan – it seemed that perhaps, without realising it, the Bulldogs had done me a favour. Like you said: things between me and Moira haven't been right for a while. A long while. And ghastly as it sounds, once it sank in that they'd taken her, I was actually quite glad. Deep down, selfishly, I thought: well, here's the answer. Here's the way out for me. Handed to me on a plate. Nothing I can do. Not my fault. She's gone. Problem solved. It felt like I'd been presented with a clean slate, a chance to start afresh. If I had the guts to take it. No, not the guts. If I could be callous enough. Calculating enough. If I had the capacity to just shut Moira off in my head, close the door on her and pretend she didn't matter any more and had never mattered.'

'But . . .'

'But I couldn't. I can't.'

'So you're—'

'So I'm going after her.' Fen took a long swig of his lager. The bubbles pricked and stung his tongue. 'I've got a plan. Well, an outline of a plan. A sketch of an outline of a plan. And I'm going to do it because I don't have a choice. It's as simple as that. That's what it comes down to. I don't have a choice.'

'But London . . .'

'Yeah, I know. London. And the M25.'

'And getting there.'

'I know.'

'And I don't think the Bulldogs, if you find wherever they are, are just going to let you have her back.'

'Me neither.'

Greeley shook his head. 'I don't know what to say. You're crazy.'

'Certifiable.'

'You'll never manage it.'

'Absolutely not.'

'It's the daftest thing I've ever heard.'

'I don't doubt it.'

'I should try and talk you out of it.'

'Don't bother.'

'Don't worry, I'm not going to. Because if it wasn't for this arm, and the fact that I have a family to consider, I'd be going with you. Really, I would.'

'I believe you.'

'I think someone else should.'

'I think I'll manage better on my own.'

'Well, I'll fix you up with some provisions. That's the least I can do.'

'Thank you for saving me having to ask.'

'I wish I could fix you up with a London permit, but you know . . . Gold dust. Hen's teeth.'

'That's all right. I know where I can try and get hold of one.'

'Cruikshank? You'll be lucky.'

'Yeah, I know.'

There was a pause, then Greeley reached out across the space between them, lager bottle extended. 'Here.'

Fen reciprocated, and the necks of their bottles clinked in mid-air.

'To noble but insane enterprises,' Greeley said.

'To doing the right thing,' Fen replied.

Later, after Greeley had gone, Fen resumed work on the hedge. Three bottles of lager had left him a little light-headed, but not so light-headed that his facility with the shears was impaired. Three bottles of lager had also encouraged him to drag up once again the doubts and questions that had been plaguing him since yesterday, when he had finally, firmly decided that he was going to go in search of Moira. These same doubts had plagued him all through last night, making him toss and turn, dog-restless in his bed. Had he developed amnesia all of a sudden? Had he completely forgotten what the past year and a half had been like? Moira wallowing in bed all day long. Her long sullen silences. Her surliness. Her petty complaints. Her pickiness. Her resentment. The different person she had become, and the compassion he had shown her, constantly, fruitlessly. Here was his chance to be shot of all that. No one would blame him. No one else in Downbourne was even thinking about doing what he intended to do.

And then there were the kids at school to think about. He would be abandoning them, for who knows how long. Maybe for good. He had undertaken a commitment to them, to their parents. Their parents, in good faith, had recompensed him in advance for his services. They wanted their children to be able to read, write, add, understand, *think*. How could he shirk that responsibility?

And even – for Christ's sake – his garden. Here he was, trimming the hedge, and a short while from now, a day, two at the most, he would be off. Even if he was only gone for a fortnight (and that was his lowest estimate, his lowest estimate by far, his if-fate-smiles-on-everything-I-do estimate), when he came back he would have lost produce to the birds and the slugs and the snails. The main picking season was at hand, that time of universal burgeoning and bearing. Without him here to harvest, so much would go to waste. He could always ask a neighbour to mind the garden for him, but could he really expect someone else to look after things as well as he could, and to take on the job without knowing when, if ever, he would return?

Such were the anchors, the gravity of obligation that held him here. Good, sound, logical, valid reasons not to leave, all of them. But at the same time, just excuses. No argument Fen could come up with against going after Moira could withstand the scorchingly irrefutable simplicity of his urge to find his wife, to get her back, to Do The Right Thing. Next to that imperative, all else fell away.

And so, even as he clipped and snipped with the shears, he knew that he wasn't going to be deflected. His doubts made him, if anything, all the more determined. They fired the clay of his resolve.

He wasn't happy about going after Moira.

He didn't believe his search for her was going to have a successful outcome.

There was, however, no other course of action that his conscience would abide. Anything else was unacceptable.

That evening, Fen presented himself at the door to Gilbert Cruik-shank's house.

Ludicrously, he had smartened himself up, like someone going for a job interview. He had washed his hair. He had shaved. He had put on his cleanest, most ironed-looking shirt. He was even wearing a tie.

All to make a good impression on a blind man.

The door opened a full two minutes after he knocked, Cruik-shank's appearance being preceded by mutters, grumbles and curses of mounting volubility that reached their climax with the pulling of the bolt and the parting of door from jamb to the maximum distance permitted by a security chain.

Out poked the spongy nose. Out peeped the sightless eyes.

'Yes?'

'Mr Cruikshank.'

'Morris. What do you want?'

'A word. Please.'

'How about "piss off"? There's *two* words.'

'First of all, I want to apologise.'

'No, you want something from me. That's the only reason anyone ever calls on me. Even the ones who bring me food. They say they do it out of the goodness of their hearts, but they want something.'

'I was out of line the other night. At the festival.'

'So?'

'So I want to say I'm sorry.'

'Do you honestly think that (a) I care, and (b) it makes any difference?'

'I hoped—'

'Morris, let's cut the crap, shall we? I know your wife has been taken, and I think I can guess what you've come here to ask for. What I don't understand is what on earth makes you think I would have any intention of parting with my London permit, for anyone and particularly for the likes of you?'

'If you'll invite me in and let me talk to you for just five minutes, Mr Cruikshank, I think I can convince you why you should lend it to me.'

'Oh, *lend* it to you, eh? *Lend* you my permit when there's very little chance I'll get it back. Interesting use of the word "lend" there, schoolteacher.'

'Please. Just five minutes of your time.'

Cruikshank's face – the slotted section of it visible to Fen – looked thoughtful. Then, abruptly, the door slammed shut. There was silence, followed by several seconds of clatter as the security chain was fumblingly disengaged. Then the door reopened, wide.

'Enter,' said Cruikshank, dipping from the waist and uncurling his arm like an unctuous *maître d'* at a high-class restaurant.

Cruikshank lived in a cul-de-sac just off Clement Road. The street consisted of two rows of identical flint-and-brick artisans' cottages, each of them two storeys tall, with a short, steep staircase, low ceilings, and cramped rooms. Cruikshank's house – strictly speaking, his sister's house – differed from its neighbours only in the extent of its filthiness, both outside and, especially, inside. A certain amount of dirt and disarray was to be expected nowadays, but Cruikshank's home was, by any standards, squalid. Upon entering, Fen found himself in a narrow hallway where the carpet was rucked and wrinkled and the wallpaper was peeling away in curls. This, along with several shelfloads of damp-swollen paperbacks, served to give the impression that he was walking into some kind of diseased, foetid throat. A couple of yards along from the front door, next to the foot of the staircase, Fen paused at the entrance to the living room. The interior of the room looked as if a lunatic decorator had been let loose with a spray-gun and several gallons of matt-black paint. Everyone knew the story. One winter's evening Cruikshank was lighting a camping stove for warmth and managed to knock it over so that it fell against the side of an armchair. The chair cover, 100% pure polyester, ignited, and by the time Cruikshank managed to fetch a bucket of water, the flames had taken hold and the room was filled with acrid smoke. Neighbours risked their lives and used gallons of their own precious rainwater to douse the fire, in return for which Cruikshank, true to form, offered not a word of thanks, complaining instead about his soaked carpet and furnishings. Nothing had been done to the room since then. Either Cruikshank still used it as it was – every object and surface in it charred and soot-caked – or else he simply avoided it, confining his solitary life to the house's three other rooms.

Cruikshank struck Fen's ankle sharply with his stick. 'Why have you stopped?' he snapped. 'Keep going, keep going. The kitchen.'

Fen moved on.

If the hallway and living room were bad, the kitchen was ten times worse. In the dim evening light, Fen saw precarious stacks of long-unwashed crockery on the sink's work-surface. There were rinds of mould in crannies and along edges, and all over the linoleum there were dried, spattered stains whose origin he did not want even to guess at. He was aware, too, of movement all around, a peripheral scuttling and hustling, tiny leggy things active among the remnants of meals, scavenging the scabs of food. The smell of rot and decay was strong but there was also a darker, mustier odour in the air which he could only assume was insect turds. Even blind, Cruikshank could not have been oblivious to the repellence of this room, so Fen had to conclude that, perversely, he relished it, and relished, too, ushering visitors into it.

'Sit down,' Cruikshank said, rapping the top of the kitchen table with a loosely clenched fist.

Fen pulled out a chair circumspectly and, discovering nothing untoward on its seat, sat.

Cruikshank remained standing. 'All right then,' he said, 'let's hear it. You want my permit? Go on. Beg for it.'

A recalcitrant urge welled up in Fen. Beg for it? Why should he? Why should he have to grovel to, of all people, Gilbert Cruikshank?

But so long as there remained a chance, however remote, that Cruikshank might let him have the permit, he had no choice.

'Mr Cruikshank,' he said, 'I need it. I can't put it any more simply than that. I need your permit so that I can get into London and find my wife and bring her back.'

'Go on.'

'Ummm . . . OK. I realise that you probably don't like me very much.'

'Not necessarily.'

'But I have to say I admire you. The way you've carried on, in spite of your disability. The way you've—'

'Oh no no no, Morris!' Cruikshank stamped his stick on the floor, causing the haphazard stacks of crockery to jump and jingle. 'No. You were doing fine up till then. Honest, straightforward, and then all of a sudden you veer off into flattery, and that won't do at all. I asked for begging, not arse-kissing.'

Fen drew in a deep breath, expelling it slowly. 'I suppose you want me to say something like "I won't be able to succeed without your help".'

'I want you to say what *you* want to say.'

Again Fen felt that recalcitrant urge. Again he damped it down. How was he meant to play this? What was Cruikshank after? Perhaps he should try an appeal to Cruikshank's better nature. Assuming Cruikshank had one, that is.

'Moira means a lot to me, Mr Cruikshank.'

Cruikshank cocked his head to one side, like someone who has detected strains of fine music. 'There, that's more like it.'

'I love her.'

'You do? Still? Despite her hating you?'

'She doesn't hate me,' Fen countered. 'She never has. It's just that things have been . . . difficult for her.'

'Things such as?'

'You know what I'm talking about.'

'Tell me about it.'

'No. Why should I?'

'Because I'm nosy. Because I like to hear about other people's miseries. Because I have a London permit and you want it.'

'So that's it, is it?' Fen said, bristling. 'That's your price?'

'Look at it from my point of view, Morris,' Cruikshank said. 'That permit is important to me. It means I can go back to London any time I want. Whether in practical terms that's possible, I don't care. I'm blind and arthritic; I'm not likely to be making any fifty-mile journeys in the near future. But that's not the point. I have an official document that says I'm not stuck here in this piss-awful little hole for ever. It says I don't have to live here indefinitely, surrounded by backward provincials like you. Now, do you think I'm going to hand over something so precious to me to just any old person who comes along and asks for it? Give it away? I'm not doing that without getting *something* in return.'

'Forget it.' Fen stood up. 'I'm not playing along.'

'Oh come on. It won't hurt. You can start by telling me how it felt when Moira became pregnant. You'd been trying for a while, hadn't you? You must have been overjoyed.'

'Cruikshank, I said forget it. I'm not doing this.'

'But what about the permit?'

'I'll manage without.'

'Oh, you will, will you?'

'I'll find a way.'

'Brave talk. But the M25 . . . Watchtowers, dogs, mines, barbed wire, and the rest. That's quite a gauntlet.'

Fen weighed it up: satisfying Cruikshank's spiteful prurience against losing the one thing without which his chances of rescuing Moira went from marginally-better-than-nil to nil.

He sank back into the chair. 'OK,' he sighed. 'All right.'

'Good man. So: when you found out Moira was pregnant – was it overjoyed, or not overjoyed?'

Fen paused, casting his mind back. 'Mixed feelings, I suppose.'

'Only natural.'

'After all, this isn't the best of worlds to bring a child into. The best of countries, I mean. Not with things the way they are. Then again, there are a lot worse places to be in England than Downbourne. And children do represent hope for the future.'

'So everyone would have us believe. I can't understand it myself. Another squalling, foul-tempered little proto-adult – how is *that* in any way hopeful? Just one more human being, destined to make a mess of things and die, like the rest of us.'

Fen almost laughed. 'But you think you can do better with each child, don't you. It's part of an ongoing process. The refining and improving of the human race. Each generation learning from the mistakes of the previous one and passing on what it's learned to the next.'

'A sentiment tidily disproved by our nation's current predicament.'

'Perhaps. Still, you've got to try. That's how I saw it. Still see it. You can't give up on the future just because the present isn't so brilliant.'

'And it was going to be twins, wasn't it? How did you feel about that? A brace of the little tykes. Was that twice as exciting?'

'We didn't know. Not at the time. It was only afterwards that . . .' Fen's voice faltered.

'That . . . ?' Cruikshank prompted.

Fen stood up again, this time shunting the chair forcibly backwards so that its feet scraped judderingly across the crusted linoleum. 'No. That's enough. I'm not going on with this. It's not worth it.'

'But Morris, things were just starting to get interesting.'

'Fuck you.' Fen pushed past Cruikshank, deliberately banging shoulders with the old man, knocking him off balance. He headed into the hallway, hurrying past the flocculent wallpaper, the bloated books, the entrance to the ruined living room. He seized the front-door handle. He needed to be out. Out of this house, away from its occupant.

'Wait.'

Cruikshank came hobbling after him, one hand spidering feelingly along the wall.

'Morris, wait.'

Fen, still grasping the door handle, waited.

'Listen. All right. Maybe I went too far. I simply wanted to find out . . .'

'What?' Fen said tersely. 'What did you want to find out?'

'How far you were prepared to go. What you'd be prepared to do.'

'Well, now you know.'

'The permit is yours, Morris. You can have it.'

Fen didn't reply, unsure whether this was just another game, a blind man's bluff.

'You do need it,' Cruikshank said. 'You deserve it.'

'Deserve it. Because my hard-luck story is sufficiently tragic.'

'No, you idiot. Because, unlike the rest of the arseholes in this town, you've actually shown some spine.'

Fen peered over his shoulder, looking into Cruikshank's eyes. The old man returned the gaze, blinkless as a lizard. Cruikshank wasn't totally blind, but sometimes it seemed his vision was better than he let on. Perhaps he exaggerated the extent of his disability, the better to earn himself charity. Alternatively, perhaps he was adept at hiding how blind he truly was. Either way, he was managing to give the impression now of scrutinising Fen's face, searching it for a response.

'Yes,' Cruikshank said, 'that caught you up short, didn't it? You weren't expecting *that*.'

'I don't understand.'

'I think you do. It's quite simple. You're the only one, Morris, the *only one* who's decided to act. Oh, certainly there's been talk of going after those Bulldog bastards. Not a lot of talk, but some. But talk is all it's been. Otherwise there's just been a bend-over-and-take-it kind of attitude. I've been hoping *someone* would have the gumption to stand up and play the hero, and it's funny but I did have a sneaking feeling that that someone would be you. You, the person who looked like he'd have most to gain from keeping his head down and staying put. The one man here who might have cause to be grateful to the Bulldogs. You know when you told me earlier that you thought I didn't like you very much? And I said, "Not necessarily"? Well, that's the truth, Morris. Don't get me wrong, I don't want you as my friend or anything, but that isn't to say I *dis*like you. I think you're tightly-buttoned, a little self-satisfied, a little priggish. I think you actually quite enjoy living in England the way it is now. You're one of those people who believes suffering is good for the soul. Hardship maketh the man. But I think there's also something else to you, something more. And I think that that's what I'm being shown right now. So yes, I admit I shouldn't have got you to talk about your marriage and your wife's pregnancy; I shouldn't have tried to make you use that as a bargaining chip. Consider it a test. An oral exam. I had to be absolutely sure you weren't wasting my time and that I'm giving my permit to the right person. And now I *am* sure.'

'Has anyone ever told you, Cruikshank, that you're an absolute shit?'

'Plenty of people,' Cruikshank replied with a shrug. 'It's not my policy to be adored. In fact, I consider it a mark of honour that I can be universally unpleasant and get away with it. I was like that when I lived in London, and still everyone rallied around when my sight started to go. That's how I got my permit, how I got down here. I was, as you so rightly put it, an absolute shit, yet people still took pity on me. You could say that by being the worst I can be, I bring out the best in others.'

'You could, if you were desperately trying to justify your short-comings as a human being.'

Cruikshank gave a dry, crackling laugh. 'Careful, Morris. It's not too late for me to change my mind, you know. Now just wait there. I won't be a moment.'

The old man groped for the staircase banister and clumped up to the next floor. Fen heard him overhead, moving around, rummaging. A short while later he reappeared, a quarter-folded piece of white paper in his hand, and cautiously descended.

'There,' he said, when he had reached the bottom of the stairs. He proffered the piece of paper to Fen.

Fen unfolded it. It was a brittle photocopy, marked with a faint blue stamp that said 'London Council'. The text on it was brief and to the point:

This entitles the bearer to access to and from the
Greater London area. Any resident/citizen presenting
this permit to the appropriate authorities at a
designated checkpoint shall be allowed free and un-
hindered passage except if at the discretion of the
authorities that person be deemed undesirable or a
threat to civic safety.

Fen read the words a couple of times, then carefully, even
reverently, refolded the permit and inserted it into his breast
pocket.

'So there you have it,' said Cruikshank. 'Your way in. Piece of
advice, though. That bit at the end? About being "a threat to civic
safety", or whatever it says? The checkpoint guards usually use that
as an excuse to extort a bribe, so I'd take something with you,
something valuable, just in case.'

'All right. Thanks. I will.'

'Now fuck off out of here.'

'Mr Cruikshank—'

'No schmaltzy nonsense, please!' snapped Cruikshank.

'I was just going to say, I *will* bring this back to you.' Fen patted
his pocket, then realised the action was probably lost on Cruikshank. 'Your permit. I swear.'

'Bollocks you will. You stand a cat's chance in hell of getting
your wife out of London. You're on a fool's errand, you're as good
as dead, and you know it. So don't give me any "coming back"
bullshit.'

'I am going to try, though.'

'Of course you are. Now bugger off and never darken my door
again!'

Awake again. Blackness. Slept for . . . one hour? Two? Body aching. Thirsty. Hungry. Hunger like a *thing* inside me, a squatting presence, filling a vacancy with pain.

The floorboards. The reek of other bodies. The stench of our waste products.

Still here. This place. This house with bricked-up windows. This room I know by feel alone. How long has it been now? Two days? Possibly three. And what time is it now? I have no idea.

I sit up and try to knead some of the stiffness out of my muscles. There's not a stick of furniture in the room, unless you count the tin bucket we've been given to relieve ourselves in. Nothing to sleep on or under, not even a blanket. It's all bare and raw. The floorboards are gritty and splintered. The walls have holes in them, patches where the concrete beneath the plasterwork has been exposed. I've explored them with my fingers. They're shallow, like moon craters.

While massaging my back and legs, I become aware of one of the other women sobbing. Gasping into her hands. It sounds like she's suffering some kind of fit. I know I ought to go over and touch her, hug her, comfort her, but I lack the energy, the will. There are four of us in here. Are both of the two who aren't sobbing asleep? Maybe. Or maybe they're just lying there, thinking the same as I'm thinking: *I can't be bothered to help her. I don't see the point.*

We've had no contact with any of the other women since we were thrown in here and the door was shut on us. Presumably they're in other rooms in this house, sitting there scared like us. We've had no contact with our captors either. No one's even walked by in the corridor outside, or at least we haven't heard anyone. It could be that we've been locked in here and abandoned, left to rot.

But I don't think so.

I think this is a cunning little ploy our captors have devised. Put the women in rooms. No food, no water. Leave them there for a few days. Weaken them. Break down their resistance.

A culinary analogy comes to mind: tenderising the meat.

And with that thought the fear returns, the fear that I've been grappling with on and off since they pulled me into that van, and I feel helpless and numb and craven and I want to sob like that other woman, just surrender and let it all gush out. I think of the men in the van, and the other men who were waiting for us here when we arrived and watched us as we were shoved and herded across the compound to the building we're in. Their brutal muscularity. The light in their eyes. You could *feel* the avarice coming off them. It wasn't just desire, it was a need so strong it was almost a hatred. Their stares could have punched through wood. As we were being paraded past them, I thought they were going to grab us then and there and tear us to pieces. I never knew what 'vulnerable' truly meant till that moment.

Those same men will be coming for us eventually, probably sooner rather than later, bringing with them violence and violation . . .

And now the fear has a tight grip on me and won't let go, and I ask myself, trying to be rational, what's the worst that can happen to me, and I think of several answers and the fear grows worse.

I try to reach for a memory. This is the trick I have developed in recent months. In order to escape the present, reach for something from my past, an image, a perfect, gemlike moment to contemplate, to find refuge in. Like that afternoon on the clifftop with Fen.

This time, however, it doesn't work. The hunger and fear in combination are too great. I grope for a happier time but all I come up with is myself screaming through labour, writhing under Anne Chase's grasp, her hands on my shoulders pushing me down onto the bed while she tries to soothe me, telling me everything's going well, breathe through the pain, breathe throooough the pain, but I know everything *isn't* going well, there's a deep and terrible wrongness to all this and I can see it in Anne's eyes, although I don't need to see her eyes to know it because I can feel it too, because deep down inside me everything's all twisted up, all sickly and rebellious, and I know I'm not giving birth, I'm giving the opposite of birth, and all this screaming and breathing throooough the pain is futile because what's coming out of me doesn't want life, never did, and then at last it emerges, the first one, in a few long, tearing minutes of agony beyond agony, and I see it and it's not moving, not making a sound, it's just lying there, stillborn.

Stillborn.

Born.

Still.

Fen holding it. Fen's hands dripping with blood, as though *he* is its murderer, *he* is the one who has killed it. Fen crying and talking to it through his tears, somehow trying to get it to live, force it to draw breath just by speaking to it and cradling it and urging it, but there's nothing he can do, he's not a miracle-worker, it's useless, and then the other one arrives, my body spitting it out into the world like it's poison, pus, something to be rid of, but Anne wraps it in a towel and offers it to me anyway, as if I would *want* to take it in my arms, as if I would *want* to embrace something my body has just rejected . . .

And now I give in to the fear, because that's all I can do, and as it surges through me I crawl over on all fours towards the sobbing woman. Plaster granules crack and crunch beneath my palms. I locate her by sound alone. Not knowing which of the other three she is, I latch on to her and she instinctively reciprocates. Our arms fumble, and then we have each other and we're trembling and sobbing together in the lost, awful dark.

A storm was brewing.

The long spell of good weather had reached its inevitable con-clusion, its climatic climax. The heat had become weary, the sunshine old, the clear skies stale. The air, humid and hayfeverish, was crying out to be sluiced, changed, renewed; all this, and more, the storm promised. From dawn onward it loitered on the horizon, a swathe of dark grey cloud hung with filmy tentacles of rain. Rumbling. Biding its time. It would move in over Downbourne when it was good and ready. Until then, it was content to portend.

And the townspeople were more than happy for it to come. Their rainwater butts begged for replenishment; their gardens gasped. They wanted a downpour. They wanted the world to be washed and returned to them sparkling and as new. They wanted pluvial England yet again to provide.

And there was another reason why the townspeople welcomed the storm's ominous rumbling and the veiled sunlight and the taste that hung in the air, the teary, back-of-the-throat taste of im-pending rain – because today was the day they buried Michael Hollingbury. In the graveyard of St Stephen's, the hole had been dug (a pagan icon, yes, but Hollingbury had been a churchgoer too, most of his life). In a winding-sheet made of old bedclothes, lodged in a small side-room at the town hall, the body waited. The service was scheduled for noon. By eleven, the route from the town hall to the church was already lined with people. They turned out to pay their last respects to their slain mayor, but they turned out, too, to mourn the passing of something else, though they weren't sure what. A kind of innocence, perhaps.

The body was carried to church on a bier, that, in another life, had been a kitchen door. Resting on the shoulders of six solemn bearers, including Henry Mullins, it wended its way past the silent crowds, up to St Stephen's, through the lychgate, across to the grave site. The vicar, the decrepit Reverend Cave, conducted the service, his quavery ceremonial intonements punctuated by the distant growls of the storm. The body was lowered. Handfuls of soil were thrown. There was, and would be, no headstone. All that marked Hollingbury's final resting place was a cross consisting of two lengths of wooden stake lashed together, the lateral one etched with his name. There were several dozen such crosses scattered about the graveyard, in various states of decay. Dating from after the unlucky gamble, they were as impermanent as the headstones from before then were lasting.

And it was while the townsfolk's attention was on the funeral, and concomitantly on themselves, that Fen emerged from the front door of 12 Crane Street with a knapsack on his back and the solidest pair of shoes he owned on his feet. Closing the gate behind him, he turned and took one last look at the house, the front garden, the meticulously clipped hedge, then turned again and set off up the road, northwards. His expression was, other than a slight jut to his jaw, impassive. In five minutes he had reached the outskirts of town. In another five minutes he was passing the signpost on which, facing away from town, the name of Downbourne was still just discernible through a film of green mould. The road ahead was craggy and overgrown, in places festooned with weeds, a decaying ribbon of tarmac that wound downhill to a copse of trees and emerged beyond into open countryside. He had travelled just over a mile along it when the first fat raindrops started to fall.

2. ON THE RAILS

After the rain, the sun. The road steamed, and as if from nowhere gnats appeared, swirling in the damp air, cycling endlessly, endlessly upwards. Fen walked past dripping trees and fields of glistening crops and great swathes of pasture where cattle munched and defecated loudly, his soaked clothes slowly drying. For a while he felt a greater optimism than he ever expected his misgivings would allow him to feel. His spirits, like the gnats, while not actually rising, at least pretended to the ascendant.

His hope was that, *en route* to London, he would be able to depend – like Blanche Dubois – on the kindness of strangers. For the first two days of his journey, however, he encountered strangers aplenty but very little kindness. The villages and small towns he passed through, many of them not much more than collections of houses sprinkled along the road, were places where itinerants were greeted with, at best, wary looks, at worst thinly disguised hostility, the latter becoming the more common reaction the further from Downbourne he went. Fen had not appreciated – perhaps, through accustomedness, had forgotten – that Downbourne was in many regards exceptional. Blessed by its location and by its adoption of a strong, charismatic leader, it was a lucky little oasis that had held steady, maybe even prospered, while everything around it fell apart. He was soon reminded that, beyond Downbourne's radius of influence, life was very different. People had less, and guarded what little they had jealously.

On the two occasions when he stopped at a house and requested water for his canteen, it was once given grudgingly and once, without apology, refused. When, in one village, he settled down on the central green to unlace his shoes and air his feet, he was approached by a delegation of five locals, one of them bearing a pickaxe, another with a Staffordshire bull terrier on a leash, and was asked – in a manner not anticipating a refusal – to move on. And when, as dusk was falling on his first night away from Downbourne in nearly a decade, he began to look for somewhere to sleep, it was not until after he had knocked on several dozen doors (and once been threatened with a shotgun) that he finally found someone prepared to offer him a bed.

'Bed', it turned out, meant a stretch of floorspace in a garden shed, but despite the pervasive reek of fertiliser, the lack of any mattress or coverlet, and the dangerous-looking array of horticultural implements hung around the walls, the place was surprisingly cosy, and Fen, exhausted from walking, slept soundly. The next morning he bandaged his blistered feet using the roll of sticking plaster that Greeley had given him, and set off again.

The road he was following was an A road which, in the days when everybody had a car and fuel with which to propel it, would have got him to London in a couple of hours if the traffic was good. How many times had he driven up and down its snaking length, on shopping trips to the West End, visits to the theatre, to see friends? Too many to count. He remembered how he used to seethe with impatience if his speed dropped below thirty because he was stuck behind a lorry or some lumbering farm vehicle; how he would drum his fingers on the steering wheel as he waited at one of the many bottlenecks along the way – crossroads, traffic lights, roundabouts. That was all the road had been then, a two-hour shuttle between home and the capital, with various obstacles to be negotiated along the way, some moving, some stationary.

On foot, it was a different entity. Its landmarks were hours, not minutes, apart. Its rises and falls, twists and turns, segued into one another, so gradually that at times Fen thought he had strayed onto the wrong road by mistake, since this one was unfurling prospects that did not accord with his recollection of it. He was used to seeing the scenery from car windows, condensed by speed. He was not used to seeing it evolve incrementally and fluently from one section to the next. Compounding the impression of unfamiliarity was the fact that, between the last time he had travelled this way and now, sizeable changes had been wrought by neglect and nature. The vegetation on either side of the road had encroached, at times narrowing it to half its width. Tree roots had thrust up through the camber, cracking the tarmac like reptile hatchlings breaking out of their eggs. The countryside around the road had altered, too. The hedgerows between fields had grown shaggy and rank so that there were no neat divisions; one field seemed to sprawl into another. It wasn't rare to come across a service station whose petrol pumps and forecourt were wreathed with weeds, or an isolated pub, now abandoned to the elements and half engulfed by rampant greenery.

Everywhere, the slow capitulation of man to Nature, and Fen could not help thinking of Michael Hollingbury's death – his murder – and how this had been an inversion of the process he was seeing around him. Nature's representative destroyed on a pyre of man-made detritus, a small setback in a war which Nature was everywhere else winning handsomely.

Near the end of the second day, Fen halted at the beginning of one of the road's infrequent stretches of dual carriageway. Sitting down on the verge and leaning his back against the signpost that encouraged overtaking for the next four hundred yards, he inventoried the contents of his knapsack and was dismayed to discover that he had consumed well over half of the dry rations supplied by Alan Greeley. The dry rations had been intended as a supplement to the warm, hearty meals Fen was to have received from warm, hearty homeowners whom he had anticipated would welcome him eagerly into their warm, hearty homes and offer him a place at their warm, hearty tables. He knew now how naïve this expectation had been, but that did not alter the fact that he was going to run out of food within a day or so unless the level of stranger-kindness improved dramatically (which, on the evidence so far, seemed unlikely, and he predicted that, with London on the horizon, it was only going to deteriorate further). He realised he was reaching, if not actually at, the point of no return. Turning back was the only sensible option.

But then – he reminded himself as he clambered wearily to his feet again – since when had 'sensible' ever been a factor in this enterprise? Indeed, if anything characterised what he was up to, it was surely an utter lack of sense.

Coldly consoled by this thought, he resumed walking.

Near the end of the stretch of dual carriageway, just before it funnelled down to a single lane again, the road traversed a railway cutting. As Fen approached this, he became aware of a delicious aroma – or an aroma that would have been more delicious had it not carried for him a memory of the Green Man's demise. Roasting meat. At first he could not pinpoint where the smell was coming from, but then he saw a narrow plume of smoke twirling up from down in the cutting. He moved to the safety fence at the edge of the road and peered over.

Two parallel sets of rust-dulled railway tracks curved away into the distance. On the left-hand of the two, parked a dozen yards along from the road bridge, was a train, or rather part of a train, a single carriage. It was painted extraordinarily, a colourful, hectic mélange of figures and patterns adorning every inch of its body-work, even the roof; and beside it, sitting on the shallow-raked embankment, was someone in a railwayman's uniform, a man, black-bearded, brown-skinned. He was squatting in front of a cooking fire, absorbed in the task of turning a spitted animal on a steel rotisserie which had once been part of a barbecue set. The animal appeared to be a rabbit, divided into halves, front and back.

Fen watched the bisected creature revolve, its skin gently charr-ing, sparks of dribbled fat fizzling in the fire, and all at once his mouth was awash with saliva. His stomach, having had nothing to digest over the past thirty-six hours but peanuts, raisins, banana chips, and some chunks of pepperoni dipped in mustard, grumbled greedily. Hunger vied with caution. There was no reason to suppose the railwayman was any friendlier than anyone else he had met on his travels so far. Caution won. Fen was just about to back away from the fence and continue on his way when the railwayman, happening to glance up, caught sight of him. Im-mediately, a smile broke through the man's beard, like a sudden white moon. He raised a hand.

'Hello, my friend!'

And that was how Fen became a passenger aboard the *Jagan-natha*.

Ravi Wickramasinghe had been a train driver for a decade and a half until the Unlucky Gamble sent England spiralling into freefall. Throughout that period he had been a diligent servant of the rail industry: never once missed a shift, often filled in for sick colleagues, did his utmost to ensure his trains arrived at their destinations on time, and if running behind schedule apologised over the intercom system in such a profuse and elaborate fashion that few of his passengers disembarked disgruntled. Indeed, his late-arrival announcements, he told Fen, had become legendary among commuters on his routes. He had heard from ticket inspectors that people often claimed they looked forward to delays, simply so that they could hear their driver offer contrition and furnish them with a not necessarily honest reason for why they were not where they were supposed to be at the time they were supposed to be there. Instead of the usual dreary litany of signalling failures and engine breakdowns and adverse leaf/track interfaces, Wickramasinghe used to offer the preposterous excuses – less truthful but also less aggravating. An escaped elephant on the line was one of his favourites. 'And what is it doing on the line? It is making a trunk call!' Another classic (to use Wickramasinghe's own description) was the somewhat surreal 'We have not slowed down at all; rather, the world has speeded up around us.' And then there was: 'For those who expected to reach the terminus by eight forty-seven, I regret to say we have not met our Waterloo.'

And everything had been fine, and then everything had gone to pot. Rail services had stumbled on, growing more erratic and unreliable with each passing day, and Wickramasinghe had done his best to keep his passengers entertained and amused even as their numbers dwindled and the frequency of hold-ups, curtailed journeys and cancellations increased. Inevitably, though, the situation had got to the point where the rail networks had had to begin laying employees off. And who had been one of the first drivers to go?

'You,' said Fen, through a mouthful of rabbit meat.

'Me,' Wickramasinghe confirmed. 'The commuter's friend. They tossed me aside like I was nothing. "Oh, let's lose the bloody Paki. No one will miss him." ' His tone was one of regret rather than rancour, the tone of someone who has shouldered more than his fair share of prejudice and abuse.

'You're Indian, though, aren't you?'

'Still a "bloody Paki" as far as most people are concerned.'

'And this.' Fen indicated the single rail carriage. 'This is where you live now.'

Wickramasinghe shook his head, beaming a splendid grin. 'I live,' he said, 'everywhere.'

It took Fen a moment to divine the meaning of this gnomic pronouncement. 'It runs?'

'She's called the *Jagannatha*, and we travel the rails together, she and I.'

Fen peered at the carriage. It was a venerable piece of rolling stock, at least forty years old, but looked younger, and jauntier, thanks to the illustrations with which it was adorned. Here and there a scrap of its original livery was visible, but mostly this was obscured beneath dramatic representations of the pantheon of Hindu gods and goddesses. Here was blue-skinned Vishnu, seated on a throne of cobras. Here was ten-armed Shiva, sword-wielding and ferocious. Here was four-headed Brahma. And here were others whom Fen could not identify, all of them interlaced with strips of curlicued Sanskrit text that wove in and out of their dramatic poses like strains of music. It was a beautiful piece of work, and he said as much to Wickramasinghe, who took the compliment well.

'I am not an artist. I had never tried anything like this before, but my hand, it seemed, was divinely guided. Ganesha, god of new ventures, blessed me.'

'Ganesha. He's the one with the elephant's head, isn't he? I don't see him.'

'He's on the other side. When you have finished eating, I will take you on a tour.'

An idea was forming in Fen's mind, a possibility. 'You know, I'm surprised you can actually move about. I really had no idea there was still electricity in the rails.'

'Oh yes, oh yes. In and around London there is. The Council has even managed to establish some regular services. I do not know how many people actually use them. I think they are a token gesture more than anything. Nevertheless . . .'

'So it is possible to get in and out of London by train.'

'It can be done, yes. This is where you are headed? London?'

Fen nodded.

'May I ask why?'

Fen told him why, gnawing rabbit all the while. Rabbit had become a dietary staple in England since the Unlucky Gamble, its stringy gaminess no longer a deterrent to its enjoyment. Hare, mink, stoat, ferret – these too had been added to the nation's gastronomic repertoire, along with most types of bird, with the inevitable consequence that English cuisine was now more of an international laughing-stock than ever, and not only that but subject to all sorts of exaggerated and distorted rumours. In the United States, for instance, it was believed that American fast-food concessions in England served a 'badger burger' (untrue, of course, since the fast-food conglomerates had closed down their English operations years ago, and it was anyway doubtful any of them would have been quite so honest about the meat content of one of their products), while in France, where just about any creature higher up the evolutionary ladder than the earthworm was considered edible, jokes about *les Anglais* and mouse pies were considered the height of topical humour. Or so it was alleged, at any rate. The provenance of such stories was dubious, and what they seemed to offer, more than anything else, was a reflection of the English attitude to foreigners' attitude to the English.

Thanks to his hunger this particular rabbit tasted better than usual to Fen, and he took frequent breaks from his account of the raid by the British Bulldogs and Moira's abduction to avail himself of fresh morsels of its flesh, which he chewed and swallowed with relish and which his stomach received with gurgling gratitude. Wickramasinghe listened attentively, eating rabbit himself but leaving the lion's share to his guest.

The rabbit was nothing but bones by the time Fen's narration was finished.

'A terrible state of affairs,' opined Wickramasinghe, sighing. 'I admire you for what you have undertaken. I know of the British Bulldogs. They have a fearsome reputation. You are a brave man.'

'Not really,' said Fen. 'Are you married?'

'I was.'

'I'm sorry. Is she—? Is your wife—?'

'No. No. Not dead. Daljit fled to India the moment things started getting shaky. Took our two sons with her and went to live in Calcutta with some cousin she barely knew.'

'Oh, I see.' It had been a common enough practice among England's immigrant community, renouncing your strife-torn adoptive land for the comparative security of the country from which you or your parents or your grandparents originally hailed.

'But I take your point,' Wickramasinghe said. 'In your shoes I would have probably done the same. What binds a husband to a wife is as powerful as it is hard to define, no? There is love. There is passion, at least to begin with. There is friendship, after the passion has faded. But there is more, too. A unity, a fusion of selves that takes place over the years, slowly, gradually, until you no longer know where you end and your other half begins. "Your other half" – that pretty much sums it up, does it not? The part of you that is not you.'

Fen murmured assent, licking rabbit grease off his fingers.

'Now listen, my friend,' Wickramasinghe said. 'I have a proposal for you.'

Fen had an inkling of what the railwayman was about to suggest. It was, indeed, the very thing he had been hoping Wickramasinghe would suggest.

His answer could not have been anything other than yes.

The *Jagannatha* was a home on wheels, neatly and narrowly self-contained. Up front was the driver's cab, which Wickramasinghe had decked out so that its interior resembled nothing so much as that of a Bombay taxi. A garland of nylon marigolds festooned the viewing window. Perched among the gauges and switches of the control desk were an incense holder (but no incense) and a small plastic figurine of Krishna playing the flute. To the pale green walls had been added more lines of Sanskrit like those on the outside of the carriage – they were prayers, Wickramasinghe informed Fen – along with an intricately-petalled lotus and a reversed swastika. Wickramasinghe was quick to assure Fen that the latter was a fylfot, a Vedic symbol of well-being, and not anything more sinister. There were also two photographs on the wall, pinned in place. One was a formal portrait of a chubby woman, posed in her best sari, regarding the camera shyly, her hair centre-parted with almost geometric precision, her *tika* neat and round in the middle of her forehead. The other was a snapshot of a pair of mischievous-looking boys, hugging and gurning in a back garden.

'Daljit,' said Wickramasinghe, pointing to the woman. He indicated each of the boys. 'Sanjay. Naz.'

'A lovely family,' said Fen.

'It was.'

Back from the cab, there were four first-class passenger compartments, one of which, with a blanket draped over the window for a curtain, was Wickramasinghe's sleeping quarters. To the rear of these was a small standard-class section, and right at the back of the carriage there was a toilet with a basin that did not work and a lavatory which Wickramasinghe had rigged up, by removing the base of the retention tank below, so that it emptied out straight onto the track without having to be flushed.

'Come and see how comfortable this is,' Wickramasinghe said, ushering Fen into one of the spare first-class compartments.

Fen tested the springs of the plush banquette seats appreciatively.

'I suppose I shouldn't ask, but I presume you stole the *Jagannatha* from your employers?'

'Not stole her,' Wickramasinghe replied, firmly and with a touch of indignation. 'Not stole. I took her from the yards because she is rightfully mine. After the way I was treated, it is only proper that I should have her. Besides, she was out of service at the time. No one will have missed her.' His previous bonhomie returned. 'But never mind that. Please make yourself at home. If there's anything you want, let me know.'

'I will. Thank you.'

'Tomorrow, we get started.'

'Not tonight?' Only then did it dawn on Fen that he was being invited to bed down for the night in the train.

'Tonight? Oh no. I never travel after dark. Too dangerous. Tomorrow.' Wickramasinghe's train, after all, and he considered himself lucky to have met the fellow. No point in pushing that luck.

'Very well then. Tomorrow it is.'

'Crack of dawn,' said Wickramasinghe.

He was as good as his word. When Fen opened his eyes the next morning, the sky outside the compartment window was a watery wash of pre-sunrise grey and the *Jagannatha* was throbbing tunefully, keen to be in motion.

He found Wickramasinghe in the driver's cabin, perusing a timetable and a map of railway lines.

'Fen! Good morning, my friend. You slept well?'

'Wonderfully well.' Fen glanced at the timetable, which was a typically no-frills London Council production: a few photocopied pages of typed text stapled down the middle. 'I take it this is to ensure that we don't crash head-on with the six-twenty out of Victoria.'

'Exactly, my friend, exactly. One cannot simply gad about the network at random. Each journey, each step of a journey, must be carefully worked out beforehand. Not to worry, I know what I am doing. You are in safe hands.'

'That's nice to know. Erm, before we set off – are you hungry?' He showed Wickramasinghe his knapsack. 'Only, I have some peanuts, some raisins, other stuff, if you're interested.'

Wickramasinghe gave a small cry of delight. 'I eat almost nothing but meat,' he said, 'and it makes me so constipated. Peanuts, raisins . . . This will be marvellous! Such a welcome change.'

And with that Wickramasinghe seized the knapsack and proceeded to wolf down much of what remained of Fen's provisions. Fen was not given a chance to object, or even to advise moderation. The railwayman just launched into the dry rations, opening packet after packet and guzzling the contents by the handful, and after a few moments of inner debate Fen decided he had no choice but to join in and match him gulp for gulp. It was only fair, he supposed. Wickramasinghe had been generous with the rabbit last night, and he *was* giving him a free ride into London. Fen mentally reapportioned the significance of the foodstuffs: not a survival necessity any more but his ticket into London, his train fare.

When they had both eaten their fill, Wickramasinghe gave a decorous little burp, patted his belly and thanked Fen for a most kind and thoughtful gesture.

'And now,' he said, lowering himself solidly onto the driver's stool, 'we commence our journey. Would you mind going back to your seat, Fen?' He jerked a thumb towards the rear of the carriage. 'Passengers are not allowed in the cab while the train is in motion.'

'Are you serious?'

Wickramasinghe looked at him levelly. 'Quite serious.'

'But what's the harm in my staying here?'

'You might distract me.'

'But—but I'll be very quiet. You won't even notice I'm here. The thing is, this may seem silly to you, but ever since I was a kid I've always wanted to ride up front in a train.' As a matter of fact, Fen had secretly been hoping that he might even be allowed to *drive* the train part of the way.

'I understand. I quite understand. Nonetheless I must insist that you go back and sit down. That is the proper thing to do.'

'The proper thing.'

'Please, my friend.'

Bemused, and not a little disappointed, Fen returned to the compartment where he had spent the night and sat down next to the window, facing forwards.

A moment later, the *Jagannatha* started to roll. At the same time there was an electric pop from the intercom speakers in all the compartments, and Wickramasinghe's voice issued forth:

'A very good morning, ladies and gentlemen. This is your driver. As you can see, we are on our way again, and there is no reason to believe that we will not reach our destination as scheduled. For those of you who joined the train at the last stop, this is the London service, calling at London and several other places beforehand. Our estimated journeying time is four days, and I hope you will have a—'

'What!' Fen leapt to his feet and hurried up the corridor. Leaning in through the doorway to the cab, he tapped Wickramasinghe on the shoulder. 'Did I just hear you right, Ravi? Did you just say four days?'

Wickramasinghe, directing a stern look at him, eased off on the power controller. 'What did I tell you about passengers in the cab while the train is in motion?' he said, as the *Jagannatha* gently decelerated.

'Never mind that. Four days?'

95

'I don't want to have to lock the door.'

'How *can* it be four days? We're twenty-five miles from London!'

Sighing, Wickramasinghe applied the brake, and the train juddered to a halt. 'It seems I did not clarify the situation to you as I should have done.'

'It seems you didn't.'

'It is a very complicated business, Fen, making this journey. There are many factors to be taken into consideration.' Wickramasinghe pointed at the rail map and timetable. 'For one thing, as you already know, we must steer clear of other users of the rails. I am sure you can appreciate that that is of vital importance. And the only way we can manage that is by making certain detours and excursions, some of them quite prolonged and convoluted. We must thread ourselves in and around everyone else, you see, every scheduled train on the timetable, and in some instances that means going many, many miles out of our way, doubling back, all sorts of manoeuvres that may seem, to the layman, illogical. This, you understand, is simply so that we can make it to London in one piece. I am sure you are as keen as I am not to collide with another train at a combined speed of, oh, say a hundred miles an hour. I am sure you would rather we avoided *that*.'

'Well, obviously.'

'Then there is the matter of points. Not every junction will be aligned in our favour, so there will be occasions when we have to stop and wait for the automatic switching systems to change them, or we will have to, again, make detours in order to locate a set of points that *are* aligned in our favour. This, too, will add time. Not travelling at night, that is another factor to consider. As is damaged track. During the worst of the bombing our friends in the International Community, deliberately or otherwise, hit the network in several places. Some repairing was done, but not all the damage was fixed. Naturally we have to go around the sections that weren't fixed. Other rail users, points, not travelling at night, damaged track.' Wickramasinghe checked the items off on his fingers. 'Oh, and of course we must take into account the unknown. Specifically, stopping for food. I have made it my rule never to pass up any meal opportunities that come my way.'

'Meal opportunities?'

'Like last night's rabbit,' Wickramasinghe said, as though explaining something patently obvious.

'The rabbit?'

'Rail kill, Fen. How else do you think I came by it?'

Fen frowned. 'I don't know. Trapped it?'

'I am no huntsman. I could not set a trap if my life depended on it. The rails provide for my needs. Either I run some animal over or it electrocutes itself on the live rail and lies beside the track waiting for me to discover it. You would be surprised, Fen, how much wildlife there is out there, eager to throw itself into my path. Why, just last week I hit a baby deer. That kept me going for three days, that did, and I must say it was most tasty!'

He smacked his lips, and Fen found himself feeling faintly queasy. It was clear now why the rabbit had been in two pieces.

'Oh, don't look like that!' Wickramasinghe admonished. 'I will not touch anything that is not reasonably fresh. If I come across a carcass the birds have already had a go at – no way. And a train's wheels – *swish!* One could not ask for a cleaner, quicker death.'

Wickramasinghe, Fen felt, had a point. If you could eat something that had lain in a snare for several hours or that had been raised in a pen and slaughtered by having its neck wrung, then you could surely have no objection to eating something that had been shocked to death by a few hundred volts of electricity or instantaneously bisected by the front bogies of a speeding locomotive. 'Fair enough,' he said. 'I accept that this isn't going to be half as straightforward as I thought. But really . . . Four days? I could walk it in one.'

'If Ganesha does not smile on us, it may even be as much as five,' Wickramasinghe said, eyeing the timetable ruminatively.

'Then much though I hate to do this, Ravi, I'm going to have to decline your offer after all. It was very kind of you to say you'd get me to London, and I'm grateful for the hospitality you've shown me, but—'

'Of course there is one major advantage to sticking with me,' said Wickramasinghe, butting in as though Fen had not been speaking at all. 'I know where the British Bulldogs live. Lewisham. And my intention is to take you to Brockley Station, or perhaps Ladywell. In other words, virtually to their doorstep. Which, of course, means you will not have to cross most of south London by yourself and on foot – which, take it from me, as a one-time Londoner, is no easy thing. I will be saving you from the most hazardous part of your journey. And there is always the possibility that if, no, *when* you find your wife, we could meet up at some prearranged rendezvous and I could escort you both back out of the capital. How about that? Does any of that give you reason to reconsider?'

It did. Wickramasinghe had not mentioned anything before to

Fen about taking him right to the Bulldogs' lair. No question, that would be a bonus. And a chance of a return trip to boot?

All at once Fen saw that his options were amplified. Assuming for a moment that he *was* able to wrest Moira from the Bulldogs' clutches – a massive assumption, but there you go – wasn't there a possibility, at least a small one, that he might be able to rescue the other Downbourne women at the same time? He might, if Wickramasinghe was on hand with the *Jagannatha* to get them all safely home. The *Jagannatha* could carry them a good half of the way to Downbourne, perhaps even further, perhaps even as far as the station at Wyndham Heath, and although it probably would not be a quick journey, it would at least be a relatively comfortable one.

He was well aware that what he was now contemplating was a task several orders of magnitude harder than the already hard task he had set himself. On the other hand, if he succeeded in pulling it off, he would restore the status quo not only in his own household but in all of Downbourne. And he was not so deficient in self-interest that he didn't quietly relish that prospect of being hailed a hero by the entire town.

'OK, let's get this straight,' Fen said to Wickramasinghe. 'It's going to take a bit of time, but you can get me all the way to where the Bulldogs live and back out of London again.'

'Certainly the one, probably the other.'

'All right. And – well, I'm not sure how to put this, but in return you get . . . ?'

'Nothing other than your company and a chance to play the Good Samaritan.'

That settled it as far as Fen was concerned.

'Then I shan't hold you up any longer. Onwards.'

Wickramasinghe grinned, then pointed down the corridor.

Obediently Fen returned to his seat, and the *Jagannatha* resumed rolling.

First, water. Then, some time later, food.

The water comes in two bottles that, by the feel of them, are the type that used to contain mineral water – although wherever the stuff that's in them now is from, it didn't come bubbling up from some scenic mountain spring such as the one that's undoubtedly depicted on the label.

As for the food: hard cheese which, if we could see it, would probably have flowers of mould on it, and some chocolate that's been in the sun and melted and resolidified. Probably more than once.

Susannah takes charge. Apportions out the food. Makes us go easy on the water, not gulp it down as we'd like to. Someone's got to do this, I suppose. Someone's got to be the practical one, the one who decides to make the best of things. I can almost hear her thinking: *I'm a town councillor, it's what's expected of me*. Maybe it helps her deal with the headachey thirst, the pain of hunger, the fear.

So we sip the water in measured doses (warm, brackish, chloriney). We chew the cheese and nibble the chocolate like we're wainscot mice. And we wait.

That's all there is to do.

That's the only way to pass the time.

Wait.

I think we're over the worst of it now. The worst of it was the anticipation of what's going to happen to us. The uncertainty of when, where, how. We're resigned to it now. We've subsided into a kind of acceptance. In a way, we're quite impatient. *Come on. Let's get it over with*.

It's Zoë I feel sorriest for. I feel sorry for myself, of course, but Zoë . . . They're bound to take her first. Young, pretty thing like her. Teenager. I can just imagine them rubbing their hands, grinning razor-sharp grins. Boasting how they're going to 'break her in'.

Then there's Jennifer. She was the one sobbing, the one I hugged.

Jennifer Franklin. She's gone all but mute now. Catatonic. She's pissed her knickers – you can smell it on her – and just sits in the dampness, not caring. She won't put up any resistance when they come for her. She'll just let them do what they want with her. Shut them out. Maybe it'll seem to her that they're doing it to someone else, someone miles away.

Susannah, I think, will fight.

I certainly am going to fight.

I'm going to fight them with all the strength I have. Weakened as I am, I'm going to kick and punch and spit and scratch and bite. They'll have me, but they won't have me easily. I'm going to make them pay for it, every second of it. If I can, I'm going to make them regret it.

In the meantime . . .

Wait.

I'm good at waiting.

'You waited for me,' Fen once said. He was being coy. Romantic. He meant because I'm a few years older than him. Because I remained single as if anticipating his arrival in my life. Because even before I met him, even though I had no idea he existed, I somehow knew he was on the horizon and so didn't become permanently attached to anyone else.

A nice conceit. Good for his ego. I didn't contradict him. I let him believe it was true.

The truth is, I wasn't holding out for him. Wasn't waiting. I wasn't some silly soppy girl with dreams of Mr Perfect. The truth is, Fen came along at the right time. I'd done with the half-arsed dates, the half-hearted boyfriends, the on-off relationships with men who couldn't make up their minds, the good-lookers who thought they could get away with murder, the ugly-bugs who couldn't believe they weren't God's gift to womankind, the so-called sensitive ones who pretended to be interested in my personality when all they were interested in was my pussy, and the married bastards, good God, the married bastards who'd swear on their children's lives that they were unattached. I was fed up with all the lies, the evasions, the meaningless flattery, the disappointing sex. I'd had enough of all that. I was tired of being available. I was tired of being Girl About Town. That's why I gave up working full-time at the magazine, went freelance and moved out of London to Downbourne. Here was a place, I thought, where I'd get a bit of peace and quiet. Here was a place where I might meet a decent man, an honest man.

And I did.

There he was, this unassuming little country schoolteacher. Handsome enough. Thoughtful in a way that London men don't have time to be. I met him at that drinks party – who gave it? Can't remember. He was introduced to me as 'Downbourne's most eligible bachelor', can you believe it. Probably true, though. I met him and I took one look at him and I thought, yes, you'll do.

No, let's be accurate here. I was introduced to him and what I thought was: Fenton? What kind of a name is that? Fenton Morris?

And shortly after we got engaged I remember thinking, Moira Morris? What kind of a name is *that*?

He told me what Moira means. At the party where we met. His artless way of chatting me up, I suppose. I'd had no idea that the name had a meaning. Mum gave it to me to remind me of her ancestry, my Irish heritage, and I'd thought that that was all it was: an ungainly, unfashionable forename that I'd been saddled with, the Celtic version of Mary.

But Fen said, 'Moira. That's Ancient Greek for "destiny". Did you know that?'

I said no. I think I might have laughed. I think I was impressed. No, I *was* impressed. And charmed.

Smart-arse, I thought. But affectionately.

A decent man. A man with a brain. Handsome enough. No dress sense, but that could be sorted out.

I didn't wait for him. He was there in the right place at the right time.

They come.

The door unlocks, rattles open. A torch beam flares in, blindingly bright.

'Her.'

It's Zoë, like I thought. They seize her by the arms. She cries out. She writhes.

I should attack them, but what good will it do? I need to conserve what little strength I have left. For when they come for me.

Zoë screams and pleads. The torch beam waves wildly around, and in its dazzle I see Susannah's face – grubby and pinched and flinching. Jennifer's face – lost. Zoë's face – a mask of terror and misery. The faces of the men – grim, greedy.

Then they're gone, Zoë with them. The door slams. The darkness is smeared with acid-green after-images. Torch flashes like Chinese script. Glowing skeletal faces.

Zoë's voice echoes along the corridor outside, growing faint, like someone drowning, slipping beneath the waves.

Who will it be next?
No idea.
But if it's me, they won't have me cheaply.

So they travelled, Fen and Wickramasinghe, shuttling around the maze of rails, brushing London like a moth flirting with a light bulb, now coming close, now darting away again. From his compartment window Fen watched the landscape change, shifting back and forth between satellite town and countryside. The distinction between the two was not easy to perceive any more. The Green Belt was far greener than anyone ever could have predicted back when the term was coined. (It was, in fact, no longer something so orderly and constrictive as a belt. Rather, Fen thought, a Green Wreath.) The parcelled-out regularity of the satellite towns had erupted into a rough verdant anarchy, so that with their unmown lawns and unmanaged parks they merged raggedly with the farmland and forest around them. And here and there was a destroyed power station, a flattened factory, even a bombed-out church, all adding to the general impression of civilisation knocked loose from its moorings.

In its roving the *Jagannatha* passed both of the capital's principal airports. Both were ruined almost beyond recognition, scorched wastelands with the shells of ruined jumbo jets lying around like used and discarded Christmas crackers. The train also passed a couple of military bases, their huts and hangars charred skeletons, their runways cratered, their parade grounds pounded to smithereens. The International Community's cruel-to-be-kind ministrations were evident everywhere, like the blundering efforts of a mad, myopic surgeon, trying to cut out a cancer he cannot find.

The journey was a stop-start affair. There was no flow to it. The great majority of the time was spent at a standstill, often in sidings where the track was barely visible among plantains and foxgloves, or else at small rural halts – cobwebbed ticket halls, waiting rooms with rotted benches, platforms wind-scoured and bare. Between, there were short hops from one place of refuge to the next. And then there were the unplanned halts, when Wickramasinghe would jam on the brakes and leap from his cabin with a yelp of predatory glee, having spied some potential repast lying defunct at the track-side. As he had told Fen, he did not touch any animal that was not reasonably fresh. He also drew the line at cats and dogs, the latter of which turned up with some frequency (hardly surprising given the number of rogue dog packs – once-domesticated canines and their descendants – which now roamed the land, a hazard to live-stock and, on occasion, humans). With these exceptions, anything was considered consumable, and normally *was* consumed.

Fen's mustard went down well at mealtimes. 'Such a rarity, such a delicacy!' Wickramasinghe enthused as he slathered the con-diment over pieces of whatever luckless mammal they were eating. In fact, Fen's presence in general seemed a source of continual pleasure to the railwayman. For one thing, as he admitted to Fen, it gave him an excuse to make the intercom announcements he was so proud of. Seldom did a leg of the journey pass without at least one wisecrack or witticism from the driver's cabin. But Fen was also someone to talk to, company, *intelligent* company – such a bonus! Wickramasinghe had been happy enough on his own, riding the rails, going wherever the whim took him, and although he would meet people occasionally, spend perhaps an hour or two with them, share some food, he had never actually offered anyone a lift in the *Jagannatha* before. He was glad that, in Fen's case, he had taken the plunge. He would not have done so if Fen had not been so friendly, or for that matter so deserving of his assistance. It was gratifying, he said, to be helping out someone so educated and so courageous.

Wickramasinghe was certainly a talkative sort, but Fen didn't mind. Often the topic of conversation was Daljit. How beautiful she was, and how cruel she had been to abandon him like that, dragging Sanjay and Naz with her off to India, where neither of them belonged nor had even visited before. It was not right for a wife to behave in such a manner. However, Wickramasinghe had found it in his heart to forgive her, and he was sure that when things in England settled down again, as they were bound to sooner or later, she and the boys would return. Fen agreed that this would happen, yes, definitely. Once things in England settled down. He did not add that he believed England wasn't going to be readmitted into the global fold for some while yet. Too many other countries were enjoying its plight. Not only did these other countries get a kick out of seeing a major-league player brought low, but England's plummet from First to Third World status was a salutary reminder of what could happen to any industrialised nation if its leaders were not careful. England was an object lesson in how *not* to handle an economic crisis, not to mention an example of just how fragile the constraints of civilised society were, and for these moral and instructive reasons the International Community had a vested interest in ensuring that its rehabilitation was not allowed to begin any time soon.

It hadn't escaped Fen's attention that Wickramasinghe was a little odd. He took the view, however, that the railwayman's eccentricity was an unavoidable by-product of his chosen lifestyle. Too much time spent in his own company had impaired his social skills, so that he had forgotten how one was expected to behave when around others. In addition, he was lost in a mild delusion of former glories, locked in the habits of the period of his life when he had felt the most functional, the most fulfilled. In this respect he reminded Fen of Reginald Bailey, or rather of Donald Bailey's frank assessment of his younger brother, as someone who chose not to think about anything that was going on around him but just let it happen. Wickramasinghe appeared to have slipped into a similar kind of fugue state, existing independently of – and immune to – the outside world, interacting with it only as far as necessity required. Denial of the present was a means as valid as any other of holding on and surviving, and Fen could not foresee a way in which, in this instance, it would entail any unwelcome consequences for himself.

In the evenings, after pegging out sheets of polythene on the ground to catch dew for drinking water, Wickramasinghe would spend a good half-hour or so poring over the rail map and time-table, plotting the next day's travels. At no point did Fen actually catch sight of any of the other users of the rails whom Wickrama-singhe was at such pains to avoid, but when he mentioned this to the railwayman, saying he was surprised that he had not seen even *one* train pass by during one of their many stoppages, Wickrama-singhe's reply was straightforward and credible enough: 'I have to leave large margins of error, Fen. Who can trust a timetable completely? If we are close enough to see another train, then we are too close for comfort.'

Fen took the point, and although he found it frustrating to travel in this way, in fits and bursts, with only the vaguest sense of his ultimate destination growing nearer, he soon began to settle into the journey's fractured rhythm and to enjoy the opportunity, enforced as it was, to see more of the nation than he had seen in ages. He was amused by the looks the *Jagannatha* drew from the people it passed – a few paid no attention, but a moving train was still a novelty and a moving train that sported a paint job like the

Jagannatha's even more so – and he began to understand the attraction to Wickramasinghe of a life perpetually on the move. Everything was there outside the train windows, England in all its crippled tenacity. Everything was there, but at one remove, and never for long.

He thought of Moira, of course. Every time there was a delay and every time there was not. When the *Jagannatha* was stationary, he would fall to wondering where she was and how she was, and he would itch for the train to be on its way again; and when the *Jagannatha* was rolling and he found himself gazing contentedly out at the view like some idle tourist, there would sometimes come a pang of guilt. How could he sit here enjoying himself when his wife was a captive of the British Bulldogs, suffering God knew what at their hands? The pangs of guilt were short-lived, however, and disturbingly mild. And grew milder still as time went on.

On the evening of their third day together, tucked away on a spur of a branch line somewhere in the depths of Berkshire, Fen and Wickramasinghe ate a dinner of spit-roasted pheasant. Wickramasinghe was in ebullient mood, pronouncing himself highly satisfied with their progress so far. 'We are, you might say, well on track,' he told Fen. 'Two more days, I should think.'

'Two. You're quite definite about that.'

'Oh, indeed. Three at the very most.'

This, of course, represented a significant upward revision of Wickramasinghe's original estimate of four days, but Fen was content to believe that the railwayman knew what he was doing. He retired to bed confident that within three days' time he and Moira would be reunited.

Not long after he got off to sleep, he was startled awake by the sound of the compartment door being rolled open.

'Ravi?'

Wickramasinghe was standing in the doorway, picked out in sharp relief against the dark blue, star-flecked sky that filled the corridor window behind him. Clad only in white Y-fronts, the railwayman stumbled into the compartment and sat down heavily on the banquette opposite. He heaved a sigh. All at once his shoulders began to jerk up and down, and Fen realised he was sobbing.

'Ravi, what's the matter?'

It took a while to coax out an answer.

'I miss her, my friend,' Wickramasinghe said.

'Daljit?'

Wickramasinghe nodded. 'I have just remembered – tomorrow is her birthday.' And he started blubbering again, helplessly, like a little boy who has fallen and barked his shin.

Fen sat up, gathering the blanket under which he had been lying and wrapping it around his waist and thighs. He, too, was wearing just his underpants. He hesitated, then reached across and laid a consoling hand on Wickramasinghe's knee.

'It must be difficult,' he said. 'I know how you feel. To be apart from someone you love . . . Believe me, I've been there. Not in the same way, but close enough.'

Wickramasinghe drew in a long, sniffling breath. 'I had a feeling you would understand.'

'But perhaps now's not the time to dwell on it. Like they say: everything seems worse at night. You should go back to bed, try and sleep. I'm certain it won't seem so bad in the morning.'

'I miss the touch of her. The feel of her hair. Her smile. The way she used to kiss me. The way we used to lie together in bed.' Wickramasinghe patted Fen's hand, and then his hand came to rest on Fen's, cupping it warmly, clammily. 'My life is such a lonely one,' he said. 'Sometimes I forget how much I need human contact.'

Very slowly and deliberately Fen extricated his hand. 'Ravi, I don't think—'

'Don't you ever feel like that too? In need of human contact?'

'This probably isn't the time and place to discuss this,' Fen said, all too conscious of his near-nakedness, and of Wickramasinghe's.

'More than just conversation. Physical contact.'

'I really think we'd be better off—'

'I'm only asking that we lie together, Fen. I'm not suggesting anything dirty. I'm not that way, not at all. But just the feel of skin on skin, body next to body . . . I think it is essential to us humans. Animals do it all the time, snuggle together for warmth, closeness, connection. Why not us?'

'Ravi, please. Just go back to your compartment.'

'You won't even consider the idea?'

'I'm not at all comfortable with the idea.'

'But don't you see—'

'The seat's too narrow, Ravi, and perhaps I'm too narrow-minded, because I take your point about animals and all that, but I'm not prepared to do it.'

Wickramasinghe gazed at him across the compartment, eyes glistening with tears which reflected the starlight. 'Too English, then,' he said, sombrely and somewhat bitterly.

'If you like.'

'Too stiff-of-lip. Too puckered-of-arse.'

'Try not to take it personally or anything.'

'Had I been a woman, you would not have thought twice about it.'

'But Ravi—Oh, fuck it, what's the point? Ravi, just go back to your compartment. That's that.'

For a while Wickramasinghe was silent and didn't move, and Fen wondered if this was going to turn nasty – if the railwayman's desire for cosy physical contact was going to turn into a desire for not-so-cosy physical contact. Thanks to his experience at the hands of the British Bulldogs, Fen was better prepared than he otherwise would have been for the likelihood and the result of an assault on his person. He didn't know how to fight now, any more than he had known back at the festival when the British Bulldogs had gate-crashed, but he did know what to expect, what being hit felt like, and so in that sense, if in no other, he was combat-hardened. And since Wickramasinghe did not appear to be in particularly good physical shape, lacking anything like the menacing, brutal tough-ness of a Bulldog, Fen thought that, if it came down to it, he had a good chance of successfully defending himself, and might even be able to wrestle Wickramasinghe into submission.

In the event, no violence occurred. Wickramasinghe, coming to a decision, got to his feet and, without another word, strode out of the compartment, returning to his own. Fen heard him stretch himself out on his banquette, and for a long time afterwards he sat, wide awake, listening intently, expecting Wickramasinghe at any moment to get up and come back and try again. He pictured the railwayman lying on his banquette, listening too, hoping Fen would have a change of heart and relent and come and join him. The silence that filled the *Jagannatha* seemed to effervesce with embarrassment and urgent longing.

Then Fen became aware of deep, low breathing coming from Wickramasinghe's compartment, unmistakably the thick, leisurely respiration of someone fast asleep, and he relaxed, sank back in the seat and wondered what the hell he should do. He was tempted to get dressed there and then, sneak out, get as far away as he could from the *Jagannatha*; but there were, he quickly realised, several drawbacks to this plan, the main one being that he had no precise idea of where he was. Somewhere in Berkshire, he knew, but that could mean as far from London as Downbourne was, perhaps further. If he was going to abandon the *Jagannatha*, he should at least do so when he was within spitting distance of the capital. Otherwise nearly a week's worth of travelling would have been in vain.

He felt, too, that there was an acceptably slight risk of the episode that had just taken place being repeated. And Wickrama-singhe's intentions *had* been innocent, hadn't they? He missed Daljit; he simply wanted the proximity of another warm body.

That was all it had been, right? And if it did happen again, it could be dealt with by the same method – gentle but persistent dissuasion.

So Fen talked himself into staying. In truth, he didn't much fancy the idea of setting out on foot in the dark, in the countryside, with no clear notion of where he was going. He decided that for the time being he was safer, on balance, remaining where he was. His best bet for getting to Moira lay with Wickramasinghe and the *Jagannatha*.

But from then on, till dawn, he slept like a cat, nervy and wire-taut, on the alert for the slightest sound.

The following morning Wickramasinghe acted as if nothing had happened. Sunny and cheerful, he peppered the day's travels with the usual amusing announcements over the intercom, and during each break in the journey he left the cab and came back to chat with Fen. If there was any discernible alteration in his behaviour, it was that he was even more solicitous towards his passenger than previously. As if to reassure Fen that all the delays and meanderings had a purpose, he kept him continually up to date with where they were on the rail map and where they were aiming for on their next stint, and when, at lunchtime, they came across a plump dead pigeon sprawled on one of the sleepers in a fluster of bloody feathers, Wickramasinghe deemed this a very good omen. 'A city pigeon,' he said, as he started to pluck the bird and prepare it for cooking. 'There'll be more of these in days to come.'

Fen was encouraged. Maybe it was his imagination, but it *had* seemed to him that they were passing through built-up areas more and more that morning, that he was looking out at countryside from the window less and less – as though, rather than the *Jagannatha* homing in on London, London was reaching out towards the train, enticing it, beckoning it with arms of concrete and brick and glass.

As they ate the pigeon, Fen quizzed Wickramasinghe about entering the capital by rail. Were there checkpoints on the rail routes, as there were on the road routes?

Wickramasinghe confirmed that there were, and predicted that the vagaries of the network were finally going to allow the *Jagannatha* to reach one tomorrow, some time in the late afternoon if all went according to plan.

'You do have a permit, don't you, my friend?' he asked.

Fen assured him that he did.

Once through the checkpoint, Wickramasinghe continued, they would pick up speed. Inside the city's perimeter the journey would become markedly easier.

'Easier? Surely there'll be more trains about.'

'Ah yes, more trains, but also more track and junctions, therefore a greater number of different routes we can take.'

Later, when they were under way again, Fen fetched his knapsack down from the luggage rack. Cruikshank's London permit was lodged in an inside zip pocket, wrapped in a polythene bag for protection. With it was the bribe, the 'something valuable' which Cruikshank had recommended Fen should bring along just in case. Fen had deliberated for a long time over what to take, what was easily portable and at the same time self-evidently costly. Now, he extracted the chosen item from the polythene bag and held it in the palm of his hand, studying it.

Moira's gold wedding band.

She had stopped wearing it – when? A few months ago, shortly after New Year. He couldn't pinpoint the exact day she removed it and its companion, her diamond engagement ring, from her finger, since he had not registered the rings' absence straight away, not consciously at any rate, and she herself had not drawn attention to what she had done. For a while he had sensed that there was something different about her, something indefinably *wrong* about her appearance, and the anomaly had nagged at him and nagged at him, until one morning, when, as he was bringing her breakfast, he had caught sight of her left hand resting pale on the counterpane, and had noticed its bareness . . . and there had been a row. It was the first time since the stillbirth that he had raised his voice to her, one of only a few times in their marriage when he had gone so far as to lose his temper. In retrospect he could see that that was exactly what she had wanted. Taking off the rings had been an act of provocation. At the time, though, he had been too enraged, and too hurt, to realise this, and had thus played right into her hands. Such a small gesture, the removal of the rings. Physically so insignificant. Yet what it had represented . . .

He remembered going to buy the rings from a jeweller's in Wyndham Heath. The engagement ring first, of course, which he had purchased on his own, and then the wedding band, which Moira had gone along with him to choose. After lengthy deliberation she had plumped for one in red gold, and it had been at the upper limit of his budget, and he had wanted it engraved, which had added to the expense, but he had not begrudged the money, not a single penny of it.

There it was, the engraving, three words in an ornate typeface around the inside of the ring:

And this was the object she had one day decided – on a casual, callous whim – she no longer wished to adorn her, and had stowed in her keepsake box on top of the chest of drawers, along with her engagement ring, as though the two items of jewellery were suddenly of no greater importance to her than any other. A calculated insult. If Fen had been sensible he would have ignored it. Since the stillbirth Moira had not been herself. She had been another Moira, embittered and aloof, a woman angry at the world, a woman robbed. He should simply have accepted the taking off of the rings as another manifestation of her illness, her depression. But it had stung him; it had wounded him to the quick. She had even tried to make out that somehow *he* was in the wrong for not noticing sooner what was missing from her hand. No wonder he had had a go at her. You can take forbearance only so far.

He held the wedding band up to one eye and watched the scenery outside chunter past, framed by the ring's circle, blurrily reflected in its russet surface. An embankment capped with crazed hawthorn. The film-reel stutter of a fence. Some tumbleweed tangles of barbed wire and then a farmhouse, apparently deserted, holes in the roof, shattered hollows for windows. Now under a brick bridge, temporary darkness. Daylight again, and what looked like an expanse of heathland until the presence of sand bunkers revealed it as the palimpsest of a golf course . . .

Then the *Jagannatha* began to slow down again for another of its spells of idleness, and Fen returned the wedding band to the polythene bag and the bag to the pocket in the knapsack. He felt – and he did not know why – that it was better if Wickramasinghe didn't find out that he had such an item with him. At the checkpoint, he would produce it only if necessary.

He wondered if Moira would appreciate the irony – as he himself did, in a grim way – that the wedding band that she had so spitefully discarded all those months ago had now been designated a major role in saving her. There was a certain aptness to that, after all, a certain inverse symmetry.

Perhaps she would not. Perhaps, when he informed her what he had used the ring for, she would not even care.

Susannah doesn't struggle. I really thought she was going to. We talked about it after they took Zoë, a quick, whispered discussion, and she seemed to agree with me – why make it easy for them? But when the time comes, she lets them lead her away, meek and compliant. And I can understand why. Rationally, it's the wise thing to do. Resistance will only bring more pain than necessary.

I can't help feeling betrayed, though. Betrayed and dispirited. If Susannah hasn't fought back, why should I?

So now it's just me and Jennifer in the room, in the dark. Dumbstruck distant Jennifer over in one corner. A few yards – and several worlds – away.

So really it's just me alone in the room.

Alone, and hating the smell of myself, the reek of my hair, my breath, my unwashed body. Alone, and sore all over from sitting and lying on bare floorboards. Alone, and thinking what's the point? What's the point in putting up a fight when they come to take me? The principle of the thing? Bugger that! Principles aren't going to improve my situation one bit. Principles are a luxury for people who aren't being held captive, who aren't waiting to be dragged out and raped.

Time pulses erratically. I try to count out sixty seconds. It seems to take an hour.

At one point I find myself scratching madly at the walls with my fingernails. I don't remember making a decision to do this. I just start doing it, spontaneously. Scratch-scrabble-scratch, like the hamster I used to have when I was small. He used to burrow furiously at the metal base of his cage. The noise used to drive me crazy. I keep going, honestly convinced I'm going to break through the wall and there'll be freedom beyond, and I recall the crater-like depressions I felt in the plaster when I first got here, and I realise I'm not the first to have tried this. Others have knelt here clawing, just like me, just like my hamster. Without success.

Some time later I realise that I've given up. My fingertips are throbbingly raw. There's no escape from here, not that way.

But . . .

Escape.

I'm calm now. Thinking hard.

Escape.

I try to recall what I saw as I arrived here. Not much, just glimpses by the light of the vans' headlamps. A sort of courtyard area surrounded by small, cubic houses. Ordinary housing-estate houses. I was aware we'd just come through a huge, heavy gate with spirals of barbed wire along the top. I was aware of walls – barricades, really – adjoining the gate. A stockade, twenty feet high, built from all kinds of household junk. After that I kept my head down and concentrated on the ground in front of me, so as to avoid the men's stares, to avoid catching anyone's eye. As we were hustled away from the courtyard, I saw only the tarmac underfoot, then threadbare grass, and then this house. This house with all its windows bricked up, blind.

So I know this is a kind of compound I'm in. A section of a housing estate commandeered by these men for themselves, cordoned off, secured. Beyond that, however, I'm in the dark (ha ha ha, very funny). I don't know how big the compound is, how many houses it contains, how far its perimeter extends. I don't even know what area of London I've wound up in.

What I do know is that escaping is a far better plan than resisting when the men come to take me. More realistic, not so short-term. All I need is a clearer idea of the layout of this place, and an opportunity. Both, I am certain, I will have soon. And then I will make my bid for freedom.

I'm so buoyed up by this new resolution of mine, this new goal – why didn't I think of it earlier? – that I feel the need to share it with Jennifer. Maybe it'll have a similar effect on her, stirring her out of her despair. Giving her something to hope for, a chink of light in this unrelenting darkness.

I crawl over to her.

When I reach her . . .

When I touch her . . .

I know.

I know almost before my groping hand finds her arm and I feel how cold her skin is.

Jennifer has found her own method of escape. A permanent one.

Over their evening meal, another rabbit, Fen recalled what Wickramasinghe had said during his nocturnal visit, that today was his wife's birthday. He hesitated about bringing this up, not wanting to be responsible for triggering another bout of lachrymose neediness, but decided there could be no harm in mentioning it. Wickramasinghe had been nothing but upbeat and good-humoured all day, more so than usual perhaps *because* it was Daljit's birthday.

The subject was delicately broached, but Wickramasinghe responded in a puzzled – and, to Fen, puzzling – fashion.

'My wife's birthday? No, no, my friend. Whatever gave you that idea? November. Daljit was born in November.'

Fen, against his better judgement, pursued the matter. He insisted that Wickramasinghe had told him that today was Daljit's birthday.

'When did I tell you this?'

'When you . . . You know. In my compartment.'

Wickramasinghe drew a blank. 'What are you talking about? When was I in your compartment?'

Nothing in the railwayman's expression intimated deceit. It seemed he genuinely had no recollection of the incident.

Immediately Fen backtracked. 'Oh no, wait, hold on,' he said, scratching his chin in feigned confusion. Several days' worth of stubble crackled under his fingernails. 'Now that I think about it . . . Yes. Yes, actually it was a dream I had.'

It had to be one of the poorest pieces of dissembling ever committed, almost childlike in its clumsiness. Fen could not believe Wickramasinghe would fall for it.

Happily, he did.

'A very strange dream. I came in and told you about my wife's birthday? Most peculiar.' And the railwayman gave a little *hmph* and nodded to himself in amusement.

Darkness fell and the two men turned in. Compartment door firmly shut, Fen took off his shoes and, without divesting himself of any other clothing, lay down on the banquette and drew the blanket up over him. After a moment's thought he pulled the shoes to within easy reach. They were the only objects he had with him that could, if necessary, be pressed into service as weapons.

He waited.

He fell asleep.

He awoke after an uninterrupted night and, looking at the shoes and at himself, fully clothed, was ashamed. As he stretched vigorously, working out various kinks and stiffnesses in his muscles and joints, he asked himself if there had really been a need for such precautions. Wickramasinghe was harmless. If what he had said was true and he had no memory of entering the compartment the previous night, then most likely he had been sleepwalking – and sleepwalkers are a danger to no one but themselves.

Perhaps, he reasoned, he was feeling awkward and on his guard because he was so much at Wickramasinghe's mercy. He had surrendered his fate to a man he barely knew, all on the basis of a quick smile and a barbecued rabbit. Perhaps – better late than never – a sense of proper caution had caught up with him.

If so, it wasn't worth heeding. He put on his shoes and stood up and slid back the door, suffused with faith and confidence. Today: the checkpoint. Tomorrow, or possibly the day after: Moira. Wickramasinghe was unquestionably going to deliver on all that he had promised.

The *Jagannatha* was silent. From the quality of the silence, its deadness, its absoluteness, Fen knew that he was the only person aboard. He searched for Wickramasinghe anyway – the cab, the first class compartments, the standard class section. He knocked on the toilet door. No reply, and the 'Engaged' sign was not showing in the slot. He opened the door. No one there. Outside, he circled the carriage. No sign of Wickramasinghe. He peered along the track, shading his eyes. He turned and peered in the other direction. A lukewarm morning breeze tickled the trees around him and set the trackside weeds quivering. Wickramasinghe was nowhere to be seen.

He remained nowhere to be seen all morning. Fen spent the time sitting in his compartment and making brief exploratory forays into the surrounding woodland, both activities carried out with mounting frequency and impatience. When he was in the *Jagannatha*, he felt he should be out searching for Wickramasinghe, but when he was out searching for Wickramasinghe he wondered why he was bothering – it was a waste of time, he wasn't going to find him, he might as well stay with the train.

The sun climbed, the day grew hot, and Fen began to worry. Not about Wickramasinghe. He was quite convinced that wherever the railwayman had gone, he had gone of his own accord, on some obscure personal mission. It was about his own mission that he began to worry. Wickramasinghe's disappearance was surely going to muck up their journey plan. If they didn't make the checkpoint today, how long until the next opportunity arose to get to one? How many days was this going to delay them?

By midday Fen began to experience the first dim stirrings of concern. It occurred to him that if Wickramasinghe *was* a sleep-walker, he could have blundered out of the carriage during the night and got lost. He hurried outside again and patrolled up and down the track, calling Wickramasinghe's name. The trees swallowed his voice. Having yelled himself hoarse, he clambered disconsolately back into the *Jagannatha*. He was very hungry by now, and there was not a scrap of food left in his knapsack other than the mustard. Motion, he realised, was vital to survival when you rode the rails. 'Meal opportunities' did not come your way if you stayed put. He headed forward to the cab. A few evenings ago he had prevailed on Wickramasinghe to give him a brief explanation of the workings of the control desk, in the hope that an invitation to drive the train might, as a natural consequence, follow. It hadn't, but he remembered well what he had been taught. There was the power controller. There was the brake valve handle. There was the slot for the control key . . .

But no control key.

That was bad news, of course, in that it meant he could not start the *Jagannatha* even if he wanted to. It was good news as well, however, in so far as it eliminated the sleepwalking hypothesis. Wherever Wickramasinghe had gone, he had gone on purpose, and that meant he would, surely, at some point come back.

Noon mellowed into afternoon, and Fen prowled inside the carriage and along the track for a hundred yards in each direction, walking to keep his mind off thoughts of food, to distract himself from the grizzling of his famished stomach. He alternated between cursing Wickramasinghe and praying for the railwayman's swift return. Back and forth he strode, inside the *Jagannatha* and outside, clocking up mile upon mile of useless distance.

It was nigh on four-thirty when Wickramasinghe finally reappeared. Fen had just stepped out of the *Jagannatha* for yet another quick turn up and down the track, and there was Wickramasinghe, sauntering towards the train like someone returning from a pleasant and bracing stroll.

By now Fen had worked himself up into a state of some agitation, and this, exacerbated by his hunger and by Wickramasinghe's manifest insouciance, boiled over into anger. As soon as the railwayman was within earshot, Fen set about lambasting him. Accusations spilled forth in a furious torrent. 'What the fuck . . . ?' 'Who the hell . . . ?' 'Where in the name of God . . . ?' Wickramasinghe continued to approach, unperturbed. It was as though such a welcome was no more than he had anticipated. When there was less than a couple of yards between them, he came to a halt and Fen stopped shouting, and for a while they stared at each other, the one red-cheeked and wild-eyed and panting, the other calm. Then Wickramasinghe said, simply, 'See?'

'See what?' Fen spluttered. 'What is this? What am I supposed to see?'

Wickramasinghe shrugged and carried on towards the *Jagannatha*.

'This was some sort of test?' Fen asked him. 'A show of strength? So we know who's boss here?'

Wickramasinghe reached up and hauled himself through the rear doorway of the carriage, between the stern sentinel figures of Shiva the destroyer and monkey-featured Hanuman with his war club.

Fen followed him inside, not prepared to let this go just yet. If Wickramasinghe had been trying to prove a point, it was useless if he didn't make explicit what that point was.

He cornered the railwayman in the standard class section.

'Listen, Ravi,' he said, reining in his temper as best he could, 'would you at least tell me what you've been up to? Where you've been all this time?'

The railwayman glanced up at the ceiling, stroking a thumb through his beard. Then, lowering his gaze, levelling it at Fen, he said: 'My friend, I fear you do not trust me.'

'Now, that's not true.'

'No?'

'No. In fact, when I got up this morning, the first thing I thought was, "Today Ravi's going to get us to the checkpoint, just like he said he would."'

'But if you trusted me, genuinely trusted me, you would not even have to think such a thought.'

'For God's sake, what chance does *that* give me?' Fen said, raising his hands and letting them drop to his sides.

'I get the impression, Fen, the *distinct* impression that you believe that I am leading you on a wild goose chase. That I am deliberately prolonging this journey. That I have invented all this stuff about avoiding other trains and junctions and damaged track and so forth.'

'Why would I believe that? Prolonging the journey? Even if you were, I can't imagine what you'd gain from it.'

'More time with you. Your company. Friendship. A purpose. I am a train driver, after all. Transporting people was what I did, was how I felt useful. Transporting *you* has made me feel useful again. It makes sense that I would try to keep that going as long as possible. To prolong my usefulness.'

Fen looked at him askance. 'Are you saying that *is* what you're doing?'

'You see?' Wickramasinghe said, with an accusatory flick of his hand. 'No trust.'

'I never said that! Although you have to admit, wandering off like that without telling me, leaving me here to stew . . . You have to see how that could make me wonder about you. And then—' Fen checked himself.

'And then?'

'Nothing.'

Wickramasinghe nodded, eyes narrowed. 'You were going to say, "And then there was that time you came into my compartment in just your underpants and asked to sleep with me."'

'You lied,' Fen said, high-voiced. 'You told me you didn't remember doing that.'

'No, *you* lied. You pretended you dreamed it.'

Fen shook his head, flabbergasted. This was daft. Ridiculous. Wickramasinghe had it all back-to-front and inside-out and wrong-way-round.

'The fact is, my friend,' the railwayman said, 'you are willing to take nothing on faith. You want proof, don't you? Proof that I have not been stringing you along these past few days.'

'I don't—'

'Fair enough. I shall give you proof.'

With that, Wickramasinghe spun on his heel and marched towards the front of the carriage. Fen remained where he was for several moments, digesting this turn of events. He heard the engine whirr, and then the *Jagannatha* gave a lurch forwards and began to pick up speed. Fen rushed out of the standard class section and along the corridor, not sure what Wickramasinghe had in mind but sensing that, whatever it was, it wasn't going to be good.

'Ravi, what are you doing?'

Hunched over the controls, Wickramasinghe intoned, 'No passengers in the driver's cab.'

'Come on, stop the train. Let's discuss this.'

'No passengers in the cab.'

Fen stepped back so that no part of him projected past the doorway. 'Right. I'm not *in* the cab. Now please – what's going on?'

'A demonstration,' Wickramasinghe said, nudging the power controller a few degrees further round. The *Jagannatha*'s wheels were chattering busily on the track. In the viewing window in front of Wickramasinghe, sleepers were laddering down out of sight at a rate of several per second.

'Of what?'

'That I have not been stringing you along. That these' – he waved a hand at the timetable and map – 'are not for show.'

Fen gave an incredulous laugh. 'What, you're going to arrange a near-miss with another train?'

Wickramasinghe turned, his face a mask of seriousness. 'That is precisely what I am going to do. At our current speed and direction, we are on a collision course with the four-eighteen out of Paddington. Our path and its will intersect at a junction approximately twelve miles from here. If my calculations are correct, we should pass each other with perhaps a hundred yards to spare. You want to see why it is taking so long to get to London, Fen? Well then, let me show you!'

Bluffing, Fen thought. He's bluffing. Trying to rattle me. He feels unappreciated. Rejected. He wants his efforts acknowledged. He wants gratitude.

But something – perhaps pride, perhaps petulance – prevented Fen from giving Wickramasinghe what he wanted.

'All right,' he said. 'Enough. This is daft. Suppose I believe you and there is a train heading this way. What if your calculations *aren't* correct? What if there *aren't* a few yards to spare?'

'Then,' said Wickramasinghe, '*boom*.'

'You'd kill us both, and maybe a lot of other people? Just to prove a point?'

'If that is what it takes.'

The *Jagannatha* continued to accelerate, urging itself forwards with intrepid eagerness. The world in the windows on either side had become a blur.

'So this is why you've been gone all day,' Fen said. 'To get the timing right.'

'How astute of you.'

'Or else to make me think that.'

'If you like. You obviously will not be convinced until you see the other train bearing down on us at the junction.'

Fen weighed this up. Wickramasinghe was right. Perhaps he would not be convinced until then. But why let it come to that?

Launching himself into the cab, Fen made a lunge for the control desk. Wickramasinghe, having anticipated this, raised an arm to fend him off. He managed to shove Fen backwards. Daljit's photograph was dislodged from the wall. Fen recovered his footing and went for the desk again, grabbing for the power controller. Fingers slithered over bunched knuckles. Wickramasinghe dug an elbow into Fen's stomach and pushed him away. With his free hand Fen wrenched at the railwayman's collar, intending to haul him off his stool. Wickramasinghe responded by yanking on the brake valve handle. The brakes were abruptly engaged, and Fen was thrown off balance and went lurching into the viewing window with head-cracking force. Sparkles and pain. The *Jagannatha* squealed deafeningly, shuddering to a complete stop. Fen, dazed, felt arms around him. He felt himself being manhandled. Then he was tumbling back into the corridor, rolling to the floor, and there was the sound of a door slamming and a bolt being shot home.

He looked up, skull throbbing, blinking through dizziness.

The door to the driver's cab was shut fast, and the *Jagannatha* was once more trundling along, gathering speed.

They took Jennifer away a while ago. An hour? Half a day? I don't know any more. I don't know what's when or who's where or the whys and the hows of anything.

They came in and took one look at her, pale and still in the torch-light, and one of them sighed, 'Oh, for fuck's sake,' while the other clucked his tongue. He didn't sound appalled, just annoyed, like someone coming out of a restaurant to find his car has been broken into.

The torch beam swung around until it located me, cowering.

'Well, at least *she's* still alive.'

Then they picked Jennifer up between them and carried her out. Where they took her, I've no idea. Disposed of her somewhere, I suppose. Somewhere outside the compound. Dumped her like rubbish.

How long had she been dead when I touched her? How long was I sharing the room with a corpse?

This is what I've been trying not to think about, and it is all I can think about.

Jennifer, silently willing herself to expire. Making this room a tomb.

Me, unwittingly present at her final moment. Inhaling air molecules she exhaled with her last breath.

The darkness enclosing me has become deeper, *thicker*, than I can bear. What I wouldn't give just to see the sun again. What I wouldn't give for warmth and light and just knowing what time of day it is, what *day* it is.

Be strong, I tell myself.

I can't.

Hold it together.

I can't.

I can't even tell if my eyes are open any more. What I see when I stare out – they may as well be tight shut.

There's floor. That's down. There are walls. That's sideways. There are legs and a torso and arms and a head and hair, and I can touch them with my hands, and that's me.

This is all I know.

It was foolish to think of escape. I'm never going to escape. I'm never even going to get out of this room. This is all I am going to know for ever. This is *my* tomb too.

I would scream, if I thought anyone could hear, anyone who cared.

Fen would care. If he heard.

Fen would. Or would pretend to, at any rate.

Where is he now? What's he doing now?

Having a party. Celebrating. He's rid of me. His millstone. He's a free man. He'll be out and about in Downbourne. Having a good time.

(This is the first time since I was captured that I've thought about Fen in the now. Not as a figment of memory. As a living person.)

'Lucky Fen,' everyone'll be saying. 'Lucky old Fen. Those blokes from London did him a favour.'

(He's better as a memory. I like him better then, because he liked me better then. There was nothing false or brittle about him then. No pretence. No call for it.)

Dancing through the town. A happy future for Fen.

Not darkness. Not limbo. Not like me.

Come *on*! What are you waiting for, you bastards? Come and get me! I don't even care any more what you want to do with me. I want out of here! Come and *get* me!

Hammering on the door produced no response. Shouting to Wickramasinghe produced no response. Reasoning with him, haranguing him – no response.

It was a bluff.

It wasn't a bluff.

The *Jagannatha* raced along, eating up distance, rocking and shimmying, its wheels beating out an implacable steely tattoo on the rails.

Fen pounded on the door again. This time he did get a response, though not an encouraging one. The intercom crackled, and the carriage was filled from end to end with the sound of Wickramasinghe intoning a poem in a loud, singsong voice:

The guard is the man,
The man in the van,
The van at the back of the train.
The driver up front
Thinks the guard is a cunt,
While the guard thinks the driver's the same.

'Ravi! Ravi! Come on! Stop this. This isn't funny.'

The intercom clicked off. Silence again.

Fen pounded on the door one last time, then took a step back, breathing hard.

OK. OK, think.

Was Wickramasinghe really going to go through with his plan? Was he that much of a nutcase? Or was this nothing more than a ploy, a way of putting Fen in his place, of reminding him who was the driver here, who the passenger? Would Wickramasinghe halt the train after another mile or so and come out of his cabin expecting contrition from Fen, abject apology?

He recalled the look on Wickramasinghe's face as he had outlined his intentions. He recalled the frank, almost dismissive way in which the railwayman had acknowledged the possibility of a collision: 'Then *boom*.'

This was no bluff.

He had to get off the train.

Turning, Fen made his way to the rear of the carriage, staggering against the judders and buffets of the train's motion. He grasped the handle of the rear door and tugged inwards, and all at once there was roar and racket and vertiginous speed. The track whisked away from beneath his feet, sleepers passing too fast to distinguish one from the next. Wind sucked at his hair.

No way. No way was he going to be able to jump out at this speed. Not without breaking his neck.

But what choice did he have?

He braced himself in the doorway. It was this or take his chances staying on the train. Either way, not an attractive proposition.

The London permit.

Shit!

His knapsack. The permit. The wedding band.

He stumbled back up the carriage to his compartment and snatched the knapsack down from the luggage rack. As he flipped the bag onto his shoulders – it weighed next to nothing now – he glanced out of the window and saw the embankment rushing past, a hectic smear of green.

Of course.

Not from the rear of the train.

From the side.

A much softer landing. A better chance of not hurting himself.

The side doors had external handles only. Back in the standard class section, Fen fought with the window of one, leaning on the metal rim-catch, struggling to shunt the thick pane of glass down. Finally! He groped for the handle. Found it. Battled to get the door open against the hurricane rush of the *Jagannatha*'s momentum. Succeeded, the door slamming back flat against the side of the carriage.

The track's gravel bed was a grey flurry at his feet. The embankment lay just an exaggerated footstep away, thick with bushes and brambles – natural shock absorbers. The embankment's height was decreasing, its gradient beginning to flatten out. Now was the moment. If Fen was going to do this, he would not get a better opportunity.

Just as he tensed, ready to leap, the sound of the train's wheels changed, becoming hollower, tinnier. All at once there was no embankment any more, instead a low brick parapet and, beyond, an unfurling vista of fields and copses, here and there a house, a barn, a glimpse of lane.

Fen shrank back from the doorway, his heart stuttering, his breath coming in short, constricted bursts. A viaduct. He had almost hurled himself over the side of a viaduct. Fuck! Fuck fuck *fuck*!

The landscape peeled by, a swooping beautiful valley, the kind of view the railway companies used to use to advertise the joys of rail travel, wanting you to believe that every mile of every journey revealed awe-inspiring sights such as this. *England, my England.* Then a hillside swelled up to meet the end of the viaduct's span and the view was whisked from sight. Fen could see no further than a hedgerow at the far end of a field, then a bell curve of embankment again, then another hedgerow at the far end of another field.

He gripped the door frame once more, and once more tired to nerve himself to jump. After his close shave at the viaduct, it was harder than ever to summon up the courage. His mind was all hysteria, his thoughts yammering in time to the wheels on the rails: *You'll kill yourself! You'll kill yourself!* It seemed to him that the *Jagannatha* was still accelerating and that the odds on him surviving the jump intact were lengthening with every passing second. Maybe he should just stay aboard. Maybe Wickramasinghe knew what he was doing. Maybe the man was not mad.

Then, distantly up ahead: a two-note blare.

Another train, sounding its horn in warning.

Jesus! No doubt about it now. He *was* mad.

The blare came again, the notes spaced much closer together this time. More urgent.

Squeezing his eyes shut and clenching his teeth, Fen leaned back. He bent his legs and, with a shout that was half scream, half prayer, propelled himself out of the doorway.

3. THE POPPY FIELD

The red admiral bumbled along on a spiralling, intricate flight path. For days – a lifetime – it had been searching for hints of pheromone in the air, skywritten come-ons, the lonely-hearts ads of its species. Wanting to mate, existing for no other purpose, it had quested and roved and flirted with the wind currents, so far in vain. Luck had kept it out of the beaks and webs of predators. The sexual imperative drove it onward.

In the soft glow of a quiet evening, the red admiral's peregrinations brought it to a field of rampant couch grass where wild poppies flourished in clusters, archipelagos of scarlet in a yellow-green ocean. At the field's edge, where it terminated in a steep, brambly embankment that led down to a railway track, the butterfly homed in on a particular stalk of grass. Descended. Settled, flattening its wings together like a penitent's praying hands.

Its weight, such as it was, caused the grass stalk to bend.

The stalk's seed-feathery tip touched the cheek of the human who lay close by, sprawled, motionless.

Briefly, Fen awoke.

A tiny, scratchy tickle on his face, but it was enough to stir him from insensibility, sparking a glimmer of consciousness in his brain.

His eyelids fluttered, not unlike a butterfly's wings.

He glimpsed hazy daylight and a jungle of grass. Heard the zip-zing-zither of crickets.

Then agony jolted up from his left leg, agony that surpassed any he had known before.

It was safer down in the dark. There was no pain there.

He happily surrendered to oblivion.

The red admiral took off, swirling back up into the air. Its search, its lust-wander, continued.

Dusk. A burnt-umber sunset. It almost blinds me. I can barely walk. A controlled stumble. Two men holding my arms, helping me along. City odours, oddly nostalgic. Grass, urban turf – acrid. Fossil-fuel fumes. Rotting things, organic matter, fruit, vegetables. I think of market stalls and summer Sundays in the park, the heady rumble of traffic and getting drunk in bars. Maybe it's because I used to be a Londoner.

We go from the bricked-up house, confinement, the place where captives get the defiance knocked out of them – we go from there across the compound. I'm grip-hauled all the way. Hurts. We go between two houses, and an Alsatian on a chain lunges at me, snarling. We pass a flotilla of white vans parked all hugger-mugger, and nearby there are jerrycans of petrol stored in neat stacks, covered in tarpaulins, hundreds of gallons of the stuff. We go towards a house that seems larger than all the rest. That's the impression it gives, though this is – was – one of those estates where every residence is identical, plonked down one after another in rows as if deposited from the rear end of some gargantuan house-excreting machine. The other houses are shabby and tumbledown. This one seems larger because it has had some effort expended on it. Someone's done up the paintwork. Someone's neatened up the small square of front garden. Someone's kept the windowpanes scrubbed and the curtains hanging straight.

The front door is open. Looks like we're expected.

In the hallway we're greeted, not by a man as I thought we would be, but by a woman. I don't recognise her. She's not from Downbourne. She has prominent yellow teeth and one of those complexions that looks like dirt is permanently engrained into her skin. Her hair is long and lank, a muddy shade of ginger. She looks thirty but she's probably younger. She might have been pretty once, back when she was a girl, back before she became so etched, so whittled, by life.

She appraises me, trying to appear indifferent. But I've spotted the flint-spark of resentment in her eyes.

'This is her?' she says to the men holding me.

'Yeah.'

She gives a small sniff. 'Nothing special.'

'You can make her nice.'

'I can try.' She fixes the men with a haughty look. She obviously has some power here, some status. 'All right. I'll deal with it from here.'

They let go of my arms. Blood flushes into the flesh where they were holding on – pins-and-needles tingle.

'If she gives you any trouble . . .'

'Don't worry. She won't.'

The men leave. It's just me and this woman. She does a circuit around me, looking me up and down, and I can't believe she doesn't know she's acting like a madame in some bad period drama, inspecting the ingenue heroine, the whorehouse's newest recruit.

'I'm Lauren,' she says, finally. 'I've been here three years. I've survived. And I've survived because I'm a hard bitch and I don't take shit from no one. You'd do well to remember that. There's been lots like you. Craig gets through you like Kleenex. You come, you go, but I'm still here. So don't get any funny ideas. Don't get thinking you could replace me. You can't. You won't. Try it and I'll kick your fucking ass.'

She isn't American. She's London through and through, and 'ass' sounds wrong coming from her like that, but I suppose she was brought up on American TV and movies; culture-bombed into believing that everything American is cool. A brave (or a stupid) belief to maintain, given which country has been the most enthusiastic advocate of the International Community broadsides against England.

'First thing I'm going to do is get you cleaned up and sorted out,' she continues. 'You look a mess, and you're no good to anyone looking a mess. Then I'm going to fill you in on what's expected of you. Craig's away at the moment. Will be for the next couple of days. So I'm going to show you around, get you familiarised with how things work round here, get you ready for him. What you have to realise is that from now on pleasing Craig is what you're all about. As long as you please him, there won't be any trouble. *Dis*please him, and . . . Well, I don't think you'd be that stupid.' She flashes a smile that isn't meant to be friendly. 'I suppose I should ask your name.'

It flits across my mind to give her a false name. I don't know why. Maybe just so as not to make things easy for her. Maybe a false name will somehow give her less of a hold over me. But I decide it isn't worth it.

'Moira.'

She raises an eyebrow. Not disdainful. Mildly surprised. 'I had you pegged as a Kate or a Jane. "Moira". Makes me think of somebody's aunt. "I'm going to visit my Aunt Moira for tea and scones." '

She's clearly missed her calling as a comedienne.

'OK, Moira. Come with me.'

We go upstairs. I'm finding this all a little disorientating. Partly because I'm so damn weak (lack of food, and all that time spent in the dark – how many days?). Partly because I thought I'd be being raped by now. And partly because I'm here in a house that's done up like someone's idea of a perfect starter home – clean white walls, a framed print here and there, chintzy curtains – yet it's sitting smack-dab in the middle of a barricaded compound inhabited by a bunch of crop-haired bullyboys who kidnap women for sex. And now – Jesus – here's a bathroom with avocado-green fixtures, brass fittings, a nice clean mould-free shower curtain, and Lauren spins the bath taps and water comes out of the mixer spout and it's steaming! Hot water! Hot water pouring into a bath!

'Take those clothes off.'

And I do. As if in a dream, I strip naked. Off come the grubby, reeking shirt and jeans and underwear, off into a pile on the floor.

A hot bath.

I can barely believe it. When the water's good and deep, I step in, and the warmth surges up my legs, and the sensation is sublime, and I'm transported back in time to when things like this were normal, when you could take a hot bath any time you felt like it. Not even a luxury. An activity you gave no more thought to than buying a newspaper or sticking a CD in the stereo. Something you did because you could. I sink down, immersing myself. Lauren watches me, sees the sheer bliss on my face, thinks I'm pathetic. I don't care.

'There's soap,' she says, 'and a face-cloth. Wash yourself. I'm not damn well doing it for you. When you're done, come downstairs.'

She leaves me to it, taking my clothes with her. I scrub myself thoroughly, removing what feels like an inch of grime. The water goes grey. A filthy soap-scum forms on the surface. When I don't think I can be any cleaner, or have ever been so clean, I lie back, water-supported, near-weightless.

There's a small window. Edges fogged with condensation like an Edwardian photograph, it frames a rectangle of London sky. There are a couple of plump, brown-orange clouds up there. A distant tower block, sporadically lit. A single star.

I gaze out.

Bizarrely, incredibly, I'm almost happy.

A sudden sharp twisting twinge, then grisly pain. It couldn't be denied any longer. He couldn't shelter from it in unconsciousness any longer.

Surging up into self-awareness, Fen began to turn himself over. A hundred white-hot daggers gouged into his left thigh, working away with sawtooth fury. He screamed and groaned and gasped out half-words, empty glottal syllables. Fingers clawing the ground, he writhed like a severed worm.

He thought: I can't endure this. I'm going to die if this doesn't stop.

It didn't stop. Gradually, though, the pain grew less jarring, less alien, becoming acquainted. It settled in, a dull, enervating throb. Fen's breathing steadied. He regained control of his thoughts. Took stock.

He had broken his leg.

Put like that, it did not seem all that drastic.

He had jumped from the *Jagannatha*, and he was all right, he hadn't killed himself. He had only broken his leg.

People were breaking bones all the time. Alan Greeley had had his wrist fractured just the other day. All things considered, Fen was lucky it was *only* his leg that he had broken.

He tried to remember what had happened, but everything after leaping from the doorway of the train was hazy. He had a vague recollection of being *bounced* like a rubber toy, of pinwheeling upwards. It made him think of footage he had seen of motorcycle racers hitting the hay-bale crash barriers, bodies yanked over the handlebars and whirling, end over end, like human boomerangs. It had always amazed him how often they escaped with nothing worse than scrapes and bruises. Helmets and padded leather accounted for some of the lack of damage, to be sure, but even so the human frame was, when put to the test, remarkably resilient.

So here he was. It was dark, and he was lying sprawled on the brow of the railway embankment, left femur fractured. How badly?

The section of his jeans surrounding the thigh felt tight, the thigh swollen, but he didn't think that bone had pierced through skin. A simple rather than a compound fracture. And (he performed a swift self-inventory) there seemed to be no other significant injuries.

Had the *Jagannatha* missed the other train? He couldn't see the track from where he was, but surely if there had been a collision he would know about it. There would be the audible aftermath of carnage, the sound of flames still burning perhaps, at the very least people injured, groaning, calling out. In the event, he could hear nothing except the sibilant hush of night-time countryside.

He glanced around. He was encircled by long, dry grass, and rising taller than the grass he could just make out the heads of flowers of some sort – poppies? At his feet lay a thicket of brambles which marked the top of the embankment. His right leg, his undamaged leg, was hooked up on the brambles, the cuff of his jeans snagged on thorns. His other leg lay stuck out to the side.

All right. First things first. To be stretched out like this, prone, chin pressed into the grass, was not exactly comfortable. If he could get himself sitting upright, that would be a start. A small improvement in circumstances.

He contemplated what he would have to do. He knew it wasn't going to be pleasant. Why not just remain as he was? It might be uncomfortable, but it was nowhere near as bad as moving himself was going to be.

The more he dwelled on it, the less eager he became to put his scheme into action.

Finally: sod it. He would give it a try.

He tugged his right leg, carefully disentangling it from the brambles. His left leg tolerated this, grumbling only a little. Next, he spread both hands on the ground, palms down, fingers splayed, as though about to do a press-up. Gently, with an even downward pressure, he raised his upper body a few inches, then lodged his right elbow under his ribs, angling his torso sideways. So far, so good. The leg was protesting, but the objections it was raising were bearable. Its voice had got a bit sharper, that was all.

He gritted his teeth and prepared to roll over onto his right side. He could do this, he could do this.

One.

Two.

Three . . .

Fen let out a howl that, had he himself been in a fit state to hear it, he would not have recognised as originating from his own throat, or indeed from the throat of any human. The howl frayed into a sob, and the sob dissipated into guttural, rasping bleats. Nothing, but nothing, was as horrible as this pain. No one on earth had ever suffered its like before. He collapsed back flat on his stomach, gritting his teeth, grimacing.

In time, his leg concluded that it had chastised him enough for having had the insolence to put it to the test. The awful agony became merely agony, and Fen was able to stop breathing in fits and bursts through his nostrils and just pant and gasp instead. He spat out a few grains of soil that had found their way into his mouth, then twisted his head round so that his ear, rather than his nose, was bearing the weight of skull and brain. His eyes burned with tears. He felt abject misery – how unfair this was, how viciously fucking *unfair* – but underlying the misery there was something else.

An inkling.

An inkling that, as bad as his situation was, it could very well get much, much worse.

Dressed in the white towelling bath-robe that I found hanging on the back of the bathroom door, I go downstairs, following sounds of activity. In the kitchen, a washing machine is churning – my clothes sloshing around and around in the window – and Lauren's preparing a meal. Nothing spectacular. Spaghetti hoops from a tin. Still, I'm all but drooling by the time it's ready. We eat sitting on opposite sides of the kitchen table. This is all so disturbingly *not* what I expected would happen, and there are dozens of questions I want to ask, but at the same time I'm not sure I want to know any of the answers. So, silence for now. Enjoy the respite.

'So where're you lot from?' Lauren asks as she chases her last few spaghetti hoops around her plate. There's a splat of tomato sauce on one corner of her mouth. Someone who liked her would point this out to her so that she could wipe it off. 'Somewhere down south, isn't it?'

'Yes. Small town, not far from the coast. Downbourne. You won't have heard of it.'

'Nope. Nice place?'

'Quiet. Primitive. Doesn't have anything like you have here – electricity, hot water. We haven't managed to get things running again. Haven't had that chance.'

'Mm,' she says, not really interested.

'I'm from London originally, though.'

'Oh?'

'Barnes. Then Islington. Lived there till my late twenties.'

'So this must be a bit like coming home for you.'

She says this entirely without irony, entirely unaware of how crass it is, and it strikes me that she's actually quite stupid. Or perhaps a bit simple. Not all there. Maybe that's how she has, as she put it, survived. Not by being a hard bitch. By not fully understanding things. Ignorance as armour.

'You?' I ask.

'What?'

'You from round here?'

'Oh. Uh-huh. Not far.'

'This may sound daft, but where *is* here?'

'South-east London.'

'Can you be a bit more specific?'

She becomes wary. 'Why d'you want to know?'

'No reason. Just nice to have some sense of where I am, that's all.'

'Lewisham,' she says finally, having thought about whether it'll make any difference if I know this information or not.

'And those men – who are they?'

'The British Bulldogs.' This she says with some pride, like a cheerleader naming her team. 'You've heard of them, I suppose.'

'Not actually.'

She rolls her eyes. 'Well, you should've. They run this borough.'

'In Downbourne we were a little, you know, out of things.'

'Yeah, I reckon you were.'

I volunteer to do the dishes. It's almost absurd how gratifying it is to run warm water into a sink, add a squirt of washing-up liquid, scrub cutlery and crockery under a layer of soap bubbles and place them rinsed and sparkling in a drying rack. I feel like one of those TV-commercial housewives discovering some wonderful new cleaning product and experiencing domestic-chore epiphany. I have to fight the urge to grin and giggle.

Afterwards, Lauren produces a beaten-up packet of cigarettes, some Dutch brand I've never heard of. She thinks about it, then holds out the pack to me. I haven't smoked in ages. I gave up before the Unlucky Gamble meant I had to give up. But it would be impolite not to accept. Impolite, and God, yes, why not?

The first drag makes me cough, but after that it's as if I never stopped. My system opens up to the nicotine, embracing an old friend. We used to smoke like chimneys at the magazine. None of that smoke-free office nonsense at *Siren*, no sir. Editorial meetings were conducted through a thickening tobacco haze, and at my desk I'd light up every time the phone rang, just about. It was almost a conditioned response. I didn't feel right taking a phone call if I wasn't firing up a cancer stick at the same time. I even penned a semi-flippant article about it for the magazine. 'Pavlov's Beagles' was the title.

So we smoke, Lauren and I, and again I think how incongruous this is. In the midst of such a shitty situation, to be doing something as normal as having a fag in somebody's nice clean kitchen . . .

'This Craig you talked about,' I say to her. 'Who is he? Does he run things around here?'

Lauren gives me a look, like: how thick *are* you? Don't you know *anything*? 'He's the King, ain't he?'

'The King?'

'King Cunt.'

'Oh. Lovely.'

'That's how 'most everyone else knows him. I'm one of the few who get to call him Craig.'

'So what should *I* call him, when I meet him?'

'Whatever he tells you to.'

'"Cunt" for short?'

She tips her head back and blows out a smoke ring. 'I wouldn't be that way around him, if I were you.'

'What way?'

'Clever. Craig doesn't like that at all.'

'OK. Thanks for the warning. I won't be clever then.'

'Just do like I said. It's not difficult. Please him, and you'll be fine.'

'And when's he coming back, did you say?'

'Weren't you listening? Couple of days. He's off negotiating with the Frantik Posse over in Camberwell. There's been a bit of friction between them and that lot in Peckham, the Riot Squad, and Craig thinks he can score points with the Frantiks if he sides with them against the Squad. Not actually makes an alliance with them. Just keeps in with them in a' – she gropes for a suitable term – 'diplomatic sort of a way. The Riot Squad aren't that strong at the moment. Been in a bit of trouble keeping people in their borough in line. So if the Frantiks try for a takeover, which they will, and they'll succeed, then we'll be in a position to take advantage of it. Expand our territory in that direction, if possible. The Frantiks won't mind because we were on their side and most of Peckham will be more than enough for them to manage. It's politics, you see.'

'I see. And what does the London Council make of all this?'

'Nothing,' she replies, quizzically. 'What's it got to do with the Council?'

'A lot, I'd have thought.'

She gives a steely little laugh. 'You really don't have a clue how things work around here, do you?'

'I think I'm beginning to.'

'The Council's there to keep the folks in the suburbs happy more than anything. It gives them the sense that everything in the inner city is fine, all under control. But the Council answers to the boroughs, not the other way round. If we need it to turn a blind eye, it always will.'

Later, Lauren asks if I'm tired. I take the hint. I *am* tired, anyway.

She shows me to an upstairs room that I can only assume is the guest bedroom. She herself normally uses this room, but while Craig's away she's been sleeping in the master bedroom across the landing. The bed's more comfortable there, apparently.

The guest bedroom isn't big. There's a single bed, a small window, some of the ghastliest wallpaper I've ever seen – but it's homely, the bed linen is clean and smooth and soft . . . We did our best in Downbourne with cold water and hand-scrubbing, but it isn't the same as soap powder, proper laundering, ironing . . . I lie down . . . Lauren switches the light out . . . There's darkness, and then there's . . .

He shouted for an hour. He shouted until his throat was sore and his yells had turned to feeble, pitiful rasps. He shouted into the night-time emptiness around him, into the whispering countryside, into the hollow cauldron of star-studded sky above. He shouted, and not even an echo answered. Nothing that heard his cries understood what they meant, or cared. Nocturnal fauna went about its business unheeding. Those that prowl prowled. Those that scurry in darkness scurried in darkness. Those that watch from tree boughs watched from tree boughs. Flowers were closed; the world was closed. Fen was stranded and crippled and almightily alone.

Still lying prone, afraid to attempt to move himself again, he struggled to marshal his thoughts, get them in some kind of order. Panic kept welling inside him, threatening to overcome him, reduce him to a quaking, witless wreck. The panic could be suppressed, but only with effort. He had to be rational. Rational thought was the control rod that kept this particular reactor from meltdown.

He was not going to die.

That was the priority here, the fact he knew he must keep at the forefront of his brain.

He was not going to die. He wasn't in some vast, uninhabited area. This was no Sahara, no Himalaya. This was England. Southeast England, to be precise. The Home Counties. One of the most densely populated regions on the surface of the planet. Not as densely populated as it used to be, for sure, but still a place where you could not go a mile without coming across some sign of human habitation. It was inconceivable that *someone* would not hear him shouting. If not now, then in the morning. There must be someone who owned and farmed the land around here. There must be a village or a town reasonably close by whose residents, for one reason or another, were wont to venture in this direction during the daytime. If he started yelling again tomorrow morning, someone would surely hear him. Come to investigate. Go and fetch help.

He was not going to die.

And he was right next to a railway track. Trains would be passing – if not tonight then sometime tomorrow. If just one person glanced out of a carriage window and spotted him lying there, obviously in difficulties, that person could raise the alarm, and in no time . . .

In no time *what?* This wasn't, as if Fen needed to remind himself, the old England any more, the old England that had had a functioning infrastructure of telecommunications networks and emergency services, where you were never more than a phone call away from a police officer or an ambulance. Such commonplace certainties were a thing of the past.

Fair enough, but it was still conceivable nonetheless. A passenger in a passing train *might* try and get assistance to him. And what if Wickramasinghe came back in the *Jagannatha* to find out what had become of him? How about that? Not terribly likely, but a possibility.

All he had to do was last out the night here. Grit his teeth, endure the pain.

A few hours, that was all.

He was not going to die.

Seldom had a few hours seemed so long. Lacking a watch, Fen's only guide to the passing of time was the moon, and the moon appeared in no hurry to go anywhere. Each time he peered up to check on its position, it was exactly where it had been the last time he looked. Even when he forced himself to wait, leaving as long an interval as he could before looking again, the moon stood still. Partially occluded on one side, its grey-shadow face leered at him like a clown peeking out from behind the circus curtain, laughing at him as though this was all just the merriest prank: Fen Morris lying helpless on the ground, waiting for a dawn that was not going to come.

The countryside was all rustle and activity. Every so often some animal or other would cough or hoot or yicker or wail. On one occasion Fen heard a creature shuffling and snuffling about nearby, sounding like something huge even though it must only be a hedgehog or a rabbit or a stoat. For a while a bat flitted overhead – its sonar chirrups were like a tiny wire being plucked inside his middle ear. Breezes swooshed through vegetation. This was the noise of the world when humankind was silenced. Raucous as any city, any factory, any rock concert.

And then the cold.

The cold seeped through his clothing, lowering his body temperature degree by imperceptible degree. Fen began shivering before he was aware of doing so. The shivering intensified, his lips turned to rubber, and his throat started making small, involuntary stammering noises. The pain from his leg, which the cold might have been expected to numb, instead sharpened, becoming glassy, crystalline, grating.

He bore it as best he could. He told himself over and over that it was just this one night, that once day broke this would all be over. All he had to do was hold out till then. Several times, though, he gave in and wept, grinding his face into the grass in despair. A similar number of times he cried out again for help, help, please, somebody, help – in the vain hope that his voice would carry to someone somewhere, some night owl, some insomniac. Once, though he was not aware of doing so, he even cried out for his mother.

An eternity later, the sky began to lighten.

No. Just a trick of the imagination. The night remained as dark as ever.

Another eternity passed, and then the moon was gone, having taken refuge at some point when Fen wasn't looking, and yes, there, distinctly, a greenish greyness to the black. The stars ever so slightly fainter, losing their lustre. A pallid glow encroaching from the east.

And at last – mundane miracle – a bird twittered.

Fen could not recall when he had heard a sound quite so welcome or quite so wonderful.

The bird was silent for a long while, as if it feared it had made a mistake. Then, tentatively, it twittered again, and some distance away, another bird responded.

After breakfast, Lauren takes me on a guided tour.

The compound covers about half a mile square, I reckon, although I'm not that hot on gauging such things. The fortifications are solid all round, nowhere less than twenty feet high. They're constructed from bits of old furniture and things like fridges and ovens, breeze blocks and heavy timber, car parts, all jumbled together, stacked high, packed tight. In most places there's barbed wire along the top or sections of spiked iron railing appropriated from the front of some town house, or else some more improvisational anti-climbing measure such as arrays of sharpened chair legs, side by side like the teeth of a comb, and planks of wood with shards of broken bottle glued to them. You could get over if you were really determined to, but not without risk of serious injury. There are a couple of lookout posts too, one beside the main gate, the other at the opposite end of the compound. They're little open-topped turrets knocked together from scaffolding and planks, accessible by ladders. Though I don't see anyone in either of them, Lauren assures me they're regularly manned.

In the centre of the compound there's the van park I passed last night – I count about twenty vehicles in all – and near that there's a kind of communal area, an expanse of open ground that was probably a children's playground when this was just an ordinary housing estate. It's got a large brick-sided barbecue pit and several tables and benches. The grass is littered with food packaging, fruit rinds, beer cans. It's a warm, bright morning, and quite a few of the British Bulldogs are out here, eating and drinking and amusing themselves. One of them is getting a new tattoo done, trying not to wince as a skull with a rose clenched between its teeth is jabbed out on his shoulderblade with the point of a compass. Another of them is giving a martial arts lesson to a few of his colleagues, demonstrating a kick technique that looks (to my untrained eye at least) just like an ordinary kick, although the Bulldog seems to think it's a move which must be studied and practised for years before it can be mastered. As Lauren and I go by, we are subjected to stares and leers and the odd building-site comment, although the men are definitely deferential to Lauren. I can't quite figure out her relationship to this King Cunt person – wife? housekeeper? – but whatever it is, her association with him protects her. Me, the men are quite happy to treat as though I'm just a vagina and tits on legs – although I get the feeling they're not – being as coarse towards me as they could be. Why? Because I'm with Lauren? Because I'm under King Cunt's protection too?

What I don't see on the guided tour is any of the other women from Downbourne. I ask Lauren about this.

'Oh, they'll be indoors,' she replies casually. 'Sleeping, if they've got any sense. Getting their strength back.'

'Getting their strength back for what?'

Lauren rolls her eyes. 'What d'you goddamn think, honey?'

I'm completely dumbfounded by that. Not by what Lauren has said but the way she's said it. It doesn't seem to impinge on her – what's being done to these women, members of her own sex. She doesn't seem to care in the least.

'Where are they?' I ask.

'There are a couple of houses set aside.'

'Brothels?'

'Well, no, actually, Moira. Duh. And here was I thinking you were all smart and knew, like, words an' shit. Brothels. Women in brothels get paid, don't they? And that's not what happens here. Craig's name for them is recreation zones.'

'Not "comfort battalions" then?'

'I don't get.'

I didn't think she would. 'And the Bulldogs can go there any time they like?'

'Pretty much. It's necessary, see. Craig calls it a release valve. Lets out the pressure. Keeps the boys happy.'

'Christ. I mean . . . Christ. That's horrible.'

'Honey, it's life,' Lauren says, with a nonchalant shrug. 'It's the way things go around here. I wouldn't spend any time worrying about it. There's nothing you can do.'

'But one of the women from our town – well, she's not even a woman. She's a fifteen-year-old girl. A *child*.'

For an instant – the merest instant – I think I glimpse something behind Lauren's studiedly casual façade, just a hint of something deeper than indifference. It's there, then it's gone. 'Well, serves her right. Shouldn't have got caught, should she?'

I ask if she'll point out to me which houses are the 'recreation zones', but she refuses.

'Think I've shown you enough for one morning. Let's go back.'

As we make our way back to the house, we pass within sight of the lookout post by the gate. There's a Bulldog in it now, lounging, enjoying a cigarette and gazing out over whatever lies beyond the walls.

That's the route out of this place, out of this fort. Not the gate, not the barricades – the lookout post. That's how I'll be getting out of Fort Bulldog.

A flock of starlings passing a few feet overhead awoke him. The rippling flap of wingbeats, the sough of wind through feathers – he opened his eyes in time to see the last of the birds disappear from view beyond the grass-bordered limits of his vision. A momentary sense of dislocation. Where? How? Then it all tumbled back into place. His leg. His throat, raw from shouting last night and again at various intervals throughout the morning. His dry mouth. Hunger – deep-rooted, throbbing hunger. The smells of sun-warmed grass and earth strong in his nose. All the components of the hellish situation he was in. And now an additional problem: he needed to urinate.

He needed to urinate quite urgently, in fact, and since he wasn't going to be able to attempt this lying face down, flat out, he knew he would have to try something drastic. He knew he was going to have to do what he had failed to do yesterday and turn over.

It was half an hour before he was able to screw up sufficient nerve to attempt the manoeuvre. It helped that in that time the urge to urinate had become a critical necessity. His bladder was hurting, and if he didn't do something about it *now* he was going to wet his pants, and that would be an indignity too far.

He assumed the position he had tried before, that sort of press-up position, bent his torso up off the ground and wriggled his right elbow into the gap between hip and ribs. Then he clamped his teeth together and squeezed his eyes shut, in expectation of the unutterable, blinding pain to come. He sent up the prayer that all agnostics resort to *in extremis,* the if-you're-there-God prayer, the bet-hedging plea for special divine intercession. Then he shunted himself sideways using his elbow as a fulcrum, the plan being that his right leg would pivot where it was and his left would be pulled across it and fall into place, knee upwards, beside it . . .

. . . lightning detonated in his left thigh . . .

. . . he was on his back but the leg was stuck, canted across the other one . . .

. . . the thigh being bent . . .

. . . femur fracture flexing . . .

He groped for the leg to shift it by hand. He was grimacing, thrashing his head up and down, ululating inarticulately. His hands found his left knee and pushed it sideways . . .

. . . another lightning burst . . .

He slumped back.

Passed out.

Pissed himself anyway.

'It's quite straightforward,' says Lauren. 'If he wants to fuck you, you let him fuck you. If he just wants to talk, you talk. You do as he says when he says. Don't do as he says, and he'll beat shit out of you. Couldn't be simpler, could it?'

We're in the back garden of the house. It's turning out to be a gorgeous day. London sunshine – hotter, harder, less forgiving than country sunshine, but always, as I remember it, more of a gift: bleaching away the sins of the city, coaxing shut-ins outdoors, putting smiles on otherwise smile-free faces. Lauren's got me on my knees beside her, digging weeds from a bed of pink busy lizzies. I haven't done work like this in ages, and the months of inactivity – con-valescence – are catching up with me. I have to stop every other minute to rest. Sweat trickles from my armpits, and I think of the bath I can have when this is done, if I want. How did I put up with it in Downbourne? The deprivations, the inconveniences? How?

That's when Lauren sets out, in the clearest terms yet, the cost of staying here. What I'm going to have to do if I want to keep enjoying hot baths and clean clothes and plentiful food.

I look at her. She looks at me.

'Is that how it was with you? When you first arrived?'

She nods. 'That was my job. For about six months.'

'King Cunt's concubine.'

'Concubine?'

'Mistress. Bed-partner.'

'Yup.'

'And then?'

'Then I'd have been thrown on the scrapheap like the rest, only Craig'd taken a shine to me because I made myself useful around the house, kept the place nice and tidy, cooked for him and all that, which none of the others had actually done before, so he let me stay on. He didn't come out and *ask* me to stay on. He just didn't tell me to go, so I didn't go.'

'But you could have gone if you'd wanted to.'

'Oh yeah. But I mean . . . I'm safe here. Life's better for me here than it ever was out there. Here, I don't have to worry about when or what I'm going to eat, and I get respect from everybody, and – and it's just better, you know what I mean?'

I do know. I can understand her point of view exactly. It's gutless and it's venal, but I can understand exactly why she's made the choice she has.

'Can I ask, then – why me? Why have I been singled out from all the others?'

'What, you mean why have *you* been chosen to be Craig's . . . What's that word again?'

'Concubine.'

'Concubine. Yeah. Well, it's obvious, ain't it?'

She strokes her hair.

I give her a blank look.

She strokes her hair again, then points to mine. 'Craig has a thing about redheads.'

'You're kidding me.'

'Straight up. It's the only kind of girl he'll sleep with.'

'Do you know why?'

'No idea. He just does.'

I remember the Bulldogs in the van discussing my hair. Saying 'he' would like it. They saw me in the street, stopped for me – a present for their boss. A red-haired gift. Jesus Christ. Now I understand. Of all the crappy, stupid reasons for this to have happened to me – a quirk of pigmentation! Were I a blonde or a brunette, they'd have passed me by. But I'm not, and that's why I've wound up here, and how ridiculous is *that*?

I'm laughing before I realise I'm laughing.

'What's so funny?' Lauren asks, suspiciously.

'Oh, nothing. Nothing at all.'

But I keep laughing, rejoicing in the absurdity of it, tickled pink at how the worst of things can happen for the most meaningless of reasons.

I'm sure Fen, if he were here, would find it funny too.

This time it was discomfort in his back that brought him round. Something protruding into his spine. Felt like a stone. No. He was lying on his knapsack. His water canteen.

Left thigh pulsing. Pain like a jellyfish wafting with the tide: clench and relax, clench and relax. Unbearable, then bearable.

Clammy wetness in the crotch of his jeans.

He fumbled with the knapsack straps, dislodging first one then the other from his shoulders. With a certain amount of judicious contortion he extricated each arm from the straps, then tugged the knapsack out from under him.

That was better.

He drew the knapsack onto his chest, undid the flap and removed the canteen from inside, hoping against hope that there was still some water left in it, even if it was no more than a trickle. Just enough to moisten his lips with would be nice. But the canteen was dry. Fen remembered shaking the last few drops from it into his mouth during Wickramasinghe's protracted absence yesterday.

Yesterday? Several decades ago!

He returned the canteen to the knapsack and fished out the only other item the knapsack contained, the mustard. This was all he had left of his provisions, thanks to Wickramasinghe. Half a pot of mustard. Not much use by itself, but still . . .

He unscrewed the lid, inserted a finger and hooked out a grainy ochre blob. Licked at it. Felt the tip of his tongue singe.

No, he wasn't going to be able to do this. Eat mustard raw. Not yet.

Besides, there *was* something to eat here. Earlier, he had noticed that the brambles at his feet were hung with blackberries – blackberries which ran the gamut of ripeness from tight green to swelling maroon to bloated purple-black. He was hungry enough to try one now.

He hauled himself up, stretched forwards, and plucked the

largest of the fruits within reach. He popped it into his mouth and crushed it between his teeth.

Acid-sour.

He spat mashed blackberry out onto the grass. Somehow he had known that the blackberries would not be edible. Not just because it was too early in the year. A source of nourishment so close to hand would have been too much like divine providence, wouldn't it? Too much like a stroke of good fortune.

He lay back.

The sun was high and searingly hot.

No train had passed yet.

Time. He told himself it was only a matter of time.

By the time a train did come, Fen had lapsed into a kind of semi-doze, neither asleep nor wholly awake. It was as if he had withdrawn into a cocoon, somewhere where he was no longer exposed to the full glare of the sun, where the relentless grating throb from his leg was dulled, where pain and thirst and heat and hunger were problems but not *pressing* problems. He was detached from himself, at one remove from his senses. Somebody else who was feeling and hearing and experiencing all that he was feeling and hearing and experiencing.

The cocoon was a fine and private place and he would gladly have stayed there for ever, but then he heard the rails start to sing out a high-pitched whine and he knew this meant something, something important, something worth emerging for. Reluctantly he roused himself, re-entering the world of dry grass and parched lips and fractured thigh and burning sunshine, the harsh world he hadn't really left at all.

The rails were humming hard, the tines of a giant tuning fork, vibrating with the approaching tonnage of the train. Fen struggled up onto his elbows, and here it came, shoving a cushion of hissing air before it . . .

Whump!

The front carriage shot into view, and the trackside foliage writhed and surged like an appreciative crowd. Windows flickered by, some with passengers' faces in them, and then here was the second carriage and only now did Fen manage to raise a hand. A third carriage, and he waved hard, urgently – *here I am, I need help* – but the passengers were being whisked past too swiftly for him to tell whether any of them even registered his presence up there on top of the embankment. A fourth and final carriage, and then Fen was waving at empty space, at the trackbed weeds shivering in the train's slipstream, at the rails now relaxing into a relieved diminuendo, sighing, subsiding into silence.

He lowered his hand. He had done what he could. He only hoped someone aboard the train had seen him and had ascertained that he was in trouble. He realised that his waving could quite easily have been mistaken for a greeting. People did that, cheerily and thoughtlessly waved at trains going by. They had at the *Jagannatha*. But it should have been obvious that that was not what he had been doing.

He settled back stiffly into the grass, which had taken on a rough imprint of his body, a coffin-shaped silhouette picked out in flattened stems. He lay there and stared upwards at a patch of sky framed by the spikes of grass and a couple of nodding poppy heads. Soon his eyelids were drooping and the sky's blue was blurring and he was sinking back into the cocoon.

Safe here. Beyond harm here.

But then a sound. A strange, succulent sucking sound, liquid and living and lively, emanating from all around him. He opened his eyes. The couch grass was growing. Right in front of him as he watched. Struggling effortfully upwards. Stems writhing, multiplying, ramifying, breeding other stems, which bred yet others. Rising with time-lapse rapidity around him, deepening the depression in which he lay, limiting his view of the sky, shutting out the light, shrouding him in shadow. He tried to reach up to claw a hole through the grass. He felt like he was suffocating, drowning. But his arms would not move. The grass was vastly tall. The stems intertwined, interlocked, closed over him. Suddenly he was in green darkness, like that of a rainforest, canopied, cool. He was paralysed. He was frightened. It was like being buried alive.

Then there was someone beside him, standing over him, framed against the meshed vault of grass, looking down.

Michael Hollingbury.

It was unmistakably Hollingbury. Downbourne's Green Man in all his green finery. Yet he looked different. Greener, for one thing, as though he had daubed on several extra coats of vegetable dye, steeping his skin in the stuff. Somewhat plumper, too, than Fen remembered. And there was a peculiar quality to his hair, beard and eyebrows. Fen was reminded of chives – thick strands, juicy with chlorophyll. And Hollingbury's eyes . . . The irises were green, a deep, sparkling jade green, and Fen was almost certain they used to be blue.

All very perplexing, but not as perplexing as the fact that Michael Hollingbury was dead. Fen had watched him die. Had watched the British Bulldogs hurl his battered body into the festival bonfire. Had heard and smelled him burn.

With a certain pardonable circumspection, Fen offered this apparition a hello.

'Ah, Mr Morris, yes.' Hollingbury smiled, shaking his head. 'Not the most marvellous of situations, eh? But then we all of us make bad choices now and then.'

'Do you think you could—?' Fen stopped. 'No, I don't even know why I'm asking. You can't help me. You're dead.'

'Am I?' Hollingbury's green eyes glinted.

'Of course you are.'

'If you say so. I, however, would beg to differ. And the evidence of your own eyes ought to furnish all the disproof you should need. Do you really think I'm so easily despatched, after all the centuries I've lived?'

'I don't know. No, I suppose. Or yes. Maybe yes.'

Hollingbury chuckled. 'I must say, Mr Morris, for a pedagogue you seem sorely lacking in certainty. A teacher should have all the answers, shouldn't he? The correct response ever at his fingertips.' There was a teasing note in his voice.

'Well, if you aren't dead,' Fen said, 'what are you?'

Hollingbury squatted down on his haunches, resting his forearms on his thighs and clasping his hands together. Fen noticed that his fingernails were as green as the rest of him. Normally they had never taken the dye quite so well. His teeth were green, too, a dark green that was almost black, each like a little hard lump of cooked spinach. This would have made anyone else's mouth look ghastly and diseased, but in Hollingbury's case it seemed somehow appropriate, not to say healthy.

'There is no death.' The Green Man's tone was perfectly matter-of-fact. 'Existences end, but nothing ever truly dies. Take that tree over there.' He gestured, and at the sweep of his hand the couch grass that had grown up around Fen was restored to its normal size, as if instantly and silently scythed.

Fen, no longer entombed, turned his head in the direction Hollingbury was inviting him to look and saw a huge, solitary sycamore, standing some hundred yards away. He did not recall the sycamore being there before. It spread its branches against the sky, its leaves fretted with light.

'That tree,' said Hollingbury, 'flourishes now, but at a certain point in time it will cease to be alive. Its sap will no longer flow, it will not grow any more, but even so it will remain standing, continuing to give support to the ivy that twines around its bark, continuing to provide a haven to the birds that nest in its branches

159

and the squirrel that hoards nuts in its trunk. Then, when the tree does at last rot through and fall, the decayed wood will be food and home to insects, and eventually will be broken down into mulch and compost, sustenance for new plant life. No death is without rebirth, just as no suffering is without gain. Do you understand?'

It was classic Hollingbury, the sort of mystical nature metaphor that had been his forte.

'Well, yes,' Fen said. 'But a tree's a bit different from a human being, don't you think?'

'Not at all. There's no difference whatsoever.'

'OK, fine, fair enough.' There was no point in arguing. Logic seemed irrelevant anyway at this moment. 'So let's accept that you aren't dead after all. Does that mean you can get me out of this?'

Hollingbury flashed him a dark green grin. 'Alas not. But I am keeping an eye on you, Mr Morris. I am on your side. Don't forget that. And everything, good or ill, happens for a reason. Don't forget that either. You will survive this. You're going to be all right. I can't promise that you're going to have an easy time of it in the near future. In fact, the opposite. But you *will* survive.'

From overhead there came a low rending sound, like scissors shearing through canvas.

Hollingbury glanced up. 'Ah yes. Behold.'

Fen glanced up too, and saw, traipsing side by side across the sky, a pair of warplanes. Sun-gold glinted on their nosecones and the leading edges of their wings. They were at too high an altitude for Fen to determine whether or not they had dropped their payloads yet.

Come, friendly bombs, and fall on Fen, he thought.

He turned his head in order to share the humorous misquotation with Hollingbury, only to find that the Green Man had gone.

But of course he had gone. He had never been there. That had been a dream, and Fen was awake now.

He refocused on the warplanes as they eased towards the edge of his field of vision. There was little left in England worth bombing, but every so often the International Community saw fit to flatten a warehouse or an office block as a reminder, the geopolitical equivalent of a clip round the ear – *we haven't forgotten you, we assume you're still misbehaving, and if you persist in refusing to toe the line then you must be prepared to pay the penalty.* Sometimes the planes weren't armed, but a reconnaissance mission was almost as effective an aide-memoire: *we're up here, we're looking down, we see everything.*

It occurred to him to try and attract the pilots' attention. He then laughed at his own foolishness. Even if the pilots *did* spot him, how insect-like he would look to them, how insignificant.

The planes disappeared from view, the roar of their jets fading soon after.

The sky was hazier than before, a hoary shade of blue. Afternoon was over and evening was coming on. Fen realised he had been out here at the top of the embankment for over twenty-four hours. Possibly, thanks to a passenger on the train that had passed, people were on their way to rescue him. Possibly. The odds were against it, though.

Hollingbury in the dream: *You will survive this.*

But that had been a dream, and this was not. This was reality, and in this reality a single thought had begun tolling in Fen's head, faintly but insistently, like a far-off church bell.

A single sentence, iterated over and over.

You are going to die.

After supper, I ask Lauren if I can go for another wander around the compound. Immediately she's suspicious. She doesn't know if she can trust me yet. For her, being trustworthy means being sufficiently intimidated, and she doesn't know yet whether I am. All afternoon I've been doing everything she's asked me to – domestic chores, helping her keep the house in tip-top condition for King Cunt's return tomorrow – and I've tried my hardest to give the impression that I'm coming to terms with what's happened to me, that I'm learning to accept my lot. It's worked. She's lowered her guard – but not completely.

'Why?' she says.

'I just want to stretch my legs.'

'I'll come with you.'

'You don't have to.'

But she thinks she does, and it doesn't make any difference to me. I just want to get a better idea of the lie of the land. So off we go.

There's a revelrous mood in the compound this evening. The Bulldogs are charging around, ragging one another. Mock fights are going on, fuelled by beer. A stereo is blaring from one of the houses, rock music, drumbeats like thunderclaps, and there's a small crowd sitting around outside listening to it, nodding along in unison as though the rhythm has all their heads on a string. In the communal area, what appears to be a weightlifting competition is in progress. Rusty barbells get shunted up and down, propelled on their way with elephantine grunts. Extra weights are clamped on, and faces get redder and the veins in necks and temples get fatter. Everywhere, the braying, bassy laughter of men. It's a cliché but the air really does seem charged with testosterone.

As Lauren and I are wandering towards an area of the compound I didn't get to see this morning, one of the Bulldogs comes striding up to us. I recognise him from the night I was captured. He was the one giving orders as we were unloaded from the vans. I remember his Gold Tooth twinkling in the headlamp's light.

'Lauren.'

'Neville.'

There's wariness in her voice. Lauren doesn't like this man. I don't think he much likes her either, but whereas she's possibly a little frightened of him, his dislike for her seems more a kind of impatience, as if he can't understand why she's still here, why she insists on hanging around when she's so clearly surplus to requirements. That, at any rate, is the impression I get from how each says the other's name and from the fact that Neville, without any further preamble, starts asking Lauren about me – how I'm shaping up, does she think Craig will like me.

Lauren's judgement is that I'm acceptable material, OK-looking, a bit inclined to speak my mind but I'll soon get out of *that* habit.

Neville eyes me up and down, then reaches out and, just like that, grabs one of my breasts. I'm too startled to protest. He paws the breast, palpating it, kneading it, and the look on his face is half sober appraisal, half smutty little schoolboy. Finally he gives the breast a tweak where he thinks the nipple ought to be (he's off-target by about an inch) then lets go. I'm still speechless but it's probably all for the best that I didn't voice my outrage or slap his hand away as I was minded to. I think I would have earned myself a punch that way.

'He likes 'em a bit bigger than that,' is Neville's assessment. 'But they'll do.'

'He wouldn't have dared if Craig was around,' Lauren confides a few moments later, after Neville's left us and we're walking on. She's indignant, although not, I feel, on my behalf. 'He wouldn't have dared lay a finger on you.'

I touch my manhandled breast. Sore. 'Who is he?'

'Neville? Craig's second-in-command, I suppose you'd call him. They used to be friends at school, best pals, though now they're, like, not such good friends any more but Craig still keeps Neville around because Craig's thoughtful that way and because a lot of the guys think Neville's OK so it wouldn't be sensible to tell him to sling his hook. Which Craig ought to, 'cause Neville's a right pain in the ass, constantly having a go at him, bugging him about this or that. All the time he's like "Are you sure, Craig, do you think that's a good idea?" I think he thinks he could do as good a job of running things here, maybe better.'

'And could he?'

'No. Oh no. Nobody could replace Craig.' This is Lauren's gospel, the central, unshakeable certainty in her life. King Cunt is king. It's sad how simply, how obviously, she adores him. 'Anyhow,' she says, 'in case you haven't figured it out for yourself already, you want to watch that Neville.'

'Thanks. I will.'

Now we're coming to a house I know far too well, even though I had only glimpses of its exterior while entering and leaving. One look at the bricked-up windows and all of a sudden I'm back in the confines of that room – the gritty floorboards, the reek of human waste, the sobbing, the helplessness, the hopelessness, and Jennifer, dead Jennifer's cold corpse, lying near me for who knows how long. And I hate these men, these Bulldogs, for putting me through that. I hate them already but my hatred is redoubled, and I know that if it were in my power I would kill them all, every last one of them.

And around a corner I come across a sight that deepens that hatred still further.

Lauren would have steered me away from here if she felt I wasn't ready to see this. Perhaps I've succeeded better than I thought at convincing her that I'm subdued and passive and not likely to give any trouble.

Three houses, their eaves hung with strings of multicoloured light bulbs that cast a jaunty glow against the gathering dusk. The windows all curtained, the front gardens enclosed by chainlink fence, and in the gardens, women. Women standing. Women seated on an assortment of plastic outdoor chairs. Women waiting. About thirty of them in all, the majority familiar to me. There's Angela Pearson, one of the first people I met after moving to Downbourne, one of the first who was friendly and didn't view me with suspicion because I was From The Big City. There's Susannah Vicks. There's Rachel Jason, or is it Jacobs? I always get her name wrong. And there, oh God, is Zoë Fothergill, sitting and being hugged by Paula Coulton, who lost her daughter last year to an infection (Ginnie Coulton, eight years old, cut her hand open on barbed wire while playing with friends, got tetanus, and there was nothing anyone could do, not even Anne Chase, though God knows she tried). There they all are beyond the wire diamonds of chainlink mesh, and some have bruises on their faces and some have eyes that are sunk in dark-circled sockets, and all of them look hollowed and harrowed and bewildered, like survivors of a plane crash or high-street shoppers who were just minding their own business when the car bomb went off. They're waiting because there's nothing else for them to do. Waiting and trying not think about what they're waiting for.

Lauren stands back, arms folded. I don't know how she can't feel any empathy for these women, but she doesn't. Maybe she just can't afford to.

Me, I move forwards to the nearest of the front gardens. As I reach the padlocked gate, some of the women notice me. Their heads turn, alarm sparking in their eyes. They're expecting men. When they see I'm not a Bulldog, a couple of them turn away again, not even curious about me. Probably they assume I've been brought to join them. The rest keep looking, and then Susannah Vicks says, 'Moira.' She says it with a certain amount of interest, but mostly she says it in the lost, deflated tone of someone who doesn't care much about anything any more. It's a tone I'm very familiar with, having heard myself use it pretty consistently for a year and a half. She says, 'Moira,' the same way I used to say, 'Fen.'

I've no idea how to respond. I don't know what I can say to these women that won't sound fatuous or patronising or otherwise offensive. I can barely begin to imagine what they've been going through, I don't want to, and even though a similar fate lies in store for me when King Cunt returns, they're behind a fence and I'm not; they're incarcerated in these 'recreation zones' and I'm walking around Fort Bulldog, not in any way free but nevertheless freer than they are.

'We've been told,' Susannah says, and points to a woman I don't recognise. 'Carla here has been filling us in. We know about the King and his redheads.'

As she speaks I hear her groping for some resentment to put into her voice, but resentment demands just that bit more emotional strength than she has at present.

'Nice of you to pay us a visit,' says Angela Pearson. She, too, is trying for something extra in her voice, in this case sarcasm. Trying and, like Susannah, failing.

I turn my attention to Zoë. Encircled by Paula Coulton's arms, she stares dazedly ahead, her face bereft of any of the liveliness you ought to see on a teenager's face. She has been hurled headlong into a world she could not have suspected existed, a world where men force and subdue and inflict hurt and disgusting humiliation over and over again. It has shattered her.

Susannah and Angela continue to snipe at me in that vigourless manner, trying to hate me for something they know isn't my fault. A couple of the other women join in. I should feel wronged, I should stick up for myself, but I don't. I ignore them, staying focused on Zoë, fixing in my mind how she looks: her slumped shoulders, every contour of her stunned, listless features.

Fuel for loathing.

We're halfway back to King Cunt's house when Lauren finally speaks. I'd forgotten she was even with me.

'I don't go there often, myself,' she says. 'Now you know why.'

'What happens to them?' I ask. 'I mean, they're not going to be held captive indefinitely, surely.'

'Oh no. After a while the guys get bored. They want to see some new faces.'

I should think that, where female physical attributes are concerned, faces come pretty low on the Bulldogs' list of priorities. 'How long does that take, usually?'

'Varies. Anything from a few weeks to a few months.'

'And then?'

'They go on another hunt.'

'No, the women. What becomes of the women when they don't want them any more?'

'They get turfed out.'

'Not . . . not killed, then.'

'Did I say that? Just turfed out.'

'And they have to make their own way home?'

'No, they get a taxi to take them wherever they want to go.' Lauren sneers, despairing of me. 'Of course they have to make their own way home!'

'But the women from Downbourne – we – live fifty miles away.'

'And a lot of them won't make it that far.'

'And what about the M25?'

'Moira, do you honestly think the guys here *care*?'

She has a point, of course. The British Bulldogs don't care about anyone but themselves. They live here in their little enclosed corral, doing as they please, taking what they need from the world outside. They certainly aren't likely to give a damn what happens to their 'recreation zone' women after they're done with them. Shove them out the gate, get the next lot in . . .

I've learned more than I bargained for this evening, and everything has changed. I was intending to make my bid for freedom tonight, before King Cunt comes back tomorrow. Arm myself with a knife from the kitchen and scale the barricade via one of the lookout posts. If I was caught in the attempt, so be it. I'd take the consequences, whatever they might be.

But now I realise that I've been given an opportunity. I've been put in a position where I may be able to do more than just save my own skin.

166

I can help these women. Paula Coulton, Susannah Vicks, Angela Pearson, Zoë. All of them. I can help them.

It could be that this is just a pretext. It could be that I'm groping for some convenient excuse not to take the risk of escaping, and these women are it. But I don't think so. I can't in all conscience leave them here, can I? If somehow I can see to it that they're treated better, or at the very least that they're returned safely back to Downbourne when the time comes . . . well then, there's no question about it. That is what I must do.

The dog pack found him not long after moonrise.

They had smelled him from miles away. The night-time air currents conveyed minuscule wafts of him to their noses, scents like phrase-fragments, gradually coalescing into an intelligible message. A human. A male. In distress. In pain. Injured. He had broken a bone. He had urinated on himself – perhaps in fear? The dogs detected the hotness of inflamed flesh. They understood that the human was hungry, tired, weakened. Their leader, a scar-faced Rottweiler, made the decision. Off he went, and the rest of the pack fell in behind.

Loping, surging, breasting, the dogs – a motley lot, all different sizes and breeds – made their way across fields, through hedgerows, along bridle paths, down tarmac lanes. Keeping to the speed of their slowest member, an elderly Jack Russell, they held their muzzles high, triangulating the human aroma as it grew stronger and richer. Soon they were within close proximity of their quarry and, as one, they slowed their pace, becoming cautious. Humans were unpredictable beasts, capable of a lot more than their ungainly, strangely-furred physiques would suggest. Just a few nights back the pack had lost one of their number, a Labrador, to a human who kept chickens. They had been breaking into the chickens' cages when the human had emerged from his house, barking at them incomprehensibly and shining a small sun in their eyes. Then had come the deafening bang, and the Labrador had yelped and tumbled over, his ribcage devastated. The rest of the pack had scattered, and while fleeing had heard a second bang and, moments later, smelled the spilled-brains-and-shit odour of the Labrador's death. So humans could be very dangerous. But they could also, under the right circumstances, be eaten.

All of the pack members could remember, albeit dimly, a time when humans were their gods. They had lived in warm homes with humans, been fed regularly by them, looked after by them, governed by them, and all in return for loving worship. Loving worship

– which came so easily to a dog. It had been a sweet deal. But then had come a fall, a period of anger and confusion and fear. Food had arrived less regularly, and then stopped arriving altogether. And soon after that, abandonment – a physical severance that was agonising, like being consigned to limbo. The dogs had each been part of a human pack, and suddenly they had become wild rovers, out on their own and having to fend for themselves.

They had come together slowly to form this new, dog-only pack. One by one they had added to its number, learning one another's scents and habits, establishing a hierarchy. Now they were of one mind, a single creature of disparate parts. A unit that had shrugged off all of the training instilled during the good years, the years of warmth and plenty, and embraced lawlessness and self-sufficiency instead. A unit that had learned to distrust and avoid humans but also, when they could, predate on them.

There was one among them that had never been close to humans, however, one that had been born into the feral life; and now, as the pack came to a halt less than a hundred leap-lengths from the human, it was this one who by mutual consent went forward to reconnoitre. The other dogs thought of her as the sly stranger, and she was a puzzling conundrum – a dog who didn't truly behave or smell like one but was one nonetheless. She had a narrow muzzle, reddish fur and a brushy tail, and most of the time she kept her distance from the pack, tagging along like an afterthought. She did, however, take an enthusiastic part in kills, and it was thanks to her that the pack had learned how to breach and raid the cages in which humans kept prey such as chickens or rabbits.

The sly stranger slunk towards the human through the couch grass, stealthy on her dainty black paws. Had the human shifted position or had the composition of his odour become tangy with anger or alarm, the Sly Stranger would have frozen, poised to retreat. But the human remained unaware of her approach, even after the sly stranger was close enough to view him clearly through the grass stalks. The human lay there, breathing irregularly, shivering . . .

An easy kill.

If not for the fact that one of the pack – the Jack Russell – became overexcited and started yapping, Fen would have had no warning of the attack and would undoubtedly have ended up literally as a dog's dinner. He was back in the cocoon, adrift inside the miserable, shiver-wracked body of Fen Morris, dreamily contemplating how easy it would be to die out here and at the same time how *miserable* – and then suddenly a small dog was yipping nearby and he could hear bodies moving through the grass.

His immediate thought was, They've done it! They've found me! Rescuers! Rescuers with sniffer dogs!

With all the energy he could summon, he began calling out, and although his vocal cords had been severely strained by earlier exertions, he nevertheless managed to produce a creditable level of volume. Relief and joy surged through him. He was saved. It was all over.

He kept shouting until it crossed his mind that no one was answering. Odd. Surely his rescuers would be telling him to hang in there, or yelling to one another, saying he was over this way, they'd located him. And then he thought: Wouldn't at least one of them be carrying a torch? Or, if they couldn't get the batteries, a lantern maybe? He saw no lights.

And then he heard growling.

A dark shape loomed through the couch grass to his right, something stocky and stout-bodied that stood not much higher than the grass itself.

All at once, Fen was staring into the face of a Rottweiler, and his surge of hope was snatched back down into a void of empty terror. In the moonlight he could make out the light-brown portions of the dog's features – jaw, jowls, pugnacious eyebrows. He saw, too, the onyx glitter of its eyes and the mesmerising white serration of its fangs. The Rottweiler continued to growl at him, and Fen, in spite of his fear, understood that it was studying him, perhaps perturbed by his shouts and wondering if he had been signalling to other humans in the vicinity. The growl was both intimidation and quizzicality, though more the former than the latter.

Peripherally, Fen became aware of other dogs lurking to either side of the Rottweiler, their eyes trained on him, glimmering through the grass stalks. Seven, perhaps eight of the animals. A pack. He kept his gaze steady on the Rottweiler. The Rottweiler had to be the alpha male. If it attacked, the rest of the pack would too.

Long seconds oozed past, the Rottweiler still indecisive. Fen's heartbeat banged in his ears, loud as timpani. The Rottweiler moved its head slightly, and he noticed that its face was cross-hatched with scars. Pale little furrows across the muzzle, over the flat forehead. Wounds from old opponents, old victims. This was a dog that had fought and killed many times, yet for all its size and sinew it had not won every battle without some cost to itself.

Partly (Fen would realise later) the notion of hitting the Rottweiler was spawned by the sight of those scars. If other creatures had defied this brute in the past, why not him?

Mostly, however, hitting the Rottweiler all at once seemed the right thing to do. A reflex action but also, in a way, an irritable one. The only fitting riposte to such a turn of events, such a ridiculously unkind adding of insult to injury. A heedless, peevish *fuck you* to whichever deity had arranged this misfortune for him.

His fist lashed out. Perfect connection was made with the Rottweiler's nose. He felt the nose squash under his knuckles, mushroom-soft; heard a satisfying moist *whack*.

The Rottweiler yelped, about-turned and fled. The rest of the pack went scuttering after it, the grass stalks quivering in their wake.

Only when his lungs felt like they were about to burst did Fen remember to breathe. He sucked in air, exultant.

A pack of dogs. He had just been cornered by, and *seen off*, a pack of wild dogs.

He marvelled at his own audacity. Bashing one of them on the nose like that. A Rottweiler no less! If he had been a fraction of a second slower the damn thing would have had his hand off, but he had timed it just right, the Rottweiler hadn't known what was coming, his aim had been true . . .

He listened to the dogs racing across the field, rustling through poppies and grass, and he felt invincible. Having survived *that*, it seemed to him that he could survive anything. Broken leg? No problem. Not now. For a man who, with a single blow, was able to send an entire dog pack packing, what difficulties did having a broken leg in a remote spot present?

The rustling continued, and it occurred to Fen that the sound was not getting quieter any more. It wasn't getting louder, either, but the dogs were clearly no longer running away. At a fixed distance from where he lay, they were milling around. Regrouping.

His sense of triumph collapsed like a pin-popped balloon.

He hadn't won a victory with that biff on the Rottweiler's nose. All he had won was a respite.

Desperate, Fen groped around for a weapon, something he might use against the dogs, a rock, a branch, *anything*.

Nothing.

He had his knapsack with its empty water canteen and half-full mustard pot, he had two fists, one foot, that was it.

He heard the dogs distantly padding to and fro, and envisaged them planning a new attack. The group-mind of the pack, debating what to do. Stratagems of canine cunning. Their prey was alone and wounded, they were many. It wouldn't take them long to figure out that their superiority in numbers was their greatest asset against him. If they attacked him together, he couldn't ward them *all* off with blows to the nose.

Out there, beneath the icy stars and the laughing moon, Fen had never felt so defenceless or so alone. He felt trapped in a nightmare, not his own but England's, the nightmare of a nation that had believed that no more shocks lay in store for it. A nation that had, like some smug, ageing plutocrat, thought its future would be all comfort and civility and the nodding collusion of its peers. A nation that could never have foreseen the penury and upheaval and ostracism it was presently suffering. England was asleep and dreaming bad dreams, and Fen yearned for it to wake up.

The dogs stopped moving. At least he couldn't hear them any more.

He levered himself up and twisted round from the waist so that he could see up the slope of the field. Couch grass and poppies waved and rippled and undulated in the moonlight. The dogs might be lying still. Equally, they might this very moment be homing in on him like sharks through the shallows, their progress masked by the field's breeze-blown restlessness.

A dim, atavistic thought sparked in Fen's brain: hide.

But hide where? There was no shelter hereabouts, nothing to crawl behind or into or under.

His eye fell on the brambles.

Yes, there was.

The next instant, Fen was pushing himself with his hands and his functional leg, pivoting around on his backside in a series of slithering shunts. His bad leg first murmured, then whined, then shrieked as it was repeatedly dragged and buffeted, but he pressed his lips tight shut and kept going. The pain became so excruciating that he twice came close to giving up. He persevered. No matter how much this was hurting him, it could not be worse than being mauled to death by dogs.

Finally – he could scarcely believe he had managed it – he was sitting with his back against the brambles.

He allowed himself a brief rest, breath whistling in and out through his teeth. His thigh felt huge and hot, like a chunk of molten ore.

Not far off, he glimpsed a shadow cleaving slowly through one of the clumps of poppies.

He snatched up the knapsack and slung its strap around his neck. Then he drew his right foot in, dug the heel into the ground, and thrust himself backwards into the brambles.

His clothing snagged. Thorns pricked. Waves of incandescent agony radiated up from his thigh.

He drew his right foot in again and thrust with it again, penetrating deeper into the brambles.

He thrust once more, but this time made no headway. The thorns had a secure grip on him now. He was in the brambles up to his waist, permitted to go that far but no further.

He struggled to detach his sleeves from the thorns. He could now discern three of those shadows slinking downslope through the field, their trajectories converging on him. The nearest was less than a dozen yards away. He thrashed his arms, managed to free them, then looked about for something to grab hold of so that he could augment pushing with pulling. There was nothing within reach but brambles. No alternative – he grasped a bunch of stems with each hand, wincing as a score of needle points stabbed his palms. Nasty but, compared with his leg, trivial. He bore down with his right foot, hauled with his hands, and succeeded in burying himself in the brambles as far as his knees.

Nearly there. One last shove should do it.

In front of him, the Rottweiler broke cover. Its massive head reared from the grass, no more than a decent lunge away from his feet.

Beside it, the head of another dog appeared. Actually, not a dog. A *fox*.

Fen had just enough time to wonder at the anomaly – a fox as part of a dog pack, an alliance forged through some sort of distant-cousin kinship – and then the Rottweiler went for him.

Sheer panic lent him the power and the coordination to save himself. Arms and good leg did exactly what was required of them. Bad leg, for the brief period that was necessary, ceased to hinder. In an ecstasy of fear Fen wrenched himself bodily backwards, hearing – *feeling* – the clunk of the Rottweiler's teeth as they snapped shut on the space where a half-second earlier his left ankle had been.

Then the world fell away beneath him and he was slipping backwards down the embankment.

It wasn't a smooth descent, rather a series of short, jerky slithers as brambles snagged him and, unable to sustain his weight, let go, passing him on. He was near the bottom when, finally, he came to a clump sufficiently thick to arrest his progress. He crunched head-first into it, and for a fleeting instant this seemed to be how he was going to stay, vertical and inverted. Gravity, however, had other ideas, and his body continued to slide, rotating slowly like the hand of a clock going from twelve to three, until he fetched up lying almost horizontal along the embankment.

He had a few seconds of stunned numbness in which to reflect on what he had done. In a sense, he had succeeded far better than he had hoped. He was even able to bemoan the countless scrapes and scratches he had received from the brambles. His face and hands stung all over. He felt grated. Lacerated.

Then his leg cut in, cancelling out these minor injuries as the sun cancels out the stars. The leg resumed its litany of pain with spectacular gusto, no longer merely drawing attention to itself but actively punishing Fen for his part in, first of all, fracturing it, and now aggravating it. The pain mounted, in a massive crescendo, and Fen threw back his head and wailed.

He wailed, and he put everything he had into the wailing, hauling up the agony, dredging up every hurt and slight and wound ever inflicted on him and hurling them out through his voice.

He wailed until the sound seemed to fill the sky and there was no room for anything else in the world except this wordless exposition of suffering.

At the top of the embankment, the thwarted dog pack circled about, ears pricked and tails at half mast, uncertain what to make of what they were hearing. One of them decided to start baying, and suddenly they were all of them baying, all trying to beat the human at his own game.

Down below, cradled in thorns, Fen bawled like a baby, oblivious to everything but the tragedy of himself.

4. NETHERHOLM COLLEGE

There was pure blinding whiteness all around him, and he thought, so this is how it happens. You don't remember dying. Life stops and, hey presto, you're elsewhere.

Squinting against the brilliance, Fen discovered that the after-life was a somewhat more mundane-looking place than he had imagined it would be. He was in a long white room with three tall, arched, curtainless windows that afforded a view of trees and sky – a march of oaks beneath a swath of cloud-patched blue. The room was furnished with beds of the military-barracks variety, half a dozen of them, including the one he was lying in. Their iron frames were painted white, with black spots here and there where the paint had chipped away. Each had a white wooden cabinet next to it. The place – some sort of hospital ward – smelled of mildew and liniment, and in one corner of the cracked-plaster ceiling there was a spider in a web.

Perhaps, he thought, all this ordinariness was meant to reassure him, to ease the period of transition. Once he had acclimatised to the idea of being deceased, he would then move on to a part of the after-life that was altogether more . . . after-life-like.

He then noticed something odd. The after-life hurt. Apparently the world's religions had got it wrong. You *did* take your bodily aches and pains with you when you passed on. Your bramble scratches smarted, your sunburned skin stung, your hoarse throat throbbed, and your broken leg . . .

. . . was in traction?

Fen peered at the makeshift device that was strapped around his left leg, keeping it suspended at a forty-five degree angle from the bed. A sling had been fashioned from a section of bright orange canvas which had, by the look of it, once been part of a tent. Laced through brass eyelets in the canvas was a length of thick cord whose ends ran up to a pair of hooks screwed into the ceiling. Within the sling there were three planks of wood, underneath and on either side of the leg, providing the necessary stabilisation.

Interesting. So the after-life wasn't all that dissimilar from England, then – a place where, when the proper equipment was not available, you improvised.

But of course it had dawned on Fen by now that he was not dead. On the contrary. He was alive. Blessedly, wondrously, miraculously alive. He had been saved from the dog pack; he had been rescued from the railway embankment.

By whom?

As if in answer, vague memory-images bubbled up in his brain. People shouting to one another as he lay among the brambles on the embankment. Lights bobbing in the dark. Hands taking hold of him by the shoulders and ankles, preparing to lift him. More pain then than he had known what to do with. He felt as if he had dreamed these things. Who were the people who had found him? Where had they brought him? It didn't matter. Doubtless he would find out soon enough. It was sufficient, for now, to be indoors and no longer in peril of his life.

Resting his head back against the pillows, Fen gazed up at the ceiling. His eye was drawn to the spider he had noticed earlier. He could see now that the creature, one of the generic brown domestic variety, was dead. Its legs were huddled about its body and it had the look of something desiccated, spindly and autumnal, something that winter winds would blow away. Its web had become its bier.

Like some arachno-coroner, Fen studied the corpse in an attempt to determine how it had died. He decided starvation must be the answer. The spider was the web's sole occupant. It had cast its net into barren waters.

He chose to interpret the spider's death by starvation as an auspicious sign: a predator denied a victim, just as the dog pack had been deprived of the opportunity of making a meal out of *him*. He rejected the notion, wickedly offered up by some malicious mental sprite, that there was a parallel to be drawn directly between the spider and himself – both of them strung up in this ward, attached to the ceiling, immobile. The spider's fate a foreshadowing of his own? That was a ridiculous idea. There was nothing to be gained by thinking like *that*.

There's a shout from outside the house.

'Oi, Lauren! He's on the approach road!'

Lauren snaps to her feet and rushes, I swear, *rushes* to the mirror in the hallway to check her face. She put make-up on after breakfast, since when she's been examining it at every opportunity. The mascara's applied too thickly and the lipstick isn't her shade, but frankly it doesn't matter – she has make-up, and that puts her one up on most other women in the country. And now, for the umpteenth time, she primps and preens in the mirror. She teases a lock of hair to one side, she fingernails a crumb of mascara away and she thumb-buffs the corner of her mouth, and then she gives herself a settled-back, approving look. *Yes, I'm all right really*. Then: 'Moira, let's go.'

Three days King Cunt has been away. Three days making overtures to the Frantik Posse, lords of Camberwell. A delicate mission, as I understand it from Lauren. The Frantiks, touchy at the best of times, don't take kindly to outsiders coming in with offers of alliances. Especially *white* outsiders. That they agreed to a meeting with King Cunt at all is, I've been assured, remarkable, a sign that even they have respect for his reputation and that of the Bulldogs. But this respect will not have been enough. In order to convince them to hear him out, King Cunt will have had to prove himself to them first, undergoing a kind of test of his manliness. Hence the negotiations taking three days. King Cunt has had to party with the Frantiks. Party hard. That's how the Frantiks take the measure of a man. King Cunt will have had to drink as much booze as the toughest-livered among them drinks. He will have had to smoke as much ganja as the biggest dopehead among them smokes. He will have had to satisfy as many of their women as their most priapic Mr Lover-man satisfies. He may even have had to engage in a round or two of 'friendly' combat with one of their top cruiserweight bruisers. He will, in short, according to Lauren, be arriving home absolutely knackered.

So I'm expecting some bedraggled, bloodshot-eyed wreck to come staggering in through the compound gate. And I'm thinking he'll be a small man. I don't know why I've pictured him that way – Napoleon Complex, I suppose. I see him as stocky, bullet-headed, bow-legged. This is the image of him that's built up in my mind over the past couple of days. I think that, when not 'absolutely knackered', he'll be cocky and coarse. Come on, anyone who calls himself King Cunt is hardly likely to be a model of sophistication. I think that, the moment I see him, I will know how to feel contempt for him and why.

All the same, I can't deny that I'm curious about him, and that I'm slightly – *slightly* – looking forward to meeting him. From an almost anthropological viewpoint he interests me. From a pragmatic, self-centred viewpoint as well. This is the man, after all, whose girlfriend I was brought here to be.

The Bulldogs converge on the entrance to the compound. They saunter, not wanting to be seen to look eager. But the eagerness is there, in clenched fists, quick grins. The King. The King is returning. They assemble just inside the gate, and jostle about, trading quips, nudges, suppositions. 'D'you think he pulled it off?' 'I think one of those curvy little Frantik girls pulled it off *for* him, ha ha ha! Know what I mean?' Then there's the rumble of an engine outside, a toot on a horn, and the man in the lookout post gives the OK signal.

Three Bulldogs heave aside the thick bar of timber that secures the gate. Another two haul the gate inwards, revealing a bare street, ramshackle houses, a few locals peering nervously from various vantage points, and of course King Cunt's van. Purring and travel-dusty, the van – which is a Mercedes, white of course – noses into the compound, the Bulldogs moving aside to make way for it. As the gate closes, the van glides to a halt, and the gold-toothed Bulldog, Neville, steps forward from the crowd.

'All right, lads. He's back. Let's hear it for the King.'

The chant starts up straight away, from a dozen throats, then several dozen. At first I think what they're saying is 'Fucking cunt! Fucking cunt!', until I realise it's a sort of pun. They're chanting 'For King Cunt! For King Cunt!' and the resemblance of this to 'fucking cunt' is intentional but, at the same time, not disrespectful. In fact I have a feeling the joke is, in a weird way, the opposite of dis-respectful.

The chant gathers volume. Fists, Neville's among the first, start punching the air in time. '*For* King *Cunt*! *For* King *Cunt*!' The Bulldogs cluster around the van. The driver's door opens.

Out he comes. He *is* small. Small and, I have to say, quite ugly, with a hook nose and a head too large for the rest of him. He acknowledges the Bulldogs' acclaim with a humble, shoulder-shrugging wave, and bows as if to say *I'm not worthy*. It beats me how this little gnome of a man can command all these individuals much bigger than him. He has no obvious leadership qualities, no *presence*.

I turn to Lauren to make a comment to this effect, and it's then that I realise my mistake. Her face is the giveaway. The little man doesn't interest her in the slightest. She's looking to the passenger door of the van. The gnome isn't King Cunt at all.

The passenger door opens, and the chanting dissolves into cheering.

The van tips to one side as he emerges; springs level again as his feet touch the ground. He's massive. He has the body of a comic-book superhero. The inverted-cone torso, the muscle-clotted arms, the swooping thighs. As with the rest of the Bulldogs he has cropped hair and is dressed in sports casualwear (his shirt is the red strip of what was once the country's most popular football team). Unlike the rest of the Bulldogs, however, he doesn't look like a thug. Oh, he has all the tangible attributes of a thug – the physique, the haircut, the jawline – but what he doesn't have is the *demeanour*. He doesn't hulk and slouch, and his face, his eyes – there's more going on there. There's an alertness. There's, dare I say it, an intelligence. He surveys the cheering throng, and he looks suitably gratified. He holds a hand aloft. He grins. He accepts the men's approbation and rewards it with precisely the right level of leaderly indulgence. But it's clear he's their superior in more than just rank. He is a different order of human being altogether. He is someone who has stratagems. Who has plans. Who has *vision*.

Or does he seem so superior simply because of who he's chosen to surround himself with? A carp amongst minnows. An ordinary man amongst pygmies.

Lauren gazes at him, rapt as an infatuated schoolgirl, and the cheering goes on, showing no sign of abating. Neville trots forward, and he and King Cunt shake hands. Lip-reading, I see Neville say something like 'Welcome back, mate,' and he claps King Cunt on the biceps. King Cunt reciprocates the gesture – but is there just the briefest of hesitations before he does so? Or am I, thanks to what Lauren's told me about Neville, simply reading too much into things?

And still the cheering goes on.

And then King Cunt looks past his men, and he catches sight of Lauren, and the next instant he's looking at me.

And he smiles.
Luckily I catch myself in time. But it's a close-run thing.
I nearly smiled back.

Suddenly it was evening. Fen awoke to find that the white room had taken on a rosy twilight blush. He blinked around, wondering why no one had come to check up on him yet. He listened, but there was nothing to be heard other than his own breathing and the distant, rustling tumult of the oaks outside. For all he knew, he was alone in the building. His rescuers had brought him here and fixed up his leg in a home-made traction apparatus, and had then abandoned him? It seemed unlikely – not unless he had been made the victim of some bizarre, incomprehensible practical joke.

He noticed something that had escaped his attention earlier. His clothes lay in a pile, neatly folded, on a chair nearby. They appeared to have been laundered. With them hung his knapsack. The chair was within reach, so he was able to grab the knapsack and look inside. Its contents were all present and correct – wedding band, London permit, not forgetting the pot of mustard. Clearly the people looking after him, whoever they were, were as honest as they were solicitous.

So where *were* they, these saintly saviours of his? Perhaps they had assumed that, when he regained consciousness, he would shout for their attention.

He tried. He put all he had into it, forcing the breath up from his lungs as hard as he could, but the best his throat was able to produce was a pitiful, aerated squeak that even someone in the same room might not have heard. His voice was ruined from all the yelling and screaming he had done during those awful hours out in the open, when it had seemed all too possible that he was going to die. His vocal cords, for the time being, had nothing left to give.

Plan B: thumping on the wall. But the wall proved solid, unresonant, dulling the smack of his fist.

Then he hit on the idea of thumping the bed frame.

The bed gonged with each blow, and the whitewashed floor-boards acted as a sounding board, amplifying nicely. For half a minute Fen hammered out a sonorous irregular peal, then stopped and waited.

Someone came.

She was a short woman, round-faced, wearing spectacles with lenses as thick as ice cubes, through which her eyes peeped like a pair of tiny asterisks. Her hair was wiry and brown and held in place by plastic clips, and there was something both brisk and anxious about the way she crossed the room – swift little strides, stubby arms swinging tautly.

'There you are!' she said. 'Back in the land of the living. I take it all that banging was to summon me.'

'I'm sorry,' Fen rasped. 'I would have shouted, but . . .'

'Ah yes. Lost your voice. And otherwise? How are you feeling generally?'

'Sore.' He nodded at his leg. 'Very sore.'

'Well, we haven't got any painkillers for you.'

This brusqueness, Fen thought, was a cover for shyness. The world snapped at this woman; she snapped back.

'It's all right,' he said. 'I'm not complaining. I'm just glad to be alive. This place.' He gestured at his surroundings. 'A nursing home of some sort? A hospital?'

The woman cast an amused glance around her. 'Does it look like a hospital?'

'Sort of.'

'As it happens, you're in the sanatorium of a school.'

'A school?'

'Netherholm College. Boys only. Ages thirteen to eighteen. Boarding. You won't have heard of it. It wasn't one of the major ones. And it isn't a school any more, of course. Closed down years ago.'

'Were you the matron?'

'Oh no. No, no.' The idea tickled her.

'But you obviously have some medical training.'

'Fourteen years with the St John's Ambulance. Hold still a moment.' She pressed a firm, dry palm against Fen's forehead, then took his pulse, timing it against her wristwatch. Satisfied with the results of both diagnostic procedures, she plumped up his pillows. 'You'll be hungry, I expect. I'll bring you some supper in an hour or so. In the meantime, do you need to do a business?'

'Do I need to—? Oh. Yes.'

'Urine? Stool?'

Fen nodded.

'Well, which is it?'

'Just urine, I think.'

'Back in a mo.'

The woman returned with a kidney-shaped enamel dish, which she slid, with little ceremony, beneath Fen's backside. The dish's rim was shockingly cold against his skin.

'There. It's none too easy if you haven't tried it before, but keep at it. You'll soon get the hang. When you're done, leave the dish on the floor. By the way, do you have a name?'

'Fen. Fen Morris.'

'Hello, Fen Morris. I'm Miriam.'

'Pleased to meet you, Miriam.'

'Likewise. Welcome.'

He's been asleep all day, flat out on the double divan in the master bedroom, fully dressed on top of the covers. Lauren and I have been tiptoeing around his presence like deer around a slumbering tiger. We haven't spoken much, and when we have it's been in whispers. The house is changed for having him in it. I was beginning to think of it as ours, mine and Lauren's. Now it is quite unmistakably King Cunt's. In the unlikely event that either of us were to forget that, there are sporadic bouts of heavy snoring to remind us.

My mind is a conveyor belt of different emotions, one trundling after another. Mainly I'm scared. I'm dreading what will happen when he wakes up, what he will want then, what he will demand. I'm also relieved, because I've seen him now, I know what he looks like now, and he's nowhere near as bad as I was expecting. He's physically impressive. He's even – in a beetle-browed, heavy-chinned way – handsome. I'm alarmed at myself for thinking about him in this manner, for even considering that he might be attractive, and then I'm cross with myself for trying to deny something that I honestly feel, and then I'm angry with myself because it doesn't really matter what King Cunt looks like because it won't make what I'm going to have to let him do to me any more bearable. Rape is rape, whoever's committing it, whatever the circumstances in which it's carried out.

I'm jittery with these conflicting feelings, and with the cigarettes I've been nabbing off Lauren throughout the day. Each time I ask her for another she says, 'Get your own darn smokes,' but then lets me have one anyway. I'm awash with nicotine in a way I haven't been for years. It's a darkly nostalgic sensation. Part of me keeps expecting a wad of page proofs to be dumped in front of me for final inspection, or someone to ask me what I'll be having to drink.

Finally, around seven p.m., King Cunt stirs. There's a lot of groaning and grunting and yawning, and then the sound of footsteps across the floorboards as he heads for the bathroom, and then the loud, echoey rattle of a man peeing. (They can never do it quietly, can they? Always right into the centre of the water, where the toilet-bowl acoustics are at their resonant best.) Then the flush, and then King Cunt comes clumping barefoot down the stairs.

Lauren's standing at attention to greet him. She clucks and fusses over his right hand, which is wrapped in a ragged strip of cloth that's brown with dried blood.

'Was it a fight?' she asks.

King Cunt glances uninterestedly at the hand. 'Nah. Just a bit of ritual malarkey. I am now, officially, a blood-sworn member of the Frantik Posse.' He turns to me. 'Hi there. We didn't get a chance to talk earlier. You are . . . ?'

I tell him, in a voice that doesn't sound quite like my own. I wait for that daft face that people usually pull when they hear *Moira*. I don't know why my name has that effect. It just does.

But not on him. King Cunt is one of the rare exceptions, just as Fen was. 'Moira, huh? Don't tell me – Scottish mum.'

'Irish.'

'Dah! Had to be one or the other. Well, nice to meet you, Moira. I hope Lauren's been looking after you.'

'She has. We've been getting along fine.' Past King Cunt's shoulder Lauren fires me a quick, grateful smile, as though I've done her a favour. But what I said wasn't a lie. We're never going to be firm friends, she and I, but all things considered, she could have been treating me a lot worse.

'Yeah, Lauren's a treasure, isn't she? Couldn't manage without her.'

Lauren positively squirms with joy.

'Now, Moira, the question that's probably uppermost in your mind is, What the fuck am I supposed to call this bloke?'

I nod. It's certainly *one* of the questions uppermost in my mind.

'Craig'll do. Most girls don't much like using the word "cunt", do they. I can understand why. It's not one of *my* favourite words, to be honest with you. But it does the business. King Cunt – 'cause I'm more of a cunt than anyone else. It's a name people remember. They hear it once, they don't forget it. But you stick with "Craig". Or "King", if you'd prefer. That's what most of the lads call me. Another question you're probably asking yourself, I reckon, Moira: Is he going to hurt me? Because I'm guessing you've formed the impression that I'm a bit of a bastard and I don't like it if I don't get my own way. And I'm betting Lauren's told you something to that effect too. She usually does. Don't you, Lauren?'

Lauren shrugs.

'She likes to make me out to be nasty, a bit of a harsh taskmaster, bless her. And I'm not. At least, I don't think I am. I think what I am –

and I'm being serious here – is moral. You don't do anything to upset me, you'll be fine. Cross me, and you won't be fine. You'll be anything *but* fine. OK?'

'OK,' I say.

'Glad we've got that sorted. Now, one last thing . . . Actually, Lauren love.' He pats his flat abdomen. 'I could do with a bite of something. Would you go and get dinner started?'

Lauren sidles off to the kitchen and begins clattering utensils around more loudly than she needs to. King Cunt moves closer to me.

'Listen, Moira,' he says, voice lowered, 'what I don't want you to do, most of all, is be scared of me. I want everyone else to be scared of me. The lads here, the other gangs, everyone in south-east London, everyone in *London*. But not you. Because it doesn't work if you're scared of me.' He steps back, and I realise he has just bared his soul, or come as close as he perhaps ever will to doing so. 'I don't expect you to like me. I certainly don't expect you to love me. But if you can just see your way to not being scared of me . . . well, that would be great.'

I don't know what to say. I mutter something like, 'I'm sure that can be arranged,' and after that we stand there for a while, facing each other. King Cunt looks searchingly into my eyes, and it's like he's imploring me for some kind of absolution in advance. I stare back, not softening, not allowing him even a glimpse of what he's after, fearing him too much not to despise him. I don't know why but I feel oddly guilty about doing this, about not giving him what he so desperately wants.

He waits a moment longer, then, understanding, drops his gaze. Off he goes to the kitchen to chat with Lauren while she cooks, and I'm left wondering if I haven't just made trouble for myself.

Maybe I have. But maybe not.

'How was the meal?' Miriam asked.

The scraped-clean bowl and empty side plate told one story, the gist of which was that Fen had wolfed down his vegetable soup and chunks of bread. Fen corroborated the story by pronouncing the meal delicious.

In truth, starving-hungry though he was, the meal had been anything but. The soup had been thin and tasteless, the bread gritty. He had eaten out of necessity and to a lesser degree politeness, but he had not eaten out of pleasure.

'Good. We're not exactly flush with provisions here but we make do.'

'Well, your chef's done a good job, whoever he is. Please pass on my compliments.'

'Better not. It was Derek's turn today, and his head's swollen enough as it is.' Miriam chuckled, her spectacles glinting softly in the light of the candle by Fen's bedside. 'Now, before I leave you for the night, is there anything else you want? Anything you need?'

'Just a couple of questions answered, Miriam.'

'Go on then.'

'How long do you think it's going to take for my leg to get better?'

'As far as I can see, it's a straightforward fracture, very little damage to the surrounding muscles . . . I'd say we'll have you on your feet in a week.'

'A week? Really?'

'But that's just to exercise the leg. I don't think you'll be walking any great distances on it for a month or so.'

A month or so.

'OK. But is there any chance someone here could get me to London, broken leg notwithstanding?'

'London?' Miriam frowned, as though he had just said Constantinople or Timbuktu. 'Well now, I don't know about that. I don't know about that at all. I take it you're hoping we have some form of transportation here – a horse and cart, maybe even a car. We don't. There are bicycles, but few of them work properly any more. Tyres gone, brakes rusted. Mostly we get around using good old-fashioned shanks' pony. So I'm afraid, Fen, you're stuck with us for a while. Best get used to the idea.'

'And that's my second question. Who's "us", Miriam?'

'We're friendly, Fen. That's all you need to know.'

After Miriam had taken away the supper tray and extinguished the candle, Fen lay in the dark and pondered. On the one hand, he was alive and being looked after by someone who seemed to know what she was doing, which was indisputably a good thing. On the other hand, his journey to London was on hiatus for at least a month, probably much more, and that was not such a good thing.

It was only then that he realised that he had not thought of Moira since . . . since leaping off the *Jagannatha*. All that time he had lain out in the open, she – the entire purpose of his journey – had not once even crossed his mind. He felt a prickling of guilt, which he absolved himself of by reasoning that he had been alone, in pain and in fear of his life. He had had, in short, other things on his mind. And with this comforting rationale came a renewed determination to reach Moira just as soon as he was able to. However soon that was.

He could see, with hindsight, that everything had started to go wrong the moment he accepted the offer of a lift from Wickramasinghe. Had he continued on towards London on foot, he would almost certainly have been reunited with Moira by now. He and she would be heading back to Downbourne together, Moira brimming with new-found admiration for the husband who had come such a distance, risked so much, in order to rescue her.

That was one possibility, at any rate. Another was that he would, by now, have reached the British Bulldogs' lair and be returning to Downbourne empty-handed and dismally alone, having failed to persuade Moira's captors to let him have her back. Another, yet worse possibility was that he, too, would have been taken prisoner by the Bulldogs, and would be undergoing God-knows-what kinds of abuse and mistreatment. He might even be dead.

Could it be that maybe, just maybe, he had never had any intention of reaching London at all? Could it be that he had accepted a lift from Wickramasinghe, and then thrown himself from the *Jagannatha* while it was travelling at high speed, simply in order to furnish himself with an excuse for not continuing with his rescue attempt? In other words, could he have deliberately (albeit subconsciously) sabotaged his own mission?

If so, a broken leg was a pretty drastic way of going about it.

Then again, anything less drastic than a broken leg would have been insufficient to waylay him. At least he could now say to himself, 'Well, I tried, didn't I? I gave it my best shot,' and, with a clear conscience, abandon the whole enterprise.

Yes. Except that he could not.

Broken leg or no, the fact remained that he had set out to rescue Moira, and he was damned well going to. Even if it took him, in the end, several weeks. Even if, by the time he got to her, she had given up all hope of ever seeing him.

He pictured Moira, in some imprecisely-realised urban setting, scanning the horizon for a sign of him. Penelope on an Ithacan promontory, praying for a glimpse of Odysseus' sails.

She isn't waiting for you at all. It hasn't even occurred to her that you might be coming.

But that was untrue.

Fen was convinced it was untrue.

Almost completely convinced.

Here we lie, like husband and wife. His weight doesn't just tilt the mattress, it seems to tilt the entire house, as though he is a collapsed star, concentrated gravity. His left arm rests across my midriff. Rests? It bears down on my stomach muscles, heavy as a slab of marble. It makes breathing difficult, but I don't want to move it off me. If I move it, he might wake up, and if he wakes . . .

His deep, slow, ponderous breathing fills the darkness. It's like lying next to an ocean cave, the waves surging in, the waves surging out. I am not going to sleep tonight. I may never sleep again.

Nothing has happened. This gives amazement and anguish in equal measure. Nothing has happened, he just turned the light out, put his arm across me and went to sleep, and I'm relieved, God yes, but I wanted it over with too, so that I wouldn't have to keep wondering what it's going to be like, how it's going to make me feel about myself. In the past, I've had sex when I didn't want to – when I wasn't in the mood for it, or just to stop a man pestering me for it. There was even that one occasion that would probably qualify as rape, in that I was too drunk to give my consent, or at least to refuse coherently. (I paid the bastard back the next morning, when I phoned his wife using the speed-dial on his mobile and told her where he was.) But I've never had sex when a man has forced me to against my will, using his superior strength or the threat of violence to subdue me, taking what will not be willingly given. I've resigned myself to enduring it with King Cunt, for the sake of the other women, for Zoë's sake most of all – but I have not had to endure it yet. Having spent all day readying myself for it, having followed King Cunt up to the master bedroom with a belly full of dread, here I am with the awful event still unrealised. He lies beside me, a giant in football shirt and boxer shorts, as dead to the world as a sleeping infant. The mattress inclines me to him, his arm denotes me as his property, but he has not yet used me for the purpose for which I am in his bed.

Perhaps he is still exhausted from his three days of exertion over in Camberwell. Perhaps the women there slaked his urges for the time being. I don't know. I don't understand this man at all, this King Cunt, this Craig. He is quite unlike any other man I have ever known. He has fists that could crush bricks and yet there's an articulacy to him, and a vulnerability, that I would never have suspected. I think of him earlier, begging me not to fear him. Does he want that in order to make things easier for me, or easier for him?

Awake in the dark, I can only wonder.

Overnight, three books had manifested on Fen's bedside cabinet. It was as if elves had placed them there while he slept. All three were paperback novels, two of them of average thickness, the third very thick indeed. Their spines were well creased and their page edges were coffee brown with age.

The very thick one was a science fiction novel called *Falling Across Forever* by Jeremiah S. Coburn. Its cover showed a spaceship in orbit around a planet. One section of the spaceship was exploding, and the planet's atmosphere was a seething swirl of reds and purples. The image promised Excitement! Adventure! Intergalactic Derring-Do! According to the publisher's blurb, *Falling Across Forever* was the second volume in 'the epic, universe-spanning *Farways* saga'.

The other two books were in the larger-dimensioned paperback format that traditionally denoted more literary fare – subtler cover design, better quality paper and printing – higher production values for a higher-brow content. Both were by someone called Jeremy Salter, who, if a reviewer for the *Daily Telegraph* was to be believed, was 'one of the foremost living exponents of the comedy of manners'. The name rang a faint bell. Fen thought he might have come across it in a bookshop once; might have briefly considered a book by that author before discarding it and picking up one by somebody else.

Idly curious, he started thumbing through the slimmer of the two Salter books, *A Charmed Life*. The novel was set at Oxford University in the early 1970s and (Fen quickly gleaned) concerned the lives and loves of a group of undergraduates at the fictitious Haldane College. A precocious lot, not to say precious, they spent most of their time drinking coffee and wine and discussing the sociopolitics of the day and, with greater enthusiasm, who among their circle of friends was bedding whom. The main protagonist was Charles Buck, devilishly handsome and something of a cad, as devilishly handsome men often are, because they can afford to be.

Women were drawn to him 'like paperclips to a magnet', as one of his friends put it, and were content to take what they could get from him, whether it was a one-night stand or even just a fond, condescending smile. His romantic misdemeanours – and they were many – were invariably forgiven, as were his academic misdemeanours, for he repeatedly turned up to tutorials with no essay prepared and his dons never reprimanded him for it. He seemed to exist (at least up until page 27, which was as far as Fen read before Miriam arrived with his breakfast) within a cloud of irresponsibility, sowing trouble and never reaping the consequences. *A Charmed Life* indeed.

'Ah, started already,' Miriam said as she set the breakfast tray on Fen's lap. On the tray were a mug of herb tea and a bowl of porridge. The tea smelled faintly of horse stables, the porridge looked a gruelling proposition. 'Enjoying it?'

Fen eyed the book, front cover and back, keeping his place with his thumb. 'It's all right. Not really my sort of thing, to be honest.'

'Oh.' Miriam was inordinately dismayed by this response, as if Fen had told her the novel was absolute rubbish and so was she. It was clear she held the work of Jeremy Salter in very high regard.

'I mean, it isn't *bad*. Just not . . . Well, I think Bradbury and Lodge have done the whole university thing better. Larkin, too, in *Jill*.' As he did his best to backtrack, Fen found that everything he said seemed to condemn *A Charmed Life* further. 'It's quite funny, I suppose. Funny in a droll way. You know, a quiet sense of humour to it. Not belly-laugh funny. Isn't it?'

Apparently the book was not supposed to be funny at all. 'It *was* his first published novel,' Miriam said, by which Fen took her to mean that *A Charmed Life*, though still an excellent piece of work, wasn't her favourite author's finest hour.

'Well, there you go. His later stuff's probably much better.'

'It's also his most autobiographical.'

'Ah.'

'Maybe,' said Miriam, 'you'd get on better with *Falling Across Forever*. For sci-fi, it's quality stuff. And much less challenging than Salter's mainstream fiction.'

Fen got the point. *A Charmed Life* was too difficult for him. He had misunderstood the novel, failed to wrap his head around its complexities. Perhaps a piece of SF fluff was more his level.

He didn't think it wise, bearing in mind his and Miriam's respective positions as care-receiver and care-giver, to try to correct her misevaluation of his intellectual capabilities. Instead he said, 'Same author, then? Jeremy Salter *is* Jeremiah S. Coburn.'

'Coburn was his mother's maiden name. He used the pseudonym so that fans of his mainstream work wouldn't pick up the *Farways* books expecting more of the same.'

'Or perhaps because he didn't want his sci-fi readers picking up his literary stuff,' Fen said, with a quick smile.

Lost on Miriam. 'Although, despite the sci-fi trappings, the *Farways* books are unmistakably his work. Well-judged dialogue, fine prose, an unparalleled grasp of character . . . and, of course, the philosophy.'

'The philosophy?'

Miriam gestured at the tray. 'Eat up before it gets cold.'

Perusal of the first few chapters of *Falling Across Forever* revealed no 'philosophy' that Fen could discern. Rather, it revealed a mediocre (at best) literary talent, all at sea within a genre that was not his natural environment. The novel made Fen think of a space explorer who had stepped out onto the surface of an unfamiliar planet, opened his helmet visor, and was staggering around, suffocating in an unbreathable atmosphere. The characters spoke in a hideously dated and clunky 'future' argot; the aliens were humanoid and seemed more like people from another country than beings from another solar system; there were spaceship battles that, but for a few differences in technical terminology, could have come straight from C. S. Forester; every female was consigned to a subsidiary role and judged according to her bra size (big chest good, flat chest bad); and even Fen, whose scientific knowledge was confined to what he had learned at school, with the addition of what he had boned up on in order to teach to his class at Downbourne, could tell that Jeremiah S. Coburn's grasp of certain principles of biology and physics was not as sure as it might have been.

As undemanding fodder for adolescents and adults still arrested at the adolescent stage, *Falling Across Forever* just about passed muster. By any other standards, it was nonsense. And if, as Miriam seemed to imply, the book expounded some particular system of beliefs, a life-doctrine, then it was so deeply embedded within the text as to be imperceptible.

By page 30, Fen was contemplating giving up on the novel. At page 51, he did so. Nothing compelled him to read further. He wasn't in the least interested in finding out whether grim-jawed hero Paul Cordwainer was going to be able to rescue his lover, the beauteous and vastly buxom Maya, from the clutches of the evil aliens, the Ch'ee-Lan, who had kidnapped Maya in revenge for Cordwainer's destruction of their home planet, which had apparently been the climax of the previous *Farways* novel. There was no doubt that Cordwainer would succeed, and Fen wasn't even curious to know how the rescue was going to be pulled off. He had a rule regarding art and entertainment: if it doesn't show you something new, it isn't worth your time. And *Falling Across Forever* contained nothing that was not hand-me-down, predictable and stale. A novel without novelty.

When Miriam next visited, she brought with her a bucket of warm water, some soap and a cloth, and invited Fen to wash himself. He obliged, using the water as sparingly as possible so that he would not have to lie in damp bedclothes afterwards. When she returned for the bucket, he asked her if by any chance she had something else he could read.

'You haven't finished already?' The incredulity in Miriam's voice contained more than a dash of scepticism.

Fen thought his best tactic was to be truthful. Truthful, and at the same time not unconditionally candid. 'I've never really been into spaceship stuff. However well it's done, it's just never grabbed me.'

'I told you to look beyond the sci-fi aspects of the book, didn't I? To delve deeper.'

'I tried, honestly I did. But, well, the spaceship stuff got in the way.' He fixed her with an appealing gaze, hoping to convince her that the fault lay with him and not the book's progenitor.

'And you haven't even considered *Noontide*?' Miriam was referring to the last of the triptych of novels, the other Jeremy Salter offering.

Fen gave a hapless shrug. 'Just not my cup of tea, your Mr Salter. My loss, I'm sure. Isn't there *anything* else to read here? I mean, this is a school. Surely there's a library.'

'A library?'

'Yes. You know, big room, full of books.'

'Thank you, Fen, yes, I do know what a library is.'

'Well?'

'Well what?'

'Is there one?'

'Burned down,' said Miriam. 'To the ground. Terrible thing. One of the pupils was responsible, apparently. The very last term, before the school closed down. Some kind of protest, I think.'

'Really?'

'Yes. Really.'

Fen knew she was lying. What he couldn't work out was why. He didn't, however, have the opportunity to pursue the matter. Before anything further could be said, Miriam snatched up the Salter books and flounced out of the room. Fen did not see her again until evening.

I found out a little more about King Cunt today. (Craig. I must try to think of him as Craig.) First, like any leader he likes his sycophants. Second, I think that secretly he hates gold-toothed Neville.

There was a meeting at the house this afternoon. Neville attended, as did Mushroom, the ugly little gnome who was King Cunt's – was *Craig's* driver yesterday. A couple of others came along whose names I didn't catch. Mushroom's called Mushroom not because he looks like he ought to live under one but, or so I've been reliably informed by Lauren, because of the shape and size of his penis. Which means I now have a particularly repellent mental image that I really wish I could get out of my head: a small, bulbous-headed penis attached to a small, bulbous-headed man.

The aim of the meeting was to discuss Craig's trip to Camberwell, and they held it round the table in the living room, while Lauren and I, in the kitchen, eavesdropped. Craig was soon describing how he finally won the trust of the Frantiks' main man, Eazy-K, by knocking cold one of Eazy-K's lieutenants in a fight that lasted all of three seconds.

'Big beast he was and all. Six foot eight if he was an inch.'

'Closer on seven foot,' Mushroom offered.

'Nah, he was never seven foot.'

'Looked that way to me.'

'Everyone looks seven foot to *you*, Mushroom,' said Neville, and they all laughed, even Mushroom.

'Anyway, bastard came at me like a windmill,' Craig went on. 'You know, arms all like that. Wurrrr! So I just ducked inside his reach, pow, one shot under the chin, and down he went. Like a chopped tree.'

'It was poetry,' said Mushroom. 'Sheer fucking poetry. Eazy-K almost popped a gasket. His face was like, "I do *not* believe this!" '

'But full credit to him, full credit to him,' Craig said, 'he came up straight afterwards and put his arm around me and called me his brother and said big respect. He meant it, too.'

'And that was that,' said Mushroom. 'Now the British Bulldogs and the Frantik Posse are the best of friends.'

'Of course, that doesn't mean they won't try and fuck us over at a later date,' Neville observed.

One of the other Bulldogs – Dean, I think his name is – asked him what he meant by that.

'Think about it for a moment. The Frantiks move in on Peckham, fine. They get control, send the Riot Squad packing, everything's cosy and rosy and nice. We're their mates, they're not going to bother us. But now we've got them bang next door, and what if they think to themselves, well, those Squadders weren't much cop, how about those Bulldogs then? Why don't we try and move in on their patch too?'

'Because now we've got a non-aggression pact with them,' Mushroom said, as if explaining the obvious. 'Because they've met the King and he impressed the fuck out of them and they're not going to take us on because they've got to be thinking, shit, if they're all like *that* where he came from . . .'

'I understand that. I'm just saying we can't trust them to keep to their side of the deal.'

'But they will if they think we're harder than them, which they do, and which we are. You don't make a non-aggression pact with someone you think you can beat, do you?'

'Maybe they're bluffing. Maybe they want us to drop our guard.'

'You weren't there, Neville. Believe me, by the end of it the King had them eating out of his hand.'

'I might not have been there, Mushroom, but I do know that you can't trust anybody and especially you can't trust a bunch like the Frantiks.'

'What, because they're black, Nev?' said Craig.

There was a pause before Neville replied, and I could imagine him darting a look of annoyance at Craig. Equally, I could imagine him smirking. 'Because they're ambitious bastards. Because they've got designs on Peckham so what's to stop them having designs on another borough as well? And yes, because they're black. That's a factor.'

'All right.' Craig's tone was lofty, cool. 'The point is made. The thing is, Mushroom's right. I impressed them. Intimidated them, even.'

'Did a blinding job of it.'

'Yes. Thank you, Mushroom. Did a blinding job of it. And they swore me in as their blood brother, too. So we have to assume that they're not going to risk moving in on our turf. I suppose to some extent we ought to pay attention to what Nev's saying. If the Frantiks get Peckham – and I say "if" because it's not a foregone conclusion – then we'll need to stay vigilant. If, as a thank-you, they want to give us some of the territory they gain, then great. We'll take it. And if they don't, well, nothing lost. But if we start hearing reports that they're muscling in on Lewisham, interfering with our supply routes, trying to shake down people who expect us to look after them because that's what they're paying us tribute for . . . If we get to hear about any of *that* shit, we come down on them like a ton of bricks.'

'Thanks, Craig,' said Neville, satisfied.

'Mushroom *is* right, though. You weren't there. I think we've got the Frantiks where we want them.'

'We'll see, won't we?'

'Yes, Nev. We'll see.'

'Only Neville would dare talk to him like that,' Lauren whispered to me. 'Only Neville.'

Well, that's what longstanding friends are for, isn't it? To say the sort of things to you that others won't or daren't.

But I get the impression that Neville's less a friend to Craig these days and more a thorn in his side. If what Lauren said is true and he's after the King's crown, I can't see him challenging Craig for it head-on. He wouldn't win. But by constantly undermining Craig's authority, chipping away at his pedestal . . .

Anyway, what do I care?

I care enough, evidently, to broach the subject with Craig now, as once again, just like last night, he switches out the bedroom light and climbs into bed beside me. Maybe it's just that I want to talk in order to postpone the inevitable. Tonight, I'm sure, he's going to want to claim what he feels is rightfully his. Zoë, I'm thinking. Susannah. Paula. All of you . . .

'Lauren says you and Neville have been friends a long time.'

'Since primary school. Why?'

'You must like him.'

'He's stuck by me through a lot of shit.'

'And he still sticks by you now.'

'Oh yeah.' He sounds definite, and perhaps surprises himself with this, because the next moment he says, 'Pretty much. We don't always see eye-to-eye. Why do you want to know about Nev anyway?'

'No reason. Just making conversation.'

'Lauren's told you to steer clear of him, hasn't she? I swear, that girl.

She really has it in for poor Nev. She's got it into her head that he's after my job.'

'Which he isn't.' I make it sound like I'm not questioning him.

Question or not, he avoids a direct answer. 'It's just Lauren being overprotective of me. Nev has a go at me now and then, yes, but that's Nev for you. If he really got uppity, I'd slap him down. If I thought he was, you know, out of line. But I've never had to yet. No, tell a lie. I did once.'

Lauren's advice: *if he wants to fuck you, you let him fuck you. If he just wants to talk, you talk.* 'What happened?'

'It was a while back. Me and Nev, we weren't much more than kids. Nineteen, twenty. Proper pair of tearaways we were. Always mixed up in one iffy scheme or another. Selling stuff that we didn't ask who we bought it from where it came from. Doing a bit of unofficial bailiff work, recovering debts from people who owed money to people you shouldn't owe money to. That type of thing. Nothing against the law, technically, but you know – treading a fine line. For a while we organised raves. That was about the most legitimate we ever got. Remember raves? Hundreds of kids in a barn or warehouse somewhere, off their tits on chemicals and dancing and hugging each other?'

'I remember. I never went to one myself.'

'Didn't think it'd have been your thing. Not someone like you. Wasn't my thing either, to be honest, but Christ, the money you could make. Silly money! There was three of us doing it. Nev, me, and this girl I was seeing at the time, Kirsty. Kirsty was the brains of the outfit. She did all the promoting, put out the flyers, signed up the DJs, greased the right palms to get licences and permits and what-have-you. Me and Nev were mainly there in case anyone she was dealing with got the wrong idea and thought they could rip her off. That's when we'd step in and, as they say, persuade whoever it was to see the error of their ways. It was a good system. Worked a treat. Kirsty was a looker as well as smart. She was the presentable face of the business. Me and Nev were the ugly fuckers who backed up her smile with force. We did well for a year or so, and then . . .'

A slow silence. I think he's not going to continue, and then he does.

'It was all a bit silly, really. Nev just kind of overstepped the mark one night. One of our raves. Sun was coming up, things were winding down. I'd gone off to talk to some local police who said they were there to arrest a few dealers but were willing to reconsider in return for a small incentive, nudge nudge. Bent coppers. There's nothing worse. Leave you feeling slimy all over, like you need a shower. I came back from sorting that out, anyway, and there was Kirsty looking all huffy and annoyed, and I asked her what was the matter and she said, "Nothing," and I hate it when there's obviously something the matter and people pretend there isn't, so I got a bit insistent with her, probably a bit angry actually, and I told her to tell me what was up, and she wouldn't, but eventually I pissed her off enough so that she did tell me. And I can remember her exact words: "You don't want to hear this, Craig, but because you're being such a prize prat . . . Neville came on to me. I told him to shove off but he wouldn't listen, and now he's out by his car nursing a sore pair of nuts." Now, any other occasion I might've thought this was funny, but I'd just had to handle those cops and I'd worked up a bit of a head of steam because Kirsty had been so evasive, and things had generally been pretty hectic and I hadn't slept for a couple of days, and . . .'

'You went and found Neville and beat him up.'

'Didn't beat him up. Just decked him. One punch to the gob. Took his tooth out. I was *that* fucking pissed off with him. But as soon as I'd landed the punch, all my anger went. Stupid twat. I just felt sorry for him then, lying on the ground, holding his mouth, blood trickling through his fingers. I mean, he's never ever had much success with women, and to try it on with his best mate's girlfriend – I mean, how daft is that?'

'Seems like he deserved what he got. Both from you and Kirsty.'

'Yeah, but . . . He was my mate. It cost me to hit him. Literally, because I paid to have that Gold Tooth put in. But it cost me in other ways too, because not only did I lose face with him, I lost face with Kirsty too. And then . . . just lost her. Not straight away, but over the next month she just sort of grew more and more . . . detached from me. She wasn't one of those girls who get a kick out of men fighting over her. She wasn't that stupid. But she thought I'd disrespected her. She'd given Nev a kick in the nads, that should have been enough, and then off I went and laid him flat and she thought that was unnecessary. Macho bollocks. So finally she left me, walked out on me, and our little business empire broke up, and it was just me and Nev again, the two of us, doing what we'd been doing before, ducking and diving, and that was that.'

'So he forgave you.'

'For decking him? Oh yeah. He knew he'd done wrong.' Craig yawns. 'But it was all a long time ago. Water under the bridge. I'm going to try and get some kip now, Moira. Goodnight.'

The arm extends across me, clamping down. Within a couple of minutes he's away and snoring.

Funny little story. A classic of its kind. Two close friends and the girl who comes between them. *Jules et Jim* in the world of cash-only business deals.

But I wonder if Neville didn't know exactly what he was doing when he came on to Kirsty. I wonder if he didn't know precisely what the outcome of his actions would be.

And I'm willing to wager good money that Kirsty had red hair.

' "... turned just in time to see Charles Buck pedal off with a valedictory trill on his handlebar bell, disappearing into the mists that seethed and swirled along the Banbury Road." '

Roy Potts looked up from the book.

'There we go. End of chapter seven. More, Fen? Or have you had enough?'

Fen refrained from saying what he wanted to say – that if he had to listen to another word of *A Charmed Life* he would probably scream. Potts possessed an air of hard-won and undependable enthusiasm, the kind that was like a confection of spun sugar, liable to crumble to pieces unless handled with the utmost delicacy. To hurt the feelings of this slouchy, insecure little man, tempting through it was, would have been ungrateful. No, worse than that. Would have been uncharitable.

'As a matter of fact, I am quite tired,' Fen said, and stifled a bogus yawn.

Potts closed *A Charmed Life*, having marked his place by folding down the page corner. 'We'll carry on later.'

He didn't leave, however. He continued to sit where he was, on the edge of the bed adjacent to Fen's, hunch-shouldered and hopeful, as if anticipating some reward.

'Thank you for reading to me,' Fen said, but this, it seemed, was not what Potts was after.

'Do you see it yet?' he asked.

'See what?'

'What the Master is getting at.'

'The Master?'

Potts held up the paperback and underlined Salter's name on the cover with his index finger.

Somewhere deep inside Fen, there was a sudden heavy click of comprehension. He felt both relieved and irritated, the way you do when you realise you and another person have been talking at cross purposes for a while. All at once the fundamental misconception becomes obvious, and you wonder, exasperated, why neither of you spotted it sooner.

When Potts had knocked on the door a couple of hours earlier, introducing himself and saying he had come to help keep Fen amused, it had seemed reasonable to assume that the book he brought along for this purpose had been chosen by Miriam – a fresh attempt by her to kindle in Fen a love for the work of Jeremy Salter. All right, Fen had thought, let's give *A Charmed Life* another crack. On the whole, when someone proselytised as vehemently about an author as Miriam was doing, that author had to have *something* to recommend them.

Now he understood that Roy Potts was a Salter fan as well. More than that. 'The Master'. A passionate admirer.

And . . .

Oh God. Surely not. Surely it wasn't possible.

'Roy?'

'Yes, Fen?'

' "The Master".'

'Yes, Fen?'

'I don't know quite how to put this, but . . .'

'Yes, Fen?'

'Well, there's a group of you here, right? At Netherholm College?'

'That's correct.'

'How many in all?'

'About fifty.'

'Fifty. And all fifty of you live here, have established a community here, because . . .'

'Yes, Fen?'

Fen gestured at *A Charmed Life*. 'Because of him. Am I right?'

'You are, Fen.'

'Because you really like what he writes.'

'Yes, Fen.'

'It . . . it speaks to you in some way.'

'Very much so.' Potts's eyes gleamed. He leaned forward on the bed, narrowing the gap between him and Fen. He was clasping the novel between his palms as ardently as a priest with his psalter. 'The Master – Jeremy – isn't simply a great writer, you see. He's a great teacher. A great thinker. This is something we all believe.' He paused. 'And it's something we'd like you to believe too, Fen.'

There were a dozen things Fen could think of to say by way of a reply, but none of them seemed appropriate, so all he said was, 'Ah,' following this up with an equally noncommittal 'Oh'.

'Let me put it this way,' Potts said. 'We've no interest in how you came to be where we found you, in the state that we found you in. That's not how we operate. Anything you did before we met you is none of our business. But we do think that there's a reason we found you, Fen. A reason you wound up injured in a place where we would hear you. Or rather, hear those dogs that had cornered you howling.'

'The reason being?' Fen said, although he wasn't sure he wanted to hear the answer to the question.

'In the past, we've had a number of strangers come our way. Not many, but in each case, once the person has stayed with us for a few days, been looked after by us, seen how welcoming we are, he or she realises that they were directed towards us. Were brought here. Something impelled them – some need, some absence in their life – to make their way to this neck of the woods. We call this type of person someone who's lost the plot.'

'Charming.'

'It's not an insult. No. All it means is they've lost sight of the overall direction of their life. Somehow or other, they can't see where they're headed any more, what everything they do is leading to.'

'Quite a common phenomenon, I'd have thought. Especially in England these days.'

'I agree.'

'No one's making plans.'

'And why should they?'

'It's all hand-to-mouth and moment-to-moment.'

'Indeed.'

'There's a lot of drift and uncertainty.'

'Quite, quite.'

'But you've got the solution to that.'

'We like to think so.'

'A way of . . . reorganising your life. Rediscovering your purpose.'

'A rather simplistic way of putting it, but yes.'

'And what if I said I'm not interested, Roy? In fact, what if I said I already had a purpose? Discovered one quite recently, as it happens?'

'I'd believe you. But then I'd have to ask you, why are you lying there in that bed?'

'Because I have a broken leg.'

'No, Fen.'

'But I do.'

'But that's not why you're there. You need to dig below the surface of things. You need to look for the subtext.'

'The subtext. This sounds like literary criticism.'

Potts nodded encouragingly.

'Literary . . . as in Jeremy Salter.'

Again Potts nodded, and Fen was reminded of the way he himself would elucidate an answer from one of his pupils, coaxing the child towards the correct solution with pertinent questions, and in the process fostering, he hoped, the capacity for deductive reasoning.

'Salter's books. His thinking. His "philosophy". He's taught you to treat life as if . . . as if it's a novel?'

Potts looked pleased, not just with Fen but with himself.

'A novel,' Fen continued, 'and each of us is the main protagonist. We're walking works of fiction. The plot runs from birth to death.'

'There. You see? It's been there all along, inside you, like a buried seed. The knowledge. A few pages of the Master's prose to water the soil, and bingo, suddenly up it comes.'

'All I'm doing is extrapolating from what you've said.'

'No, you *think* that's all you're doing.'

'No, I *know* that's all I'm doing.'

'Oh, Fen,' Potts said, shaking his head, 'we still have some way to go with you, I can tell. But not to worry. We're nothing if not patient.' He stood up. 'I've given you something to think about, at any rate. I'll leave you to get some sleep now. You did say you were tired.'

'Oh, I am.' Fen thought about feigning another yawn; decided it would be over-egging the pudding; opted instead for a slow, sleepy blink.

'You're fortunate to have fetched up where you have, you know.' Potts waved *A Charmed Life* at Fen. 'You'd do well to remember that.'

'I will,' Fen replied.

He would also, he decided, do well to remember the way in which Potts had said, 'We're nothing if not patient.'

He didn't want to think of terms like prisoner. Captive. Helpless victim. He didn't like to compare the bare white sanatorium room to a cell, the makeshift traction apparatus to shackles. He didn't relish the scary little notions that kept popping into his head – that he was trapped, that his hosts weren't entirely *compos mentis*, that what had first seemed like salvation was beginning to look more like the opposite.

He tried, instead, to adopt a positive outlook. Tried to feel that this situation was something he could endure, something he could survive so long as he kept a sense of humour and a sense of perspective. Potts, Miriam, the rest of the people at Netherholm College, these disciples of author Jeremy Salter, these literary acolytes, these Salterites – they were just human beings. Being members of some odd little sect, some weird hybrid of fan club and secular cult, didn't necessarily make them mad. Or bad. Or, for that matter, dangerous to know. It just made them different, and perhaps a little more difficult to deal with than ordinary people. But he could deal with them, as long as he kept his wits about him.

The trick would be to remain friendly and, if he could, open-minded. He knew Potts would be back to evangelise further about the wonderful credo he and his friends lived by. All he had to do was smile and nod and keep saying how very fascinating it all was while at the same time make clear that what was being advocated, this fiction-based method of making sense of life, was not for him. Potts would get the message soon enough.

Fen was wrong, however. He was right about the evangelising, but he had underestimated the Salterites' persistence.

It became a kind of siege.

The first few exploratory forays had already been made, testing the strength of Fen's fortifications – Miriam with the paperbacks, Potts giving a reading. Now, the assault began in earnest. Potts returned the following morning to give another reading, picking up from where they had left off. Two more hours of *A Charmed Life*, and then a further two later that same day. With the book nearly finished, Fen professed – lying – that he had found it enjoyable, much more so than he might have expected.

'Enjoyable,' said Potts, 'and illuminating?'

'Perhaps.'

The next day Potts polished off the last couple of chapters, and not long after he left, someone else turned up to begin another Salter novel. This new person was stiff, elderly Leonard, who suffered from an infrequent but severe tic that caused the whole of the left side of his face to crease in spasm, eye winking, mouth wrenching up at the corner. Naturally, this condition interfered with his reading. Without warning, Leonard would break off in the middle of a sentence, sometimes between syllables of a word, and twitch silently for anything up to a minute before resuming his recitation, his mind entering stasis while his facial muscles danced their little jig. The marvellous thing was that he never gave any indication of having halted. He carried on after each hiatus just as if it had never happened, not losing the cadence of the prose. It was like somebody randomly pressing the pause button while a spoken-word CD played.

Fen took a shine to Leonard but not to the book he was reading, *The House of Janus*, which was intended as a satire on the publishing industry but came across more as the peevish rantings of someone who had not attained the level of success and renown that he felt he merited. It was a tale of two authors, boyhood friends who tirelessly encouraged each other in their fledgling literary efforts until one day one of them sold a novel which, when published, became a best-selling sensation. Then the cracks appeared in the friendship, as the successful author failed to honour the pact the two of them had made when young, that if either hit the big time he would do all he could to help the other's career. Festering in a mire of bitterness and rejection slips, the unsuccessful author – by far the more sympathetically drawn of the two characters, not to mention (oh, irony!) the better writer – began to plot his estranged chum's downfall. This involved a bogus publishing imprint and a pair of jailed but still powerful East End mob boss brothers. The resulting shenanigans stretched credulity to breaking point. Towards the end of the novel Fen was praying that the mob bosses, the Kray twins in all but name, would go ahead and give the order to have both of the authors killed, thus putting *everybody* out of their misery.

He and Leonard discussed the book afterwards. Leonard was

214

keen for Fen to see that *The House of Janus* was all about duality, the good and bad that existed in everyone, while Fen attempted to persuade Leonard that it was nothing more than a rather silly revenge comedy (although phrasing his argument somewhat more daintily than this). Leonard, of course, was not to be convinced.

Then came Pamela.

Pamela read *I Am Watching*, a dark, grimy little novel about a voyeur, as though it were an adventure story for children. It didn't help that she lacked breath control, so that she would accelerate towards the end of each paragraph and then gasp for air like a swimmer surfacing. Nor did it help that she had a naturally high-pitched and girlish voice, which rendered the seamier portions of the novel incongruously naïve-sounding. The disparity between her vocal style and the book's subject matter made the reading a deeply disconcerting experience. There were times when Fen felt as if he had side-slipped into a parallel universe, one where Enid Blyton's preferred topics were not faraway trees and gangs of intrepid junior detectives but lingerie, binoculars, and relentless masturbation.

Though she sounded unsophisticated, Pamela was anything but. She offered up a spirited defence of *I Am Watching* as an honest and uninhibited exploration of the sweatier crevices of male sexuality, while at the same time conceding that Fen's description of the novel as pornography might be justified.

'Not that there's necessarily anything wrong with pornography,' Fen said. 'Do you think the Master read a lot of it as part of research for the book? Or do you think all the dirty bits just came naturally to him?'

'I don't know, Fen. What do *you* think?'

'I can't say. I really haven't read enough porn to comment.'

Then Leonard returned to deliver a pause-strewn rendition of the contents of Salter's one and only collection of short stories, *Inhuman Nature*. All of these were twist-in-the-tail squibs in the manner of Saki and Roald Dahl, and Fen's sole source of amusement while having them read to him lay in seeing how early on he could guess the upcoming 'surprise' ending. More often than not, he had it within the first minute: the child was not telling lies, there really *was* a tiger in the back garden; the narrator of the story was neglecting to reveal one crucial item of information, namely that he was dead; the murderer managed to convince the jury he had not committed the crime when – ta-daa! – actually he had; and so on. The only yarn in the entire collection that displayed a modicum of ingenuity was one in which a cuckolded husband, having heard his wife's pet parrot squawk the name of her lover, went after the wrong man, persecuting and eventually killing innocent Phil Liphook instead of guilty Philip Hook.

Leonard insisted that there was a lesson to be drawn from *Inhuman Nature*, something along the lines of you could never foresee the pitfalls that life might put in your path. Fen, though Jeremy Salter's pitfalls were anything but unforeseeable, didn't demur. He simply said that some shocks were greater than others.

Miriam manned the siege engines next, treating Fen to *Noontide*, which she deemed Salter's very best work. Her reading style was idiosyncratic, to say the least – a hectoring combination of pace and bombast that left Fen deafened and reeling. *Noontide* was a study of a young man's sexual awakening, the kind of coming-of-age tale that traditionally strives to evoke such epithets as 'sensitive' and 'moving'. Whatever niceties and subtleties Salter might have woven into the prose, however, were bulldozed flat by Miriam. For her, it seemed, a nuance was a crease to be ironed out; a shade of meaning a weed that should be trampled. At times she was almost declaiming the novel, like an orator on a podium.

And so, with work of fiction after work of fiction, the pressure was applied, but Fen held out, refusing either to succumb or to retaliate. Like London during the Blitz, he maintained an attitude of cheery resilience in the face of constant bombardment. What else could he do? The Salterites wanted to open his eyes to the manifold and multifarious brilliance of their favourite author, but even if Salter had been indisputably a genius, Fen would have refused, on principle, to acknowledge it. There was a streak of bolshiness in him that responded badly to browbeating. At the same time, he wasn't about to risk offending his hosts – captors, assailants, whatever they were – by telling them to bugger off and leave him alone. Much though he would have liked to, his sense of self-preservation counselled against it. He remembered only too well what had happened when he had confronted Wickramasinghe and invoked the railwayman's wrath. If he had learned anything from that episode it was that you should never aggravate someone who has power over your continued health and wellbeing, especially if you suspect that person to be somewhat slightly unhinged.

Day by day, as the siege wore on, Fen felt his leg getting better. The pain was abating. On a number of occasions he realised that he wasn't noticing it at all. There was a sensation of healing, nothing he could precisely define, not a tingle or an itch or a glow, just the distinct impression that events were going on inside his thigh, the body's wondrous self-repairing mechanisms hard at work. Tiny fissures being bridged, damaged bone and tissue being microscopically patched up. A fizzing cellular industriousness. And with each day that passed and each incremental improvement in his leg, he was pleased to think he was getting closer to resuming his quest for Moira. He wished he could somehow transmit his thoughts to her. Psychically tell her to hang on, not give up hope, he was coming for her.

He knew the Salterites meant well. That was the most galling, the most frustrating thing about the whole situation. They weren't bad people. They were harrying him in the same way that the International Community was harrying England, with the best of intentions. They had something to share with him that they genuinely believed would improve his life. The novels of Jeremy Salter were not mere works of fiction but sacred texts, riddled with messages and lessons and meanings. In their pages, for those with the wit to perceive it, could be found the answer to everything. The scales presently covering Fen's eyes would fall away, the Salterites were sure, if only he were exposed to enough of the Master's prose.

How Salter had become their guru was revealed by Miriam on the evening she finished *Noontide*. As she and Fen talked the book over, he parrying her thrusts of argument with deft, sideswiping evasions, the conversation strayed into the arena of writing in general, whereupon Fen made a comment to the effect that the relationship between author and reader was a paradoxical one, at once intimate and distant.

'You don't actually know the person whose stuff you're reading,' he said, 'you've never met them, and yet it's like you've been given privileged access to the inside of their head.'

Not at all an original opinion, but Miriam responded as though a major breakthrough had occurred, as though the Salterite battering ram had finally breached Fen's outer gates.

'Yes! Yes! Almost a kind of thought transference. You know the author better, I'd say, than if you actually met him or her in the flesh.'

'Have you met Mr Salter in the flesh ever?'

'Of course.'

'And what's he like?'

Miriam paused to think, her asterisk eyes contracting to full stops. 'How to put it into words? It's not easy. Very relaxed, I suppose you could say. Very affable. Always ready with a smile. Modest. But behind that, an incisive intellect.'

'Was this at a book signing?'

'The Master doing a book signing? Not likely. No, this was on his creative writing course.'

'He held a creative writing course?'

'Every year here, during the summer holidays. It was a way for Netherholm College to make some extra money outside term-time. Two weeks of intensive study and practice of the literary craft. Cost a bit to attend, I can tell you, but it was worth every penny. I came four years running. I would have come a fifth, but the course was cancelled because . . . well, the obvious reason. The school had closed. All the posh families were fleeing the country. No point keeping a fee-paying school open when your fee-payers are emigrating.'

'And this was something Salter did – teach creative writing – for the love of it?'

'Of course.'

'And not for the income.'

'That, too. The Master has never been one of those who can earn an acceptable living just from writing alone. Nothing to be ashamed of in that. Not many authors do, and those who can are the ones who produce dreadful tripe. Lowest-common-denominator stuff. The potboilers, the airport-lounge thrillers. It's one of the terrible ironies of publishing that the really good books sell poorly while the rubbish gets snapped up by the bucketful.'

A debatable point, but Fen let it slide. He also refrained from commenting that Salter's Jeremiah S. Coburn SF novels had quite clearly been an attempt to tap into the lucrative 'rubbish' market.

'But I do believe,' Miriam went on, 'that the Master taught the course simply because he wanted to impart his love of fiction to others, and because he wanted to share his vision with others.' She nodded to herself. 'I do believe that.'

'So you studied under him. You learned at his feet.'

'Initially I went along with a view to improving my writing skills. I had ambitions in that direction, as you can probably guess. But as the fortnight progressed, more and more the Master's lessons came to be about things outside writing, about the wider world and the role of fiction in it. And we liked that. There was a group of us, you see. I suppose you could call it a core. It had started forming the year before I went. I fitted in pretty quickly. We were all of us Salter aficionados already, and after the course was over we kept in touch with one another, and there were meetings. Informal at first. In pubs, people's houses. We'd get together and discuss the Master's work: And it just snowballed. Each summer we'd come back here and renew contact with the Master, and he saw how fervent we were about his books and how we were drawing life-lessons from them, and it was as though we had been searching for him and he had been searching for us. It was mutually beneficial. He realised from us what he could be, and vice versa. And that was why, as everything began to fall apart, that awful time, the riots and lawlessness, and then the bombing . . .'

Miriam shivered, and Fen shivered too in entirely sincere fellow-feeling. The events that had followed immediately after the Unlucky

Gamble had left a scar in every Englander's psyche, a communal trauma that still ignited nightmares and haunted waking thoughts. No one talked about it much. No one had to.

'Netherholm College seemed to us a safe place,' Miriam said. 'Remote. Self-contained. No one else wanted these buildings. Why shouldn't *we* use them? So we just converged on here, and here we've stayed ever since, quietly getting on with things.'

'And the Master?'

'What about him?'

'Do you know what's become of him?'

Miriam changed the subject as clumsily as a learner driver shifting gears. 'I think tomorrow we should get you up and outdoors, Fen. Put some colour in those cheeks.'

'Sounds good to me.'

'Can't have you wasting away in bed, can we?'

'You don't actually know where Salter is, do you?'

She let out an impatient huff. 'I know that he's fine and that he's hard at work on a new novel.'

'Really? A new one?'

'Oh yes, and we're all looking forward to it immensely. It's going to be his greatest literary endeavour yet. His masterpiece.'

'Well, that's something. Beavering away amid all this mess. He must reckon the country's going to be back on its feet soon, then.'

Miriam's eyebrows popped up, inquisitively, above the rims of her spectacles. 'What makes you say that?'

'Stands to reason. If he's writing a book, he must expect someone's going to be able to publish it for him when it's finished.' Fen kept to himself his astonishment that Miriam could imagine even a leaflet being published in the present circumstances, let alone a full-blown novel.

'Fen' – suddenly Miriam was beaming – 'you are so right.'

'I am?'

'The Master wouldn't write a book that nobody would get a chance to read. Sometimes I've had my doubts. You wonder, don't you, if what you're waiting for, really waiting for, is ever going to come. But then . . . Thank you, Fen. Thank you.'

'No problem,' said Fen, bemused, not sure what he was being thanked for. 'Glad to be of service.'

It's hardly a routine, but I really don't know what else to call the shape of our days here. We've fallen into a pattern. It's not a smooth one, there's no strictly-adhered-to timetable, but still, things go in their habitual order. I wouldn't say life is dull. My nerves are at full stretch and I feel like I'm walking on tiptoe all the time. There's something a little anticlimactic about all this, however, as if I've turned up at a theatre expecting to see a Webster play and they've put on Pinter instead. Not that I'm not grateful. Who would prefer blood-and-guts over drab domesticity? It's just that I keep expecting the sudden explosion, the whirr of action, the descent into nightmare, and it hasn't happened. Is this the lull before the storm, or is this simply how things are *chez* King Cunt, one long perpetual round of unreleased tension? The undercurrent of threat always there. Just like in Pinter.

Craig wakes up around seven-thirty. More often than not I'm awake already. Lauren makes breakfast for all of us. Craig then goes out, mucks around with the lads, works out with the barbells, maybe does a little sparring. Lauren and I, like a pair of redheaded charladies, clean the house. Craig likes a clean house, he does. We get lunch ready for him and whomever he feels like inviting over, usually the charming Neville, often Mushroom too. After lunch, he carries out his official duties as man in charge of Lewisham. He receives tribute from the locals, in the form of food, petrol, clothing, other essential items. God knows how these people get hold of the stuff, what they have to do in exchange for it, but some of it has to come Craig's way, a kind of tithe. And in return, he extends them the Bulldogs' protection. It's a version of the feudal system, and whether or not it's right and just, I have to say it seems to work. All across central London these little fiefdoms maintain a delicate, interconnected balance, keeping the heart of the city tamed and under control.

Sometimes Craig's called upon to judge disputes among his 'subjects'. Like some latterday Solomon he listens and arbitrates, and his word is law, his decision binding. Sometimes he has to punish, although this hasn't yet occurred while I've been here. Lauren tells me there are occasions when nothing except a beating will sort a problem out. Craig is fair but, when he has to be, he is harsh too. When it comes to maintaining order, there's nothing like a short, sharp burst of violence, is there? It's an inoculation, a tiny dose of disease to stimulate immunity.

Come evening, Craig's back for his tea, and then he's out again, loose in the compound, seeing what the rest of the boys are up to. They watch movies on tape, I hear. Hollywood and Hong Kong action blockbusters. Someone's got a collection – aliens and killer robots and kung fu spectaculars and lone cops in skyscrapers battling terrorists, a classy selection, only the best. The Bulldogs have watched them over and over till they know every line of dialogue and the tapes are so worn there's more snow on screen than image. Or they sit around and listen to music and drink beer. Or they mess about with the engines of their vans, ostensibly to keep the vehicles running, really because they just enjoy having the bonnets up and being able to tinker around and talk in motor-speak. It makes them feel skilled and arcane, like initiates into a mystery, a cadre of mechanic-Masons.

Around nine or ten, Craig comes home and we go to bed. Usually I can smell alcohol on him, but he never has so much to drink that he's drunk. I don't think he likes the lack of self-control that comes with being drunk. I think for Craig self-control is very important, the attribute he prizes the most. It wouldn't do him any good to be pissed and incapable in front of his Bulldogs, of course. He would lose face. But also, I'm not sure he wholly trusts himself. That story about punching Neville suggests his temper is fearsome when aroused and so he has to keep it buried deep where it won't easily be disturbed. Being drunk and uninhibited carries too many risks for him.

The other Bulldogs, at this hour, troop off to the recreation zones to round off their evenings with some coerced sex. Craig has that option here at his house – I wouldn't be able to fend him off if he forced himself on me – but he doesn't take it. We get into our nightclothes discreetly, keeping our nakedness from each other. The light goes out. Sometimes we talk, sometimes not. When we do, it's Craig telling me about his day, what he's been up to, the decisions he's had to make. He doesn't ever ask me about me. He doesn't ask about where I come from or what I used to do for a living or anything like that. He hasn't even asked if I'm married or not. Does he know already? I don't see how he *can*. Perhaps it doesn't matter to him. Perhaps he assumes I'm not. (I'm not wearing a ring, am I?) Or perhaps it's simply that he doesn't want to know either way.

If he did ask, I've no idea what I would tell him. *Yes, I am married.* Technically, that's true. *No, I'm not married.* Emotionally, that's true. Fen and I were in a state of separation. There was a distance between us that might as well be called a divorce.

But, for whatever reason, the question doesn't arise. All I do, when we talk in bed, is what's expected of me: listen; comment occasionally; let Craig unburden himself until he's ready to go to sleep. And then we go to sleep, and another day is over.

After more than a week of this, I have to confess I'm starting to become restless. Keeping house may be all right for Lauren – I think she actively enjoys it – but I'm nobody's skivvy. The idea of escape suggests itself again, but I remind myself I've resolved to stay and help the others, the women from Downbourne, if somehow I can. The problem is, now that it comes down to it, I really have no idea what I can do for them. I've been racking my brains and come up with nothing. According to Lauren they get fed regularly, they have bathing and clothes-washing facilities, and Craig is adamant that his men always use condoms. Anyone reported not to be doing so will, I am assured, 'get the living shit kicked out of him'. What I really want, of course, is these women freed and got back home safely. I know that I'm in a position of influence here. I have the ear of the Bulldogs' leader every night. I just haven't yet figured out how to take advantage of that.

An idea will come, I'm sure. All I have to do is bide my time, tread softly through the days, be alert, be aware, wait, watch, not cause any trouble, above all be patient. An idea will come.

Netherholm College was laid out like a university campus, with large buildings separated by quads and lawns. But there was, too, something of the monastery about the place. Windows were arched, doorways likewise, and everywhere there were cloisters through which Fen could picture well-scrubbed boys filing on wet winter days, books in hand, as pious and orderly as friars going to prayer.

A buttressed clock tower, resembling a sort of brick rocket, was the school's geographical epicentre, the hub from which all else radiated. Predictably no longer functioning, its four dials told an eternal twenty-five to six. Immediately adjacent was a dining hall, and, set at right angles to this, a chapel. From outside, both edifices looked the same, both lofty, boastful, conscious of their importance. A small spire topped by a stone crucifix identified which of them was the venue for the taking of spiritual, as opposed to physical, sustenance.

To the south lay a long driveway which sloped downhill to a distant gate. Next to the driveway there were playing fields, an expanse of greensward still set up for the rugby season. The grass had grown shin-high and several of the goalposts had lost their crossbars or else collapsed completely. Nonetheless it was possible to envisage packs of pink-legged youngsters out there chasing balls to and fro, clustering, yelping, heaving, rucking, covering themselves in mud and sometimes in glory, while classmates, house masters and parents stood scarf-wrapped and huddled on the touchlines, filling the air with vaporous cheers. *Come on, Netherholm! Get in there! Tackle him! Tackle him! Pass the ball! Pass it! Yes! Yes!! Yes!!!*

In every brick, in every architrave and flagstone, in every finial and stained-glass pane, in every single swipe of mortar that had gone into its construction, Netherholm College embodied tradition, but more than that, changelessness. Nothing had been different here for ages. Oh, doubtless there had, every now and then, been concessions to modernity. The innovations of the outside world would have to have been acknowledged, some of them even incorporated into the fabric of school life, but invariably they would have been embraced with circumspection, looked on as passing fads, trinkets that paled into insignificance beside the jewels of hierarchy and religion and rote-learning. Netherholm College was a place designed to stand the test of time, founded on immutable values, rooted in certain solid, unquestionable verities. It struck Fen as more than apt that the hands on the dials of the clock tower now stood still.

While Miriam pushed him around in a wheelchair, showing him the sights, he kept drawing comparisons with his school back at Downbourne, then chiding himself for doing so. It was no contest. Netherholm College was in an altogether different league. Macmillan-era modesty could not hope to compete with Victorian grandiosity. Establishment wealth trumped post-war state funding every time.

All the same, he could not help wondering what he might have done, as a teacher, with facilities such as these. He had never once entertained the notion of entering the independent sector. Fresh from obtaining his PGCE he had had only one goal, to educate ordinary kids and make them the best they could be. He had known that he was choosing the harder of two options. He had known that a more comfortable and lucrative existence awaited in places like Netherholm, where the pupils arrived eager to learn, having been brought up with the understanding that this was what they must do in order to be awarded the bright futures that gleamed alluringly on their horizons. So much easier it would have been for him to slip into this well-pelfed world, to coast through the short terms and long holidays, to rise gradually, effortlessly, through the common-room ranks to the top. He could have done it. But why? Why, when there were pupils from normal backgrounds, normal homes, many of them with no inculcated desire for an education, who needed him more? A job at a public school was a sinecure. A job at a comprehensive was a vocation. It was a rougher, rowdier existence, to be sure, but the sense of achievement was commensurately greater. The extra effort you had to put in made every success, every good exam result and university place, that much more gratifying.

He had no regrets about the career path he had chosen to follow . . . and yet these immense, impressive buildings, these huge spaces – what power they might have conferred on him. What paedagogical muscles they might have allowed him to flex.

The things he could have done with the minds of the scions of the well-to-do. The difference he might have made.

Miriam halted the wheelchair. The tour of the school premises had come full circle, ending where it had begun, at the entrance to the sanatorium.

'You're very quiet,' she remarked. 'Leg bothering you?'

Fen glanced down. The leg stuck out in front of him, still in its sheath of canvas and plank, pointing the way forward like a tank's gun barrel. The cord that had tethered the sling to the ceiling hooks was now wrapped tightly around it, binding the whole package together like parcel string. By this simple expedient, traction apparatus had been transformed into cast.

'It feels fine. I've been thinking, that's all.'

'Anything you want to tell me about?'

Fen felt a flash of irritation. Weren't his thoughts his own business? Then he remembered that this was a woman who, at least twice a day, carted away his bodily waste products in a dish. Hardly surprising that she should feel a proprietorship over him, a right of access to his inner workings.

'I was just wondering why we haven't seen anybody.' Well, it *was* something that had crossed his mind. 'I'd have thought, what with there being fifty-odd of you here and it being such a nice morning and everything, we'd have bumped into *someone*.'

'This is writing time,' Miriam replied. 'Between nine and one, we stay in our rooms and set down on paper what we did yesterday and what we're thinking about and where we feel the shape of our current personal chapter arc is taking us.' (Fen didn't interrupt her to ask what 'personal chapter arc' meant. The term seemed pretty self-explanatory.) 'I, of course, have been given special exemption from that while I look after you. As have the people who've been reading to you.'

'But doesn't it get a bit, well, repetitive? Don't take this the wrong way, but I can't see that an awful lot actually happens here to write about.'

'We're encouraged to elaborate in our writing. To fantasise. It's all part of the process. Fabulating the real, we call it.'

'I see. And the afternoons? What do you get up to then?'

'There are chores, of course, but once those are done we gather in the dining hall to read out what we've written, and then workshop it together, suggesting changes, improvements. The point isn't so much the writing itself, you see, as the act of giving definition to our lives.'

'And the ritual of it too, I imagine.'

'The ritual,' Miriam said, construing the word to mean what she wanted it to mean, perhaps deliberately, 'is the Master's own. He himself has always done his first-drafting between nine and one every day. That's his discipline, so we observe it too.'

'It's really made a difference to you, hasn't it? Being a Salterite.'

'A what?'

'Sorry. Just a name I came up with.'

Miriam tried it out for size: 'Salterite. I like that. We've never called ourselves anything. When something occurs so spontane-ously, like us, a name doesn't really seem necessary. Salterite.'

'I thought of "Jeremiads" as well, but . . .'

'No, Salterite is better. Much better. I'll mention it to everyone this afternoon, see what they think. Well done, Fen. Very good.' She bent down and – what he was least expecting – planted a kiss on his cheek. 'You certainly fit in here. And being a Salterite is really going to make a difference to you too.'

It was then that Fen understood, once and for all, what he was going to have to do. That kiss. That remark about fitting in. He was going to have to get the hell out of Netherholm College just as soon as he could.

How, though? That was the question. As Miriam helped him out of the wheelchair and then provided a supportive shoulder while he hopped in an ungainly fashion backwards up the sanatorium stairs, Fen felt more acutely than ever his crippledness, his dependence on others. I am Gilbert Cruikshank, he thought bitterly. Surrounded by people I regard as simpletons. Obliged to rely on them for my survival.

In the ward, he lowered himself onto his bed, then watched as Miriam unwrapped the cord from his leg and set about reconnecting it – him – to the ceiling hooks. He reckoned that, if it came to it, he would be able to unpick the cord from the sling and detach himself. He would probably be able to hobble downstairs, using the banister for support. But thereafter . . . ?

Miriam had told him she had searched the whole school but had failed to locate a pair of crutches. The wheelchair had been a lucky find, folded away at the back of the props cupboard in the school theatre. (Fen postulated that it must have been used in a production of *The Man Who Came To Dinner*.) Crutches, however, would have been preferable. With crutches, he would have been able to make a reasonable stab at a getaway. Why couldn't the Netherholm College drama society have put on *Richard III* instead?

Of course, the wheelchair itself was a potential means of escape. He pictured himself struggling into it, then propelling himself out of the sanatorium, down the driveway, out through the front gates, off into the wild blue yonder . . .

And then? Realistically, he was not going to get very far in a wheelchair on roads that were only just passable on foot. And what if he came to a steep hill?

But then that wasn't really the point. The point was liberating himself from the clutches of the Salterites. Whatever hazards and difficulties lay beyond the boundaries of Netherholm College, he was surely better off taking his chances out there than staying here among these people, these kindly but deluded bookworms. How long before their persistence wore him down? How long before he started swallowing all this guff about 'personal chapter arcs' and 'fabulating the real'? How long before they succeeded in making a brainwashed convert out of him?

Hell, the process might already have begun. How would he know if he wasn't already secretly succumbing to the Salterites' influence? Mad people kept believing they were sane, didn't they? They were never aware of going mad. And the same here. The mutation in his thought patterns could be creeping over him silently and surreptitiously. He could be sliding into convertdom without even realising it. Turning into a Salterite while remaining convinced he was perfectly all right and normal. That was how cults operated, wasn't it? An insidious drip-drip-drip, wearing the subject down without his knowledge.

One mark of his resistance was the subtle digs he kept working into his conversation, as just now, that comment he had made to Miriam about not an awful lot happening at Netherholm College. Little sniping potshots fired from behind a camouflage of disingenuousness. Verbal barbs the Salterites were too blinkered to notice, too thick-hided to feel. As long as he kept those up, he was fine. Right? It meant he was still himself, still wary, sceptical old Fen. Still the same person who had all his life avoided the octopus embrace of any one particular creed or philosophy, who had dodged dogma, ducked doctrine, steered his own course through the world, striven to remain individualistic and ideology-free. Right?

The fact was, he did not know how much longer he was going to be able to last. His determination to escape, however, was outweighed by the obstacles that stood in the way of that escape being a success. Which was definitely a problem. But it was not, he was certain, going to be a problem for ever. Sometime soon, he would have absolutely no choice but to flee. Something would provide the impetus he needed, the shove to set the ball rolling. He could not know what that something would be. He could only hope that he was in a fit state of mind to recognise it when it came along.

And then, just like that, we go from Pinter to Webster.

Everyone in our happy little household is getting ready for bed when Mushroom arrives hotfoot with the news. He hammers on the front door. Craig opens the bedroom window and sticks his head out.

'What's up?'

'Trouble at the recreation zones, King.'

As Craig pulls on his shoes and tracksuit bottoms, I ask him if I can come along.

'What for?'

There's no obvious answer to that. I'm curious? I want to help?

He decides it doesn't matter. 'Oh, all right then. Get your kit on. Hurry up.'

I'm only partially undressed, so it doesn't take me long to get ready. On our way out, we pass Lauren, standing in the doorway to her bedroom. She perceives instantly that I'm not merely accompanying Craig to the front door, that I'm going outside with him. I ignore the look she gives me, half envy, half spite. Ignore it, and at the same time am amused by it.

Across the compound Craig and I go, following Mushroom, who bounds ahead of us, impatiently like a spaniel.

At the recreation zones, in the jaunty glow of the coloured light-bulbs, I see clusters of Bulldogs, clusters of women, standing, murmuring. Their attention is focused on the rightmost of the three houses, and specifically on a small group of people in that house's fenced-in front garden. A trio of Bulldogs, several women. One of the Bulldogs is slumped in a chair, clutching the side of his face and letting out a stream of pained profanities. There's blood running down his neck, glistening like fresh paint. The top of his T-shirt is soaked with the stuff. The other two Bulldogs are hurling abuse at the women, who shout back. The women are fearful but defiant. There's an insane look about them. Women cornered, with their backs to the wall, become Furies.

'It's Gary,' Mushroom says, pointing to the bleeding Bulldog. 'Seems like one of the bitches went berserk on him.'

A Bulldog stationed outside the fence gate unlocks and opens it. Craig strides through, closely followed by Mushroom. Although I'm not invited to go with them, I'm not instructed to stay put either. I approach the gate with a sufficiently authoritative air that the Bulldog guard doesn't think to bar me from entering.

The moment they catch sight of King Cunt, the shouters fall silent. That's presence for you: the ability to bring hush without even saying a word, just by being there.

'Gaz? How bad is it?'

'She just fucking went for me, King!' Gary moans. 'I didn't do anything. Honest. She just—'

'I didn't ask what happened. I asked how bad is it.'

Gary takes his hand away from his face. There's a hole in his cheek like a crimson rosette, a chunk of skin and flesh missing, ragged meat revealed. Blood's still oozing out.

Craig glances round at Mushroom. 'Get the first-aid kit, will you?' As Mushroom scuttles off, Craig turns to face the women. 'OK, which of you was it?'

The women exchange glances. One of them raises a trembling hand. It's Paula Coulton.

Craig studies her for a moment, then sighs. 'Which of you *really*?'

'Me,' Paula insists.

'Don't fuck me about, eh?'

Paula hesitates, then lowers her head, and then her hand. Another hand goes up. Someone at the back of the group of women, hidden by the others. They part to reveal her.

Zoë.

Craig seems startled. It never occurred to me that he might not know that one of the recently gathered crop of 'bitches' is so young. I assumed Neville, or one of the others, would have bragged to him about it. Apparently not.

He beckons her forward. Zoë looks tiny and wretched in front of him, barely half his size.

'What's your name?' he asks her.

'Zoë. Zoë Fothergill.'

'Why did you attack this man, Zoë?'

Zoë shakes her head.

Craig repeats the question, more sternly this time.

Finally Zoë says, 'I didn't want him touching me.' The words spill out. 'I hate him. I hate all of them. I'm sick of them and what they do. I don't want any of them touching me ever again.'

'She bit me,' Gary interjects. 'We went up to a room and the little slut just turned around and *bit* me. I hadn't even done anything. She's a fucking animal!'

Well, of course she is. She's a *bitch*, isn't she?

'Zoë,' says Craig, 'you realise you're in big trouble, don't you?'

'Don't care.'

'I can't have you – any of you – attacking my men.'

Zoë mutters something.

'Beg pardon? I didn't catch that.'

Loudly, in a burst of truculence, Zoë says, 'Piss off, you horrid bastard.'

There's a gasp from everyone watching. Myself, I'm appalled – doesn't she realise who this man is? – yet I can't help but admire her too. She has nerve, that's for sure. Nerve, and nothing to lose.

Then a voice calls out from the next-door front garden: 'Oi, Craig! You're not going to let her talk to you like that, are you?'

Who else but Neville? He steps up to the intervening fence, showing us his grin with that glint of gold in it.

'Tart needs to be taught some manners, she does,' he adds.

'Leave this to me, Nev,' Craig says, and while his voice is steady and controlled, I can see the muscles in his right forearm flexing, as though he's having to fight the urge to make a fist. 'Zoë? Best not make things any worse for yourself than they already are.'

Zoë shrugs, resigned to her fate.

'I'll do it if you want,' says Neville. 'Dish out the beating. If you're too squeamish.'

'I said, Nev' – now Craig's patience is really being tried – 'leave this to me.'

'Keep your hair on. I was only offering.'

'She doesn't need to be punished.'

Who said that? Was it me? Jesus Christ, it *was*.

Craig spins round. Stares.

My heart's in my belly, kicking there like a rabbit.

Everyone's looking at me.

In a much feebler voice, the sound of someone who knows it's too late to backtrack now, I repeat myself: 'She doesn't need to be punished.' And add: 'She's fifteen. She ought not to be here. She's suffered enough.'

Craig's eyes go from wide-surprised to narrow-shrewd. I see him considering. Appraising. He realises what I've just presented him with. A face-saver. A get-out. I could tell he didn't have any stomach for giving Zoë a beating. He'd have gone through with it if he felt he had to, but this way he has a choice. It all depends on whether he can make it look as though he was already thinking what I said, as though I've merely articulated what was already on his mind.

If he doesn't think he can pull it off, then not only will Zoë have to be punished but so will I. Can't have a bitch mouthing off like that. Especially not King Cunt's bitch. Sets a bad example to the rest, doesn't it?

'Fifteen,' he says.

I think what I am, he said the other day, *is moral*.

'Nev?'

'Yeah?'

'Did you know how old she is? First time you saw her?'

Neville senses which way this is going, and replies, 'I'd no idea. News to me.' Whether this is the truth or not, it's a sensible stratagem. Backside firmly covered. 'Some girls, you know, they look more mature than they are.'

Craig studies Zoë. Now, after all she's been through, she seems older than her years, but before, back in Downbourne, no one could have mistaken her for anything other than the age she is.

'She doesn't belong here,' he says finally. 'She shouldn't have been brought here. It was wrong.' He turns to me. 'Moira? She's coming back to the house with us. She's your responsibility now. All right?'

I want to smile. I want to sink to my knees with relief. I don't do either. I simply nod.

'She's still going to be punished, right?' says blood-drenched, grimacing Gary.

'No.'

'But, King! My fucking face!'

'I said no, Gaz.'

Gary gets to his feet. 'I'll do it myself, then.'

He takes a step towards Zoë.

If he wasn't so angry, and in so much pain, he'd never have been so stupid.

I don't even see Craig's arm move. There's just a sudden, meaty *smack*, and then Gary's on the ground, doubled up and writhing.

'Don't,' Craig says, standing over him, 'you ever fucking do that again. Don't you ever even *think* about it. I say something, it's an order, you little shit-head.'

'I'm sorry, King,' Gary mewls. 'I'm sorry, I'm sorry.'

'Yeah, you are now.'

'It won't happen again, I swear.'

'Too sodding right it won't.' Craig looks up. Looks around. Sees that his authority has been reasserted. The brief, one-man mutiny has been quelled with sufficient speed and force. No one is in any doubt that King Cunt is still boss around here. Not even Neville. At least, whatever Neville's really thinking, his expression displays nothing but approval for the King's action.

'OK, everyone,' Craig says. 'As you were. Show's over.'

Mushroom arrives with the first-aid kit, now needed by Gary more than ever.

Paula Coulton guides Zoë over to me. 'Look after her,' is all she says. I take Zoë's hand and nod.

Craig stalks out of the garden. I want to say more to Paula, but I think it's best to leave. Get out while the going's good. I offer her what I can in the way of a reassuring look – *there, you see, I'm on your side, I'm trying to help* – and she seems to understand.

All the way back to the house, Zoë by my side, I feel the breathless exultation of a gambler who's staked everything and won. It's not the jackpot by any means, but it's a start. A victory I can build on.

I make up a bed for Zoë on the sofa in the living room. Exhausted, traumatised, she lies down and goes to sleep almost immediately.

Upstairs, Craig's waiting for me. He's sitting on the edge of the bed, looking . . . *discombobulated* is the only word for it.

'You stuck your neck out there, Moira.'

'I know.'

'Big risk.'

'I realise.'

'Thanks, though.'

'I did what I felt I had to.'

'Thanks anyway.'

'That's OK.'

He pauses, then: 'You're still scared of me, aren't you?'

'I'd be foolish not to be.' The honest answer.

'Ah well. Never mind.'

'I'm sorry.'

'It's OK. I just hoped that . . . Forget it.' He shrugs, turning his head away.

I spy an opportunity here. 'Craig, can I say something?'

'Yeah?'

'The recreation zones . . .' I hesitate.

'Yeah. Yeah. I know what you're going to say, Moira. Not humane, not right, blah blah blah. If I'm being honest, I'd have to agree with you. But we have to have them. That's all there is to it. Have to. No choice. Now look, I'm tired.' He yawns and begins to undress. Conversation terminated. Subject closed.

And so to bed.

Tonight, however, no arm comes over to pin me down.

Strangely, I find myself missing it. The contact.

And so, once Craig is sound asleep, I reach over and gently rest *my* arm on *him*.

The weight of my arm is so light, and he is so massive, that I don't think he'll notice. But he does.

Briefly, ever so briefly, my touch makes him stir.

Two days later, Miriam wheeled Fen out into afternoon sunshine and steered him past the clock tower to the dining hall.

There, surrounded by linenfold oak panelling and glowering oil portraits of past headmasters, he was introduced to the entire Salterite contingent, all fifty-plus of them. They were as jumbled and shamblesome a collection of human beings as he had ever met, the odds and ends from God's attic trunk. Everywhere he looked he saw protruding teeth and flustered hair, chewed fingernails and patterns of beard that could just as likely have been accidental as intentional. There were unusual sartorial combinations of waistcoat and T-shirt and full-length skirt and knee sock and sandal; there were hats – deerstalker, fedora, Tyrolean, Homburg, kepi – worn as badges of individuality, headgear that protested *I am different, I am special, I am not run-of-the-mill*; and there were spectacles, dozens of pairs of them; thin, thick, large, small, round, rectangular, bifocals, trifocals, bottle-bottom, rimless, a large proportion with sticking-plaster or scotch-tape repairs to their frames, a whole glinting thicket of optical aids.

The Salterites smiled at Fen. He smiled back, paying particular attention to the three of them he already knew – Pamela, creaky, twitching Leonard, hunched-up Roy Potts. He kept smiling, and tried not to feel like some anthropological curiosity, presented before a gathering of scientists for study and dissection.

It was Roy Potts's turn to moderate today. He got the proceedings under way by extending a formal welcome to the new addition to their group. (Fen winced inwardly: *new addition*.) The Salterites were invited to greet Fen with a round of applause, which echoed ripplingly up to the hall's high rafters.

'This is the man,' Potts added, 'who has christened us.'

There was more applause, and a few shy cheers.

Then it was down to business.

One after another, the Salterites stood up and read aloud their morning's work. They wrote in exercise books with the Netherholm College crest on the front cover. They wrote with pencils and ballpoint pens obtained, evidently, from the same bountiful stationery cupboard as the exercise books. They wrote about themselves, but what they wrote was not mere autobiography. As Fen had surmised, not enough went on at Netherholm College to make a straightforward chronicling of each day's events worthwhile. Instead, the Salterites cast themselves as first-person narrators of novels, recounting the minutiae of their daily exploits in story form, with all the heightened drama and tension that it entailed. They replayed conversations they had had, the prism of imagination transforming what must have been banal exchanges of dialogue into colourful cut-and-thrust repartee. They took mundane rituals – washing, cooking, eating, cleaning, digging out weeds in the kitchen garden – and developed them into allegories, extrapolating macrocosmic struggles from microcosmic endeavours, the ordinary becoming extraordinary, the humdrum Herculean. Some of them, perhaps inspired by Blake's line about seeing a world in a grain of sand, described in intense detail, at often enervating length, a scene or object they had come across. Several related their dreams (in Fen's view, there was nothing more fascinating than your own dreams, and nothing more boring to other people). A few offered up poems, lolloping doggerel mostly, or free-form meditations that borrowed clumsily from the Beats – the angst, the heart-cry, the repetition, yes, the repetition. One man seemed to think he was Raymond Chandler, another James Joyce, while among the women there were a couple of Dorothy Parkers and one Jane Austen wannabe. What they all had in common was that every one of them, without exception, believed that he or she was the most important entity on Earth, the focal point of everything. The world revolved around each of them. They were the heroes of their own lives.

The readings were breathtaking in their solipsism and self-absorption. Breathtaking, too – though for a different reason – was the workshop session that followed each one. The frankness of the Salterites' criticism of one another's work verged on the lacerating, and Fen quickly discerned that they were anything but objective in their opinions. In the guise of honest commentary, scores were being settled, feuds waged, rivalries aired, personal animosities given vent. The Salterites were not the happy, collaborative bunch they might like to think they were. When one of them found fault with another's use of, say, metaphor and alliteration, what was really at issue was neither of these things but the writer himself or herself. Because writing and individual were so closely linked, it was impossible to discuss the one without discussing the other. As a result, tempers frequently flared. Umbrage was taken. Voices were raised. 'There's nothing wrong with my adverbs!' 'Nothing that cutting half of them wouldn't cure!' 'You wouldn't know a decent simile if it came up and hit you in the face!' 'I would if it hit me like a wet ten-pound salmon!' And so on. It was a critical bear pit, and several of the Salterites were reduced to tears by the maulings they received. They would sit and sob while the next member of the group read, and then they would, often as not, lay into that person's work, alleviating their hurt feelings by hurting someone else's. What surprised Fen was that no one stormed out and no one declined to read. Willingly the Salterites exposed their writing, and themselves, to the harsh scrutiny of their peers, perhaps in the belief that there was no gain without pain. He couldn't make up his mind whether this was inestimably brave or inestimably stupid. Probably, he decided, both.

It went on, this brutal, bruising exercise, and on. After a couple of hours, whatever mean-spirited delight Fen might have derived from watching the Salterites verbally savage one another had evaporated, and all he wanted was fresh air and silence. The baton of reading passed to a man called Roger, a sallow, lizardy type whose spectacles had tinted lenses (tinted lenses always made the person wearing them look – Fen had no idea why – like a pervert). As Roger launched into an elaborate account of making his bed that morning, Fen realised he couldn't stand any more of this. He nudged Miriam and whispered that he needed to be excused.

'Can't it wait?'

He indicated, with a grimace, that it could not. 'But look. I can wheel myself out.'

'Are you sure you'll be able to manage?'

'Wheeling? Of course.'

'Relieving yourself.'

'I'll just find a patch of grass and slide myself down and . . . you know. I only need to pee. I'll be fine. Really.'

Miriam looked doubtful, but he could tell she had no desire to leave before the readings ended. She had proved to be a vituperative judge of others' work, her tongue one of the most caustic in the room. Fen wondered if this had anything to do with the fact that, thanks to her special exemption, she herself had no piece of prose or poetry to offer. She was, for the time being, safe on the sidelines, a commentator rather than a participant. She could shoot down without fear of being shot down in return. Then again, perhaps this was how she always was.

'All right,' she said. 'But don't go far.'

Fen began nudging the wheelchair slowly backwards, hoping to make a discreet exit. Unfortunately, Roger spotted him, and interrupted a digression on various symbolic interpretations of folding a hospital corner in order to say, 'Excuse me, Fen, is there something the matter?'

Fen halted. All eyes were on him. 'Call of nature. Sorry. Please, carry on.'

Roger was haughtily dismayed. 'It's not considered polite to leave in the middle of someone's reading.'

There were mutters of agreement, a few tuts. Fen sensed that among the Salterites his stock had just fallen sharply. Well, so what? Fuck them.

'I'll be as quick as I can,' he said, and turned the wheelchair around and aimed for the door. Reaching it seemed to take forever, and then the handle proved hard to budge, and then there was the whole rigmarole of shunting the door open and manoeuvring the wheelchair through the gap, and meanwhile he could feel fifty-odd gazes fixed on him, the back of his neck tingling as though under hot lights . . . but finally he was out of the dining hall, out in the open, out in the late-afternoon brightness, out, thank God, out!

He rested a while, sun on his face, sturdy and silent clock tower beside him. Then a thought came: here was his chance. While the Salterites were busy with their vicious group-therapy. He should aim for the driveway and just keep on going. See where he ended up by nightfall. Surely he would find someone out there who would offer him board and lodging, someone who would take pity on a poor, wheelchair-bound gimp.

But no. Damn it. He didn't have his knapsack with him. It was still hanging on the chair in the sanatorium. And he wasn't going anywhere without his knapsack, or rather what it contained.

He decided, instead, to take the opportunity to explore the school further. Apart from anything else, if he was going to escape at a later date, he needed some practice with the wheelchair.

He circumnavigated the clock tower a couple of times, then trundled past the squash courts and the tuck shop and took a left into one of the larger quads. A dead fountain stood in the middle, pretty but incomplete without its plume of water, like a vase without flowers. He pulled up beside a window and peered in through a grubby pane. A classroom. Desks waited in their rows, marshalled and forlorn. On the blackboard somebody had scrawled *SEE YOU NEXT TERM* – a promise not kept. Geography had been taught in this room. There was a globe on the teacher's table, and a couple of maps on the wall, one of the world, the other of the British Isles. On the latter, three thick red lines had been added by hand, denoting the fortified frontiers between Scotland and England, Wales and England, and St Piran's Peninsula and England. Hadrian's Wall was now a rampart, Offa's Dyke a trench, and the Devon/Cornwall border both, for the Cornish took their secession seriously. There ought to have been a fourth line, a red ring around London, and Fen could only assume that the capital's self-isolation had occurred after Netherholm College broke up for the final time. Yes, that would make sense. The M25 became a cordon only after the London Council was formed, and that was a little less than five years ago, after things had settled down in the city and all the central boroughs had become established as pocket principalities, firmly under the control of quasi-militias like the British Bulldogs.

London. Bulldogs. Moira.

Fen put his hands to the wheel rims and rolled himself disconsolately on. Some rescuer he had turned out to be. But he would, of course, be resuming his journey to the capital any day now. Just as soon as he felt completely fit and well and ready to do so.

In flagrant disregard of Miriam's admonition not to go far, he crossed the quad and propelled himself through a vaulted passageway, emerging into another, smaller quad. It was not one he had visited with Miriam during the tour the day before yesterday. There was a great, chunky, bolt-studded door at the far end, with a row of curtained windows on either side. The door seemed to indicate that what lay inside was of some importance. The curtains too, closed against prying eyes. Fen couldn't resist the temptation to investigate.

The handle rotated rustily. The door swung ponderously inward. Along the threshold there was a low lip of stone, which Fen managed to negotiate without too much difficulty.

Towering bookcases, densely tomed. The piquant bouquet of decomposing paper. Buttoned-leather armchairs, designed for the long, lounging perusal of text. A lectern with a huge venerable volume laid out on it, pages spread like angel wings.

The school library.

The place Miriam had said had burned to the ground.

Echoes of the door's opening skittered through the gloom, disappearing into far-off corners, book-shadowed deeps. Fen edged tentatively forwards, waiting for his eyes to adjust to the lack of light. There was something that didn't seem quite right here (other than the fact that Miriam had lied to him so flagrantly about the library's continued existence). He had every reason to think that he was alone, yet he sensed somehow that he was not.

'Hello?'

Silence. Yet it was a stifled silence, not pure absence of noise but noise being withheld. The sound of someone listening.

'Hello?'

Finally, a distant answer: 'What, is it supper time already?'

Fen, now more curious than ever, headed in the direction the voice had come from.

Deep within the library's dimness he passed a bookcase aisle in which there was a camp bed, a sleeping bag draped over it like a slab of melted cheese over a slice of toast. A little further on he came to a double row of carrels. A man was ensconced at one of them, reading by candlelight. Probably in his early sixties, he was wearing leather slippers and a silk dressing gown that was threadbare, with seams split at one armpit and on one pocket. He hadn't shaved in over a week, and his skin had the pallor of someone who had not seen the sun in ages. As Fen came into his line of view, he looked up and blinked, mole-like.

'Who are you? I've not seen you before.'

'Fen,' said Fen.

'Oh yes, the new boy.' The man appraised him: face, wheelchair, splinted leg. 'Where's my meal?'

'Meal?'

'You aren't here to bring me my supper?'

'Sorry, no. It's a bit early, actually.'

The man consulted his wrist – a reflex action, since he wasn't wearing a watch. 'Yes. So then why aren't you with the others, workshopping?'

'I bailed. I was finding it a little . . . I wearing.'

The man laughed.

'Why aren't *you* there?'

'I used to go. Regularly. But like you, it got on my nerves, so now I just leave them to it.'

'Seems wise.'

'I don't know how they do it. Every day, including weekends. How do their egos survive?'

'Flagellants.'

The man laughed again, warmly this time. Fen sensed a kinship kindling between them, both of them outsiders, positioned by choice at the periphery of the Salterite flock.

'How did that happen?' The man pointed at Fen's leg. 'No one here seems to know.'

'No one's asked. It's a long story.'

'Go on. I like long stories.'

Fen saw no reason not to tell him. He began with his adventures aboard the *Jagannatha*, then filled in the background – Down-bourne, the arrival of the British Bulldogs, Moira's kidnap – and concluded with his time spent out in the wild, broken-limbed and helpless.

'Nasty,' said the man, with a wince of sympathy. 'Still, at least you're alive and, after a fashion, kicking. And lucky you were found by such nice people, eh?'

'Very lucky,' said Fen, surprised by the other's note of sarcasm and only too happy to match it. 'So how come you've managed to not be a part of all this? To keep your distance? I mean, you're here, but it's obvious you don't really belong.'

'Is it? Don't you know who I am?'

Fen didn't until that moment. As soon as the man asked the question, the penny dropped.

'Jeremy Salter?' he said. '*You're* Jeremy Salter?'

'Don't look much like my jacket photograph, do I?'

'I haven't seen your jacket photograph. The only editions of your books I've seen are paperbacks.'

'Take it from me, it doesn't do me justice. And of course, it is rather out of date. That's the beauty and the tragedy of jacket photographs. They're ageless, while their subject ages. It's often a bit of a shock for readers, first time they meet you. I see it in their eyes: *blimey, he's old!*'

'Jeremy Salter.' Fen shook his head, bemused. 'I've got to say, it never even occurred to me you'd be hanging around this place. I pictured you in, I don't know, a nice little cottage somewhere on the coast. Book-lined study, desk, typewriter, view of the sea.'

'How about a one-bedroom flat in Hackney with a view of a Turkish restaurant?'

'That would have been my second guess.' Fen threaded a chuckle through the remark.

'Believe me, if I had a cottage like you describe, I'd be there right now.'

'I don't know. Hackney's not so bad, is it?'

'It used to be fine. I liked it. But rumours are, there was trouble there a couple of years back. An outbreak of fighting. The International Community weighed in. Now most of the area is rubble.'

'Better off here then.'

'Quite. I have peace and quiet, my meals brought to me, and all the books I can read.'

'Plus lots of time to work on your new novel.'

'Ah, you know about that.'

'Miriam told me. She said you're hard at it.' He saw Salter flinch slightly. 'Aren't you?'

'Miriam,' said the novelist, with a sigh, 'would like to believe I am. They all would. They're all looking forward to it desperately. Salivating at the prospect. The new Jeremy Salter. It's an article of faith for them, that that book is coming. And a sign.'

'A sign?'

'When the novel is ready for publication, that will be when England returns to normal. Didn't Miriam explain that bit?'

'Not exactly.' Although she had hinted, hadn't she? When she had talked about waiting for something, wondering if it was ever going to come.

'Well, she probably thought you weren't ready.' Salter stood up and ground his knuckles into his lower back, baring his teeth with the ache. 'Jesus. Bad posture, that's my trouble.' He glanced down. His dressing gown had fallen open, and he was wearing nothing underneath. A glimpse of pubic hair and peeping pink. He tightened the cord to restore his modesty. 'It's really very simple,' he said. 'To them, at any rate. Once my book is finished, all will be right with England again.'

'How do they reckon that?'

'Because when the book is ready, there *has* to be a publisher to publish it, because it's a book by me, Jeremy Salter, the Master. And if there's a publisher to publish it, there must be booksellers to sell it, and if there are booksellers then there'll be other shops, and if there are other shops . . . and so on and so on.'

'Very logical.'

'Isn't it? The whole country will spring back to life, just like that, because of me. There'll be petrol and electricity and cars and buses again. There'll be supermarkets full of food, and the BBC back on the air. Phones will work, and you'll be able to listen to the shipping forecast once more. You'll be able to go on holiday once more. You'll be able to visit the chemist's to buy your toothpaste and your tampons and your headache tablets. There'll be doctors and 'flu jabs, pub landlords and sandwich shops, dustmen and plastic carrier bags . . .'

Salter shook his head, the vision vanishing.

'Albion will rise again,' he said, 'just as soon as my book is done.'

'And you don't believe it.'

'No, of course I don't believe it. It's just a fucking book we're talking about. Its appearance isn't going to change things over-night, like waving a magic wand.'

'So why haven't you told them that? Everybody here?'

Salter, with a rueful laugh, picked up the book he had been reading, closed it and searched for a slot on a shelf to insert it into. 'As if they'd listen.'

'But you're nothing short of a religion to these people. Miriam, Leonard, all of them. They've organised their lives around you.'

'Tell me about it. It was never my intention. It's these damn times we're living in. People are desperate for new leaders, new gods. Anyone'll do, anyone who even vaguely fits the bill. Even a washed-up and never-very-successful author. Whatever offers them just a little glimpse of stability, they'll take it. Don't think I don't know I'm the proverbial "any port in a storm".'

'But what I mean is, they'd listen to you. If you told them their book might not be coming. They'd listen to you and they'd under-stand.'

'Really? And even if they did, how can I do that to them? I'm Jeremy Salter. I'm their Master. They love me. I can't let them down. Can't disappoint my fans.'

'Have you even started this novel?'

Another rueful laugh.

'Writer's block?'

'To a certain degree, yes. I've been "silent", as they say, for a while. Not produced anything of any note. Bred "not one work that wakes".'

'Hopkins.'

'Well done. Mainly, though, it's the weight of expectation. I can hardly deliver the book, can I? Not when my devotees have so much hope invested in it. What happens when I complete a manu-script and nothing changes, England just continues to stumble along in its buggered-up way? How crushing is that going to be for them? The Master promised the country's rebirth and it didn't come. Not that I *did* promise it. It's just an idea they got into their heads: delivery of new novel equals dawn of new era.'

'I see,' said Fen. 'That does leave you rather up the creek, doesn't it?'

'I should say so. Even if I could write a book, I don't dare. And so this is what I get up to instead.' Salter gestured around the library. 'Read. Look busy. I tell them I'm doing research. Seeking wisdom and inspiration among the words of others. Preparing the ground. Stoking up my creativity. And writing too, although that part's a lie. Not a *complete* lie. Occasionally I do jot something down, maybe in the margin of a book – an idea, a fragment, a line or two, a character sketch, a few paragraphs of cross-talk. But usually it's no good, or else I lose the book or the scrap of paper I've written it down on. By and large, I just kill time. There's a lot of interesting stuff on these shelves. Some absolute crap, too. You'd be amazed the kind of junk a public-school library accumulates over the decades. Cricketing almanacs from way back when. Obscure novels by even obscurer novelists. Bound collections of Victorian-era *Punch*. Some of the most recondite non-fiction works you can ever imagine. Who'd have thought somebody would have written, let alone published, a survey of British gas-lamp designs, eighteen-fifty to nineteen-twenty?'

Fen's next question – *How long have you been here?* – he decided against asking. He didn't think he wanted to know the answer. He rolled himself closer to Salter, not by much, just a couple of wheel revolutions, and lowered his voice, as if someone might be eavesdropping, as if books had ears to go along with jackets and spines.

'Leave,' he said. 'I hear what you've been saying, but leave. You don't have to stay here. Come with me. We'll go together.'

Salter peered round at him, frowning. 'You're deserting Nether-holm? Already?'

'I've been putting it off, but yes. I can't stand it here, and I've been sidetracked long enough from what I have to do.'

'But your leg . . .'

'Won't be too much of a hindrance. Not if I have your help. Come with me.'

'What about' – Salter gestured in the general direction of the dining hall – 'them?'

'What *about* them? They'll be upset to lose you, sure, but I imagine they'll get over it. Eventually.'

'I'm not so sure.'

'You didn't ask to be their Master, Jeremy.'

'I didn't exactly discourage them. I was . . . flattered by the attention they gave me. Not to mention the adulation. They really love my books.'

'Fine. But you didn't ask them to make the nation's recovery your responsibility. They've elevated you to a role you can't possibly live up to. So forget them. It's time to move on. Don't you want to get back to your flat in Hackney?'

'If it's there any more.'

'You can at least check up on it, see for yourself. I need to get to London too, remember. And if we go together . . .'

Was he being too forceful? Pushing Salter too hard? But Salter needed to escape, even if he didn't realise it, and with his assistance Fen's own bid for freedom would be markedly easier. Fen could see the pair of them, Salter at the handles of the wheelchair, wending their way towards the capital. (Presumably Salter had some proper clothes lying around somewhere – shoes, socks, trousers, all that. And a London permit. He must do, as an ex-Londoner.) It was perfect, wasn't it? Two predicaments solved at a stroke.

'I don't know.' The corners of Salter's mouth were turned down in a grimace of reluctance. 'They look after me here. I get fed. I get respect. I'll have to think about it.'

'OK,' said Fen. 'Of course it isn't something you should rush into. But, not to put pressure on or anything, I do want to get out of here pretty soon.'

'I understand.'

'Perhaps I could come back and visit you tomorrow? Assuming I can find a way to.'

'I can't say I'll have made up my mind by then.'

'Nonetheless.'

Salter deliberated for a moment, then said: 'All right. Tomorrow.'

When the Salterites emerged from the dining hall, they found Fen next to the clock tower. He was asleep in the wheelchair, or at any rate seemed to be, for when Miriam shook him by the shoulder, he acted very much like someone waking up – blinking, smacking his lips, squinting around him.

Miriam was not best pleased. Nor were the others. Fen had shown them great disrespect. It appeared he was not taking their way of life as seriously as he should. There were grumbles and murmurings – a definite discontent about the new addition's attitude.

Fen apologised and apologised. He was still not a hundred per cent well, and it had been such a warm afternoon – he had just nodded off, nothing he could do about it. Very poor show, he knew. Could they find it in their hearts to forgive him? Just this once?

The Salterites could, and in the end, impressed with his contrition, did. Miriam alone remained unmollified. Fen was in her care. He had embarrassed her. She wheeled him back to the sanatorium by the bumpiest route possible, jerking the chair around corners and braking sharply more often than was strictly necessary. Up in the ward, she tied his leg up to the hooks – tight knots – then left him for a long time with nothing to do except watch dusk gather outside, the sky purpling, the oaks clouding into silhouettes, a last twilight fling for the birds. Supper arrived, and then, when he had eaten, out went the bedside candle.

But tomorrow afternoon. Tomorrow afternoon he would know. Whether or not he had a new-found ally. A fellow escapee.

Fen opened his eyes, aware that he had just awoken from a very vivid dream. Dawn light, barging in through the curtainless windows, flooded every inch of the room, liquid brightness. Outside, the wind-busied oaks were all writhe and bluster, shouldering against one another, boisterous as drunken soldiers. It was early. Five, five-thirty. Today, he felt, was the day.

The day for what?

For fleeing, he hoped.

Through the windows he gazed at the oaks. He was both drowsy and nervously excited. He might sleep again before Miriam arrived with breakfast; he might not. Like a sea view, the oaks were comforting to watch: the graceful filigreed flutter of their leaves, and now and then a deep cavity appearing where the wind punched a hole. On one particular tree he could make out what looked like a face forming amid the heaving green. Yes, thanks to the configuration of its branches and the efforts of the wind, the oak definitely seemed to have facial characteristics. Sunken eyes, a thick nose, a mouth opening and closing. The more Fen searched for the face, the more apparent it became. Not just a nose but a nose with nostrils. Not just a mouth but a mouth surrounded by beard. And in the eyes . . . It was daylight showing through the leaves, but the resemblance to the gleam of real eyes was uncanny. There was a clear differentiation between white and iris. Remarkable. He would point the phenomenon out to Miriam when she came.

And then the oak spoke.

And its voice was Michael Hollingbury's. And so, Fen realised, was its face.

'Be ready, Mr Morris,' it said.

The voice was vibrant and multifaceted, exactly as one might expect a voice to sound when formed from thousands of rustling leaves. It was shimmering and sonorous, both reassuringly familiar and disquietingly strange.

'Ready as the seed pod,' it said, 'waiting to be freed by a gust of wind.'

Fen felt a chill run through him and he wanted the voice to be quiet; he didn't want to see and hear this tree talk to him, however much it looked and sounded like Hollingbury.

'Ready as the fungus spore, waiting for the raindrop that will burst it loose into the world.'

He tried to ignore what it was saying. Tried, through disbelief, to will it into non-existence.

'Ready as the pollen grain for the questing bee.'

Shut up! he yelled in his head. *Shut up!*

'Be ready for your opportunity.'

Fen opened his eyes, aware that he had just awoken from a very vivid dream. Dawn light, barging in through the curtainless windows, flooded every inch of the room, liquid brightness. Outside, the wind-busied oaks were all writhe and bluster, shouldering against one another, boisterous as drunk soldiers. It was early. Five, five-thirty. Today, he felt, was the day.

The day for what?

For fleeing, he knew.

Through the windows he gazed at the oaks. The oaks had been part of the dream, integral to it. He remembered them as being sensible. Sensible, and familiar, and alarming. With some effort, because the dream was rapidly dimming in his memory, he recalled Michael Hollingbury's face appearing in the leaves and branches of one of the oaks, and then the face speaking to him. He recalled his fear at the apparition, and realised that the fear was still with him, an echo of itself, fainter but still resonating away in his insides.

Twice now. Twice he had been visited in a dream by Downbourne's dead mayor. Was it right that he should be dreaming so intensely about the man? Was it *sane*?

At least this time, instead of vague reassurances like last time, Hollingbury had had some practical advice for him. Something along the lines of . . .

What was it?

Be ready.

That was it. But what did that mean? In what way 'ready'?

Ready as he had not been ready yesterday, when he could have made his getaway but for the fact that he hadn't had the London permit and Moira's wedding band with him.

A lack of foresight that was easily remedied.

Fen reached for his knapsack.

' "Why?" I had to ask myself. "Why has he chosen this moment, of all moments, to make his exit?" My flow was broken. I felt betrayed. This new member whom we had invited into our circle, clasped to our bosom, had had the impertinence, or so I thought, to make to leave whilst *I* was reading.

' "Fen, my lame-legged friend," I said, peering at him coolly, "I trust you aren't going anywhere."

'How furtive he looked then, like a burglar caught in the beam of a policeman's torch.

' "I'm enjoying your piece immensely, Roger," came the reply, and there was a murmur of assent throughout the dining hall, a general acknowledgement that, with these words, Fen had spoken for all. "It's powerful," he added. "Almost too powerful. I need to go outside and ponder a while." '

Fen managed to suppress a snigger, but it hurt to do so, like containing a sneeze. A couple of the Salterites seemed bemused by Roger's outrageously distorted version of yesterday's events, but most appeared not to find it extraordinary at all. They regularly performed the same kind of alchemy themselves, turning base reality into literary gold.

'I smiled at him,' read Roger, 'the warm, wise smile of a man who knows he has done his job properly. To provoke another to contemplation, to stir the depths of another's soul – this is the one true goal of the author. And so with Fen. It was his first-ever attendance at one of our meetings, and I had succeeded in – *oh, what now?*'

Behind the tinted lenses, Roger's eyes flashed with irritation. Who could it be, opening the dining-hall door? Who was the late arrival whose entrance meant that for the second day running his reading was interrupted?

Then Roger remembered that all of the Salterites were present and accounted for, so the late arrival could only be—

'Master,' he gasped.

Jeremy Salter's head poked round the door. He regarded every-one nervously, debating whether or not to enter. After a moment he did, sidling warily into the room. An absolute hush had fallen. On every Salterite's face there was mingled delight and disbelief. The Master, paying them a visit. Could it be that he had left the library for a very specific reason? Could he be here to give them a progress report on the new book? Might it be nearing completion? Might it even be – no, surely not, it was too much to hope for – be *finished*?

'Master,' said Roger, 'forgive me, please. I didn't mean to sound so annoyed. My temper got the better of me. I'm sorry.'

Salter barely heard the apology. He was gazing around at his assembled acolytes, and Fen wondered when was the last time he had faced them all together like this. By the look of him, it had been a while. The devotion, the *need* of such a number of people, was overwhelming to him. He hadn't bargained for this when, willingly or otherwise, he had become their messiah.

It took him the best part of a minute to gather himself together. He toyed with one end of the cord of his dressing gown, coughed, thrust a hand into the dressing gown's unfrayed pocket, took it out again, looked down at his feet, looked up, ran his fingers through his hair, and finally summoned up the nerve to speak.

'Everyone,' he said.

A long pause.

'Everyone, I have something to tell you.'

A wordless whisper went around the room, a susurrant rustle as Salterite turned to Salterite, exchanged a look, nodded. *Here it comes. This is it.*

Fen, for his part, had the fear that Salter was about to land him in trouble. *This man came to the library yesterday afternoon and tried to talk me into abandoning you all.* He hated to think how the Salterites might respond. Beneath that meek bookishness ran a current of restive, ill-focused anger. He had had numerous glimpses of it yesterday, during and immediately after the workshop session. He could see it, given sufficient provocation, welling up and erupt-ing. Violently. And here he was, in a wheelchair. Never had he been less capable of defending himself.

In the event, what Salter had to say gave hope to the perturbed Fen and perturbed the hopeful Salterites.

'For a while now, I've been distant from you,' Salter said. 'Hidden away in the library, I've left you to carry on pretty much under your own steam. You may feel that I've been neglecting you.'

There were cries of *no, no* and *of course not*. 'You may feel that my aloofness has meant that I want nothing to do with you.' Again, the Salterites loyally contradicted him. 'You may have found it insulting that I, your Master, have withdrawn from all contact with you save for brief meetings at mealtimes.'

'We don't mind,' said Pamela.

'You need your solitude, Master,' said another of the Salterites.

'The fact is,' said Salter, 'it's true.'

There was silence as the Salterites attempted to decipher this remark. *What* was true? That he needed his solitude? That he only saw any of them when they brought him his meals at the library? Or that . . . ?

'Master?' said Roy Potts. 'What are you saying?'

'I'm saying' – Salter looked both patient and scared, making Fen think of a saint in the throes of martyrdom – 'I'm fed up with the lot of you. This is absurd. Crazy. I should never have allowed things to get out of hand the way they have. Look at yourselves. Go on. Take a good, long, hard look. What are you doing here? What are you achieving? What does writing about yourselves do for you? Where does it get you, putting yourselves through the mill like this day after day? Do you honestly feel better for it?'

Several of the Salterites nodded. They honestly did. The rest were just puzzled.

'And waiting for my next novel,' Salter went on. 'Waiting for it like it's some kind of magical solution, the talisman that's going to save the day. Here's a newsflash. It's not coming. It's never coming. I haven't written a word of it. I've been sitting there in that library with my thumb up my arse, pretending to be creating. I've been stringing you along, simply because I can. Because you've let me. And it's time this whole . . . this whole *charade* was at an end. I'm not what you think I am. Nor am I what you hope me to be. I'm just an ordinary person who's been promoted way above his station and who's sick and tired of being hailed as something he isn't. Let's stop this now. Let's call it a day and go back to our homes. It was fun while it lasted; now it's over. And I'm sorry. I hope we can still be friends after this, but I appreciate that's most likely impossible. I'm sorry I misled you. I'm sorry that we all got into such a mess. But there you are. It's all over. Please, let's just agree that it's all over.'

The Master had delivered this illusion-shattering speech in such a hesitant and understated manner that for a while the Salterites wondered if he was genuinely telling them what he seemed to be telling them. A couple of them murmured something to the effect that this was a test of faith, an attempt to discover which of them were his true devotees and which merely playing at it. Another mentioned a scene in one of the Master's Jeremiah S. Coburn books wherein an evil Paul Cordwainer duplicate comes to Earth and tries to persuade the planetary government to call off the war with the Ch'ee-Lan. This, surely, was the Master acting out a similar scene, perhaps in order to establish how familiar they were with the *Farways* novels (as if such a thing needed establishing!). A few of them had simply not heard a word Salter had said, their cerebral cortices refusing to believe what their ears were telling them.

For most present, however, it became apparent soon enough that the Master was not fooling around. This was no attempt to wrong-foot them, to shock them into some precipitous and self-revelatory response. This was no demand for proof, no trial by fire. This was really happening. The Master had had enough of them. The Master was a sham. The Master had just confessed that he had been lying to them, leading them on, avoiding them because he thought them . . .

Absurd.

Ridiculous.

Contemptible.

And in that instant of dreadful realisation, the Salterites switched from adoration to loathing. Fen could feel the animosity lunge out of them at Salter. Salter felt it, too. He took an involuntary step backwards, as though recoiling under the impact of a physical blow. Behind dozens of pairs of spectacles, eyes went narrow and dark. The atmosphere in the dining hall drummed with dissident rage.

Roy Potts stood up. 'You shit,' he growled. 'You absolute *turd*.'

Then Leonard got to his feet. 'How could you have' – half of his face jerked and writhed for several seconds – 'done this to us? All we did was' – more jerking and writhing – 'admire you.'

Now Roger: 'A joke. That's all we've been to you, isn't it? A big stupid joke.'

Salter was shaking his head. He was suddenly calm. Surprisingly so, Fen thought, given the circumstances. 'Please understand,' he said, 'it was never my intention to hurt anybody's feelings. This has been long overdue. I had to get it out into the open. For all our sakes. I couldn't go on deluding you, letting you delude your-selves.'

'We were happy!' someone shouted.

'You've ruined everything!' someone else shouted.

All the Salterites were on their feet by now. Slowly, menacingly, they began to move on Salter. Some were yelling and gesticulating, others were grimly tight-lipped. Among the latter, Miriam looked the grimmest and tightest-lipped. Her face was white, her mouth a barely visible slit. In her asterisk eyes Fen saw pure murder.

It did not take a psychic to predict that the situation was about to turn very nasty. Certainly Salter seemed aware what was going to happen, but, although he retreated before his acolytes' advance, he did not turn and attempt to flee. It was almost as if he had been expecting something along these lines. Almost as if he welcomed it. As he backed up against a wall and the Salterites encircled him, he looked relieved that the option of escape was no longer available. It was out of his hands now. He had set a train of events in motion. He had no choice any more but to ride it to its final destination.

Briefly Fen considered intervening. But what could he do, wheelchair-bound as he was? The expression on Salter's face decided him. The resigned acceptance. A price was about to be paid. Fen aimed the wheelchair for the door, which Salter had left ajar. The last thing he saw before he propelled himself through it was the Salterites pouncing on their disgraced, dressing-gowned Master. The last thing he heard was a howl from several dozen throats, a cry of pure, maenad fury.

And then he was off, hurtling past the clock tower, past the science block, onto the driveway. Thrust, thrust, thrust with his hands, the wheelchair jouncing and juddering over uncertain tarmac. In his trouser pocket: Gilbert Cruikshank's London permit, Moira's wedding band. Farewell to the knapsack – he had had no choice but to leave it on the chair in the sanatorium, but it wasn't such a great loss really. Frantically down the driveway, with the Salterites' howl still echoing in his ears. Were they following him? Were they behind him? Or were they still in the dining hall, exacting their terrible revenge on Salter? He didn't dare look. He should have helped Salter. No, he couldn't have done a thing. Wheel spokes a blur. Palms and fingers slipping on the steel rims. Breathing rough. But thrust, thrust, thrust, and out through the gateway and into the world beyond Netherholm, and on, and on, as if all the devils in hell were giving chase, on along a pocked, pitted road, with no direction other than Away, no goal other than putting as much distance as he could between him and the school. And on into the emptiness of England, and on.

5. FAIRFIELD HALL

Hands blistered, arms aching, Fen homed in on the hum.

He had been two and a half hours on the road. Urgent impetus had become painful effort had become exhausted trudge. The going had not been as difficult as he anticipated, but neither had it been easy, thanks to one of the wheelchair's front castors, which had developed shopping-trolley syndrome, that propensity to stick when least expected and least wanted. More and more, with his shoulders tiring and his palms turning raw, Fen had had to fight against the chair's leftward veer and force the damn thing around right-hand bends. Wearisomeness adding to weariness.

Then, the hum.

Shortly before he first heard it, he had been reconciling himself to two uncomfortable facts: that evening was coming on, and that he was hopelessly lost. From Netherholm, he had hurtled headlong into a network of country lanes, single-track, high-banked, an open-topped labyrinth. At junctions there were signposts – the old-fashioned kind, wooden with black lettering, not needing to be replaced by anything newer, their mile-truths still accurate – but the names on them were of no help to him. The signposts weren't giving directions to any major towns, merely offering guidance to the immediate vicinity. Evidently you weren't supposed to enter this rural backwater unless you already had some idea where within it you were headed.

There had been hills, but none steep. There had been ruts and potholes, nothing he could not steer the wheelchair over or around. But then, as the light began to fade, the despairing sense had crept into him that he was getting nowhere. Where were the houses around here? Where *were* the villages named on the signposts? Hemmed in by tall hedgerows, he was afforded no prospects, no glimpses of a potential destination. It could be that he was going round in circles. What if he wound up by accident back at Netherholm? Netherholm, and those betrayed bookworms who had vengefully turned on their god. Not an appealing thought.

Then he had come to the wall – mossy brick, waist-high, round-capped, portions of it collapsed, other portions sagging with intent to collapse. The wall curved with the road, extending a protective arm around a deep margin of woodland. Wall meant habitation. Fen, with renewed vigour, had followed its course, and after quarter of a mile had become aware of the first faint strains of a threnodic thrumming, as though a distant choir of bass singers was intoning a minor-key chord. The sound originated from up ahead, further along the path of the wall, and as Fen shunted himself closer it deepened and intensified and developed weird harmonics, skittering piccolo trills like a knife scraping ice. Closer still, and the world seemed to shiver with it – sky, trees, lane, trembling to its eddying vibration and swirl. A power drill? A chainsaw? What?

He rounded a corner, and the wall rose in a swooping parabola and became a pillar, crowned with a limestone lion. Five yards on, there was an identical lion atop an identical pillar, after which the wall resumed at its previous level. Between the two lions, a pair of imposing gates might once have stood, but now there was just an open entrance. On each pillar a brass plaque was attached, and on each plaque were etched two words, still legible under the verdigris:

> ## FAIRFIELD
> ## HALL

Fen eased himself onto the incurving apron of gravelled tarmac which, beyond the gateway, became a winding drive. The source of the hum lay along the drive, somewhere past the point where the margin of woodland ended. The wheel rims were tacky with blood from his flayed palms. His knitting, splinted femur throbbed from all the jostling and bumping it had had to endure over the past few hours. His arms ached so much, they no longer felt part of him; they were hollow, unwieldy prostheses. What kept him going was the thought that the hum, whatever it was, had to mean human activity of some sort, human industry consequently someone on whose mercy he could throw himself.

A hundred yards of stiff, wincing progress brought him clear of the trees. He was at the top of a rise. The drive wound downwards, into a valley. All Fen could see of the house to which it led, was a dozen red chimney tops, standing proud amid a cluster of cedars.

Beyond was a flank of green hill where sheep, tiny as maggots, grazed.

A bee buzzed across his field of vision. He turned to look in the direction it had come from.

Of course.

Hives. A couple of dozen wooden hives, like miniature white tower blocks, each with a cloud of bees cycling attentively around it.

And next to one of the hives, a man dressed in a beekeeper's veiled hat and thick, tight-cuffed gloves.

The man had removed the hive's top two levels. As Fen watched, he leaned down, extracted a frame from inside the hive and held it up to peer at the comb it contained. Drones and workers crawled off the frame onto his gloves, like a glossy black contagion, but the man seemed unconcerned, his the fearlessness of someone who has been stung often, or never stung at all. Having satisfied himself that all was as it should be with the comb, he slotted the frame back into place and commenced the delicate task of removing the bees from himself. It was while he was doing this, gently wiping one hand against the other, that he noticed Fen.

He let out an oath, more in bemusement than in shock. Next moment, he began laughing – a rich, throaty chortle. His whole body, which was of some considerable size, rocked and wobbled, and the last few bees still clinging to his gloves took flight, dispersing agitatedly.

Fen, for all his various pains and discomforts, could not help but smile. The man's laughter was so unexpected and so obviously heartfelt that it was impossible not to relish it. Even though he, Fen, was its cause – and he realised how absurd and incongruous he must look, broken-legged in a wheelchair, here in the heart of the countryside – he was not offended. Rather, he was relieved that he had given the beekeeper something to laugh about. A better response he could not have hoped for.

The man carefully reconstructed the hive, then walked over to Fen, lifting his veil as he went and securing it over the hat brim. Something about his revealed face made Fen instinctively want to trust him. He was somewhat surprised that, given his experiences with Wickramasinghe and the Salterites, he still had it in him to trust a complete stranger. Nevertheless . . .

'I need some help,' he said.

'I'll say you do,' the man replied, and not long after that he was wheeling Fen down the drive, away from the hive hum, through the stately acres towards the house where Fen was to spend the next two months of his life.

Fairfield Hall had been Beam's family's principal residence since the Restoration. Legend had it that the duke who built it was given the land and the funds for its construction by Charles II himself as a reward for his loyalty and financial support during the king's exile. (Legend also had it that the duke was one of the royalists who helped hide Charles after his defeat at Worcester, although in Beam's view this was merely an instance of the family lily being gilded.) The one condition attached to the king's munificence was that he was entitled to visit the house whenever he wished and have his way with the duke's wife, by all accounts a great beauty. Such an arrangement seemed to suit the duke, no doubt because he, in turn, was exercising *droit du seigneur* over various of his female servants. As for the duchess, she got a large and impressive country seat out of the deal, and what woman of that era, or indeed any era, could resist the blandishments of the monarch? Besides, when the king was not around and her husband was otherwise engaged, there was always a discreet footman or a handsome, horny-handed stable lad whom she could, as it were, fall back on.

So licentiousness had reigned in the household, and had continued to reign for several generations, with the result that the routes by which the Hall passed from one owner to the next were not necessarily the most direct and straightforward. Every time a resident duke died, he left behind at least two heirs, usually more, each with more-or-less equal claim to his title and estate. For a couple of centuries the family tree was a tangle of half-siblings and bastards and bigamy and morganatic marriages – less a tree, in fact, more a briar patch – and often the question of inheritance could only be settled by who was the better shot in a duel, or, as time went by, who employed the better lawyers.

By the middle 1800s things began to settle down, as conventional morality asserted itself and the system of eldest-son-of-sole-spouse-gets-everything became the norm – generally a more satisfactory method of establishing right of succession, and less costly in terms of both money and life. The promiscuity that had characterised the early years of Fairfield's existence was eschewed, and a prudish veil drawn over that era of the house's history. A shame, in Beam's view, but there you go. The Victorians were unlikely to believe, as he did, that not only had the family benefited from the misbehaviour of its first owner and his immediate descendants, the Hall itself had too. The house, he reckoned, had received a kind of erotic christening, an infusion of energy from the sexual shenanigans that had taken place within its walls during its formative years, a baptism by fornication that had imbued it with a vibrant, playful atmosphere of the sort you wouldn't find in, say, a cathedral; while the admixture of commoner genes to the bloodline meant that, whereas many an aristocratic family dwindled away through inbreeding and hereditary disorders, becoming an anaemic ghost of its former self, Beam's had remained robust and vital down through the decades. For an example of this, you only had to look at his grandfather, who had survived appalling wounds at Anzio and a three-bottles-of-claret-a-day drinking habit to live to the ripe old age of ninety-four. War took one of his arms, alcohol-related circulatory problems cost him both of his legs, but he had soldiered on regardless.

'When I was young, it used to be my job to push the old bugger around in a wheelchair,' Beam told Fen as they trundled down the drive. 'Just like I'm pushing you now. I was only a strip of a lad, but it wasn't that hard work. So much of him was missing, he hardly weighed a thing. We got along great, Grandfather and I. He taught me all the dirty jokes I'll ever need to know. But d'you know what impressed me the most about him? How he never let his disability get in the way. He'd shoot game, uncork bottles, rattle off long, choleric letters to the *Spectator* on his typewriter . . . No mean feat if you've only one functioning limb. Fondled the ladies, too, and always knew he could get away with it because they couldn't possibly slap a one-armed war veteran in the face, could they? Naturally enough, I grew up wanting to be exactly like him.'

'With all your parts intact, of course.'

Beam laughed, in the very same way that he had laughed when he had caught sight of Fen at the hives. Fen got the impression that Beam laughed a lot; a lot of things amused Beam. His face seemed designed for little else: the small, twinkling eyes; the clownish bulb of nose; the nub of chin that rested on a roll of dewlap; the parallel grooves in his jowly cheeks that reminded Fen of a cut of meat from the butcher's, segmented with string. A face that was the very epitome of the term jovial.

'My father was much the same,' Beam continued, after his laughing fit had run its course. 'When he took over the Hall, we were getting fucked five ways to Sunday by the government. Taxes on this, taxes on that. At the time, they were treating the landed gentry like a disease that had to be eradicated. And who knows, maybe they're right. Maybe we are. But that's another argument. The thing is, Dad refused to let it get to him. I never once heard him even grumble. You'd see these arsehole politicians come on the television and talk about social equality when what they were really talking about was paying off their debts at our expense. And Dad would just smile. He took the view that we'd been around for a while, and we'd continue to be around for a while, come what may. That's what lineage does for a family: roots it hard, like an old tree. So a few paintings, a few heirlooms, went off to the Middle East and Silicon Valley. It was sad to see them go, but they saved us. A small portion of our past bought us our future. I think there's a kind of justice in that, a kind of balance. And it meant Fairfield didn't have to become a country-house hotel, the way so many other stately homes did.'

Fen asked, in the tone of someone both amused and baffled, how Beam had come to be called Beam.

'Because it's my name,' was the straightforward reply. 'Well, part of my name. Part of one part of my name. I've got more barrels than a brewery. Beam's a useful shorthand. That's how everybody knows me. And I think it rather suits me, don't you?'

It did, Fen thought. Beam, as in ray of light. Beam, as in big smile. Beam, as in 'broad in the . . .'

'But perhaps we should steer clear of the subject of un-conventional names, *Fen*.'

Now the drive was flattening out, settling in for a final long, straight run. The Hall itself was still masked from view by its stockade of cedars but Fen saw outbuildings, stables, which had been converted into an open-sided garage. He saw cars within, half a dozen of them in a row, snug under dustsheets. He saw a stream winding through a deep groove in the valley, decanting into a lake. He saw a great, undulating expanse of lawn on which clumps of rhododendron squatted, somehow calling to mind giant green armadillos. He saw a tennis court, and a huge ancient oak whose boughs played host to a rope-and-tyre swing and a ramshackle treehouse. He saw people. A group of children haring around in a field. Two men walking back to the house from the stream, toiling under the burden of filled buckets. Women sitting out on the grass, preparing vegetables, nattering. Everyone lit sidelong, gilt-edged, by the early evening sun. The women waved to Beam as he and Fen passed by. Beam waved back, and Fen, not knowing what else to do, waved too. One of the women shouted out, 'What have you found there, Beam?' and Beam replied, '*He* found *me*.'

Then, at last, the Hall. Aged. Pondering. Crimson beside the dusky blue of the cedars. Three storeys tall, with the chimney stacks adding the height of a further storey. A spread of ivy embracing most of one wing, like a viridian pelt. An interlocking to-and-fro of pitched roofs. Windows large and true. Something so solid, so sempiternal about the place that you could quite see Beam's father's point. What could destroy *this*? No act of Parliament, of International Community, even of God, had power sufficient. Netherholm College had been founded on principles, and in the end had failed to survive. Fairfield Hall had been founded on land and lust, earth and earthiness, and had endured.

A pair of Irish wolfhounds appeared from nowhere and came charging up the drive towards Beam and Fen, barking wildly. Fen gripped the arms of the wheelchair, his mind whirling back to that night on the railway embankment, the dog pack, the lunging Rottweiler. His heart was quick-thumping, and he would have, if he could have, stood and run.

The great grey shaggy beasts zeroed in on him and subjected him to the impertinent sniffing and slobbering with which domestic dogs traditionally greet new arrivals to their territory. Fen held himself utterly still, not wanting to give them the least excuse to take offence. He knew, he *knew*, the wolfhounds would not attack. Their tails were lashing to and fro. They were just being friendly. But they were huge creatures, and set into the grizzled muzzles with which they were probing him there were teeth. Huge, sharp teeth. And the smells of dog fur, dog breath, were rank, overpowering, all too horribly reminiscent . . .

'Crap! Piss!' Beam yelled, somewhat belatedly noticing Fen's discomfiture. 'Off! Get off, you buggers!'

Obediently both wolfhounds moved away from Fen. Still wagging their tails, they circled round until they were flanking Beam.

'I do apologise, Fen. They don't mean any harm. Just very excitable. You're not a big fan of dogs, by the looks of things.'

'Got put off them quite recently,' Fen said, with a forced laugh. 'Crap? Piss?'

'It's all they did when they were puppies. And chew shoes.'

'So which is which?'

'Honestly don't know.'

Beam left Fen by the front door, saying he would only be a moment. He disappeared into the house, but Crap and Piss, instead of following their master, remained with Fen, stationing themselves on either side of the wheelchair. Their heads were on a level with his. They peered at him with their big, rough-browed eyes, beseeching. He realised all he had to do was give one of them a pat and he would have a friend for life. He could not bring himself to. He kept thinking of the Rottweiler, of punching it on the nose. Someone else had done that, someone terrified to the point of recklessness. That someone was still inside him, and had sworn for all time to detest dogs, and no amount of logic was going to persuade him to change his mind.

Several minutes later Beam emerged, bearing a dusty wooden crutch. 'My grandfather's,' he said, brushing cobwebs off it. 'Between losing one leg and losing the other. He used to race around the house on this. It's been in the attic a few years. I hope it's still all right.' He banged the rubber ferrule on the ground. 'I mean, it seems pretty sturdy, and I can't see any signs of woodworm. But if you don't want to take the risk . . .'

With Beam's help Fen eased himself up out of the wheelchair. He lodged the crutch under his left arm. He took a few exploratory steps, with Crap and Piss padding alongside, perhaps thinking they were being helpful. The crutch creaked but did not seem in any immediate danger of snapping. It felt strange. His first independent steps in over a fortnight. It felt good.

He turned around and headed back towards Beam, gaining confidence with the crutch.

Beam, he saw, was beaming.

Fen started beaming, too.

Supper was a raucous, convivial affair. Only then, with the full complement of residents gathered in the dining room, did Fen begin to appreciate how things worked at Fairfield Hall and what Beam had achieved here.

All told, adults and children, there were thirty people present. The table they sat around was a great long slab of mahogany, scuffed and coarsened, the wood slowly reverting through usage to a semblance of its original raw state. They ate off ironstone china, using good silverware. They ate well. And there was wine – wine! – from a cellar stocked so generously that, by Beam's reckoning, it would take a decade of hard boozing to empty it. His grandfather's legacy. The old bugger had acquired the stuff even faster than he could guzzle it. He'd had a morbid fear of the house running dry. There was water on offer, too, cool and clear from the stream. Perfectly safe to drink, Beam assured Fen. The stream had its source a short way up the valley, bubbling up from a deep underground spring, so unlike most waterways in England it hadn't been polluted by the outspill from destroyed factories and power stations. Proof? They were eating the proof. Trout from the lake. Lake was teeming with the buggers. So many, you got a bite almost before your bait hit the surface.

The wolfhounds hunkered by Beam's chair, waiting for scraps which he fed them even while scolding them – *greedy devils!* – for begging. Beam, as you might expect, was seated at the head of the table. Fen was accorded the guest of honour's place at his right hand. And throughout the meal everyone chattered and bickered and hooted, filling the room with noise. The adults discussed the day just ended and what needed to be done tomorrow, and teased one another about working too hard or not hard enough, while the children yelped and squabbled and, between courses, played hide-and-seek under the chairs. Gradually Fen picked up names. Annabel, Simon, Ed, Lucinda, Corin, Jessica . . . He chatted with a couple of them, but Beam monopolised him, wanting to know all about him, genuinely interested. A dessert course – honey pudding – was brought in, fresh from the wood-burning range in the kitchen, still warm. More wine. Yes, he was a schoolteacher. Lived down south, not far from the coast. Yes, yes, he *was* a long way from home. Thereby hung a tale. Tell me, said Beam, so yet again Fen rehearsed his litany of travels and tribulations, not forgetting to tack on the latest addition at the end, Netherholm College. Oh, Beam knew about those people over at Netherholm. Everyone around here just left them to get on with it. All sorts of rumours. Artists' colony of some kind. Writers, eh? And they had done *what*? Killed someone! *Maybe* had killed someone. Ah yes. So Fen hadn't seen this Salter fellow actually die. But he was pretty sure the chap had met a sticky end. Brrrr. How ghastly. Still, Fen had got away from 'em, and by the sound of it he'd had a lucky escape.

In the windows the tail-end of twilight deepened into night – violet, indigo, black. Candelabra were lit. The children were taken up to bed, each having kissed Uncle Beam goodnight. It was like a family, Fen thought, a big, rumbustious family, presided over by a portly, avuncular patriarch. He had established that the majority of the people here were old friends of Beam's. As the effects of the Unlucky Gamble began to take hold, they had gravitated towards the Hall. Before, they used to come for weekends, for a break from their pressured working lives. A place of refuge then. Now more so. Beam had welcomed them in under his roof. Then had come one or two outsiders, drifting in as Fen had drifted in: friends of Beam's friends, who knew of the Hall and had made their way there in the hope of finding sanctuary too. They had been welcomed, of course. There was room enough. As long as you did your bit, you could stay. That was the one rule here, according to Beam. The only rule. There was always work to be done, and as long as you chipped in, you fit in.

'Seems a fair system,' Fen observed.

'Probably isn't,' came the reply, with a wink, 'but I like to think it is.'

More wine, and still more. The candle glow mellowed, refracted. The faces ranged around the table were golden moons. A little boy came downstairs in his pyjamas, unable to sleep. He sat on Beam's lap and everyone listened as Beam told a story about a chocolate moose. The boy had no idea what a moose was and only a vague concept of chocolate, but he loved the story, which Beam made up as he went along and which contained very little plot other than the various different methods the moose employed to keep from melting in the sun. The wolfhounds snored at Beam's feet.

Later, the dribs-and-drabs decampment to bed.

Later still, Beam and Fen stood on the Hall's west-facing terrace, last survivors of the evening. Crap and Piss busied themselves, dim loping shapes in the dark, carrying out their eponymous bodily functions. The night was black and brilliant, the bowl of the valley crisply silhouetted against the stars. A barn owl screeched. Other than that, the world was so hushed and still that Fen could hear the wolfhounds' panting, the bump of their paws on the grass, and his own heartbeat, accelerated and erratic from the wine, bounding in his ears. Everything that had happened to get him here suddenly seemed remote, someone else's sufferings. Even Downbourne seemed remote. And what seemed remotest of all was Moira. He pictured her face. The last time he had seen her. It felt like long, long ago.

'Lovely out here, eh?' Beam said.

Fen concurred. 'And what a meal. It's ages since I've eaten that well. I'm so full my trousers are tight.'

'Better than being so tight your trousers are full!'

Beam laughed mightily at his own witticism. Fen joined in.

'So tell me,' Beam said, 'any idea what your plans are? I mean, in the immediate future?'

'London,' Fen replied. London, in his drunkenness, seemed all at once the London of old, the London of cliché, red double-deckers and Tower Bridge and pigeons and Hyde Park and newspaper vendors barking out headlines on street corners. Disney London, Swinging London, Ealing Comedy London. Faraway and lost. Big Ben chiming through the fog. Black cabs on rain-glassed roads. A fantasy capital that he could no more reach than he could reach Xanadu or Shangri-La.

'But not straight away,' said Beam.

'I suppose not.' Why not? Moira was there, and he wasn't a captive here as he had been in the *Jagannatha*, on the embankment, at Netherholm. He could leave any time.

'Even with a crutch.'

'Yes. Even with.'

'We're happy to have you here for as long as you want to stay. That's what I'm trying, in my clumsy way, to get at.'

'Thank you. But I'm not sure . . .'

'Not sure . . . ?'

Not sure he should stay. 'Not sure what work I can do.' He tapped the crutch.

'Teaching,' Beam said, with a shrug, as if it was the most obvious

272

thing in the world. 'Take that mob of little tearaways you met this evening and knock a bit of knowledge into 'em. Think you could manage that?'

Fen thought about it. Thought he could. But: 'It'd only be until my leg's usable. Would it be worth it?'

'A little bit of learning's better than none. Might stop 'em from turning into *complete* savages. We have books. The library can be your classroom. What d'you say?'

As Fen said yes, OK, he saw Beam grin and nod to himself. Though it might have been a trick of the starlight, he thought he glimpsed not just satisfaction in the grin but also regret, as if Beam was acknowledging some brief, private twinge of pessimism – the impossibility of bringing children up wise and true in a shattered, unmoored country like this one. Fen himself had had to battle with this pessimism on a regular basis. He laid a hand on Beam's shoulder.

'I'll do what I can in the time available.'

Beam did not speak for a while, then said: 'Words we should all live by. "Do what you can in the time available." A good philosophy. Yes.'

Coming back through the dark from a tour of the borough's borders. Mushroom and me crammed together on the Mercedes's passenger seat, which is wider than a single but not quite a double. Craig at the wheel, peering ahead into the headlamps' projected glare. Slow going, the roadways treacherous at night, hidden holes, lumps of debris, a minefield of obstacles. Every so often, a glimpse of a figure scuttling into a doorway or down an alley, scared by the van. Like cockroaches running for cover when the kitchen light comes on. Lewisham eerie after nightfall, fitfully illuminated by the few streetlamps that haven't been vandalised, the occasional stray chink from an uncurtained window, the jump-and-flicker of a dustbin fire. A shadow land. Shadows folded over shadows. King Cunt's kingdom, but after sunset it belongs to others too, or so it seems. Furtive fugitives engaged on errands I don't dare speculate about. Sealed in the white van, we thread our way cautiously. I keep reiterating a small prayer: *thank God Craig's with me, thank God I'm with Craig.*

We've spent the day over by the western edge of Lewisham, where it folds into Peckham. Honor Oak Park, Brockley, and up towards New Cross, St John's. Partly a state visit, partly an intelligence-gathering patrol. Word has come: the Frantiks have finally made their move. And so Craig's been consulting the locals. What have they heard? What have they seen? There are rumours. Running battles around Peckham Rye Common and Nunhead Cemetery. Fires towards the south, down Dulwich way. Nothing substantiated, but no reason to think the rumours aren't true. Everybody, understandably, is pretty anxious. Where reassurance is called for, Craig has reassured. Where scolding is called for, Craig has scolded. King Cunt has the situation under control. Lewisham is not going to be affected. The Frantiks and the Bulldogs have an agreement. O ye of little faith! The King is looking out for his subjects. He has their best interests at heart. Never fret. Never worry.

Beside me, Mushroom picks his nose, coring out a long brown rind of dried snot. Either he thinks I don't see or he doesn't care if I do. He studies the snot, turning it this way and that on his fingertip, then pops it into his mouth. Yum. I really hate Mushroom. But I'd far rather it was him sitting squashed up against me than, say, Neville. Mushroom, at least, is openly repellent. With Neville, it's worse because it's all inside. He makes my skin crawl.

Craig seems all right with what we've found out today. Nothing more or less than he expected. He estimates that Peckham will be fully under the Frantik Posse's control within a fortnight. Those members of the Riot Squad that the Frantiks don't kill, they'll chase out. Some of them, inevitably, will fetch up in Lewisham, where they'll get pretty short shrift from the locals and from the Bulldogs.

The only thing that troubles him – slightly – is the International Community noticing what's happening. It's a slim possibility, but all it takes is a chance flyby, a wink from a spy satellite, and down will come fire and great punishment from heaven. He doesn't give a shit about Peckham getting pounded, but the International Community isn't noted for its pinpoint accuracy. The odd stray missile may land on Lewisham. All the same, a slim possibility. A risk factor he can live with.

At last the gate to the compound comes into view. I never, ever thought I would be glad to see it. It opens as we approach; Craig doesn't even have to decelerate. We glide through, we're in. The gate closes. Safe.

A vague thought: *I'm trapped again*. But it doesn't feel like that any more. It feels like that less than ever. This trip outside has been instructive. Apart from making me realise I'm safer off here in Fort Bulldog than out there in the wilds of the city, it's also made plain the extent to which Craig trusts me. There were several times today when I could have made a bid for freedom. Craig was busy talking to people, and Mushroom, obviously at Craig's instruction, was hovering close by me all the time, but I'm pretty sure I could have given him the slip and outrun him if I'd wanted to. And I'm pretty sure Craig knew that. He also knows I wouldn't leave Zoë behind. But still, he trusts me. And he wanted me to come on the trip. He asked me to. He wanted me to see him at work. And every now and then he's asked me for my opinion. A vote of confidence there.

There's something going on between us, that's for sure. Developing. I just have no idea what it is. The closest I can get to a name for it is an *understanding*. Not like in a Jane Austen novel, though. 'Reader, it seemed that Mr Cunt and I had come to an understanding which would, when in the fullness of time it reached fruition, grant the both of us much happiness.' No, not like that at all. But an understanding nonetheless.

Soon as we've parked the van, Craig heads off to share with the lads the info he's gathered today. Mushroom goes with him. I traipse back to the house. *Our* house.

Lauren's taking a bath, running through a medley of tunes as she lies soaking. *La la, tum de tee, mmm-mmmm, will always love yoooou*. She hasn't got a bad voice, just not as good as she thinks it is. I find Zoë in the living room. She's flicking through one of the magazines she found yesterday. There was a whole stash of them at the back of a cupboard. Time capsules from a healthier, wealthier age. Including an issue of *Siren*, one I worked on. I checked for my name in the contributors' credits. There it was: Deputy Chief Sub-Editor – Moira Grainger. It was like finding an old snapshot of myself. *God yes, that's me*. No, it didn't have quite that sense of familiarity. It was more as if I'd come across a name in print that just so happened to be the same as mine. Who was she, this Moira Grainger? Well-paid, career-obsessed, determined to succeed, enjoying a hectic social life, interested in nothing but the world immediately around her, happy with that. If we met, the two of us, we'd hardly recognise each other.

The magazine Zoë is reading is one of those teen-girl titles. (There were several of them in the stash. A girl Zoë's age must have lived here, before.) Garish fluorescent layout. All those hunky pop stars, those fashion tips, those tricks for losing weight, those photo-love stories. Messages from another planet, to Zoë. When I come into the living room, I see she's looking at the problem page. No agony aunt could offer advice for what *she* has been through.

'How are you, Zoë? How's your day been?'

'Oh, fine. Bit boring.'

Boring's good. Thank heaven for boring. Once again I marvel at how well she's bearing up. She seems to sleep a lot, but otherwise there's little outward sign of trauma. She says she barely remembers anything that happened to her in the recreation zones. Perhaps she believes this. Perhaps it's even true.

She asks how the trip went. I tell her about it. She isn't that interested, but listens anyway.

'Will we be all right? The fighting and that?'

'We'll be fine. Are you hungry?'

'Yeah. Lauren said it's your turn to cook tonight, so we've had to wait for you.'

She accompanies me to the kitchen and for a while just watches as I put on a pan of water to boil and start cutting up some potatoes. I don't know teenage girls. I used to be one but I don't remember it well enough. I don't realise that Zoë wants to talk about something but requires some cue from me to get her going. Eventually, seeing she's not going to receive it, she starts talking anyway.

'Moira . . . I heard something today. Something I wasn't supposed to.'

'Oh?' It comes out more curt than I intended. I'm just about to hear some trivial piece of gossip, aren't I? Some comment Lauren made about me, probably not complimentary.

'Um, yeah. That bloke came round this afternoon. That one who was in Downbourne. He was the leader there. The one with the tooth.'

'Neville.' Now she has my attention. 'He came round? But he knew Craig was out today.'

'He wanted to see American Lauren.' Children have a knack for nicknames. They never come up with anything subtle, but they always get it dead on. 'I was having a snooze. At least, I was till Neville arrived. I woke up when I heard him come in. He asked Lauren if they were alone. She said hold on a moment and came upstairs and looked in on me. I was in your room, because you said I could go in there during the day if I wanted to?'

She's checking to make sure the offer is still valid. She has to sleep on the sofa down here at night, so I made sure with Craig that she could use our bed in the daytime, somewhere more comfortable if she wants a nap. I nod.

'I pretended I was still asleep,' she continues. 'Lauren said my name but I didn't move or anything. So they went out into the garden and they started talking. They thought they were being quiet but I could still hear them, because, well . . .' Here she looks guilty. 'Because I went into the bathroom and listened. The window was open. I knelt right by it. I know I was being nosy, but it was strange him visiting, Neville, because Lauren always says how much she doesn't like him, doesn't she, and here he was being all friendly and nice and wanting to talk to her and that. And I think it was good I listened, because what they talked about was you. You and Craig.'

I hold up a hand – *ssh a moment*. I listen at the kitchen door. Upstairs, Lauren's still warbling away.

'All right. Go on. Just keep it low. Me and Craig?' I still have a vague feeling that this is going to be just gossip, Neville saying he doesn't think much of me, something along those lines. I still have that feeling, but it's more hope than expectation.

'I didn't catch every single word of it,' Zoë says. 'They *were* being quiet. Especially Neville. But they chatted about this and that for a while and then he asked Lauren about you, what she thought about you, and she said . . . you're not her favourite person in the world.'

Can't fault Zoë for her discretion. I'm sure what Lauren said about me was a lot less polite. 'Well, she isn't mine either, so that's all right.'

'She said she thinks you're bad for Craig.'

'Did she say why?'

'She might've. I missed a bit. Someone in one of the other houses turned on some music very loud, then turned it down, and then she was talking about me, not you any more, about how it was a "pain in the ass" having me here because the house isn't big enough for all of us. And Neville said yeah, like he didn't really care, and then he started going on about the other night, you know, at the houses where all the women are, when you and Craig came, and there was that arguing because I'd . . .' She shies away from mentioning what she did. She doesn't want to think about it. 'He said because of me you'd made Craig look stupid. Stupid and . . . "pussy-whipped"?'

'It's another way of saying stupid.'

'Oh.' Not quite convinced, but she gives me the benefit of the doubt. 'And he said a lot of "the boys" have been grumbling about you. And about Craig. Apparently they think he should never have made a pact with that lot in Camberwell, and he's losing his edge. They aren't respecting him as much as they used to.'

Is that true? Or is it just what Neville wants to believe? 'I bet Lauren stood up for Craig.'

'Well, she did, but it was funny because it was like she really had to try. Like her heart wasn't in it. She said she was surprised by herself but even *she* was beginning to wonder about him. And she said she thought you were to blame. She said if there was some way to get rid of you . . .'

A soft, sudden chill. 'Get rid of me?'

'I don't think that was exactly her words. Maybe get you out of the house. Away from Craig. Anyhow, Neville said he didn't think Craig would stand for that, and besides the problem was more him than you, and Lauren said, "There's a problem?" and Neville said, "There's definitely a problem." I remember that clearly. "There's definitely a problem." And Lauren had a cigarette then because she needed to think, she said. And while she was thinking, Neville went on about the Bulldogs getting more and more unhappy with the way things are being run here, and about how there's talk of maybe someone should make a challenge for the leadership, and about how if that was going to happen then now would be a good time, or soon, while this

Peckham business is going on, while Craig's distracted. And . . . That's about all I can remember. Yeah.'

'You're sure? Nothing else?'

'Yeah. At the end, though, Lauren was being much nicer to Neville than when he arrived. When he arrived she was all "Craig's not in, what do you want?" but when she was showing him out she was more "Well, you know, I'm glad you came and told me all this, I don't know if there's much we can do but maybe we should have another chat soon, honey". She didn't say "honey" actually, but it was kind of like when she *does* say "honey", you know, when she's talking to Craig, all soft and caring.'

Good old Lauren. I doubt she really believes the King's throne is under threat. I certainly don't think it is, and she's ten times more loyal to him than I am. But still, it never hurts to keep on the pretender's good side. Just in case.

'Does this mean you're in trouble, Moira? Over what you did for me?'

'I don't think so.'

'Because if you are, I'm really sorry.'

'Don't worry about it.'

'What about Craig? Is *he* in trouble?'

'If he is, it's nothing he can't handle.'

'So are you going to tell him?'

A very good question. Am I?

'I don't know, Zoë. We'll have to see.'

They tested him at first, but this was no more than he expected. It was what children, in groups, did when someone new was put in charge of them. That exploratory prod-and-probe. *How much can we get away with?* The trick, he knew, was not to let them rile him. Rise above it. Assert his authority gently, calmly. Allow them some leeway to begin with, not put them in their place too soon, give them the sense that he was patient, amenable; draw them up to his tolerance threshold and slightly over, so that they would never be quite sure where it was, then snap them back down with a single, sharp, well-chosen comment. That was how it worked. That was how you turned a mob into a class.

In this instance, it did not work.

The seven children at Fairfield Hall were not a *tabula rasa*. That much Fen swiftly established. From the youngest, five, to the oldest, thirteen, they were numerate and literate. Some parental educating had gone on so he did not have to start from scratch, which was a relief. But they were part-feral, too. With the adults preoccupied with planting and cultivating and gathering, pickling and pre-serving and cold-storing, herding and hewing and generally keeping on top of the basic necessities of existence, the children had been left pretty much to their own devices. And children who have been left to their own devices will, as Golding, Barrie, Ballard and others have shown, run wild.

So they did not like being cooped up every morning in the library with Fen. They did not like being read to and having to read. Being made to do sums. Being made to learn about England and Europe and the other nations and continents of the world. Being asked to wrap their tongues around the strange new syllables of French and German. Being expected to find interesting such outlandishly irrelevant concepts as atoms and history and moon landings and monarchic succession. Where was the fun in all that? It wasn't anywhere near as exciting as, say, climbing a tree to its topmost branches, or watching a lamb being born or slaughtered, or damming up the stream, or swimming starkers in the lake, or investigating the Hall's many attics with their plethora of dust-coated artefacts (always something new and inexplicable to discover). The children fidgeted and champed and chafed, and at the end of each morning, when Fen finally allowed them to leave, they exploded out of the library like peas out of a malfunctioning pressure cooker.

He thought the problem would right itself with time. If he just hung on, the children would soon come to realise that the lessons were to their benefit.

Then they started not turning up.

The first time, it was just the one absentee, the eldest child there, the leader of the pack, Christopher. Fen decided not to waste time looking for him. The boy could be anywhere. He taught his remaining six pupils as normal, as if nothing was awry, and later, when Christopher put in an appearance at lunch, he took him aside and had a gentle word. Shouldn't set a bad example to the rest, et cetera.

The following day, Christopher dutifully showed up, but three of the others were missing. This was unacceptable. Fen enlisted the four attendees' aid in finding them. The hunt took up most of the morning, and everyone except Fen found it hilarious. Up in the attics, out among the rhododendra, down by the stables – to the children it was one big romp, a supervised version of the games they normally played. One after another the truants were rounded up, and in the hour remaining before lunch Fen drilled the class on *être*, *avoir* and *aller*, making them chant the conjugations till they, and he, were heartily sick of irregular French verbs.

'I'm not sure about this,' he confessed to Beam that afternoon. They were down in the damp of the wine cellar – vintage-packed vault leading to vintage-packed vault, like the tomb of some bibulous pharaoh. 'I don't know if it isn't too late for these kids.'

'Hmmm,' said Beam. It was unclear whether he was musing on what Fen had just said or on the bottle of Beaujolais whose label he was examining by torchlight.

'They're just not responding to me. They're bright, all of them, very bright, but they've no discipline, no attention span.'

'Perhaps . . .' Beam said.

'Perhaps . . . ?'

'Or perhaps not.' Beam returned the bottle to its place in the rack. 'Too flowery. One needs something "bigger" with lamb casserole.'

Beam, to Fen's chagrin, did not seem in a mood to discuss the subject of the children's education. It wasn't until they were leaving the cellar, each carrying as many bottles of Cabernet Sauvignon as he could, that Beam gave any indication he had been listening to Fen at all, and then all he said was: 'Keep at it, old chap. I know you can do it. Be prepared to meet them halfway.'

Fen was of the opinion that he had already met the children halfway. Had, indeed, gone further than that. But he resolved to persevere with the lessons. He owed it to Beam to keep trying, at least.

The next morning, all seven pupils failed to show. They had got it into their heads that hiding from their teacher was not only an enjoyable exercise but an honourable one as well, and perhaps even an educational one. They set themselves the goal of finding places to stow away that were so abstruse, so cunning, that they would remain undiscovered all morning. It was a test of their wits against Fen's, their ingenuity versus his perspicacity.

They won. And, in another sense, they lost.

Fen did not go looking for them. He stayed in the library, quietly thumbing through a copy of *The Jungle Book*. He stayed there even through lunch. When he didn't appear for the meal, and his absence was remarked upon by the adults, the children exchanged questioning glances. Afterwards, *they* went searching for *him*. Perhaps he had chosen to turn the tables. Perhaps *he* had gone hiding, expecting to be found.

The last place any of them thought to look, because it seemed too obvious a place for their teacher to hide, was the room in which he taught them. But one by one they eventually wound up at the library, having exhausted all other possibilities. Each entered, saw Fen sitting, calmly reading, and went straight to the big table in the middle of the room and pulled up a chair. They none of them could understand why, precisely, they did this. Something to do with the way Fen had been waiting for them, the way he said nothing when they came in, the way this made them feel. Awkward. A bit unhappy. They sensed they had hurt his feelings. They had never meant to hurt his feelings.

From then on, there was no more playing truant. A lesson of a different kind had been taught, and learned. The children began to take to Fen, and to tutelage. They recognised that he had out-psyched them, and it earned him their admiration. If he could beat them at their own game like that, he must have *something* going for him, therefore his lessons must have *something* going for them too, therefore it might be wise to pay attention.

For his part, Fen began tailoring his usual teaching style to accommodate this group of children's particular waywardness. He took them out of the library whenever he could, giving them fresh air and sunshine and a sense, if not the actuality, of freedom. He encouraged exploration of the environment, drawing instructive examples from trees and fields and buildings and animals and the contents of the Hall's attics. He chaired round-table discussions, nudging the proceedings along with simple, reflexive questions that were intended to lead his pupils to an understanding of their own ignorance – the Socratic method. He kept rote-learning to a minimum. And he began to enjoy his job in a way he had not for years. At Downbourne teaching had become, while not a chore, something he did only because he was not fitted for much else. Sometimes, especially after Moira lost the babies, he had had to drag himself to school in the mornings. What good was it, he had wondered, instilling knowledge in kids who might never get the chance to make use of it. The hope of every Englander was that present circumstances could not pertain for ever. That was just about all that kept people going, belief in an inevitable end to the hardships and exigencies of post-Gamble life. But what if there was never going to be any end? What if the International Community kept up its war of attrition indefinitely, whittling and whittling until England was no more? Why bother, if that was the case? Why bother teaching? Why bother doing anything? He had grappled with these doubts. Everyone had to. And most of the time he had got the better of them, but sometimes they had got the better of him.

Now, he was sure – as sure as he could be – that his efforts were not in vain. Christopher, Toby, Megan, little Scarlett – he felt them burgeoning under his care. Hungry young minds opening like flowers. William, who had a surreal sense of humour. Gap-toothed Serena, away in her own little world half the time. The aptly-named Storm, with his touchpaper temper. Fen forged a relationship with them closer than the usual teacher-and-class. The seven-strong gang embraced him. He became one of them, their eighth member and, Christopher graciously abdicating the role, their leader. He assumed responsibility for organising their afternoons as well as their mornings. A tennis racquet and ball, unearthed by Beam at Fen's request, provided – along with some wooden fence-stakes – the wherewithal for games of cricket and rounders. Crutch-hampered, Fen umpired. The other adults postponed their after-lunch labours in order to spectate. Usually one of them could be persuaded to take part, making up numbers so that there were two even teams. On a couple of occasions the adult was Beam himself. Not much of a runner, it must be said, but the children made allowances, fielding in slow motion so as to give him time to waddle and huff his way between the wickets or from rounders post to rounders post. Crap and Piss liked to join in too, but since their involvement invariably culminated in one or other of them making off with the ball and refusing to give it up, it was soon agreed that they be banished indoors for the duration of play.

Dealing with the children full-time, being one of them, took a lot out of Fen. Every night, he would clump upstairs to bed exhausted, his left leg a symphony of aches. His room lay at the far end of the Hall's west wing, two doors down from where Megan and her parents, Ben and Sally, were quartered. He slept in a creaking four-poster with a capacious trough in the middle of its mattress. He never closed the curtains. He liked to drift off watching the night outside, pure and ancient, with the window casements left open so as to invite in breezes and the countryside's whisperings.

Gradually the sufferings he had endured prior to arriving at the Hall began to fade, slipping into that recess of memory in which everything seems to have been exaggerated and you're pretty certain that what happened to you was nowhere near as bad as it felt at the time. He could almost laugh now about being beaten up by a Bulldog, and about the non-physical, though no less thorough-going, assault he had undergone at the hands of the Salterites. Ordeals were metamorphosising into anecdotes. He was incorporating his recent experiences, becoming someone shaped by them rather than someone still reeling from them. It was amazing what a difference a few days, a regularly filled belly, beautiful surroundings, and a renewed sense of job satisfaction, could make. It was as if he had entered a whole new country; had, just a handful of miles from the railway embankment and Netherholm College, crossed a border into a realm so utterly unlike either of those places that it was hard sometimes to believe it even existed.

There has to be a catch. Something, somehow, has to be wrong with this situation.

But the days passed and no fly garnished the ointment, no bump appeared in the road, no serpent hissed in Eden. Fairfield Hall was nothing other than it appeared to be, and thank heavens for that.

For Fen felt he had found something here. Something like home, but not quite. Something more fundamental than that.

Increasingly he found himself thinking, *I could stay here.*
Not just till his leg was better.
I could stay here for good.

The four Riot Squadders kneel on the ground and weep and beg for their lives.

You'd think they were tough nuts, to judge by their thick necks, their combat trousers and boots, the ragged red 'R' of scar tissue that each of them sports on the underside of his left forearm, razor-etched there. Hard as nails. You'd think they wouldn't even know *how* to cry. But they're crying now, like four man-sized babies. Blubbing and pleading with King Cunt. The Frantiks have overrun Peckham, they tell him. They're killing any Riot Squadders they find. The 'R' on their arms is as good as a death sentence. Please, they implore. They'll do anything. Join the Bulldogs, anything. Just please spare them.

Unfortunately for them, Craig isn't going to. Unfortunately for Craig, he has no choice in the matter.

It wasn't easy, letting him know about Neville's conversation with Lauren. It wasn't easy finding a way and an opportunity to broach the subject. For one thing, he's been hellishly busy with the Peckham situation this past couple of weeks – sifting through the reports coming in from the borough border, sending out Bulldog patrols both to repel fleeing Riot Squad members and as a show of strength to reassure the local populace, keeping channels of communication open with the Frantik Posse, marshalling his resources so that he'll be able to take advantage of the Riot Squad's capitulation when it comes (and it's pretty much a foregone conclusion now; Craig just requires confirmation of the fact from the Frantiks themselves). We've barely had a quiet moment together, he and I, since the Frantiks' attack was launched. At night, he comes to bed so late that I'm already asleep, and, if I happen to be awake, he zonks out as soon as his head hits the pillow, without time for much more than a mumbled 'g'night'.

But the problem didn't only lie with how busy he's been. It lay with me, too. The number of times I almost came out and told him, and then balked. Neville's his friend, his best mate. Would he believe me if I told him his schoolboy pal was plotting against him? And my source being Zoë – it's not as if she doesn't have an axe to grind.

Neville was the one who took her captive in the first place, the one who offered to beat her up at the recreation zones when Craig wouldn't. *I* have no reason to think she made up the stuff she heard, but Craig might.

There was never the right moment.

Then there was.

Last night.

It wasn't premeditated.

In fact, nothing about last night was premeditated.

It just happened.

And I'm not ashamed of it. Any of it.

It was the way Craig looked as he was getting undressed. The hour was late, past one, and he thought I was asleep and so, as usual, he didn't turn on the main bedroom light, just left the bedroom door open and used the light coming in from the landing to see by. Courteous.

And it was the tiredness of his actions, the clumsy way he removed his football shirt, fumbling it over his head as though it was a conundrum whose solution he could not quite fathom.

And it was the contours of his torso – that magnificent torso – combined with the slight stoop in his shoulders that I hadn't noticed there before: the weight of care, the burden of leadership.

And it was the lost look on his face, the expression people get when the only thing that'll help them is the oblivion of sleep.

I felt sorry for him.

I wasn't scared of him, not now, not any more.

I wanted to comfort him.

It just happened.

He got into bed. I took the initiative. I reached across. My hand between his legs. Took hold of him. Kindled him. Quickened him. Straddled him. Rode him. It was over with in no time. He took part, distantly, a little puzzled, but his hands were strong on me, and the digging grip of his fingers deepened, and he gasped, and it was over with. I can't say I found it earthshattering, but I can't deny there was pleasure in it. The sight of his face relaxing afterwards, tension ebbing out, tightness unclenching. This giant underneath me, eased by my ministrations.

I thought that, after I rolled off him, he would doze off straight away, but he didn't.

'You know why I'm called King Cunt, Moira?' he said, after a minute or so of silence.

'You're "more of a cunt than anyone else".'

'Yeah. Yeah, that's what I tell people. It's less complicated. Saves bother. It's not really why, though.'

For one terrible moment I think he's going to start boasting about his sexual prowess. Talk about inappropriate!

But he says: 'You've heard of King Canute, right? Course you have. Bloke who sat on a beach, commanded the tide to go back, got his feet wet. Every schoolkid knows that story. Well, I read about him once, in a magazine, or maybe a book. Or maybe it was something I saw on the telly. Can't remember. Anyway, apparently the way we spell his name isn't the way his name's supposed to be spelled. You know, we spell it "can-yoot", but actually in Norwegian or whatever, it's "ker-nut". See, en, you, tee. Which, when written down, looks a lot like "cunt". Just swap the middle two letters round. Amazing what a difference swapping two letters round can make to a word. And I thought it was quite funny. "King Cunt". It just stuck in my head. One of those things you don't forget. One of those things you tuck away for later use and you don't know why. And then, when things started falling apart a few years back . . . It was like a tide. A tide of chaos. Remember?'

I remember.

'Crashing over everything. The country going mad. England going under. And as things began to fall apart, I realised . . . If I say I realised my destiny, I'll sound like a total ponce. I realised what I had to do. Somebody had to pull things together. Somebody had to try and hold back that tide. But it had to be by force. That was the only way it could be done. Just words alone, grand gestures, wouldn't work.'

'As King Canute showed.'

'Yeah. Exactly. And I knew that, even by force, I couldn't bring the whole of London under control, let alone the whole country.' He laughs at the absurdity of *that*, which suggests to me that at one point he did consider it. 'But maybe a small area of London. Maybe where I lived, here, Lewisham. Maybe with foot-soldiers under me, a small army, I could do it. I wasn't alone in having this idea, of course. The Unlucky Gamble gave rise to a lot of people like me, especially in the big cities. Selected us, in a way. Remade us. Moulded us into the thing we had to be. People who under other circumstances probably wouldn't ever have made much of an impact on the world – suddenly it was our time. We were needed. Here, in London, we were needed most of all. And so I stopped being Craig Smith and started being someone else.'

'King Cunt.'

'Seemed like the right name for the job. And it worked. The whole thing worked. The name, what I wanted to do. It wasn't easy. God, all that fighting, that staking out territory and defending it. Getting the Bulldogs together, moulding them into shape, giving them an identity they could be proud of. And then seeing off other gangs. One long constant struggle. But eventually the effort paid off and things settled down, and I'd achieved something. I knew it. I'd brought some stability and order back into people's lives. I hadn't made things perfect again, but King Cunt had done what King Canute couldn't do. He'd held back the tide. Only, now it looks like . . .'

All at once he seemed to be speaking from deep inside himself, his voice thick, cracked with exhaustion.

'I'm trying to keep it all together, Moira,' he said. 'You can see that, can't you? I'm trying to, but it's not easy. It's not enough just to make the right decisions. You have to make the *best* decisions. All the time. Or else you lose respect, and then you lose everything.'

And I realised I'd never heard him so vulnerable.

'They want you to be infallible, and if you're not, they'll turn on you. One wrong move is all it takes, and it's gone. Everything you've worked for, fought for. Gone.'

Or so lonely. I never realised how lonely till then.

'You think you have trust. You don't. All you have is whatever people find it convenient to give you.'

Now.

'I think there's something you should know about Neville . . .' I began.

I didn't have to say much more.

Craig wasn't angry. I'd expected rage, I'd expected cursing, but all that came was bitter acknowledgement. He told me how he'd been aware for some time that all was not right within the Bulldog ranks. He told me that Neville was the main source of the unrest, Neville waging a covert campaign against him, Neville spreading discontent through the compound, but doing it quietly, subtly, insidiously, planting a seed of doubt here, a seed of doubt there, always with the knowledge that, as King Cunt's best friend and second-in-command, he was above suspicion, no one in their right mind would believe *him* capable of treachery, not *Neville*.

Craig, it transpired, had known about all this for quite some while.

And when I asked him why he hadn't taken steps to remedy the situation, he said he couldn't, at least not openly. 'The lads see me and Neville as inseparable. He's been with me right from the very beginning. I can't turn on him. I'd be finished for sure if I did.

Reputation would be shot to shit. The only way I can handle what he's doing is by being better than ever at my job. Keep the lads on my side by continuing to set an example.'

And I saw then – and see even more clearly right now, with the four captured Riot Squadders awaiting King Cunt's verdict on whether they are to live or die – how well Neville has manipulated things. He's manoeuvred Craig onto a knife-edge pathway, with a sheer precipice either side. Craig has no choice but to keep going forwards, to prove himself time and time again to the Bulldogs, to be more and more the King Cunt they expect him to be, ruthless leader, hardest of the hard, to continue to pull off this precarious balancing act. Because the slightest misstep now, and he will fall.

And Zoë. She, I understand now, was part of it, part of Neville's scheme. A test. A provocation. How would King Cunt react when he found a fifteen-year-old in the recreation zones? He reacted, with my help, according to his sense of morality . . . and the decision gave Neville yet more ammunition against him.

Which is why these four members of the Peckham Riot Squad have to die. It's their lives against Craig's credibility. And while he could show leniency towards a fifteen-year-old girl and just about get away with it, he can't do the same with members of a rival gang.

It's there in the Bulldogs' eyes as they look on. It was there before, but I mistook it for admiration. It's zeal. Fanaticism. Thanks to Neville's machinations, the Bulldogs now believe in King Cunt, the ideal, far more than in King Cunt, the man.

Which makes him more, not less, vulnerable. A man cannot disappoint. An ideal can.

The Bulldogs need Craig to be what they want him to be. As they stand here in a ring around the Riot Squadders, restless, bloodthirsty, they're waiting for King Cunt to give the word, waiting for him to demonstrate that he truly deserves their worship.

And he does give the word.

Because, this time around, he has no choice.

'Do it.'

There's a roar of approval, and the Bulldogs move in on the four Riot Squadders.

The compound was formerly a housing estate. There are lampposts. The Bulldogs have rope.

I don't stay to watch. Neither does Craig. As the Riot Squadders are hauled off struggling and screaming, he stalks away, head down, not looking at me, not looking at anyone. I go with him, but I might as well be walking alone.

It doesn't take long. I hear, behind me, four separate sets of jeers and yells, and then it's over with.

Afterwards, a sated silence descends on the compound.

The British Bulldogs are content again.

For now.

It got better.

Christopher's mother, Jessica Myers, was a divorcee. At first Fen assumed she was Beam's girlfriend. The two flirted constantly, teased each other brutally, were often to be found in a conspiratorial clinch, giggling over some private joke. She was a small, robust woman, very pretty, with big round eyes that gave her a look of perpetual wonderment. (Fen found out later she was severely short-sighted but too vain for spectacles.) Among her faults, she had a laugh which, had she been any less pretty, would have made you want to throttle her. Indeed, when she laughed it sounded as though she *was* being throttled. Torture to listen to. She was, moreover, one of the most artless and tactless people Fen had ever met.

And yet, and yet . . .

It soon became clear to him that she was not Beam's girlfriend. She and Beam had known each other since childhood. Theirs was an intricate intimacy, established during innocence and adolescence, playful and sexually charged but always quite perfectly platonic.

And as the only unattached woman at the Hall, it was not long before she was sizing Fen up as a potential partner. She knew about Moira, of course, but Fen was nonetheless, to all intents and purposes, unattached too. It was not as if Moira was anywhere nearby. London was another country, another *world*. Nor was it as if Fen was likely to be departing for the capital any day soon. That, indeed, was looking an ever more remote prospect. Everyone at the Hall could see that. They could see how Fen was settling in, how comfortable he was becoming in his role as the children's pedago-gue-cum-ringleader. He was fitting quite nicely, thank you, into the warp and weft of Fairfield life. They could sense his growing desire to remain, his dwindling eagerness to leave. He was mentioning Moira and London less and less. His mission, his quest, was receding in importance. Perhaps he had already abandoned it but had yet to admit this to himself.

So, by this way of thinking, Jessica was perfectly entitled to go after him if she wanted to. And he, in turn, was perfectly entitled to reciprocate.

He didn't, though. At least, not to begin with. He was flattered by her advances. Jessica was, her laugh notwithstanding, an enticing proposition, and it gave him a delicious and queerly nostalgic thrill to be the target of a female's attentions once again. As a husband, you kind of got out of the habit of thinking that just any woman could find you sexually desirable. You took it for granted that your wife did, and there seemed little need to consider the prospects any further than that. To be reminded that you were appealing to a broader section of womankind, that you were, besides all else, a *man* – this was not an unpleasurable thing.

All the same, he *was* married, that fact had not changed, so for a while he kept Jessica at arm's length, and this he did through a combination of evasion and obtuseness. He pretended to be oblivious to her interest in him. Though her intentions could not have been more obvious, nor her overtures less subtle, he still managed to give the impression that he had no idea what she was up to. When, for example, she told him that there was nothing sexier than a man who got on well with kids, he replied, 'And nothing more likely to get that man arrested.' When she complained one evening about the size of her bed – 'I can't think of anything more depressing than a double bed with only one person to occupy it' – he suggested she get crap and piss to join her in it. When she expounded a philosophy to the effect that nowadays, with England in the precarious state it was in, people shouldn't hang about, there was no point putting off till tomorrow what you could do today, 'gather ye rosebuds' and all that, Fen's reply was: 'You know, I always used to think *carpe diem* was Latin for "death to fishes!".'

There was, he could not deny, some delight to be had in frustrating his admirer like this, in being so deliberately knuckleheaded. However, the fun wore thin pretty quickly, and at the back of his mind there was always that feeling of *why not?* Jessica fancied him. She was lonely. She was lovely. Moira was miles away and probably lost to him for ever; had, in a sense, been lost to him a long time back. Why not take advantage of what Jessica was offering? Why not treat himself to her? Why not? Why the damn hell not?

Late on a drizzly Sunday afternoon, Fen and Beam were playing billiards in the games room. Low leaden light came in through the rain-ticked windows. Crap and Piss were sprawled in a corner, with only the occasional whistling sigh from either to prove they weren't completely comatose. Throughout the house there was a similar air of profound repose. Sunday was, by Beam's decree, a day of rest. No work, other than culinary-related activities, could be done on a Sunday.

'A lack of real responsibility,' Beam said, squaring up for his next shot. 'That's always been the problem.' With a deft, deceptively soft thrust of his cue he ricocheted the red ball into one of the side pockets. 'Fourteen.'

Fen fished the ball out of the pocket and placed it on its spot. This task, along with supervision of the scoreboard, was pretty much the extent of his involvement in the game. Beam was a billiards expert, his skills honed by a lifetime of practice on this very table. Fen had played pub pool a few times, but to no great success, and anyway billiards, as Beam said, was an altogether higher order of game, as far removed from pool as Picasso is from painting-by-numbers. A game of refinement, of space and angles, of rebounds and strategy and a wonderfully pure simplicity. A game that demanded an archer's eye and a surgeon's hand. Whereas pool – well, pool was, for want of a better word, *American*.

'You mean politicians aren't directly accountable for anything they do,' Fen said.

'Precisely. Precisely.' Beam moved around the table, sized up his options, leaned over, and assertively scored a cannon. 'Take this last lot we had,' he said, as the balls rolled to a rest. 'Perfect example. The ones who buggered everything up for everybody. The ones to blame for the mess this country's in. Where are they now, eh?'

'Bermuda, last I heard.'

'Exactly. Bermuda. Holed up in the tropics. Soaking up the sun while the rest of us get shat on.'

' "Parliament in exile".'

'Ah, yes.' Beam recognised the quotation, part of the speech made by the Prime Minister shortly before the House of Commons voted *nem. con.* to up stakes and relocate to the Caribbean.

' "Waiting until national circumstances are conducive to the re-establishment of effective control",' Fen added.

'Ha!' Beam careened his cue ball off Fen's and into a corner pocket. 'Eighteen.' He stepped back, appraising, while Fen returned the ball to the baize. 'Always were a lying, weaselly lot, weren't they? Trouble is, that's par for the course where politicians are concerned. Like I said, a lack of real responsibility. Tell me, when was the last time you saw a cabinet minister get it in the neck because of some poor decision he made, some catastrophic error of judgement that ruined dozens, perhaps even hundreds of lives? I mean *really* get it in the neck?' He allowed Fen a second to answer, or rather, not answer. 'I'll tell you. Never. At worst he might have had to resign, but even then you can bet there'd be some other government post waiting for him, or a seat on the board of a blue-chip corporation, a job in broadcasting, a lucrative publishing deal for his memoirs. Something like that to cushion his fall. And he might show remorse for his mistakes, might even *feel* remorse, but he's still got away scot-free while the people he shafted are left to suffer. If the owner of a business screws up, his livelihood is on the line, isn't it? If a sea captain blunders, his ship goes down and most likely him with it. But a cabinet minister?' He bent down, his belly doubling over the cushion, and lined up his cue. 'See my point?'

Fen dutifully asked the question he knew Beam wanted him to ask. 'So how would you do it? How would you go about introducing a level of accountability into government?'

Beam stroked the cue back and forth, as if storing up kinetic energy for the shot. 'Simple. Link every politician's fortunes intimately with those of the nation. If a Chancellor of the Exchequer, say, wastes taxpayers' money recklessly – and Chancellors of the Exchequer usually do – then instead of him using nothing but more taxpayers' money to make up the loss, he ought to have to contribute a significant sum out of his own pocket. And the Defence Secretary. It should be decreed that, in the event of war, the Defence Secretary's nearest and dearest are flown straight to the front line. That way, as it's *his* next of kin at risk rather than someone else's, he'll be much more inclined to choose diplomatic resolution over conflict. And the Home Secretary should be made to live in the most run-down, most crime-ridden housing estate in the land. Policing problems would be solved in no time!' At last Beam unleashed the shot, and there was a ripple of clacks as his cue ball met both the other balls and all three scattered across the table, rebounded chaotically and collided again. 'Double cannon. Twenty-two.'

'And the Health Secretary should never be allowed to go private for an operation,' said Fen.

'Exactly.'

'The Transport Minister should have to travel everywhere by bus or train.'

'See? It's a very easy system to get the hang of.'

'Never work.'

'Why not?'

'Nobody'd be willing to become a politician under those conditions.'

'Oh, I'm not saying it should be all stick. There'd be carrot as well. Financial incentives. Bonus payouts for particularly commendable pieces of governance.'

'Decided on how? By whom?'

'An administrative body drawn from a representative cross-section of the electorate. They'd deliver annual reports on the government's performance and mete out rewards and punishments as they saw fit. What I think you'd get, you see, if this scheme were put into action, is a better class of politician. Men and women keen to do their best, to do what's right instead of what's expedient.'

'I'm getting the distinct impression you don't think much of politicians.'

'Line 'em all up and shoot 'em,' Beam said cheerfully. 'Of course, I don't ever expect this little utopian fantasy of mine to come to pass. It's just a dream I have. A dream of leaders who do us justice rather than do us over.' He fired off a quick shot which unaccountably failed to score and thus brought his break to an end. 'Your turn, old chap.'

Fen picked up his cue and hobbled over to the table. He had recently graduated from the crutch to a walking stick – a walking stick which, like almost everything else at Fairfield, came with a detailed provenance, an oral history. Beam's Great Aunt Ernestine had been its first user. Beam's father had availed himself of it next, as his arthritis set in. A venerable stick, a well-scuffed stick, now helping a third generation of the halt and lame to get about. Fen hooked it on the edge of the table by its deerhorn handle and, taking his weight on his good leg, crouched down with the cue.

'Bit of topspin,' Beam advised, and it was good advice. 'Well done!'

The game proceeded, and so did Beam's disquisition on leadership. For a model of sensible ruling, he said, one only had to consider the beehive, specifically the type he used, the British National Hive, in which the queen was confined to the bottom section, the brood chamber, by means of a partition which had holes in it big enough to let drones and workers through but not the queen herself, who was, of course, of somewhat larger proportions. Down there in the brood chamber, Her Majesty had two basic functions. One was to squeeze out eggs – up to a couple of thousand per day during spring, the equivalent of her own body weight – and the other was to send out a continuous pheromone signal informing her loyal subjects that she was alive and well. ('Like a Christmas Day message,' Beam said, 'all the time.') In other words, the queen was both the hive's figurehead and its most menial member. She was stuck in the basement with nothing to do except procreate and keep up morale. A true servant of the people.

'And you think a system like that would work with humans?' said Fen.

'Possibly. Possibly not. It's the interdependence of it that I find so alluring. The queen has a vested interest in the welfare of her subjects and vice versa. They cosset her, keep her sweet, and in return she works harder than any of them. She's both above and below them in the social order. Interesting, eh?'

Fen nodded, unconvinced. 'With the greatest of respect, Beam . . .'

'Oh dear, *that* euphemism.'

'. . . the trouble with nature analogies is that you can find one to apply to any situation, can't you, and that makes them essentially valueless. You can say a beehive is a good model for human society, and someone else can say yes, but a pride of lions is too. You know, the females do all the hunting and rearing while the males loll around, rousing themselves for a mating session every so often. Or a school of fish, which has no leaders at all and operates as a kind of mass entity, every member playing an equal part – pure communism. Or a flock of migrating geese, each taking it in turns at the head of the formation, doing its stint of the navigating and pace-setting, like a committee with a rotating chairmanship. Nature analogies are like biblical quotations in that respect. There's one to suit every occasion.'

Beam found this highly amusing. He pointed his cue at Fen. 'I *do* like you, Fen!' he exclaimed, chuckling. 'Liked you the moment I laid eyes on you. You've a good heart and a good brain and you're not afraid to use either. I hardly need add that everyone else here likes you too. Apart from anything, the difference you've made with those children is remarkable. What is it, a month? And they're scarcely recognisable as the urchins who used to tear around the place and get up to no end of trouble. Quiet and thoughtful and polite as can be. Everyone's come up and said to me how much they appreciate what you've done. What you're doing.'

'That's very nice to hear. Thank you.'

Beam rested the end of the cue on the floor and leaned on it like a shepherd on his crook. His face was serious now, as serious as Fen had ever seen it. 'But I think the thing we all want to know, old chap, is whether you plan to stay on or not. Your leg's definitely on the mend. I'd say you could be on your way in a fortnight or so. Now, I'm not expecting you to give me an answer right here and now. There's a lot for you to consider, I understand that. For my own selfish reasons I'd like to think you *are* going to stay, but that's not to put pressure on you or anything. Just a statement of fact. And, my God, it's your wife up there in London, and no one admires you more than I do for trying to go after her and bring her home. You're a braver man than I am, Gunga Din. But if you've come to the conclusion that rescuing her is a lost cause, no one here's going to fault you for it. Quite the opposite. And the children *do* think that you're the best thing since sliced bread. And' – Beam winked – 'it's no secret that there's a certain lady here who's quite smitten with you. What I'm getting at is, you have good reasons for going and good reasons for not going, Fen, and I think now's the time for you to ask yourself, frankly, honestly, which you have more of.'

A visit from Eazy-K.

The head of the Frantik Posse is tall, languid, graceful, and cocky (as well he might be, given that he's just masterminded the takeover of a neighbouring borough). He wears a dark blue bandanna tied around his head, gypsy-fashion. So do the two lieutenants he's brought with him. His eyes are profoundly bloodshot, their black irises surrounded by flaring coronas of red. He greets Craig with a complex configuration of handshakes. 'My brother.' He's all smiles and back-pats and compliments.

Then he and Craig disappear into the dining room together for a powwow. Eazy-K's two lieutenants are left to loiter in the living room with Neville and Mushroom. There are attempts at idle chitchat. They come to nothing. There's little love lost here. The roots of tribal rivalry run too deep.

As the women of the household, Lauren, Zoë and I are called on to play happy hostess. *Tea? Coffee? Snack of some kind?* 'I'll have *you*,' one of Eazy-K's men replies, leering at Zoë, a great creamy grin on his face. I pull Zoë out of the room before she, or I, can do something we might regret.

The powwow goes on for half an hour. Voices in the dining room rise. Tension in the living room grows. Another quarter of an hour. Then Craig comes out, fuming. Eazy-K saunters out after him. 'Don't take it bad, man,' he says. 'We don't want much.'

Craig whirls, and for one terrible moment it looks like he's going to hit Eazy-K, and I envision an explosion of violence, Bulldogs and Frantiks at each other's throats, with Zoë and me caught in the crossfire.

'We had,' Craig says, spitting out the words, 'a deal.'

'Still do,' comes the reply. 'Only, it's changed a lickle bit.'

'I swore blood loyalty to the Posse.'

Eazy-K shrugs. 'Yeah, well. You in't the right colour, knowah mean?'

'You're fucking with the wrong person here, Eazy. You do realise that, don't you?'

'I ain't fucking with nobody, man. I come here, I been straight with you . . . It ain't *my* problem you don't like what I'm offering.'

'I think you'd better go.' Craig jerks a thumb. 'Go on, get the fuck out.'

Eazy-K makes an air-patting gesture, his long fingers splayed. 'OK, OK. I can see you need some time to think about this.'

'I don't need any time. You try anything you shouldn't, and it's war. Right? Can I make myself any clearer?'

Eazy-K and his lieutenants leave the house, swaggering back to the stereo-on-wheels they arrived in. They drive out of the compound with rap music on at full volume, the car throbbing like a Titan's pulsebeat.

Tight-lipped, terse, Craig sketches us in on the content of his and Eazy-K's discussion.

The Frantiks, it turns out, want some of Lewisham. They want Brockley. They have Peckham and they've decided to extend their new territory a little further east. They want to make Brockley Road the boundary between their turf and the Bulldogs'. Until now, the boundary between Peckham and Lewisham has always been, by common consent, the railway line.

'No fucking way!' exclaims Mushroom.

'Told you so,' says Neville.

'They wouldn't dare,' I say.

'Who asked *you*?' Neville snaps.

'Shut your face, Nev,' says Craig.

Neville doesn't bat an eyelid. 'I told you you should never have trusted them, didn't I, Craig. I warned you, but would you listen to me? Wankers! We should've kicked shit out of them while they were here.'

'It wouldn't have achieved anything,' says Craig. 'Anyway, safe passage through each other's territory was part of the agreement.'

'The agreement they've just broken.'

'They haven't yet. Eazy-K was trying it on. Seeing how I'd react.'

'Bollocks.'

'Neville, unless you have anything constructive to say, kindly either shut up or piss off.'

Neville strides up to his old friend, his former school chum, his leader, and thrusts his face up to Craig's and looks him straight in the eye.

'You've lost it, you know that, mate,' he says. 'You've let yourself get shafted. You've fucked everything up good and proper.'

Craig towers over Neville. He could break him in two. He could crush his skull with his bare hands. For all that, it's easy to see which of them has the advantage right now. Neville has Craig right where he wants him.

'Out, Nev. Now. Go. Leave.'

Neville turns to Lauren, who has been standing at the entrance to the kitchen along with me and Zoë, watching this drama unfold. 'You want to stay here, Lauren? With Captain Loser? You still think he's such a big shot now?'

Lauren bites her lip, thinking hard. Her eyes flick from Craig to Neville, Neville to Craig. Finally, she comes to a decision.

'Let me get my things,' she says, and pushes past Zoë and me.

Five minutes later, she's gathered up her belongings in a bundle. They don't amount to much – an armful of clothing and cosmetics. Neville's ready to leave, but Lauren keeps prevaricating. I know what she's waiting for. She's waiting for Craig to ask her not to go. All he has to do is say the word and she'll stay.

But Craig doesn't care any more. About Lauren, about anything. He sits slumped in an armchair in the living room, head bowed, hands locked at the back of his skull, gazing down at his feet.

Neville opens the front door. 'All right?' he says to Lauren.

Lauren looks like she's about to have a last-minute change of heart. She's fighting back tears.

She peers through the living-room doorway at Craig.

Craig doesn't move.

She draws in a deep, self-strengthening breath and says, 'Yeah, I'm fine. Let's get outta here.'

Barely has the front door closed when Zoë taps me on the shoulder and whispers, 'Does this mean I can have her room?'

Under other circumstances I'd laugh.

But this now – the way Craig is.

This is not good.

Early the next morning, Fen took himself down to the stream and sat for a while on the bank with his bare feet dangling in the limpid water. The valley, refreshed by yesterday's rain, was an exultation of green. Sheep bleated to one another distantly in the stillness. The lake reflected the emerging sun as a sheen of glittering gold, broken here and there by the small plopping roundel of a fish-rise.

A religious person, gazing around, might have called this spot God-blessed. A secular person like Fen could admire it as a sublime synthesis of Man and Nature.

How did he get here? He reviewed the chain of event and circumstance, the causes and effects, that had brought him to Beam's door.

A religious person could have unravelled a thread of divine intent from the tangle of error and impulse that was the story of the past few weeks of Fen's life. Fen himself could perceive only human will and the odd nudge from his subconscious, nothing that could be considered, even in retrospect, a supernatural plan.

What was he to do? *You have good reasons for going and good reasons for not going, Fen, and I think now's the time for you to ask yourself, frankly, honestly, which you have more of.*

A religious person could have prayed to his or her deity for guidance. Fen had only himself to consult, his heart and his gut instinct to put forward the various arguments for and against staying.

He found himself vaguely wishing for another appearance from Michael Hollingbury. Surely here, if anywhere, the Green Man would feel at home and be happy to manifest himself. Just some words of advice, that was all Fen needed. Just something to tip him in one direction or the other.

Don't be foolish, he chided himself. Don't be so childish.

The Green Man came only when he was asleep. The Green Man was a dream-vision. You couldn't expect him just to pop up out of the grass when you wanted him to, could you?

Could you?

Shadows steepened. Sunshine deepened. From behind him Fen heard the sounds of Fairfield Hall waking up – windows being opened, indoor shouts, the wolfhounds barking, the first stirrings of another day of cheerful industry. His feet went numb in the chilling stream. The damp ground soaked the seat of his jeans.

It was up to him.

What was life but a series of choices, some far harder than others?

These were exceptional times.

He had been through so much. Had he been through enough?

The wise man knew when to call it quits.

The unknown was sometimes more welcoming than the known.

Another shot at happiness.

A new leaf.

A fresh start.

And just like that, Fen realised that his mind was made up. He got to his feet, picked up the walking stick, gathered up his shoes and socks, turned towards the Hall . . .

Forgive me, Moira.

. . . and, feeling lighter inside than he had for a long time, ambled across the grass towards his new home.

Then Beam died.

Nobody had the least inkling that all was not well with the lord and master of Fairfield Hall until, one suppertime, he collapsed. More accurately, he *sagged*, since he was seated at the time and the arms and back of his chair kept him mostly upright. Those at the table who witnessed the actual event saw Beam slump forwards, saw his eyes close and his chin sink into its hammock folds of jowl, saw his fork tumble from his suddenly nerveless fingers, and assumed, quite reasonably, that he was playing a prank. No one, just then, was talking to him, and Beam dearly loved to be the centre of attention. Hence he had feigned falling asleep. A narcoleptic attack, brought on by boredom. Any moment now, once he was sure that people were looking at him, he would open his eyes and grin and wink.

Someone laughed.

Beam did not stir.

Someone else laughed, uneasily this time. Beam was taking the pretence a little further than was comfortable.

'Uncle Beam's not moving very much,' observed one of the children.

An ugly silence fell.

Jessica was the first to her feet. She hurried to Beam's side, took hold of his arm and shook him. His head rolled and his eyelids fluttered and he murmured something. Thereafter he swiftly regained consciousness and, while protesting that they shouldn't make such a fuss, allowed Jessica and Sally to lead him out of the room and upstairs.

After he was gone, there was muted consternation. None of the adults, because there were children present, wanted to voice too much concern, but the children picked up on the general mood of anxiety and became fretful and agitated, demanding to know what was wrong with Uncle Beam and why he had had to leave the room like that. Since the meal was almost finished anyway, Fen proposed that the youngsters should go up, get into their nightclothes, come back down to the drawing room, and there he would read them a Sherlock Holmes story. The diversionary tactic worked, and an hour later the mystery of the Red-Headed League had been solved and the children trooped contentedly to their rooms, yawning hard.

Back in the dining room, Fen learned the worst. Jessica said that when she and Sally undressed Beam, they had found blood in his underpants. He was still bleeding. There was a chance it might just be a perforated stomach ulcer. That was the best they could hope for. But even a perforated stomach ulcer was hardly good news.

Fen asked – for the sake of asking, not expecting the answer to be yes – if there was a doctor living somewhere hereabouts, in one of the nearby villages perhaps. He was told there was not. In one of the big towns? Maybe, but the nearest of those was over ten miles away. Besides, how much help was a doctor going to be? To which Fen could only nod. As he himself knew only too well, under present constraints there were limits to what a medical practitioner could do, especially in cases as serious as this. Medicine had been thrown back to the days of poultices and cold compresses and faith in the body's ability to heal itself. At best a doctor could diagnose what Beam was suffering from, but as for treating him . . .

It was a long night. The adults sat downstairs, unwilling to retire to bed, as if to do so would constitute a betrayal, as if by staying up, remaining awake, they could somehow assist Beam's recovery. To keep their spirits up, they swapped Beam-related reminiscences – tales from before the Unlucky Gamble, from prelapsarian England, a more innocent age. That time Beam swam across the lake at night for a drunken bet and, when he came out, they had hidden his clothes, but he just spent the rest of the evening walking around naked, his revenge on them. That time he set up an abseiling rope on the side of the house and got into difficulties halfway down and was left dangling there for over an hour before anybody came looking for him. That time he drove his convertible Beetle up onto the terrace and crashed it into his mother's favourite urn, the one she had brought all the way home from a holiday in Sardinia, insisting on taking it aboard the plane with her as hand luggage even though it was nearly as big as she was. At first they found it invigorating to recollect Beam's life in this manner but after a while it started to feel ghoulish so they stopped. They drowsed. They waited. Upstairs, Jessica and Sally kept vigil at Beam's bedside. There was nothing anyone else could do. Drowse. Wait. The empty hours of darkness crept by.

At dawn, Jessica delivered the latest update. It was not encouraging. More blood, a lot of it. Beam was conscious, he was talking, but he was terribly weak. Things did not look good.

Life tried to go on as normal. Exhausted as they were from their sleepless night, the adults still had the children to consider and still had tasks to do. Breakfast was prepared and, in desultory fashion, eaten. Fen took the children off to the library and coached them for an hour on Venn diagrams. Their hearts weren't in it. Neither was his. Megan asked him if Uncle Beam was going to die. 'Of course not,' he said, and wondered if the children could tell he did not believe it.

The day was overshadowed. Always it was *there*, unspoken, unacknowledged, always *there*, the fact that Beam was lying upstairs in his room, not well, ill, deathly ill. The Hall was dulled, subdued, filled with hollow whispers and muffled echoes. Crap and Piss were not their usual exuberant selves. They sensed what was up, and skulked and moped, looking so mournful, so hangdog, that even Fen, recently confirmed canophobe that he was, was moved to ruffle their ears consolingly. Outside, the sun shone. Inside, the Hall was all the gloomier for its brilliance.

By evening, the prognosis was very bleak indeed, and the mood in the house likewise. Of all of them, only Beam was facing up to the inevitable with anything like equanimity. He had told Jessica he had suspected for some while that things weren't right with him. Odd cramping pains every now and then. A feeling of bloatedness that he had put down to his being, not to put too fine a point on it, a fat bastard with poor digestion and a fondness for the booze. If you really wanted to get down to the nitty-gritty: for several weeks now he'd been suffering from the most chronic wind. His farts had reeked like Italian bank notes. Always a bad sign, when you found the smell of your own farts offensive. Yes, he'd had a pretty good idea that something was up. He hadn't mentioned anything to anyone because, well, after all, who wants to hear about stuff like that?

All this Jessica relayed to the assembled household after the supper dishes had been cleared away and the children put to bed. She was doing her best not to cry. Beam had expressly forbidden any of, as he called it, *that weepy stuff*. 'Not in my house,' he had told her, 'not from any of you, so long as I'm alive.' She said he was resolutely upbeat, despite being in considerable pain. And she said he had requested that no one should see him except her and Sally. He wanted everyone's last memory of him to be of him as he always had been, not as he was now.

'What, no one see him at all?' said Corin. 'We can't even say a goodbye?'

'It's what he wishes,' Jessica replied firmly.

There was a numbed, silent exodus to bed. Fen, in his room, lay on his back and stared up into the shadowed recesses of the four-poster's canopy and tried not to think what would become of the Hall with Beam no longer alive. Cliché though it was, Beam was the place's heart and soul. Without him, would this oddly effective little community be able to survive?

He had no idea he had fallen asleep till he became aware of Jessica beside him, prodding him.

'Fen? Fen? Wake up. Beam would like a word.'

The smell of death was in the room. Fen did not have to know it to recognise it. It was a smell as insinuatingly familiar as a door-to-door salesman or a prize-draw letter. With a leer on its face and your name on its lips, it greeted him like an old friend he never knew he had. *This is me*, it said, in silky, sickly tones, *and one day this will be you.*

Beam turned his head as Fen entered, and the smile he offered was a ghost of itself, a faint copy of the original. He looked half the man he had been. Still of the same proportions, but undeniably diminished, he sat propped up on pillows with his hands resting limp by his sides. His face was riven with lines, its slack pulled in by pain. The candlelight lent his skin a ghastly jaundiced pallor.

On the way here, Fen had decided that humorousness would be the best attitude to adopt. Do what he usually did with Beam: intelligently amuse him. But it took several moments to adjust to the sight of the reduced, wretched figure in the bed; to get over the changes that less than a day and a half had wrought, to tune out the death odour. It was an effort to come up with something suitably jaunty to say.

'Nice pyjamas.'

'D'you like 'em? I think it's the monogram that gives them real class.' Beam patted his breast pocket, on which was embroidered an elaborate 'B'.

'Oh, definitely. But you know, this hypochondria, Beam . . . Enough's enough. It's got a lot of people upset, and it's time you leapt out of bed and admitted you're just putting this on to get you some sympathy.'

'Curses! Rumbled!'

'Nothing escapes my eagle eye.'

There was more brittle banter, then Beam signalled to Jessica and Sally that he wanted to speak to Fen alone.

After the women had gone, Beam allowed himself to drop the mask of bravado. 'Christ, this is fucking awful, Fen.'

'I don't know what to say.'

'Well, that's good. I don't want to hear any crap. Especially none of that nonsense about a better place and eternal life. I've never believed in any of that and I'm not about to start now.'

'I've never believed in it either, if that's any consolation.'

'Funnily enough, it is. Damn, this has all happened so quickly. I suppose I was in denial for quite some time, but even so.'

'It *is* cancer, isn't it?'

'Oh, I think so. No question, really. I've been incubating a nice little tumour for myself. A nice *big* tumour, I should say. And it's bleeding me dry.' Beam winced, although whether at a twinge of pain or merely at the thought of the homicidal growth he was harbouring inside him, Fen could not tell. 'What I hate most,' he said, 'is having to leave all this behind. Life. Life's a marvellous old thing, really. There's so much to it.'

'You've had a good one, Beam. Last night everyone was telling stories about you. You've had a lot of fun, by the sound of it. You've made people happy. You've done good things. This' – Fen waved around him, indicating the Hall – 'is a good thing.'

'You think so? I hope so. And actually, Fairfield's the reason I asked to see you, Fen. You see, someone has to take over from me. Someone has to keep the old place going. Someone—Why are you shaking your head?'

'Not me, Beam.'

'Why ever not?'

'I can't. I'm the new boy. The others – they've known each other for years.'

'And that makes you ideal for the job. You're from outside the circle. You have no history with any of the others. Think of the tensions it would cause if one of them was elevated above the rest. Would *you* like it if suddenly you had to start deferring to a long-standing friend of yours? Whereas an outsider . . .'

'Even so, they won't take kindly to me telling them what to do.'

'It isn't about telling people what to do. Not really. It's about being there. Queen bee, Fen. Queen bee. Top *and* bottom of the social ladder. Overlord *and* underling. Ruler *and* drudge. You have it in you. I know you do.'

'I know I don't. I'll happily carry on with the kids, but as for being in charge of everyone else . . . How about Jessica? Or Ben? Or Simon? Any of them rather than me.'

'I want you to do it, Fen.'

'Do I have a choice?'

'No. And if you continue to object, I'm going to have to pull rank on you. I'm the one dying. That means you're obliged to honour any last requests of mine.'

'That's not fair, Beam.'

'No, it isn't. Tough. You're my successor. I'm going to tell Jessica and Sally that when they come back. Like it or not, the job is yours. Now, we can keep arguing about it if you want, but that'll probably hasten my demise. Best you just accept, eh?'

He lasted another three days.

He did not go prettily. He did not sink sighing into the embrace of everlasting sleep. He went writhing and groaning amid soiled bedclothes. He departed from life in much the same way as he had arrived, swaddled, blood-drenched, gasping for breath.

The day they buried him was a gorgeous one, summer in its full ripeness, with just a hint of the decline to come – autumn's bloat and shrivel – discernible in the air.

The wolfhounds keened from morning till dusk.

A bad atmosphere. Not just in our house, throughout the whole compound. Perhaps because I'm looking for it now, I see it everywhere I go – anger, uncertainty, mistrust. The unity isn't there any more. Inside them, the Bulldogs sense the power struggle Neville's initiated; they feel it tugging them this way, that way. They want to stay loyal to King Cunt. They do. But Neville is talking to them, and he's being so persuasive, so convincing. And then there's the evidence. You can't turn ignore the evidence. The Frantik Posse, planning to make inroads into Bulldog turf. Mistake to have trusted them, wasn't it? And Lauren has moved out of the King's house. She's gone and shacked up with Neville. Lauren! Just in Neville's spare room, mind. He's not knocking her off or anything, just letting her stay with him (and in return she does his housework because that's what she does best, housework). But Lauren! If *she's* abandoned King Cunt, then something's got to be up with him, hasn't it? So maybe it's time to have a good hard think about who should be leading them. Maybe Neville's right. Maybe the King *is* past his best. Maybe – they can scarcely believe it – maybe they should be looking for someone to replace him.

Several of them, I notice, have taken to wearing football scarves around their necks, or long-sleeved shirts. Hiding their KING CUNT tattoos.

What's so ludicrous is, Craig could put a stop to all this if he wanted to, no trouble. All the Bulldogs need is to be reminded again who's boss, and he could do this easily, if only he had the will to. A show of decisiveness, a firm, forthright display of action. That's all it would take, and the Bulldogs would fall back into line.

Craig, though, hasn't been out of the house in days. Craig prowls about indoors, sullen, uncommunicative, eating, sleeping, mechanically going through the motions of living. He just can't be bothered any more. And I don't need to ask why. There's been too much treachery. He's surrounded by Judases. Neville, Eazy-K, Lauren. All he's done for his men, for Lewisham, and this is how he's rewarded. This is the thanks he gets. Craig has had enough. He just wants everybody to fuck off and leave him alone.

God, I've known exactly how *that* feels!

There's nothing I can say or do that'll bring him out of it, however. I try talking to him and get nothing in response but monosyllables. I try nuzzling up to him at night and get pushed away. Some nights I don't even get *that* much of a response, because he's drunk heavily, a couple of six-packs of beer at least, and by bedtime he's in a virtual coma.

Zoë does her best. She asks him questions, cracks jokes, even gently teases him about the way he's behaving, as if he were her big brother. Sometimes he looks at her and it's as if he'd like to be amused by her antics but can't bring himself to. Other times he looks at her and his expression is so murderous I have to warn her to give it a rest.

One small side-benefit. Now that I don't have Lauren breathing down my neck all day, and since I'm not able to achieve much with Craig at the moment, I've started paying regular visits to the recreation zones. I went along initially in order to keep the women there abreast of the situation within the compound, but they, it turns out, know as much as I do about what's going on, perhaps more. The men who screw them can be very talkative at times, so they're well aware how things have begun to deteriorate. Paula Coulton is my main point of contact. We talk through the chainlink. She says she and the others are worried what'll happen if Neville succeeds in overthrowing Craig. 'At least he's the devil you know,' she says, with reference to Craig. 'That Neville, on the other hand. A bastard, he is. Although . . .' And then she tells me something we both have a good long laugh about. Neville, it seems, has a slight problem in the bedroom department. A bit of a *shortcoming*, you might say. He's a little too, as it were, easy to please. In fact, the women have taken to referring to him as Nine-Second Neville (although never to his face, of course). Nine seconds is his record, allegedly.

It's jokes like this that help keep them going, help keep them brave. I admire these women beyond all reckoning.

'There's a chance, of course, that we can turn what's happening to our advantage,' I tell Paula one afternoon.

'Go on,' she says, looking dubious.

'There's going to come a point,' I say, 'when Neville will have to make a stand. He's going to have to face Craig in front of all the other Bulldogs and tell him it's over and someone else is in charge. A public confrontation. That's the only sure-fire way Neville's going to be able to dethrone Craig and take his place.'

'So?'

'So then one of two things can happen. Either Craig slaps Neville down once and for all, or he lets him win. It's not about what Neville does, you see. It's about how Craig responds, what *he* does or doesn't do. He can give in to Neville or he can sort him out good and proper.'

'"Sort him out good and proper". You're starting to sound like one of them, Moira.'

She's right. I *am* taking on Bulldog cadences and inflections. Sometimes I catch myself at it. Mostly I don't notice any more. Camouflage, I tell myself. Blending in.

Fitting in?

'Yeah, well, when in sarf-east Lahndan . . .'

Paula tuts and rolls her eyes.

'Anyway,' I say, reverting to the good middle-class tones I was brought up to speak, 'my point is, Neville confronts Craig, Neville loses, all well and good.'

'Why? Nothing will have changed.'

'No, everything will have changed. Neville's no longer undermining Craig all the time, Craig has full control over his domain again, and then I can start to work on him. Get all this' – I indicate the recreation zones – 'dismantled.'

'You think you can do that?'

'I don't know,' I admit. 'But I can have a damn good crack at it. Craig trusts me. I think he's even quite fond of me. We have a working relationship.' Is that entirely right? We've had sex once, and since then there's been too much going on for the event to be repeated, and Craig was so distracted at the time, and has been so distracted since, that I can't be a hundred per cent sure he even remembers it happened. A working relationship? Not right now, not in any real, practical sense. 'And with Neville out of the way, Craig'll be much more amenable to listening to me. Much more open to my influence.' That part, at least, I do believe is true.

'And if Neville takes over?'

'Then we have a chance – a slim one, but still a chance – to try and get out of here.'

Now Paula looks openly incredulous.

'There'll be confusion for a while,' I tell her. 'Disarray. Neville won't be able to get a handle on things immediately. The transition won't be smooth. That'll be our window of opportunity. While the Bulldogs are adjusting to their new boss.'

'I like the first alternative better.'

'So do I.'

'Escape just seems' – Paula shakes the fence – 'a bit unlikely.'

'Agreed. Which means what I have to do is make sure Craig *does* stand up to Neville when the moment comes. The mood he's in right now, I doubt he will. I think he'd much rather be shot of the whole thing.'

'Then you have to work on him.'

'If I can. I *am* trying, but he's not especially receptive at present.'

'Then,' says Paula sternly, 'you have to keep trying.'

And she's right. But I get back to the house and nothing's changed, Craig's still this hulking great thundercloud in the shape of a human being, all grumbles and brooding silences and pent-up menace, and I begin to wonder if anyone can do anything at all to stop Neville's challenge to the throne.

I'm scared what may happen if Neville takes over this place.

I'm especially scared what may happen to me.

Fen found Jessica at the grave. They had buried Beam close to the edge of the Hall's apple orchard, a spot he used to love, especially in spring when there was blossom on the trees and a mauve mist of bluebells beneath. In the grave's turned earth, a few shoots of grass had already appeared, fine as hairs.

Jessica didn't look round as Fen approached but signalled she had heard him coming by straightening her spine, squaring her shoulders and raising her head.

'How are you?' he asked.

'How do you think?'

He hesitated, then placed a hand on the lower slope of her neck, just at the base of her bobbed brown hair. A paternalistic gesture. He was trying – although he didn't like it and didn't think he was very good at it – to be exactly as Beam had been. Continuity, for now, was what the household needed, and he *was* Beam's replacement, no matter how undemocratically he had been appointed to the role.

Jessica's big eyes were red-rimmed and swollen. 'It's not right, Fen. It's just not fucking right at all. Why him? Why, of all people, him?'

Because life's a bitch and fate's a bastard, Fen thought, but said, 'At least it was quick. Relatively quick.'

'No, "quick" is a heart attack, a car crash, a fall off a cliff. Bang, you're dead. This was five days. Longer, considering he'd known a while back he was going to die.'

Fen recalled his first evening at the Hall, him and Beam out on the terrace, Beam echoing a certain remark he had made: *do what you can in the time available.* How could someone live with the knowledge of impending death like that and not crumble in despair? Out on the railway embankment, Fen had truly believed he was a goner and had been terrified. Yet Beam had been able to joke and smile almost to the very end. Courage? Or was there a certain point past which it became possible to accept what was going to happen, courage no longer called for? The two deaths Fen had hitherto had first-hand experience of, those of his parents, had been slow, incremental slides into oblivion, eased by medication. In hospital beds, drip-fed and cathetered and pumped with drugs strong enough to obliterate almost all conscious thought, first his mother and then a year later his father had slipped away, scarcely knowing where they were or why they were there. A miracle of modern science: the insensible demise. But now that that kind of easy get-out was unavailable and would probably not be available again for some time, it was necessary once again to face up to death as people had done down through the centuries, tackling it, taking it by the horns, wrestling it to its knees. Beam, it seemed, had managed this feat. Fen hoped he might learn from the example.

'I was just trying to say something positive,' he said.

'I know, Fen.' Jessica patted his arm. 'I know. I didn't mean to snap. I'm sorry.'

His hand was still on her neck. Her skin was soft, warm, faintly sticky from the summer heat. He felt a sudden, sharp uncoiling of lust. Shameful, at Beam's graveside, but there was nothing he could do about that. He wanted her. He knew that now for sure. If she was still keen, he wanted her.

'What did you come out here for?' she asked.

'Oh, no particular reason. See if you were all right. And to tell you that lunch is on the table, if you want some.'

'How kind.'

'Not at all.'

'I've not got much of an appetite at the moment.'

'You ought to eat *something*.'

'Fen . . .' Hesitantly.

'Yes?' Expectantly.

She let him down with remarkable gentleness. All in all, for someone in the habit of just saying the first thing that came into her head, she was extremely considerate. She told him she had been doing a lot of soul-searching over the past few days. She told him her perspective on a lot of things had changed. She told him her outlook was different now. She said she felt the world was a great deal colder and emptier than she used to believe. More brutal, less favourably disposed towards human endeavours. Things one started might not necessarily finish well.

In that way that many foreigners regard as peculiarly English, she avoided direct mention of what she was actually talking about. She skirted around the subject like a swordsman around a practice dummy, taking oblique feints at it. By this method she hoped to spare herself, and Fen, feelings of awkwardness. To a large extent she succeeded. When she stopped speaking, all Fen had to do to acknowledge that he understood her meaning was take his hand from her neck and nod. He managed both actions with surprising ease. He was nowhere near as crestfallen as he might have expected. All at once he realised how little he in fact liked Jessica. What a shallow person she was! It said everything about her that her reasons for spurning him were so tenuous, so contrived. Did she honestly expect him to believe that she had only just now realised that life was unfair, that the world always worked against you, that everything always turned to shit in the end? How naïve of her to think he could think her so naïve.

All the rest of that day Fen was elated. He felt like he had dodged an assassin's bullet. Jessica's manners, her mannerisms, that wide-eyed look of hers that she thought so winning – come to think of it, he couldn't stand her. If they had started an affair, she would driven him up the wall within days. A lucky escape he had had. Definitely. No question about it.

Besides, he was Beam now. Beam had not had a girlfriend. Accordingly, nor should Fen. He couldn't be allowed to play favourites, could he? He had a duty to run things impartially. Like Beam, he had to be wedded to the Hall. The Hall came first, his personal desires a poor second.

Brimming with self-justification, Fen began to feel that Beam's mantle might indeed fit him after all. He started to behave less like a copy of Beam and more like the version of himself that he thought Beam would have wanted him to be. He did not take on airs. He was rigorous with himself on that front. No swanning about the place acting as if he was better than everyone else. Humility was his watchword. The walking stick, he thought, helped with that. It accentuated his lameness, reminding the others that he lacked a basic function that they all retained, full mobility. He was unstinting with his courtesies. Pleases and thank-yous and words of praise were forever coming from his mouth. He was careful, at the same time, never to patronise. Above all, he worked as hard as anyone. Teaching the children remained his primary duty, but no longer was he able to supervise them in the afternoons as well as the mornings. The morning lessons continued in the library as before, but after lunch Fen went off and helped where he could around the estate, indoors, outdoors, wherever an extra pair of hands was needed. He handed dominion over the gang back to Christopher.

Christopher accepted the returned responsibility without pleasure. He had quite liked not having to think on behalf of all the other children, most of whom, let's face it, were scarcely older than *babies*. He had also quite liked the way Fen used to discuss with him on what they all should and shouldn't do together. Being unofficial aide-de-camp to Fen had made Christopher feel rather grown up. Now, all of a sudden, he was just another kid again.

Miffed and a little betrayed, the children started to slide back into their old ways. Restive during lessons, unruly at other times, they punished Fen for, as they saw it, abandoning them. It was understandable, he thought. And it could not be helped. Sacrifices had to be made, and the children's untarnished admiration was one of them. They came up with a nickname for him – No Fun Fen – and he let them use it in his presence, or rather did not react when they used it in his presence, so as to demonstrate that he understood their feelings of hurt and sympathised. They could hurt him back if they wanted to, because then they might appreciate that he, too, was not happy about the way things had had to change. The children might be unfamiliar with the word *martyr*, but he was sure they would grasp the concept soon enough.

So Fen did his best to lead by example, and for a while the other members of the household seemed content to have him in charge. After the shock of Beam's death, the loss of an old, dear friend, they were stunned, numbed, rendered docile. They allowed Fen to take over because, yes, that was what Beam had decreed, of course, but also because none of them felt up to objecting. If Fen wanted to step into Beam's shoes, fine, go ahead, let him. It made sense. Fen wasn't suffering to the extent that they were. He had known Beam for a little over a month. His bereavement was nowhere near as great as theirs.

Gradually, though, the shock wore off, and that was when Fen's troubles really started.

Little signs at first, a grumble here, a muttering there, snippy remarks that Fen could ascribe to grief, that probably *were* the result of grief. On one occasion it was his choice of suppertime wine. His choice of wine! Someone said only an idiot would choose *that* wine to go with *this* main course. He overlooked the comment, treating it with the disregard it deserved. On another occasion, one of the wolfhounds stole an untended raw chicken from the kitchen table and left scraps of skin and flesh and gnawed bone all over the drawing room. For this misdemeanour Fen was expected to shoulder at least part of the blame. As if Crap and Piss were his dogs now. As if he was supposed to be able to control them. He didn't even like the bloody animals!

Little signs. Snippets of conversation that he happened to over-hear and was perhaps meant to overhear. Was it proper that Fen should sit at the head of the table at mealtimes? Why had Fen given up minding the kids in the afternoons? Did Fen really think, when he was supposedly helping the adults, that he was actually being useful? With that leg of his he was more a hindrance than a help. Got in the way. He couldn't dig. He couldn't kneel. It was nice that he made the effort, you couldn't fault him for that, but all the same . . .

Little signs. People being curt with him. When he asked someone to do something, receiving a frosty reply, usually along the lines of 'I was just about to' or 'I'm not stupid, you know'. Simon one day addressing him as *mein Führer*, meant as a joke, naturally, just a little tease, and Fen took it in good part, but others who were present laughed in that cackling, spiteful way which adults never grow out of using, no matter how many decades separate them from the school playground, and thereafter *mein Führer* and German accents were frequently to be heard in Fen's presence.

It was never open rebellion, and was all the worse for that. Open rebellion would at least have been honest. Instead, it was furtive, corrosive, a process of constant undermining, a campaign of dissent conducted behind smiles that were broad and fine and friendly and fooled no one. Day after day Fen endured the genial needlings, the snide provocations. At no point did he lose his temper, although several times he came close. He forbore, he tolerated, and he hoped that, as time passed, things would settle down. But time passed, and the dissent only intensified, becoming an attitude of entrenched resentment. As autumn crept in, its drying touch turning first this leaf brown then that one, its chill slowing the ardour of growing, its dampness stiffening the air, Fen realised that his days as head of the household were numbered. Either he would have to step down or he would be deposed. Sooner or later, one or the other would have to happen. The situation could not continue as it was.

He was reluctant to step down. It not only smacked of failure but seemed a betrayal of Beam's dying wishes. Then again, Beam would not have wanted life at the Hall to carry on amid such an atmosphere of distrust and antagonism, nor would he have wanted Fen to remain in charge when everyone else was so against it. If only Beam had foreseen that Fen might not work out as his replacement. If only he had made provision for that possibility by assigning Fen a second-in-command, an obvious next-in-line should the need for one arise. But Beam, on his deathbed, had had a fixed, single-minded vision for the future of the Hall. It had been a consolation to him to believe that all would pan out exactly as he intended. He had not allowed room in his head for uncertainty. Perhaps had not dared.

Fen, by contrast, had room in his head for little else *but* uncertainty. The dilemma gnawed at him. Should he abdicate now or should he stick it out till he was forcibly ousted? Which would be healthier for the household as a whole? The latter, he suspected, for the simple reason that ousting him would require the others to organise themselves; it would require focus, a deliberate act of will; and in that act of will a new leader would emerge from their ranks, naturally, organically, as part of the process. One of them would inevitably come to the forefront as spokesman, voice of the aggrieved masses. That person would then, once the overthrow was successfully completed, find himself or herself being asked to take Fen's place. That was how revolutions worked. That was how new regimes were established.

Fen steeled himself for the impending coup d'état. He became impatient for it to happen, just so that it could be over and done with. Maintaining the pretence of business-as-usual was an effort. It would be a relief not to have to act the innocent any more, not to have to carry on as if he didn't know the others were going to rise up against him. He would be glad when the sniping stopped, when he was no longer the household's whipping boy, when it was no longer them versus him. Everything could then go back to the way it was before.

Except that it couldn't, of course. With Beam gone, nothing at Fairfield could ever be the same again.

This became clear the morning Ben and Sally left.

They took off in one of the cars. Fen had had no idea the cars were still in working order. He had assumed that beneath the dustsheets they were mouldering away, becoming useless, static sculptures of perished rubber and oxidised metal. Nobody had told him, not even Beam, that efforts had been made to keep them viable, and that quantities of petrol were stored with them in the garage. Nobody had mentioned this to him because, it seemed, nobody had thought it of any importance. Beam had wanted the cars maintained for no other purpose than that they would not go to waste. There were a couple of vintage models, there was an E-Type that had belonged to Beam's father, there was Beam's beloved convertible Beetle – beautiful machines, all of them, well worth preserving. When the day came that England was allowed back on its feet again, Beam had wanted them driveable. It hadn't required much effort, turning the engines over every so often, keeping the batteries topped up, that sort of thing. However, the first Fen knew about any of this was when he and the rest of the household were rudely awoken one morning by the sound of a motor revving, followed shortly by the sound of a car disappearing up the drive.

Fen ran to his window but knew it was useless. There was nothing to see but cedar fronds. He listened to the putter of exhaust and the rumble of tyres, fading into the distance. When silence finally returned, it was a strange kind of silence. There was a feeling that something more than just the tranquillity of the morning had been broken.

Ben and Sally – along with daughter Megan, of course – had made off in Beam's MG. The note they left to explain their sudden departure was succinct, if also somewhat disingenuous:

We've borrowed the MG. Hopefully we can bring it back some-time.

Things aren't working out. Maybe you'll be better off without us.

Sorry.

– B, S and M –

'Bastards!' exclaimed Corin, after the note was read out. 'What utter bastards! How dare they!'

Similar sentiments were expressed by many of the others. Ed, a tall, rangy man whom Fen considered to be Beam's best friend after Jessica, was quick to point the finger of blame at Sally, saying she had never been entirely happy here. Whether or not this was true – and Fen was of the opinion that it was not – there was general agreement that Ben wouldn't have left of his own accord. He and Beam had been at school together. They had shared digs at university. And Ben loved Fairfield.

In no time at all, Sally had been transformed into an Aunt Sally. Everyone at the Hall, in her absence, turned on her, dredging up every slightly waspish comment she had ever made, every small *faux pas* she had ever committed, every cause for mild grievance she had ever given, treating these peccadilloes as if they were cardinal sins. In a way Fen was glad that, for once, someone other than him was taking the flak, but the novelty of this soon wore off, and as he watched Sally's former friends vindictively pull her to shreds, he realised – with a profound and wearying sense of regret – that Fairfield Hall was falling apart.

And it was nothing to do with him. It was not his fault. He had done everything he could to hold the household together, and the fact that he had not succeeded said nothing about his leadership qualities and everything about the depth of influence Beam had had over these people. They had not merely respected Beam, they had needed him in a manner so fundamental that not even they themselves understood it. He had been more than simply their friend: he had been their father-figure, their magnetic north, their confessor, their idol, their liege lord, their arbiter, their all. They had abdicated responsibility for their lives to him, and now that he was dead, they did not like having that responsibility back. They did not know what to do with it.

Fairfield was doomed. No matter what Fen, what *anyone* did, the community was not going to last. Ben and Sally had realised this a little earlier than everyone else. They had jumped ship while they could.

Who would be next?

Fen could see it in everyone's eyes. Even as they lambasted Sally, they were all of them thinking the same thought: *maybe I should leave too.*

It was a matter of days, he reckoned. A couple of weeks at most. No one would be willing to follow Ben and Sally's example straight away – how could you emulate someone you were so busy denouncing? – but after a reasonable interval had elapsed, perhaps forty-eight hours, there would be another departure. And then another, and then another. A steady trickling away that would rapidly become a gush.

And nobody would want to linger on after the majority had gone. Nobody would want to be the last one left here. The only thing sadder than an outdated dream was the person still clinging adamantly to it.

It was not difficult for Fen to decide what course of action he should take. Unlike the others, he did not care what anyone thought of him. Not only that but he felt he was owed something for the slights and resentment he had had to endure these past few days.

At first light the following morning, he was out at the garage, hauling the dustsheet off the Beetle.

6. LONDON

The fight began in the grass beside a rotted tree stump. Head to head, mandible to mandible, the stag beetles shoved and buffeted, each seeking advantage, each looking to flip the other over. It was, unquestionably, a grim battle – two males in mating season, horns locked in competitive fury – but there was something delicate in its execution, too, something dance-like: the stateliness of a waltz, the precision of a pavane. The beetles, for all the tenacity with which they gripped each other, seemed in no hurry for the contest to be over. Eventually, inevitably, one of them would have to triumph, but until then there were steps to follow, beats to count, a silent music to heed. Looking down on this minute minuet, one might even imagine the beetles were enjoying themselves.

From the grass, the beetles' pushing and pulling brought them out onto the rugged grey plain of a road. Whether they registered the change in terrain is hard to say. It would be tempting to conjecture that each was concentrating so intently on his opponent as to be oblivious to all else. Equally, the tarmac provided a clearer field of play than the grass. The stag beetles' movements became more surefooted, and they must, at some dim level of insect sentience, have been aware of this.

What they were not aware of was the possibility of imminent destruction.

It came with a roar too loud for the beetles' crude nervous systems to assimilate. It came at a speed that these deliberate little creatures, even when airborne, could never hope to match. It came with earthshaking suddenness, with thunder and immensity, like a fit of divine rage.

In the event, it took only one of them. A few millimetres further into the road and both beetles would have been obliterated, crushed to coleopterous paste. As it was, one was flattened and the other was sent scuttering away, fetching up on its back some yards distant. After much struggling, it managed to right itself. Moments later it was on its way, the fight seemingly forgotten.

The unwitting agent of the other beetle's demise drove on, whistling to himself, a blameless angel of death.

It was, Fen thought, a lovely morning.

Three hours was all it took to reach the M25 from Fairfield. Three hours, travelling not very fast over road surfaces that varied in quality from passable to atrocious. Three hours, including time spent doubling back and detouring around obstacles – a fallen tree, a bomb crater, a town with such an antipathy to through traffic that the residents had erected barricades across the roads leading in.

Three hours.

Half a morning.

Fen drove with the Beetle's roof peeled back, the sun full on his head, and a sense of ridiculousness in his heart. Because getting to London was, after all, proving to be simple. Absurdly simple. *This* simple. And hadn't he made such heavy weather of it till now! All those mistakes, all those setbacks. Certainly, were it not for the mistakes and setbacks, he would not now be at the wheel of this car. But still, he had wasted so much time. Ten weeks, give or take. When he could have done the journey, there and back, in less than a day.

It was something to laugh about, self-deprecatingly, as the M25 neared. An irony that was palatable only because at last he was on the right track, at last things were going swimmingly.

Well, almost. The clutch on the Beetle was stiff and temperamental, not helped by the fact that Fen's left leg was still weak. On several occasions he was unable to push the pedal all the way down and his attempt at a shift in gears ended in an ugly, wrenching crunch of cog teeth. This, though, all things considered, was a minor inconvenience. Otherwise the car behaved itself impeccably. The miles clocked up on the odometer. And suddenly, almost before he knew it, Fen was within sight of the M25.

What he first saw was a watchtower, a teetering breeze-block edifice so poorly constructed that it seemed as much of a hazard to the lives and safety of the armed sentries who were posted at its summit as the armed sentries were to the lives and safety of anyone who might attempt to cross the motorway illegally.

The next thing he saw was the gridlock.

Stationary, bumper to bumper, they stretched in both directions as far as the eye could see – lorries, coaches, vans, cars, cars with trailers, cars with caravans, great parallel chains of multicoloured metal. At first glance they looked like part of some immense traffic snarl-up that would, in time, clear. But Fen knew this wasn't the case, and even if he hadn't known, the lack of noise was a clue. Absent were the sounds commonly generated by traffic at a stand-still, the horn toots and the impatient shouts and above all the massed rumbling of engines in neutral. Hundreds of vehicles, sitting in stark silence, empty – it was a surprisingly eerie sight, like the chaos left behind after some unspeakable holocaust.

Which, in a sense, was just what it was.

The gridlock had, in fact, occurred years ago. Londoners, having withstood months of so-called 'precision strikes' designed to bring them back into line, and having failed to be brought back into line, had been subjected to an all-out, no-holds-barred assault, an apocalyptic rain of high explosives that lasted a week and that left few of the capital's landmarks standing and many of the capital's citizens in no doubt that it was time to flee. This they all chose to do at once and by motorised means rather than on foot. Result: few of them got further than the M25. Accidents happened, junctions became blocked, fuel tanks ran dry, the orbital motorway seized up, and gradually it became clear to the would-be refugees that they were unlikely to make any further progress, and so, for lack of an alternative, they abandoned their transportation and trudged back home. Some of them, perhaps conditioned by the fact that hold-ups were once commonplace on the M25, or perhaps out of sheer desperation, had stayed put for days before at last allowing them-selves to admit that the gridlock was permanent and irremediable. It was even rumoured that here and there along the motorway's circuit small pockets of humanity remained, communities that had adapted to their automobile-bound environment, using belongings they had brought with them and items scavenged from other vehicles to erect shelters that hid them from the prying eyes of the watchtower sentries. Fen was intrigued by the idea of people living this rat-like existence, scurrying secretly among the rows of im-mobilised traffic, but his feeling was that this particular rumour consisted far more of fable than of fact.

Inarguably, though, the gridlock had proved advantageous to somebody, namely the London Council. To those who might wish to enter or leave the Greater London area without valid documentation, six lanes (in some places eight) of packed-solid automobiles formed a daunting psychological barrier. The gridlock was the detritus of an abortive exodus, the husks of failed escape, and as such it was perhaps as efficient a deterrent as all the physical barriers – the watchtowers, the mined areas, the armed guards, the fifteen-foot fences that ran all the way around the motorway's inner perimeter – put together.

Fen had managed to get himself onto one of the A-roads that, if memory served, traversed the M25 on its south-western arc by means of a narrow bridge. He hoped that, since the bridge was one of the motorway's minor crossings, its checkpoint might be unattended, and that there might not even be a checkpoint at all. No such luck. Reaching the bridge, he entered a chicane of rock-weighted oildrums, and having negotiated this, he found two large piles of sandbags ahead of him, stacked on either side of the road so as to create a bottleneck just one vehicle wide. Drawn across the bottleneck were sturdy-looking sawhorses wreathed with barbed wire, and stationed to one side of this obstruction were three men with rifles.

They were ex-soldiers, and looked it. They wore camouflage uniforms that were patched and threadbare and hung tiredly off their bodies – drab fatigues displaying more than a few signs of drabness and fatigue – and they themselves were long-haired, rough-shaven and lean in a way that they would never have been allowed to become were they still in the army. Immediately, Fen felt a twinge of apprehension. As he came closer to the checkpoint, one of the men unshouldered his rifle and wandered out in front of the sawhorses, there to stand louchely with the weapon cradled across his belly, looking towards Fen with an expression that seemed to say: *who are you and why do I hate you?* Fen considered making a three-point turn and getting the hell out of there. But that, surely, would arouse the guard's suspicions, and he could not afford to arouse the suspicions of someone with a warrant to deploy lethal force as and when he saw fit. Besides, he had a permit, didn't he? And, if necessary, a bribe.

He continued forward, maintaining such a low speed that the needle on the speedometer failed to register it. As he drew to a halt in front of the guard, he put on a smile that felt face-crackingly false. He could feel his heart hammering away inside his ribs. Was it really possible for the human heart to beat that fast?

The guard came around to the side of the car and, as if this was no more than a casual meeting between two strangers, as if one of them was not in uniform and toting a loaded rifle, made some innocuous comment about the weather, to which Fen, warily, responded in kind. The guard eyed the Beetle and said that it looked like a nice little runabout; Fen said it was. The guard nodded at Fen's walking stick, which was propped up against the passenger seat, and said that it looked like a nice stick; Fen said it was.

During this exchange of pleasantries, Fen dared to dart a glance at the other two guards. Theirs were the faces of people who have front-row seats at a show and are fully expecting to be entertained.

His apprehension deepened.

'Permit,' said the guard beside the car, and Fen delved into his trouser pocket, slowly, cautiously, making the action as open and demonstrative as possible so that the guard would not somehow get it into his head that he was reaching for, oh, say, a concealed pistol or something.

He slid the permit out. Should he get out the wedding band too? No, not yet. Wait and see.

The guard studied the permit. He seemed to study it for a very long time. So long that it occurred to Fen that perhaps the permit was a fake. Had Cruikshank played a cruel trick on him? He wouldn't have put it past the old blind bastard.

He told himself the worst that could happen was that the guard would turn him back.

That was the worst.

The very worst.

'Hmm,' said the guard, in such a way that it was impossible to tell whether he was pleased or displeased with what he was looking at.

'It *is* quite an old one,' Fen said. 'I haven't used it in a while.' It had dawned on him that the problem might be that the permit was out of date. The London Council might have issued a new version of the document since Cruikshank left for Downbourne.

'Hmm,' said the guard again, and his two colleagues shared a quiet snigger. Lording it over people at the checkpoint, tormenting them – it was one of the perks of the job. 'Yes, well, it does look like it's been sitting in a drawer for a while. But I don't suppose that matters. Reason for journey?'

'Visit. I'm making a visit. Visiting someone.'

'Who?'

A trace of indignation – just a trace – entered Fen's voice. 'Is that relevant?'

'If it is to you, it is to me.'

'It's . . .' There was no point telling him the whole saga. 'A friend.'

'Anyone I know?'

'Doubt it.'

'Try me.'

'London's a big place.'

'Not as big as it used to be.'

'All right, his name's' – *quick, think* – 'Jeremy. Jeremy Salter.'

Why this, of all names, should have popped into his head, Fen couldn't say. Possibly it had something to do with the fact that Salter had once lived in London. Fen had long ago learned that he was one of those people who could not lie plausibly unless the lie contained an element, however small, of honesty.

'Jerry Salter? You know Jerry Salter?'

Oh fuck.

'Fancy that!' The guard turned to his companions. 'This bloke's a mate of Jerry's.'

The other two laughed and nodded, and there was a lot of *Jerry this* and *Jerry that* and *ah, good old Jerry*.

And then the first guard said, 'Never heard of him.'

Fen, who had already worked out that he was having his leg pulled, said nothing, but quietly wished some horrible accident would befall all three of the guards. He wondered how many times they had perpetrated this feeble gag on people using the checkpoint. Not enough times, clearly, to have grown bored of it.

'All right, here you go.' The guard offered the permit back to Fen. All at once he had become a smiling, beneficent presence, his manner saying don't mind us, just our sense of humour, bit of piss-taking, dull job, breaks up the routine, you know how it is.

Fen took the permit. He was relieved that the ordeal was over, but peeved, too, at the way he had been treated – so much so that the *thank you* he offered the guard, while as ingratiating as he could make it, was also not a little supercilious.

The other two guards began moving the sawhorses aside, shunting them with their booted feet on account of the barbed wire. Fen bore down on the clutch and was all set to put the car into gear when the guard beside him said, 'Hang on.'

Fen eased his foot off the clutch and looked round.

The guard had changed the way he was holding his rifle. A subtle but unmistakable repositioning. His left hand was now clamped around the barrel, while his right had moved to within twitching distance of the trigger.

'Now I might just be being over-sensitive,' he said, 'but d'you know what? I don't think you sounded all that grateful just now. For me letting you through.'

Fen assured him he was grateful. He conveyed his gratitude with words, with tone of voice, with his eyes, his face, his entire body. He *radiated* gratitude. It was conceivable that no one had been more grateful to anyone in the history of the world ever.

'Well, still,' the guard said, 'I am a little hurt. Perhaps it'd make me feel better if you gave me something. Yeah. Something as compensation.'

'Something as—'

'Like, for example, your car.'

'My car.'

'It's a lovely little car.'

You can't have it, Fen thought.

But of course he could. The man with the rifle could have whatever he wanted.

'Or maybe your walking stick there. I quite fancy that, as a matter of fact. I'm no expert, but it looks like an antique to me.'

Fen handed over the walking stick without a quibble. What choice did he have? None, and both he and the guard knew it.

He was sorry to lose the stick, but he would, he thought, be able to manage without it. For the past few days it had been more of a stage prop than a necessity, anyway, and seeing as he had a car now, he didn't anticipate having to do a great deal of walking in the near future.

The guard brandished the stick at him in a kind of ironic salute and waved him on his way.

And at long last, London.

Half a mile past the checkpoint, Fen could still hardly believe it. Finally, after all this time, he had made it into the capital. He steered his way through suburbs, maintaining a low speed partly because he had to – the quality of the roads inside London was little better than that of the roads outside – but partly because he wanted to. There was much to gaze at as he went, and gaze at it he did, with something of the curiosity of a tourist and something of the bewilderment of a dreamer.

Suburban London was, as it had always been, the overlap between two distinct modes of being. Once, those two modes had been city and country. Now they were past and present. So, while everywhere there was evidence of International Community intervention and of the civic disturbances that had prompted that intervention, there was also the clear impression of old ways having been re-established and, where possible, retained.

Houses were missing (Fen saw semi-detached homes that were now fully detached, and terraced rows with gaping absences like pulled teeth). He passed a shopping mall and several municipal buildings that had been reduced to blackened, burned-out skeletons. There were tower blocks which, with many of their windows patched over with sheets of polythene, resembled vast, three-dimensional crossword puzzles.

And yet, amid all the devastation and dereliction, there were high-street shops open for business, selling basic goods and supplies, including food tins retrieved from International Community airdrops. At intersections there were traffic lights that ran through their signal cycles for the benefit of road-users who, though there were too few of them to make it strictly necessary, obeyed the lights' instructions nonetheless. There were black taxis, grumbling along, their drivers likewise grumbling along, either to themselves or to their fares. There were pubs, and midday drinkers at tables outside, supping pints and shorts. There were schools whose play-

337

grounds were thronged with howling, whirling, delirious children, some of them clad in uniforms, some in home-sewn approximations of uniforms. There were people who looked unmistakably like people with office jobs, and their suits and shoes might not have been of the newest but still they comported themselves with an air of tidy diligence as they strode along pavements or – Fen caught the occasional glimpse through a window – sat at desks and performed whatever clerical or administrative duties it was that they were paid to perform. If they *were* paid, that is. It occurred to him that they might visit their workplaces simply because that was what they had always done before the Unlucky Gamble.

It was like some ghostly display, with phantoms of normality flitting to and fro against a backdrop of semi-ruin. Although Fen had known that in London, specifically outer London, life had got back pretty close to the way it was before, he had had no idea, till now, just how close. Hearing about the high standard of amenities and actually seeing it for himself were two very different things. Perhaps the most arresting symbol of the suburbs' regeneration he encountered was a municipal fountain in full working order. Drinkable water, that most valuable commodity in Downbourne, the resource the townsfolk assiduously conserved and prayed for, was here being jetted into the air in profligate amounts, merely for the purpose of providing a public spectacle.

No wonder Londoners had to have permits. No wonder they were so jealously protective about what they had. No wonder they had turned the M25 into their castle moat.

Weirdly enchanted, Fen drove on.

Thanks to Wickramasinghe, he knew where he was headed. Lewisham. The precise route he should take to get there he wasn't sure of, but he was familiar enough with the basic layout of the capital to know that Lewisham was somewhere in the south-east, not far from the Thames, somewhere around Catford, Greenwich, that area – so as long as he continued going northward and eastward and kept an eye on the road signs, he would eventually wind up in the general vicinity of his destination. And having got near, doubtless he would be able to prevail on some helpful passer-by to tell him where, exactly, he might find the British Bulldogs.

It was a nice, sensible, straightforward plan, and it might well have succeeded, had the Beetle not had other ideas.

One moment, the clutch was merely troublesome. The next, it was broken. Fen, needing to downshift from third to second in order to negotiate a sharp bend, put his foot on the pedal and pressed. The pedal did not budge. He pressed harder. Still the pedal would not budge. In a paroxysm of panic, he stamped on the brake. The Beetle juddered, stalled, swerved sideways, and went veering into the kerb.

Since he had not been going particularly fast, the impact, while shocking, caused no injury. He sat for a minute till his jangled nerves steadied, and then he unclamped his hands from the steering wheel and tried to restart the engine. He twisted the ignition key, and the Beetle gave an unhappy gargle and jolted into the kerb again.

Of course. Still in gear.

He wrestled with the gearstick but could not move it. It was locked in place.

Great. Absolutely great.

Fen swore at the Beetle for a while, leaving it in no doubt how he felt about it. He hammered on the clutch pedal with his good foot, hoping that brute force might solve the problem, as brute force so seldom did. Neither the verbal nor the physical assault yielded results. The car was useless. Beam's pride and joy, Fen's easy means of getting to Lewisham, had become an inert, inoperable heap of junk.

So it was back to walking again. As he had commenced his journey, so he would complete it.

After a brisk-paced mile, Fen remained confident. His left leg was bearing up. He was beginning to regret that he had not had the foresight to take some food with him from Fairfield, but he couldn't have known that the car would break down, could he? Besides, he was only slightly hungry. Otherwise he was in good spirits.

After two miles, he was wishing he still had his stick.

Three miles, and he was limping, and he was very hungry indeed, and he had no idea where he was. Somewhere north of Croydon, but that was as accurate as he could be. He had entered the zone where outer London shaded into inner. True suburb was behind him and, with it, the orderliness he had found so remarkable. Here, the city looked depressingly as he had expected it would: worn-out, bombed-out, scoured, rubbled, harrowed. Little was as he remembered, little readily identifiable. Now and then he would come to a section that was sufficiently intact for him to recognise it, but it was like finding a patterned shard amid a heap of broken chinaware, familiar but no longer integrated.

He soldiered on, noting as he went that there were considerably fewer people out and about compared with the suburbs, and they walked quickly and purposefully, those that *were* out and about, and kept their heads down, and resisted catching anyone's eye.

At around the same time as this, he became aware of a piece of graffiti. When he first spotted it, he thought nothing of it. He soon realised, however, that it was everywhere. On walls. On signposts and shop façades. On the hollowed-out frames of phone boxes and bus shelters. Across the torn scraps of poster that still clung to advertising billboards. Spaced out down the white sections of a Belisha beacon pole. A single word, scrawled in marker pen or clumsily spray-painted:

RAZORBOYS

What the graffiti actually signified did not become clear to him until, as he was sitting perched on the wall of somebody's front garden, taking a rest, a couple of young men came strolling by, wearing T-shirts with the same word emblazoned across the front. The young men scrutinised him as they passed, subjecting him to the sort of stare that manages to be both appraising and contemptuous, the sort of stare that policeman and security guard and doorman and every other thug with authority struggles to perfect, and all at once it dawned on Fen that they were looking at him in this way because he had strayed onto their territory. He was now in that region of London that was nominally under the control of the London Council and really under the control of people like these two. The graffiti marked the area as theirs. Their T-shirts confirmed the fact. They were entitled, by dint of proprietorship, to look at him in whatever way they wanted.

In the event, the two Razorboys did not give him any grief, although undoubtedly they would have if they had felt the urge. They sauntered on by, and then one of them let rip an immense fart, which prompted his friend to punch him and call him a disgusting pig and say it sounded like he had bust his ringpiece, and this kept them both guffawing all the way to the end of the street and around the corner.

From there on, Fen proceeded with extreme caution. He was in the badlands now, and frankly, it scared him. Taking his cue from the other pedestrians, he moved like a shuffling tramp, gaze fixed on the ground, spine hunched so that he would seem small, unimportant, beneath notice. Northward still, and eastward, he zigzagged through the shattered capital, pausing every so often to take his bearings from the sun, or try to, for the sun appeared to want no part in his plans and dodged erratically across the sky, travelling in any direction except, it seemed, west. Soon its light was filtering sideways, and the city took on a skewed geometry, jagged purplish shadows everywhere. By now, Fen was ravenous, but hadn't a clue what to do about it. He traipsed past restaurants, and what remained of the frontage and decor of each evoked pangs of hunger strong enough to make him groan. A curry house: he could taste the spices. A Chinese take-away: what he wouldn't have given for a heaped-high plate of chow mein. A burger bar: Christ, french fries, french fries, *french fries*! In the partly-demolished interior of a pizza parlour he rooted around for half an hour in the hope that somehow, by some miracle, some item of non-perishable foodstuff had survived, tucked away in a corner, in an undiscovered store cupboard – a tin of tomatoes, some vacuum-packed meat product, *something*. All he turned up, however, was a menu, which he tortured himself by reading and then reading again. The menu even smelled of the various permutations of pizza toppings it advertised, its cardboard impregnated with the wondrous aromas that at one time had swirled wantonly around it. He put it to his nose and inhaled and inhaled and inhaled.

It was hard to concentrate on finding his way when an unfilled stomach commanded so much of his attention. Obtaining something to eat was now a dark, hounding obsession. He approached strangers in the street – people who looked safe – hoping to cadge a meal, but no one was prepared even to listen to what he had to say. It was all too obvious from the way he approached that he was going to ask a favour, and whatever the favour was, they weren't in a position to grant it. It wasn't that kind of world any more. Maybe it had never been. They shooed him away like a stray dog.

Lost, light-headed, despairing, he stumbled on into the thickening haze of evening. A few streetlamps popped into life and brightened from buzzing pink to silent amber. Stars blinked awake in the dirtying sky. Blinds were drawn, hatches battened. In the gathering dark London did not come to life with light and activity as it had used to. It hushed and grew still. And then nightfall.

With the onset of night, Fen knew he had to find shelter. Somewhere to hole up, hide, sleep. He came to a set of railings in front of a church. The church was still used for worship but its door was not locked. All that was worth stealing from inside had been stolen long ago.

He drank from the font, spooning holy water into his mouth with a cupped hand. The water filled his belly, and that made things better.

Curled up on one of the pews, a hassock for a pillow, he fell asleep to the rustle of pigeons in the rafters.

I had a dream last night that Fen came for me. He fetched me away from here, whisked me back to Downbourne, and everything was well. Downbourne was its old self, unbusy little country town. I filed my articles – detox this, de-stress that, how to improve your love life, bigger breasts, firmer buttocks, the usual. Fen taught his kids. We got by. We got along. Everything was well.

This morning, everything is *not* well.

It turns out I underestimated Neville. Or rather, I overestimated how bold he would be. I fully thought he would offer some sort of formal challenge to Craig. Not so. He's sidestepped that whole process and crowned himself king anyway. So no Neville/Craig confrontation. Nothing to force Craig to get off his backside and act.

Neville, to all intents and purposes, is the new leader of the Bulldogs.

'Men,' he says. He's standing on one of the picnic tables. In front of him: an eager, milling throng – dozens upon dozens of close-cropped haircuts, of muscled necks, of transfixed eyes. Weapons are carried. Bats and two-by-four at the ready. Neville has these men in the palm of his hand. Perhaps he's learned a trick or two hanging around Craig. He speaks with the skill of a practised orator, and he looks – I wish I could deny it but I can't – he looks statesman-like.

'This is the time,' he says. 'This is the hour. This is when we decide whether or not we're going to allow ourselves to be pushed around. Because let's not be under any illusion here. The Frantik Posse are taking the piss. Somehow' – ironic emphasis – 'they've got it into their heads that we're a bunch of pushovers. Somehow they seem to think they can just waltz in and steal a piece of our turf and we won't do anything about it. Now, is that true?'

The assembled British Bulldogs mutter and grunt and grumble their negatives.

'No,' says Neville, 'it isn't fucking true, because that's not how things work around here. That's not how we are. That's not *who* we are. We're called Bulldogs for a reason. You mess with us, we'll bite your sodding leg off!'

343

Laughter. Some cheering.

'So listen. We all know what's happened. The Frantiks have gone into Brockley, like they said they would, they're lah-di-dah-ing around like they own the place, and I don't even want to get into why they thought they could do this and get away with it, because, well, it's not a subject I much enjoy talking about.'

He leaves a pause there, so that the Bulldogs can appreciate not merely what he's referring to but his tact in referring to it so obliquely.

He then makes a minor misstep by deciding to go into detail. 'King Cunt thought he was doing the right thing by striking a deal with Eazy-K. All along he was being warned against it but he went and did it anyway, and now that he realises he made a mistake, where is he? What's become of him? Why haven't we seen him lately? I'll tell you why. Because he can't face us. Because he's ashamed.'

Some of the Bulldogs sound appropriately disgusted, but a few speak up in favour of Craig. One of them's Mushroom, who – bless his stubby little penis – says: 'Fair do's, Nev, he thought he was doing what's best for us.'

Neville realises then that he would have been better off not mentioning Craig directly; leaving unsaid what he said would be unsaid. Briefly he flounders, lost for words, and I think (but it's more of a hope than an expectation) that his whole scheme is going to unravel there and then, and the Bulldogs are going to turn on him and heckle him off his makeshift podium and chase him out of the compound and that will be that.

But he recovers. This is his moment. He knows it. His self-belief is riding high. He's silver-tongued. Unstoppable.

'Craig did think that, yeah. His intentions were good. But let's face it, good intentions and smart decisions don't always go hand-in-hand.'

He allows time for the epigram sink in. You can see the Bulldogs working it through. *Good intentions. Smart decisions. Oh yeah. Huh. Clever.* They stop scratching their heads and start nodding them.

'And here we are,' says Neville. 'Left with a right mess to tidy up. We've got people inside our borders who shouldn't be inside our borders. Today it's Brockley. Tomorrow, who knows? Crofton Park? Loampit Hill? Hilly Fields? *Here*? Because that's what's going to happen. You mark my words. The Frantiks aren't going to stop at Brockley. They'll come all the fucking way in, just like they did in Peckham. Or they will if we don't send them packing.'

He has the Bulldogs back under his sway again. All of them, even the Craig loyalists like Mushroom, I think. He's appealing to their instinct for self-preservation, their desire to keep the good times rolling for themselves, above all their innate love of a good scrap. What he's also doing – a tactic beloved of monarchs and emperors and politicians throughout the ages – is creating a distraction from an internal problem by directing attention elsewhere, onto an external problem. The Frantiks are a genuine threat to the Bulldogs, no question about it, but for Neville they're also a convenient bogeyman. They're there and he can use them to rally the Bulldogs behind him and in the process cement his popularity as leader, and so that's what he's doing. And he's doing it well, damn him, he's doing it very well indeed.

'What I'm asking from you lot,' he continues, 'is nothing more than you'd be happy to do anyway. Kicking the Frantiks' arses. They won't be expecting us to come after them. They certainly won't be ready for it. And look at us. *Look* at us. Look how fucking tough we are. I get the shits just seeing all you lot's ugly faces.'

That one gets a huge round of laughter.

'And them? Bunch of fucking dopeheads. "Yah mon, jus' wait till I roll dis spliff before you kick shit outta me, a'right?"'

This time the Bulldogs' laughter is more like a snarl.

'So what are we going to do? I'll tell you what. We're going to hit 'em like a lightning strike. Swift. Sharp. Clean. Sudden. Like we're fucking cobras.'

The snarl again, rising in tone, deep, like magma welling up in a volcano.

'Shove 'em back into Peckham. Further, if we can. That's what we're going to do. But I need to know, lads, I need to hear you tell me, are you ready for this?'

A massed assent, an enormous, greedy YES!

'Are you ready to give the Frantiks the kicking they deserve?'

Again YES!

'Are you sure?'

One more YES! – yelled, howled, roared, thundered.

Neville raises his fists aloft, like a demagogue, a dictator. On his face there's a passionate, an almost beatific smile. 'Then let's go *get* the fuckers!'

And for a while it's all stampede and frenzy and weapons aloft, and when the dust settles there's just me left behind and, I discover, Lauren. The two of us, standing on opposite sides of the space where, a few moments ago, the Bulldogs were congregated.

We eye each other awkwardly, warily, and then Lauren decides to give me this weird, superior waggle of the eyebrows, like she's someone who's just won a crucial point in a debate. 'He was good, wasn't he?' she says.

I feel the urge to call her all sorts of names. Stupid cow. Silly bitch. Can't she see what Neville *is*? He's not a true leader of men, like Craig. He's a rabble-rouser. A shrewd little opportunist who's bided his time and got lucky. I want to say this to her, but then I realise if I do, I'll sound just like she used to before she changed allegiance, before she became Neville's live-in skivvy rather than Craig's. I'll sound like I'm just as head-over-heels about Craig as she used to be.

So instead I say, 'Lauren, this isn't going to end well. You know that. For either of us. For all of the women here.'

'How d'you reckon that, Moira?'

'Neville's dangerous.'

'Oh really?'

'And declaring war on the Frantiks – he may have bitten off more than he can chew.'

She sneers at me. 'D'you really think that, Moira? Or are you just saying that because you're stuck with Craig? Because Craig's a waste of space now and you just can't bring yourself to admit it?

'A waste of space?'

'You know it, I know it. But only one of us has had the guts to do something about it. Am I right, huh?'

She's got me there. But not in the way she thinks she has. Doing something about Craig – yes, I haven't had the guts. But that's because what I have in mind to do about Craig isn't run away, à la Lauren. What I have in mind is a great deal harder and riskier, which is, of course, the reason I've been putting it off.

I know now that I can't put it off any longer.

'Lauren.' I inject defeat into my voice. Let her think she's won. Simpler that way. 'You're right. Nailed my colours to the wrong mast. I'm a fool.'

'Oh, don't be so hard on yourself, Moira.' She sounds almost genuinely sympathetic. 'I'm sure you'll get on fine in the recreation zones. Craig's ex-concubine.' Well done her, mastering that word. 'You'll be amazingly popular. The guys'll be queuing up for you.'

With that, she flounces away.

Queuing up for you. Nice image.

I begin trudging back to the house.

I've gone over this and over this, and it's the only method I can think of for getting Craig to come to his senses.

Am I happy at the prospect of what I'm going to have to do?

I think not.
Is there an alternative?
I think not.

He found a dead pigeon lying on the floor in the nave. No obvious indication of how it died. Just lying there on the flagstones, as though it had quite literally dropped off its perch. He thought it was a dove at first, and the symbolism seemed too absurd to be true. Closer to, he realised the bird was just a pigeon after all, a freakishly white one with a few tiny specks of brown in its plumage.

He didn't eat it.

He was tempted. He picked it up. Weighed it in his hand. Plump, limp little body. Lolling head. Contemplated how he might pluck its feathers, tear its skin open, pull off bits of its flesh, shove them raw into his mouth . . .

But he didn't.

Repulsed by the idea, and by himself for entertaining the idea, he threw the bird down and stumbled out of the church into the daylight.

It was an overcast morning. Warmish but not warm. A light wind gusting. Mealy-coloured clouds lidding the city. He began walking straight away, at first to put distance between him and the church (and the pigeon, and the temptation) but once the church was out of sight he kept going because he was already in motion and it seemed easier to continue than to stop. Then he did stop. After half a mile, he felt a sudden, hollowing onrush of dizziness. Weak-kneed, woozy, he looked for the nearest thing to sit down on, which was the stump of a tree. Since the winter that followed the worst of the bombing, very few trees in the inner London area had been left standing, arboreal beautification having had to give way to the need for firewood. He lowered himself onto the stump and stayed there till his head cleared and he felt strong enough to carry on. In the interim, he watched the wind pluck at the edge of a bin-liner that had been fixed, none too securely, over a hole in a roof. The bin-liner wavered, lifting, descending, lifting, descending, never quite touching down, like a nervous lover's hand. Fen was mesmerised. He could have sat and watched it all day.

But on he went.

It was all he could do. All he had left to him. He had come this far. To give up now was unthinkable. He knew that she was somewhere near. Moira. Somewhere near. If he kept going long enough, if he could just keep going long enough, he would find her.

Right foot, then left.

Along buckled roadways, over uneven pavement, treading the contours of London's hills – on he went.

Right foot, then left.

Momentum propelling him. The accumulated weight of the distance he had travelled to get to here. A last few ergs of inertial energy, spinning themselves out, bearing him along on their ebb.

Right foot, then left.

A final, desperate, all-or-nothing push. No sense of direction, only purpose. No sense of destination, only hope.

Right foot, then left.

He paid no attention to his weaker leg, which pleaded with him to stop. He blanked out the hunger, miserable in his belly, that dragged, nagged, ached, enervated. Mind over body. Him versus himself.

Right foot, then left.

And on, and on, and on. One step after another. Thinking no further ahead than where to place which foot next.

Right foot, then left.

Who was he? Not Fen Morris but gradually, receding now, an entity inside Fen Morris. Sharer of his own body. Passenger in his own skull. Staring out.

Right foot, then left.

Viewing the world like a rider on horseback or a sailor on a ship's deck. Watching the scenery sway up and down, lurch from side to side. Watching people pass by as indifferent to him as stalks of corn in a field.

Right foot, then left.

A bus depot. Every one of the parked red double-deckers with its windows and headlamps smashed. Methodical, systematic vandalism.

Right foot, then left.

A flyover, broken in two. A landslide of concrete boulders. Snapped reinforcement bars protruding from their sheared edges, like iron bristles. Some children treating the rubble as though it had been put there for their benefit, a place to clamber over and explore.

Right foot, then left.

A shanty village occupying what had once been a construction yard. Huddled, ramshackle shelters cobbled together from pieces of plywood, timber, corrugated iron, other scavenged scraps. Leaning against one another, mutually supportive. Homes for the displaced, the dispossessed, the despondent.

Right foot, then left.

A rat, hunkered inside an overturned dustbin like a bear in its cave. Doing what Fen had not been able to bring himself to do: gnawing on the corpse of a pigeon. Blood on feathers. Tiny yellow incisors. Little jealous eyes.

Right foot, then left.

A bomb crater on a common, as though some gigantic hand had reached down with an equally gigantic trowel and scooped out a section of the planet. And not far away, another missile that had landed but, unlike its fellow, failed to detonate. Embedded nose-first in the earth. Surrounded by a carpet of weather-worn offerings: flowers, keepsakes, handwritten messages, items of clothing, cuddly toys. Propitiatory tributes at a shrine.

Right foot, then left.

A municipal park. Shorn of trees. Stripped, too, of the play apparatus in its children's activity area. Swings, seesaw, slide, climbing frame – all dismantled, taken away for use elsewhere, leaving just empty oblongs of rubbery all-weather base, dented by the impacts of a thousand minor tumbles.

Right foot, then left.

The Thames. Surly and slow and grey-green. Easing eastwards. Its waters swirling in lagoons where the river bank had been breached by bombs. On the foreshore, mudlarks scavenging.

Right foot, then left.

Canary Wharf tower, rising high above the rooftops. The immense glass-and-steel obelisk having been used, it would appear, for aerial target practice. Gouged, bruised, scarred.

Right foot, then left.

A street with few pedestrians about, and then an adjoining street with ever fewer. A feeling. Something he could not put his finger on. An tingle in the atmosphere. The sense that there was a reason why people were suddenly not around. A rhythm he was not attuned to but they were. Invisible signs he did not know how to read.

And then, around a corner: men, fighting. Scuffles up and down the length of a street. Black men with dark blue bandannas knotted around their heads. White men with next to no hair. Laying into one another with brutal intensity. A clamour of shouting. Bared teeth. Bloodied, pummelling knuckles. Contorted faces. Pistoning arms. Weapons pounding. Combatants running to and fro, seeking fresh opponents, launching themselves frenziedly into existing brawls. Black against white. White against black. A rhythmless choreography of fist, knee, foot, elbow, forehead, wood on flesh, impact, impact, impact. And there: a nose getting mashed by a hard, sharp, sidelong chop with a broom-handle truncheon. And there: a man on his knees, clutching his groin, ashen-faced, vomiting. And there: someone yelling defiance even as his arms were pinioned behind his back by one opponent and he was punched repeatedly in the mouth by another. And there: someone on the ground, having his fingers whacked with a baseball bat until every one of them was broken. And there: an ear being bitten, an indignant scream, a chunk of cartilaginous flesh being spat out . . .

And now Fen, being seized by the arm, being yanked into a doorway, through the doorway, inside.

Door slamming.

'Jesus Christ! You ruddy great moron, are you *trying* to get yourself killed?'

The man was angry. Angry like a father whose child has just performed some staggeringly foolish stunt and avoided injury thanks only to a timely parental intervention. He bolted the door and went off muttering, leaving Fen alone. *And you can stay there while you think about what you've done.* Outside, the fighting raged on, dimly, a conflict in another world. Fen peered around. A large room. Windows on two sides, boarded over. The shapes of furnishings gradually loomed into visibility through dust-hazed stripes of sunlight. Chairs and tables, leafy anaglypta wallpaper, the squarish bulk of what looked to be a jukebox, and was that a dartboard? And over there, filling out the far end of the room – a bar?

He pulled up a chair and dumped himself gratefully into it. His feet throbbed with relief; his bad leg, too.

Some time later, his rescuer returned.

'Listen.' He was a raw-skinned, big-bearded man. Used to be professionally jolly, you could tell. Brawny, too. A laughing, no-nonsense type. Though not any more. 'About earlier. Sorry. For shouting at you. But I mean, honestly, what did you think you were up to? Standing out there like a prize chump.'

Fen couldn't think of a reply to that.

'The Frantiks wouldn't have known the difference, not with their blood up like that. Just one more white guy needing to have his face bashed in.'

'Pub,' said Fen.

The man blinked. 'That's right, yes.' Mentally downgrading Fen from berk to nutter, he took a precautionary step backwards. 'A pub. Used to be, anyway.'

'Yours?'

'Of course. And before you ask, no, I don't have anything to drink. Not a drop.'

'Eat,' said Fen. 'What about eat?'

'Nor that either. I don't have anything except what I need to survive. Look, you're welcome to stay, but only till things calm down outside. After that, out. It's the most I can offer.'

Fen nodded, accepting. It was the most he could expect.

Slowly things did calm down outside. The shouts and the stamped-ing and the unholy smackings of wood on flesh faded away as the fighting moved on elsewhere. The publican kept watch by the window, peering out through the gaps between boards. Fen sat in his chair with his arms wrapped tight around his belly, drifting back and forth between full consciousness and semi-trance. The numerous scratches and indentations on the tabletop in front of him, the crudely carved words, the stains etched into the varnish by alcohol spillages, all kept swirling before his eyes, forming them-selves into patterns. Not just patterns but symbols, hieroglyphs whose meaning, if he could only interpret it, would, he knew, explain everything he had ever wanted to know. He was forever on the brink of a great understanding, but then the patterns would break up, dispersing back into randomness, all intelligibility gone, and he would be left with the tantalising sense of a wonderful opportunity lost. He hoped, each time, that order might be extracted from disarray. Each time, he was disappointed.

Finally the publican said, 'Well, that looks like that. All clear. Time you were on your way.'

Fen rose to his feet.

Then he was lying flat on the floor.

How had *that* happened?

He heard the publican hiss through his teeth. 'Fuck's sake! What is *wrong* with you?'

'Food,' Fen mumbled. 'Hungry.'

For a while there was silence, and then he heard the publican sigh. It was the sigh of someone who has decided, against his better judgement, against every instinct he has, to do good.

The meal came from tins – baked beans, processed ham, peach slices in syrup – and was served up with the minimum of presentation. The publican opened the tins, handed Fen a fork, wielded another fork himself, and together they took it in turns, digging in, prising out, shovelling into their mouths.

It was hardly *haute cuisine*, but it was one of the best meals Fen had ever had the pleasure of putting into his body, and once he had finished he was appropriately grateful.

'Don't thank me, thank the International Community,' said the publican. 'It giveth as well as taketh away. Though not so often.'

Fen now felt well enough to explain how he had come to be standing outside the publican's door in the middle of that pitched battle. In return, the publican explained how the pitched battle had come about and who the two sets of combatants were.

'Bulldogs?' said Fen. '*British* Bulldogs?'

'Our local landlords, you might call them. Although how long they remain that way is anybody's guess.'

'But it's them.' Fen felt a prickle of excitement. 'They're the ones. They're the ones. There's only one gang in London called the British Bulldogs, right?'

'Far as I know.'

'And this *is* Lewisham.'

'Edge of.'

'So they come from round here. I mean, they have some sort of headquarters here.'

'About a mile due east.'

Fen sat back. That was it, then. *A mile due east.* Half an hour's walk. Less.

'Will you give me directions?' he asked. 'How to get there?'

'If you like. I don't recommend you try, though.'

'Why not?'

The publican gestured towards the windows. 'You've seen for yourself – we're in the middle of a territory war. Not sensible to get caught up in that. Again. And then there's the small matter of actually gaining access to the Bulldogs' lair. It's pretty much a fortress. Certain specific times, outsiders are allowed in. The rest of the time, not. What do you have in mind? Stroll up to the gate and demand entry?'

'Won't that work?'

'It might. Most likely not. Please understand, I'm not trying to pour cold water on your plans. It's just that you couldn't have picked a worse time to turn up. The Bulldogs are fighting to keep control of the borough, and word is that King Cunt's no longer in charge. Nobody's seen him in a while. I've even heard it said that the Bulldogs have kicked him out and he's left London.'

Fen recalled the tattoos on the Bulldogs' forearms and necks. King Cunt. Their leader.

'All the same,' he said.

'All the same,' said the publican, nodding. 'They took your wife. Here you are. The circumstances are far from ideal, but there's not a lot you can do about that. All right . . .' With a heavy exhalation, he stood up, left the room, and returned moments later with a pen. He peeled the label off the tin of baked beans and smoothed it out flat on the table, unprinted side up. 'Here we go.' He began drawing. 'This is the pub, here. First off, you need to head down this way. And then . . .'

It was quiet as Fen stepped outside. The street seemed strangely unaltered by the violence to which it had played host just an hour earlier, as though human carnage were a phenomenon it was well accustomed to. There were spatters of blood here and there, already hardened and black, and a puddle of vomit which a scrawny, jittery cat was hurriedly lapping up. Otherwise, little trace. The wounded were gone. The street looked no more or less ravaged than any other street in the area. The fighting might as well never have happened.

The publican, in the doorway, wished him luck and godspeed. 'If you don't make it,' he added, 'or they don't let you in, come back here.'

Fen shook his head. 'You've done enough.'

'Hey. In for a penny . . .'

Fen smiled gratefully, then looked down at the map the publican had drawn for him and turned it till it was correctly orientated. When he looked up again, the publican had withdrawn indoors. He heard the sound of bolts sliding to.

He realised then – to his surprise and, it must be said, shame – that he had failed to learn the man's name. True, the publican had neglected to introduce himself, but that was no excuse. When someone helped you like that, the least you could do was find out who he or she was. It was only proper.

Well, he thought, if nothing else I can make sure I remember the name of the pub, which is . . .

His gaze travelled up to the long, narrow board on the side of the building, where faded gold letters on a flaking black background spelled out three simple words.

And he stared.

And then he laughed.

And then suddenly his amusement curdled, and a feeling of disquiet stole over him. It was all right to laugh, but not when there was a good chance that he himself was the butt of the joke.

A pub called The Green Man?

He looked across to the sign that hung from the corner of the building. There, too, was the pub's name, along with a depiction of a man wreathed in foliage, with twinkling eyes, a merry smile, holding a foaming tankard aloft. He did not resemble the late mayor of Downbourne in any way, this apple-cheeked, boozy charmer whose features were criss-crossed with horizontal fissures where the wood of the sign had warped and split. Nor did he resemble the figure Fen had seen twice in his dreams, once on the railway embankment, once in the sanatorium at Netherholm: that transformed and transforming version of Michael Hollingbury, the first time a man with tree-like attributes, the second time a tree with man-like attributes. *This* Green Man looked exactly as a picture of a Green Man painted on a pub sign ought to look.

There was something about him, nevertheless.

The smile.

The knowing cast of his features.

No.

Rubbish.

It was easy to read too much into this sort of thing. Coincidences, Fen felt, existed solely in order to disprove the notion of a planned, rigid universe. If everything wasn't entirely random, if some guiding force did run the show, then coincidences would never happen, because a guiding force would never choose to be that obvious. Like the author of a novel, it stood to gain by remaining hidden, submerged within its material, its machinations well masked. To reveal itself time and time again was to jeopardise the illusion it had worked to hard to foster in humans – the illusion that their lives were their own, their destinies malleable, their decisions all a matter of free will; that they weren't puppets whose every action, from birth to death, was preplanned. In a universe that was entirely driven by chance, coincidences – by the laws of statistics and averages – *had* to happen.

In fact, looked at objectively, the manifestation of a Green Man three times in Fen's recent history was hardly worthy of being called a coincidence at all.

A couple of dreams and the name of a pub, that was all it amounted to. The memory of someone he had seen die horribly. A very common British pub name.

And just like that, Fen was able to dispel the eerie tingle he had been feeling. Nothing to it. Simply apply a bit of cold, hard rationality to the problem and it went away.

And he wasn't troubled as he walked away from the pub, following the route indicated by the publican's map.

Wasn't glad to leave the pub behind him.

Wasn't relieved when he turned a corner and there was no longer the pub's presence at his back and no longer the fear that, if he glanced over his shoulder, the man in the sign would have changed and his face would now very much resemble that of Michael Hollingbury. Or, worse, that of the publican.

None of that.

Oh no.

Not looking forward to this. So not looking forward to this.

Each step I take up the staircase – the condemned prisoner walking towards the electric chair.

Get a grip, Moira! Don't be so melodramatic.

But still . . .

Out of the corner of my eye I catch Zoë peering up from the living-room doorway. I wave angrily: *I told you, stay in there, keep the door shut.* She retreats, closing the door.

Good girl.

Craig's fast asleep on our bed. I wanted to wait till he woke up, but it seems he's out for the count. Which means I'm going to have to wake him up, which isn't going to help at all.

Deep breath. Here goes.

Nudge.

'Craig.'

Another nudge.'

'Craig.'

A low, burbling murmur that ends with 'Go away.'

'Craig, we have to talk.'

That does the trick. Four words every man dreads to hear from a woman: *we have to talk.*

He lifts his head from the pillows, puffy-eyed, not happy. 'What the fuck is it?'

'We have to talk' – my mouth is so dry – 'about Kirsty.'

He looks at me like I'm mad.

Then he looks at me like I'm stupid.

Then he slams his head back down onto the pillow.

'Piss off, Moira.'

I sense that this is the point of no return. My last chance to back out. But I can't. There's too much at stake. So . . .

'You gave up on her, didn't you?'

No reply.

'After that night at the rave when you punched Neville and she got cross with you for it. It all started to go wrong from there. Your relationship. All started to turn sour.'

Still no reply, other than a brief, testy sigh.

'You loved her, though. You still do. She's the only woman you've ever really loved.'

Now Craig looks up again, and his face is blank contempt, but I can see it in his eyes – I'm getting to him.

'Moira, I don't know why you think I'm interested in hearing any of this,' he says, coldly, precisely, 'but I promise you, I'm not. In fact, I promise you that right now this is the very last thing I'm interested in hearing.'

The threat could not be more explicit. Leave him be or else.

But of course, what else can I do except forge on?

'That's why you have a thing for redheads. You can't have Kirsty back, much as you wish you could. So what do you have instead? A string of Kirsty substitutes. That way you can be reminded of her but, because none of us is ever going to be her, you don't have to worry about falling in love. We remind you of her just enough to remind you that we're *not* her. And falling in love is something you really don't want to do because look at all the hassle and the pain it brought you the last time you did. You can't bear to go through all that again, so best avoid it, eh?'

He waits a moment, then says, 'Finished?'

I shake my head.

'Then, before you go any further, a word of advice. This isn't clever, Moira, this psychoanalytical bollocks. I don't know what you're hoping to achieve, but you're wrong on so many counts. So many counts. So just give it a rest, all right? For your sake, not mine.'

'You gave up on her, Craig. You know you did. The moment things started to get difficult, you gave up on her. You let her slip through your fingers, and all because you were too proud.'

'What?'

'Too proud to admit you'd done something wrong. Too proud to apologise. That's all Kirsty was waiting for – you to say sorry, to say that you acted like a big fat idiot, you shouldn't have, please forgive me. But you didn't. You couldn't.'

'Moira . . .' Not so much my name, more a growl.

'She didn't leave you, Craig. Kirsty didn't give you the elbow. You let her go. And you did it knowingly, and it was the single biggest mistake of your life, and you've been bitterly regretting it ever since.'

He sits upright, slides off the bed, stands, one swift agile movement. So big but so fast. Now I'm looking up at his face instead of down. Now we're one yard apart instead of three.

I'm within his reach. Within striking distance.

I should be terrified.

But I'm the woman the Bulldogs kidnapped and kept in a bricked-up room for God knows how many days. I'm the woman who's managed to survive all this time in Fort Bulldog and maintain her sanity and her dignity. Most of all: I'm the woman Craig has allowed to share his house, to accompany him on trips, the woman he has confided in, slept with, the woman he trusts, perhaps even respects.

He will not hit me. He will not.

'You were a coward. Big King Cunt, a coward.'

His face reddens. His eyes bulge.

'You were a coward then, and you're being a coward now.'

His fist clenches. A part of me can hardly believe I'm saying these things to him. Another part of me knows I have to, no matter what the consequences.

'And you know why you're a coward? Because whenever you have a problem, not a practical problem, an emotional problem, a *personal* problem, you refuse to face up to it. Oh sure, King Cunt can handle anything. King Cunt's the fixer, the fighter, the organiser, the ruler. There's nothing *he* can't deal with. But Craig? Once you get to Craig, it's a whole different story. Like now. Neville's stolen your empire right from under your nose, and you've let him. He's undermined everything you ever worked for, just like he undermined everything you had with Kirsty. You know this. You told me you've been wise to his game all along. But why haven't you done anything? Because Neville's your blind spot. Your great weakness. The flaw in this marvellous moral code you live by. You've let him stay with you all this time, tag along in your slipstream, because you somehow think you owe it to him. You think you need him, perhaps so that you won't forget where you came from, your youth, your background, your origins – or perhaps because every time he grins and you see his Gold Tooth you remember how it felt to lose control and hit him, how it felt to turn on someone you're still for some reason convinced is your best friend. Christ, Craig, that's what Neville plays on. That's his great advantage over you. He grins all the time when he's around you, have you noticed that? And you can bet whenever he does it, part of the reason is to make sure that tooth of his reminds you what you did to him. But then was it really so bad, hitting him? Didn't he deserve it? Wasn't he *asking* for it?'

I have to keep talking now, if only to forestall a reaction from Craig.

Keep talking. Let it all come tumbling out. All these words that I've planned, rehearsed in my head over and over for days, but still somehow never expected to hear myself say out loud.

'If that guilt has been eating at you ever since, it's time you bloody well stopped letting it. You are King Cunt. Hardest of the hard. You are King Canute. You stood up to the tide, to a whole tsunami of troubles, and turned it back. You did that. You can do the same now. The only difference now is that this time the enemy isn't outside. It's in you. It's *you*. All that mess that's in your head, all those conflicts between what you think you ought to be and who you really are.'

He raises his arm. Fist the size of a wrecking ball at the end of it.

'You can give up,' I tell him, 'or you can fight back. Which is it to be? Because it's not too late. Neville's running things for now, but you're still here and your Bulldogs still aren't completely convinced their future lies with anyone other than you. You can pull this back from the brink, even now. *If* you choose to. That's what it boils down to, Craig. You have to make the decision. You have to want your kingdom back, otherwise you won't get it.'

No more. I've run out. I've stated my case. Nothing more to say.

His fist hovers in the air.

It occurs to me: in attempting to save my own skin, it could be that all I've done is put myself in line for a severe beating.

But I knew the risks in goading him like this.

I had to get him angry, and I've succeeded.

The fist hovers.

This is just a few seconds. This is forever.

No man has ever laid a finger on me before.

Craig will not hit me.

The fist hovers.

Pure silence. We are in a bubble, the two of us. There is nothing in the world but us.

I look him in the eye.

The fist hovers.

It will only be pain.

He moves.

I flinch.

He wheels away.

He lets out a guttural yell.

A lamp goes flying.

A bedside table does a backflip.

The bed is hurled over onto its end, covers sliding off, mattress bouncing.

The curtains are torn down.

He starts pounding the wall. Thump after thump after thump, until the plaster begins to crack and fall away in chips and then in chunks and then bare brick is exposed, and still he keeps pounding. As though he can break through. As though, if he keeps at it long enough, hard enough, he can bring the whole house down.

He curses all the while, spitting out a long chain of profanities, giving vent to the frustration he has been feeling, articulating the injustices that have been done to him, naming the principal source of his pain: *Nev, Nev, Nev* . . .

Women cry. Men cry out.

He grunts and swears and rails and pounds away, and the house reverberates to the damage being inflicted upon it, a huge sounding board for King Cunt's anger and anguish.

He would not stop, he would keep at it till every bone in his hands was broken and probably even after that . . .

. . . but I touch his arm.

Squeeze ever so gently.

And he halts.

His head droops. He stares down at his hands.

The knuckles are split open, red raw. Blood is flowing freely.

He stares down wonderingly, as if his hands don't belong to him, are not part of him.

Then, after about a minute, he turns his gaze on me.

He seems lost, confused. A small boy in a giant's body.

But little by little, the confusion clears. Certainty enters his eyes. His face relaxes, the redness suffusing away.

We look at each other.

'Moira,' he says.

He sounds grim, but also cool and clear-headed. For the first time in – what is it, a fortnight? – he sounds something close to his old self.

'Hi.'

Tentatively, like he's recognising me after a lengthy absence.

'We have work to do, don't we?'

And I nod.

'All right then,' he says

And I smile.

And he says, 'What's the plan?'

The hue and cry of men in combat drifted across the rooftops and resounded along the empty streets. Sometimes it was far away, sometimes dangerously close. It almost seemed to be searching for Fen, like some rapacious, amoeboid monster, roving around, feeling blindly for him, but in the event he reached the Bulldog compound without finding himself in the thick of battle again and, indeed, without encountering another living soul along the way.

The compound gate cut across the end of a road, just as indicated on the publican's map. On either side there was a jumble of junk, piled high, every piece of it seemingly locked in place, a wall it would be difficult to scale or dismantle. Looming high over the gate there was a lookout post, with two Bulldogs stationed in it. Fen squared his shoulders and strode towards them with all the self-possession and erectness of bearing he could muster, hoping to convince them, even before he spoke to them, that he meant business.

It didn't work. The two Bulldogs watched him approach, and when he was close enough, one of them made a turning-around gesture in the air.

'Not today, mate.'

'Back indoors,' the other added. 'It's not safe.'

'I'm here,' Fen said simply, 'for my wife.'

The two Bulldogs exchanged frowns.

'You what?'

'My wife. She was taken a couple of months back by you lot. I want her back.'

The reasonableness of this seemed to confuse them.

'Are you mad?'

'You're having a laugh.'

'I've come a long way for her,' Fen said, 'and I'm not leaving without her.'

One of the Bulldogs puffed out his cheeks, then shook his head in a world-weary fashion. 'I don't know if you've noticed, pal, but – not to put too fine a point on it – there's a war on.'

'Anyway,' said the other, 'you can't come wandering up like a big twat and think we're going to open up for you and let you in just because you ask us to.'

With, of course, the exception of the 'like a big twat' part, this was a pretty accurate summation of Fen's plan of action.

Well, the publican had said it was unlikely to work.

What now?

'Then I'll wait,' he said.

'Beg pardon?'

'I'll stand here and wait.'

'You've got to be fucking kidding.'

'I've come fifty miles. I've been through hell and high water to get here. I'll wait.'

The two Bulldogs had not heard anything so preposterous in a long time, a fact they conveyed to Fen in no uncertain terms. Beyond that, however, there was little they could say or do. The moron down below wanted to wait, fine, he could wait. For all the good it would do him.

For a while Fen stood at the gate. The two Bulldogs stood in the lookout post. They taunted him sporadically. *Bored yet? Didn't you bring a book to read? Oh, all right then, you can come in – oops, no, sorry, you can't.* He shrugged it off.

Gradually, though, the needling took a nastier turn. The Bulldogs found it irksome that they couldn't get a rise out of him. His refusal to be annoyed, annoyed.

'This wife of yours,' said one. 'What she look like? I mean, she must be a bit of all right if you've come fifty miles for her.'

Fen stuck to his policy of silence.

'See, the reason I'm asking is, I've probably had her.'

'Me, too,' the other Bulldog chimed in.

'So I thought we can maybe compare notes. She like it missionary?'

'Doggy-fashion?'

'Up the arse?'

'Bet she loves it up the arse.'

'All the girls do.'

'Not the first time, but once you've broken 'em in . . .'

'Can't get enough of it, once they've been broken in.'

Finally: a reaction.

'She's medium build.' Fen kept his face as impassive, his voice as steady, as he could. 'About so high. Attractive. She has auburn hair. Her name is Moira Morris.'

The two Bulldogs went quiet, as though slapped, and then broke into disbelieving laughter.

'You're *Moira's* husband?'

'Fucking hell.'

'The ginge minge.'

'King Cunt's private totty.'

Fen wasn't sure whether to be encouraged by these remarks or not. 'She's with him, then? Your leader? This King Cunt person?'

'In a manner of speaking.'

'She isn't with him?'

'The "our leader" bit, is what I meant. Yeah, she's with him all right.'

'But he's not here any more,' Fen said, recalling what the publican had told him.

And just like that, he understood that it had all been for nothing. His journey. His sufferings. Moira had left. King Cunt had gone and had dragged her with him, God knows where. He was never going to find her now.

'Who told you that?' one of the Bulldogs wanted to know.

'That's what I heard,' Fen replied. 'King Cunt has left London.'

'Well, whoever said that, they're wrong. He's still here. He just—'

There, the Bulldog broke off and turned to his companion. Fen was too far below them to hear the brief, whispered discussion that followed. All he knew was that, a moment later, both men were looking down at him with a very much altered demeanour.

'Listen,' one said. 'We've decided to bend the rules a bit. Make a special case for you.'

'Seeing as you look an OK sort of bloke,' said the other. 'And you have come a long way.'

'And we're not total wankers.'

'We're not wankers at all.'

'So this is what we're going to do.' The Bulldog pointed to his companion. 'Trevor here is going to come down and open the gate and take you to King Cunt's house to see your missus. How about that, eh? Can't say fairer than that.'

Fen made the appropriate appreciative noises, but remained sceptical. Even as he watched the Bulldog called Trevor climb out of the lookout post and disappear from view, he was prepared for the possibility that it was all a pretence. Any moment, Trevor would pop back up and both Bulldogs would start laughing and jeering at him again. What was it about men who guarded entry-points, he wondered, that made them so prone to sarcasm, scorn and silly little games? The dullness of the job, he supposed, combined with the absolute power it gave them over people's futures.

Then from behind the gate he heard a loud *clunk* – the sound of something heavy being drawn back. A moment later, the gate was open and there was Trevor, beckoning him inside.

Fen entered the compound on a small but heartening high of gratification. Clearly something about him – his words, his plight, his abundant sincerity – had struck a chord with the two Bulldogs and had won him access through the final obstacle on his long journey. It was a victory of decency over thuggishness. Or perhaps tenacity over thuggishness. A victory over thuggishness, at any rate.

He followed Trevor across the compound, struggling to match the forthright pace set by the Bulldog. There was, as far as he could see, not a great deal of difference between what lay inside the compound wall and what lay outside. Here was the same shabbiness, the same cracked window-panes and paving slabs, the same treeless spaces, the same level of disrepair, the same intensity of decline. The wall, it seemed to him, had been thrown arbitrarily around a section of the city. The compound was a fortified piece of anywhere.

He wondered what effect ten weeks in this place would have had on Moira. It was hardly likely that it had not left its mark on her in some way or other. He was, after all, under no illusion as to the purpose for which she and the other Downbourne women had been kidnapped. It wasn't a matter to which he had so far devoted a great deal of thought, by deliberate choice. Only now, with their reunion imminent, did he permit himself to begin to contemplate what would have been done to Moira while she'd been here – what she would have had no choice but to allow to be done. The thought stirred up an angry nausea, which he forced back down. Pointless wasting energy on rage. He was better off waiting to see how Moira herself had been affected by her ordeal. If she could cope with it, so could he.

'Tell me,' he said, in the hope that conversation would oblige Trevor to reduce his speed. 'This King Cunt – is he a reasonable sort of person? Do you think he can be bargained with?'

'Can't say, really. You catch him on a good day, then maybe.'

'And today's a good day?'

'Oh no.'

Fen was startled by the offhand malice of the reply. 'But you're still taking me to see him.'

'It's *why* I'm taking you to see him. We thought it would be amusing.'

'You thought it would be amusing. Your and your friend on lookout detail.'

'Yeah, me and Larry.' Trevor grinned. 'See, the King's kind of not the King any more. He doesn't have much to do with the rest of us any more. He's all shacked up with his redhead, your missus, and this kid, this girl. Playing happy families. Or *un*happy families, it could be, possibly, who knows. Who cares? Anyhow, me and Larry, we thought it'd be funny to drag you along and throw you into the mix. Just for a laugh, as it were.'

'Ah. I see.'

'Sort of, I don't know, a spanner in the works, along those lines.'

Fen laced his voice with as much sarcasm as he dared. 'How very ingenious of you.'

Trevor simply shrugged. 'Yeah, well, look at it this way. I'm not the one who's come fifty miles to try and get his wife back from a bloke twice his size and ten times tougher. Who's ingenious *now*, eh?'

There was, Fen realised, no good answer to that.

I can tremble now. Now that it's over. Now that it worked.

I can berate myself for not doing it sooner.

I can say to myself, *well, that was easier than you thought it was going to be*, and feel a wry inward smile forming.

Easy? Well, maybe not.

But I judged him exactly right. I gauged which buttons to press and I pressed them.

I *knew* him.

I don't think I've ever felt this exhilarated.

In the living room, I apply bandages to Craig's hands, binding them tight. Meanwhile, Craig apologises to Zoë. He doesn't have to do this but he wants to. He tells her he's sorry for the way he's been acting this past couple of weeks, although it's clear (to me, at least) that he's saying sorry for a great deal more. Zoë hears him out graciously. She doesn't go so far as to say she forgives him, and I don't think that's what he's looking for anyway, but she lets him know she appreciates the gesture. She asks him if his hands hurt. He tells her they do but it's a pain he can cope with, a pain he thinks is useful.

That out of the way, Craig gets me to bring him up to speed on what's been going on lately in the compound and outside. When I tell him that Neville has gone to war against the Frantik Posse, he nods gravely. Absolutely the right thing to do, of course, but he wonders what sort of battle strategy Neville has adopted.

'On the evidence I've seen,' I say, 'none at all. Just hit them hard and hope for the best.'

'They're tough, the Frantiks. They're no cowards.' Craig winces slightly over that last word, as though it's a thorn that's snagged in his brain. 'It'll take more than sheer brute force to beat them. If Neville doesn't win today . . .'

'That'll be bad, yes. Very bad. But, as far as the three of us are concerned, there is a worse possibility.'

'What's that?'

'If Neville *does* win. Then he'll no longer be just leader, he'll be a hero. And consequently, anyone who goes up against him will auto-matically be the villain.'

'Even me.'

'Even you.'

'So where does that leave us?'

Before we have a chance to explore this vexed question, there's a knock at the door.

Zoë goes to answer it.

I can scarcely believe the words I hear her say next.

'Mr Morris? What-what are *you* doing here?'

Fen had to smile. When was the last time anyone had been quite so pleased and astonished to see him? Apart from Beam, that is.

'Hello, Zoë. I'm not surprised you're surprised. As a matter of fact, I'm pretty surprised to be here myself.'

'But—But—' Zoë spun round and called excitedly into the house, 'Moira! Come and see who it is! You'll never guess!' She turned back to Fen. 'This is terrific. You've come to take us back to Downbourne, haven't you? That's why you're here.'

Fen bit his lip. 'I hope so, Zoë. If I'm allowed.' He threw a glance at Trevor, who answered him with a remorseless grin.

'Fen?'

Moira appeared in the doorway beside Zoë. Behind her was one of the biggest human beings Fen had ever seen, a Bulldog whose hulking massiveness made the hallway of the house, indeed the house itself, seem ridiculously tiny, as though it had been built for dwarves. Fen saw the man's face, didn't like the look of it; noticed his bandaged hands, didn't like the look of those either. He concentrated his attention exclusively on Moira.

She had changed, no question about it. She was not the woman he had said a curt thank-you to in their kitchen all those weeks ago, shortly before he walked out of 12 Crane Street. No longer was there that air of wounded exhaustion about her. Gone, too, was the tightness around her mouth which he had become so used to seeing and which had given the impression that she was forever restraining herself, that even harsher comments than the ones she let out were queuing up on her tongue, effortfully withheld. She seemed taller and she seemed younger, more like the Moira he had known when they were first going out. The light was there in her grey eyes again, the intelligence, the willingness to engage with the world.

She had, in a word, flourished.

And that was wrong. That was not supposed to be.

The weeks of mistreatment at the hands of the Bulldogs should have left her a wreck. She should have been haggard, empty, bewildered. She should have taken one look at him and thrown herself into his arms. That was the reception he had been expecting. The reception he deserved, damn it. An outpouring of relief. Exclamations of joy and gratitude. Tears.

She should have been glad to see him. As glad as Zoë was. Gladder.

And she was not.

Instead, she was looking at him with her eyebrows knotted slightly, her head canted to one side. Something in her face said *irritation*. Something else said *unease*.

He wanted to believe that it was simply that his turning up like this, out of the blue, had startled her. Moira was so taken aback, she didn't know how to react.

But as the seconds ticked by, her expression did not soften into delight. If anything, the opposite.

At first it's like seeing a ghost. How can he be here? He's in Down-bourne. Fifty miles south. He has no place being here. He does not fit. His presence jars.

Slowly, though, I accept that it's really him. No ghost. No illusion. No doppelgänger. Fen. Here. Looking a little dusty, a little grubby. His hair needs cutting. He could do with a shave. But Fen. Same old Fen. Stalwart, dependable Fen. Essentially unchanged since I last saw him. As though, as soon as he walked out of our house, he was snatched up by some magical whirlwind, whisked across space and time, and deposited here only slightly the worse for wear. From doorstep to doorstep in a twinkling.

What can I say to him? What does he expect from me?

I don't know.

But then I become aware of Craig standing behind me, and all of a sudden it's as if there are two of me inside me, two Moiras, the Moira I was and the Moira I am, and neither seems real. Each is a part I've played, a costume I've worn. One lived with the man in front of me in a small country town and fell into despair and thought she would never come out. The other lives with the man behind me in this cordoned-off pocket of a South London housing estate and has just pulled off one of the most courageous feats she has ever attempted. In the midst of her triumph, the partner from her old life appears. Past gatecrashes present. Doors burst. Clocks spin out of true. The world warps.

And then comes guilt.

Beside Fen, Trevor shuffled his feet. Of all the possible outcomes of the husband-and-wife reunion that he and Larry had anticipated, dumbstruck staring was, quite clearly, not one. In a way Fen was glad to disappoint, but he himself, of course, had also been hoping for something a little more positive, a little less underwhelming, than this. He groped for words to say to end the deadlock.

'I broke my leg,' was what he came up with. To him it had been a crucial moment, the point at which his journey had gone from straightforward to wayward. But stated baldly, out of context, it seemed unimpressive. Banal.

'Oh dear.' Somehow Moira managed to sound both intrigued and indifferent, as if one part of her brain was registering the fact that he had suffered a serious injury and supplying the correct sympathetic response while another part was concentrating on a different matter altogether.

'It's what kept me.'

'I see.'

'I did set out the day after you were kidnapped. Well, the day after the day after.'

'Ah.'

'But what with one thing and another . . . You wouldn't believe some of the stuff that's happened to me. Not extraordinary, but still . . . Stuff.'

How eloquent he was being. He felt like one of his own pupils, fumbling out excuses for tardiness.

'There was this stately home . . .'

He thought a character sketch of Beam might bring a smile to her face, but then remembered that it was at Fairfield that he had abandoned his quest to find her. *Temporarily* abandoned, as it turned out, but the decision had been made in the full and firm belief that it was a permanent one. It was at Fairfield, too, that he had fallen for Jessica, and even though in the end nothing had come of the mutual attraction between her and him, nevertheless he had been prepared to start up a relationship with another woman. Were it not for Beam's death, doubtless he would still be at the Hall right now (perhaps living in adulterous bliss with Jessica, perhaps not, depending on whether his desire for her remained strong enough to blind him to her personality flaws). He would never have embarked at all on his final push to London.

It wasn't that he had come close to giving up on Moira. He *had* given up on her.

Suddenly, he could no longer look her in the eye.

He starts gibbering about breaking a leg, my being kidnapped, things that have happened to him, and I'm sure I'm replying to what he says but all I can think about is that I feel like someone who's been caught red-handed. I tell myself not to turn round. It's what I want to do, more than anything. I force myself to focus on Fen and continue to look as if I'm paying attention. Don't turn round. He mentions something about a stately home. A stately home? Then he goes quiet. His gaze flicks around. Don't turn, I tell myself.

Because I've realised at last, in these past few moments, a truth I've been hiding from myself. Not denying, just not acknowledging.

Don't turn.

Because if I do turn and look at Craig, I will know for sure.

And so, I fear, will Fen.

'Your husband,' said the massive Bulldog, who it seemed sensible to assume was none other than King Cunt.

Moira, not taking her eyes off Fen, nodded.

King Cunt turned to Trevor. 'Well done. Thanks. Nice one.'

The sarcasm would have amused Trevor, were it not for the steely glare that went with it. All at once, he was not quite as cocky as he had been. His shoulders rounded. If he had been a dog, his tail would have curled under his balls to protect them.

King Cunt continued to glare at him until the point was well and truly made. Then he looked back at Moira.

'You never said you were married.'

'You never asked,' Moira replied, thinly.

'You don't have a wedding ring.'

'Perhaps I wouldn't wear one in a place like this. Perhaps one of your men stole it off me.'

'I assumed . . .'

'But you never asked. Would it have made a difference? Does it?'

King Cunt frowned. 'I don't know.'

Now she turned to him. She had been waiting, Fen understood, till she was sure she had the moral high ground. That was like her. That was Moira all over.

He thinks it isn't obvious. Hard man. So hard, nothing soft ever shows.

But the eyes. The eyes are always the giveaway.

His are hurt. As though, somehow, I've deceived him.

I never deceived him.

His discomfort, though, tells me all I need to know.

And my indignation tells him all *he* needs to know.

Moments pass in which nothing is said and nothing has to be.

I look at him and see the image of me, reflected twice in his corneas. Or the image of someone who closely resembles me.

Then the hurt melts from his eyes, and in its place there's a sudden, certain fire.

And in that instant, the reflection shifts, flickers, changes, and now *is* me. Definitely, undeniably me. The other person, the lookalike, is gone.

Behind me, I hear a click in Fen's throat, a stifled gasp.

Then, from far off, comes a shout.

A dozen disparate thoughts crashed into Fen's brain, all jostling for attention, like a mob of irate shareholders storming the bankruptcy hearings, demanding to know why their investments are now worthless, why the bubble has burst. He was unable to give one precedence over another. All was tumult. All was incoherence.

Moira . . .

King Cunt . . .

He had a vague conception of the enormity of the joke that fate had played on him. He could perceive the folly of his journey, how monstrously misbegotten an undertaking it had been, perhaps from the very outset.

But to frame these impressions into words? To give voice to his outrage, his sense of betrayal, his mortification?

Beyond him. His throat was stopped. Nothing would emerge.

He did not hear the shout that came from the direction of the gate. All he knew was that King Cunt and Trevor were all of a sudden talking to each other in urgent tones. He grasped that it was something to do with the fighting, the 'war' he had inadvertently strayed into earlier that morning.

It didn't seem important. Nothing seemed important.

'The approach road,' says Trevor, wide-eyed, disbelieving. 'Frantiks on the approach road.'

'I heard,' says Craig. 'Who's on lookout?'

'Me and Larry at the gate. Dave and Carl, I think, at the back.'

'That's it?'

'Everyone else went with Neville to Brockley.'

'All right. Go get Dave and Carl, then meet me at the gate. Hurry!'

Off Trevor runs. No hesitation, no pause to question who it is who's giving him his orders, not a trace of the insolence he was so full of a moment ago.

'Moira.'

'Yes.'

'You and Zoë – indoors. Take hubby here with you.'

He doesn't wait for an answer, just spins round and sets off toward the gate at a sprint.

I turn to Fen. He looks crushed, dazed, a million miles away. We ought to talk about what's happened, but is there actually anything to talk about? Besides, now is not the time.

I say his name. Twice. Three times.

'Come on, Fen. Best do as we're told.'

I reach for his arm. He snatches it back, as though my hand is a snake's head, my fingers fangs. He scans my face, and I get the impression that for the first time in ages he's seeing me, not as he thinks I am, but as I am.

Though it couldn't have come at a worse moment, it is, all the same, a breakthrough. For so long he's been content with the idea of me, denying the unpalatable reality. And it's obvious that that's what he has pursued to London: the idea of me. Me as I used to be. Me as he hoped I could be again. He can't accept that some changes are permanent. For all those months he was holding out, waiting for me to recover, just as we're all waiting for England to recover. Our private country of two, our broken little kingdom, was, he was sure, going to rise again.

382

He was wrong, and now he knows it, and I'm sorry he had to find out this way. I'm sorry for him. But that's all. That's all I feel for him. Pity.

'Come *on*, Fen.'

'Come *on*, Fen.'

No point. Indoors? With her? Why?

He didn't want to spend even another minute in her company.

The world whirled around him, as if it, not he, was doing the about-turn. The world began to travel, flowing in reverse on either side of him, hauling him back along the route he had taken from the gate to the house. It was like being on one of those pedestrian conveyor belts in airports, motion without volition. He retraced his steps across the compound, scarcely aware that he himself was supplying the impetus, his legs fulfilling their nature-intended role.

In no time at all, or so it seemed, he was nearing the gate. From the other side of it he could hear the noise-creature that had hunted him after he left the pub. The shouting. The clamouring. The howls and yells.

He wasn't frightened. He was too numbed, too shrivelled inside, to be frightened.

Someone was opening the gate. The big man. Moira's new lover. King Cunt. Trevor's lookout partner, Larry, was with him.

Good, thought Fen. Convenient. The gate being opened. Now all I have to do is walk through.

And that was all he wanted to do. To walk through, walk out of the compound, walk away, leave. There was nothing for him here. And he was well practised at the art of leaving places. Fairfield. Netherholm. The *Jagannatha*. He was a tried-and-tested leaver. Master of the timely departure.

'Fen! Don't!'

Moira's voice – she had followed him? – but there was his exit a few yards away, a widening and welcoming gap between gate and wall, and the street visible through it.

'Craig! Stop him!'

King Cunt, also on the point of leaving the compound, paused. Scowled at Fen, as you would at any hopeless nuisance. Seemed all set on ignoring Moira's plea and letting him pass. Changed his mind at the last moment.

'Fucking hell,' King Cunt sighed, and swung his fist.

Thereafter all Fen could see was sky. The cloud cover, riven by low-altitude winds, was beginning to break up. Sunshine was piercing through. It was one of the most awe-inspiring sights he had ever beheld. The slow, soft tearing apart, the glowing-edged holes created, the white fibrous wracks that bridged the fissures, the glimpses of stratospheric blue – a mighty work. He knew that he was in pain. That was how he had come to be lying on the ground, gazing up. His skull rang dully. A bruise was tightening the side of his jaw, just below the ear. There was all sorts of commotion nearby, he knew that too. But above it all, literally above it all, the clouds were parting and it was his privilege to be in a position to watch the whole sublime process unfold, and so he did watch, transfixed, transported, as the nebulous awning over London gradually and inexorably disintegrated, exposing the city once more to the gaze of God.

At first it's hard to make out what's going on. Everything's maul and mêlée out there. Swift, darting attacks, a lot of shirt-grabbing and savage punching, taunts, battle cries, yelps of pain, the flail of weapons, men running. It appears it's not just Frantiks on the approach road, it's Bulldogs too. And then the penny drops: the Bulldogs are losing. The Frantiks have driven them back. It's a rout.

I can't believe it. I don't want to believe it. But the couple of dozen Bulldogs I can see are quite plainly in retreat. They're still fighting, but the Frantiks outnumber them and the battle is moving inexorably in the direction of the gate. The Bulldogs keep giving ground, perhaps because they're aware that they're close to the compound. Inside its walls there will, they hope, be refuge and respite. The Frantiks press home the advantage.

I see Mushroom. He flings himself at a Frantik twice his size. With a sweep of his arm the Frantik repels him. Mushroom scrambles to his feet. The Frantik takes him by the collar, thumps him twice, then tosses him aside like a sack of rubbish. Mushroom picks himself up and, undeterred, staggers once again towards the man.

I see Gary, the Bulldog that Zoë bit. I recognise him only by the wad of dressing on his cheek. One of his eyes is swollen to the size and colour of a plum. His nose is bent out of true and gushing blood. He's limping along, being harried by a pair of Frantiks. He lashes out at them, but for every one of his blows that usefully connects, several of theirs strike home.

I see Neville, bloodied, bug-eyed, yelling. He's ordering the Bulldogs to stand firm, not give way, keep at them. But even as he yells this, he's getting nearer the gate himself. Repeatedly he takes one step towards the advancing Frantiks then two towards the compound.

On they come, the implacable Frantiks, the battered, bedraggled Bulldogs.

Craig, at the gate, hasn't moved. It's almost as if the scene before him is too much for him to take in. Larry likewise.

Then Trevor comes charging past me, with another two Bulldogs – Dave and Carl, it must be – in tow. The three of them pull up alongside Craig, and Craig gives them the once-over, then gestures grimly at the fighting.

'We can win this,' he says.

The three new arrivals, Larry also, nod. They believe him. It's as simple as that. They hear Craig utter four little words, and such is the conviction in his voice that all their misgivings are dispelled. They stiffen. Their hands bunch into fists. Their jaws jut. Craig has told them they can win. Any doubts they may have had about that fact, and about him, are washed clean away. They don't even think to question him.

As if I didn't know already, now it's well and truly confirmed.

King Cunt is back.

Craig launches himself out from the gateway, the other four following close behind. Up the road they go, into the midst of the conflict, to collide head-on with the oncoming Frantiks. I go over to where Fen is lying and crouch down beside him. Sprawled on his back, concussed, he gazes up at the sky. His face is strangely, unblinkingly serene. Knocking him cold is not exactly what I had in mind when I told Craig to stop him, but then under the circumstances it's the only thing Craig could have done, and probably the best thing. I reach down and stroke his hair, for the comfort of human contact, the reassurance, as I watch the battle continue to unfurl.

For a while it seems as though Craig's involvement isn't going to make any difference. The Bulldogs are still outnumbered, still on the defensive. They're in worse shape, too, than the Frantiks, many more of them sporting injuries (although it does cross my mind that blood and bruises don't show up as obviously on dark skin). Skirmishes are taking place close to the gate now, just a few feet away from where I am. The Frantiks are almost inside the compound, and I realise that the moment one of them sets foot across the entrance, that will be it. A vital psychological line will have been crossed. It occurs to me to shut the gate, but I reject the idea. And leave the Bulldogs trapped, with nowhere to fall back to? It also occurs to me to take refuge somewhere indoors, just as Craig advised. But I can't leave Fen here, and I can't carry him with me. Nor can I abandon Craig.

No, all I can do is wait here and watch. And hope.

The light brightens and keeps brightening, shafts of sunshine stabbing down onto the battle scene, haloing the heads of the men fighting. I can't make out where Craig is, then I can. I lose him amid the chaos and find him again. Now he's slamming a Frantik's head against a lamp-post. Now he's delivering a volley of punches to an opponent's ribs. Now Frantiks are swarming over him, and they bring him down through sheer weight of numbers, but then, with a great grimacing grunt of fury, he rises up and throws them off one by one.

And around him the Bulldogs are fighting hard. Not just the four who were on lookout and have come fresh to the fray. All of them. Fighting harder. Fighting back. They have seen Craig in the thick of things. They have seen their King knocking down, swatting aside, pulverising the foe. They take heart from his example. Inspired, they turn on the Frantiks with renewed ferocity.

The chant starts with Craig:

British Bulldogs!
We're tough, we're brave, we're class . . .

Almost straight away, every other Bulldog is singing it. It ripples rapidly outwards from Craig, a chorus of defiance and aggression, gaining volume as it spreads:

British Bulldogs!
We're tough, we're brave, we're class . . .

Louder and louder it gets, until the Bulldogs are all but howling the words.

And that's when the Frantiks know. They look around at one another in consternation. That's when they know that everything has changed, the conflict isn't going their way any more. The chant is a force, a weapon. It gives the Bulldogs strength, unity, identity. Roaring the same seven words over and over at the top of their lungs, they are fearless. Imperious. Impervious to pain.

The Frantiks have no adequate response. They struggle on, but slowly, ineluctably, remorselessly, the tide of battle turns. With King Cunt in the vanguard dishing out punishment left, right and centre, the Bulldogs start pressing the Frantiks back, away from the compound. Stragglers are given short shrift: floored, hammered into submission, bludgeoned senseless, or hurled forwards to join their retreating comrades.

I stop stroking Fen's hair and stand up, barely able to contain my elation. The Frantiks are now at the far end of the approach road. They start to scatter and run.

And then the sky falls to earth, with a sound like a million doors slamming shut.

The ground bucked. Fen felt himself being tossed up and caught like a palmful of loose change. Once, twice, three times, and by the third time he was aware of detonations and screaming. A white needle streaked overhead, there and gone in a split second, and then came a flash, an instantaneous bloom of smoke and fire, a *boom*, another mini-earthquake. Débris came scattering down like sown seed.

Fen rolled his head to the side. On the approach road, men were dancing. They moved jerkily, without rhythm, dancing to no tune, no waltz or song, just a series of slow, huge thunderclap drumbeats that arrived at irregular intervals, anything from five to fifteen seconds apart. Now another white needle, now another thumping explosion, and the men staggered in response, sidestepped, twisted into balletic postures, and some clutched each other in a masculine *pas de deux* and some sagged to the ground like dying swans. Black man pirouetted with white man. Pale shaven scalp and dark blue bandanna capered side by side. And the drumbeats continued, slugging, repetitive, deafening, until Fen's ears were overloaded and all he could hear was a continuous tintinnabulation that fluctuated briefly with the pressure wave from each successive impact, dull muddy thud after dull muddy thud amid a general rumbling. Beside him Moira was either screaming or laughing, he couldn't tell which, and then a nearby section of the compound wall disintegrated into its component parts – an office chair, a TV set, a microwave oven, a door, a night-storage radiator, a car tyre, a bathtub, a whole slew of domestic jetsam hurled in all directions, discarded once again, the Bulldogs' hard work undone in the blink of an eye. Then a house on the approach road emptied itself out, voiding dust and glass fragments and shreds of curtain through its windows, then slumping in on itself, depleted. A man on the road did likewise, sinking to his knees, blood blurting from his mouth, nose and ears, his belly burst like a pierced egg sac, his guts unspooling.

Fen was beyond horror. Beyond fear, too. It didn't once cross his mind that one of the missiles – that was what the white needles were, missiles – might have the spot where he was lying as its final destination. At some primal, animal level he understood that death was present, death was imminent, but in the dazed upper levels of consciousness his brain was working with a dreamlike detachment, calmly assessing and assimilating. He was able to marvel at the wondrous strangeness of it all. The changes that destruction wrought. The ungainly dancing of the men on the road. The way his hearing had capitulated to the stunning percussive immensity of the missile hits. Above all how utterly alike everyone here had become – himself, Moira, King Cunt, the British Bulldogs, the Bulldogs' opponents, the people of Lewisham, all of them equally blameless in the face of this awesome, relentless assault from above, their sins and foibles as nothing compared with the grotesque overkill of the International Community, which had granted itself the right to bomb where and when it wished and to decide who deserved to live and who to die. Down here, there were no guilty parties. Down here, in the teeth of this minor apocalypse, there were only innocents.

At what point the bombardment ceased, Fen had no idea. It resounded in his eardrums long after the last missile landed. He realised things were not as they had been only when Moira was suddenly no longer next to him. She was off along the approach road, walking delicately, precariously, her arms outstretched for balance, as though the ground underfoot were made of chunks of chopped rubber. Smoke poured around her, thinning, thickening, thinning again. She skirted bodies, heaps of rubble, bodies half buried in heaps of rubble, bodies that looked like heaps of rubble. She was searching for something. Someone. Fen thought he knew who. Finally she found him, or so he gathered. She halted halfway along the road and, silhouetted by the smoke, became a statue of grief, head lowered, shoulders sunk. It was impossible to tell for sure, but he thought that she was weeping. If so, he sympathised. He knew what it was like to lose love. And he knew, too, that in feeling sorry for her he was, in effect, accepting that he did not hate her for falling in love with another man. He couldn't for the life of him understand what she had seen in King Cunt. *His* Moira would have had nothing but contempt for someone who looked like that, dressed that way, thought a name like King Cunt was impressive and clever. But then she was not *his* Moira any more. It was that simple. She was somebody else now, and it didn't matter why. Why should it matter why, when everyone was blameless, when there were no guilty parties, when there were only innocents?

Slowly, totteringly, Fen got to his feet. On the approach road other survivors were doing the same, rising like ghosts from among the damaged and the dead. Their faces were blank with shock, but in their eyes there was the gradually dawning awareness: *I'm alive.* No triumph in the realisation, just a sweet intake of reprieve. The worst had happened. The worst was over. Ignoring the distinction between friend and foe, the uninjured began tending to the injured. Helping hands were extended. Fen looked for Moira again, but the smoke where she was standing was denser than ever. She was hidden from him. He could not see her at all. She was gone. And he was surprised how little difference this made to him. Surprised, and relieved, and – this was the true revelation, this was what really counted – pleased.

7. DOWNBOURNE

He only narrowly avoided treading on the dead cat.

It lay amid the waste ground's thickets of weed, hind legs protruding onto the pathway. A slender little tabby, flat on its side, eyes half-shut, as though it were merely napping. Not long lifeless, and no marks of violence on its body. Dead of natural causes, then. For what *that* diagnosis was worth. Causes of death, for an animal living wild, were seldom anything other than natural.

Gently Fen bent and touched it, running his fingers across its cold fur, feeling the solid stillness of the flesh beneath. He uttered a few words, an informal requiem, expressing a wish that the cat had had a relatively contented life, then drew his hand away. Immediately, as if on cue, a fly homed in. It alighted at the corner of the cat's mouth and began exploring, prospecting across the pink rim of exposed gum. There would be more flies soon, and in a day or so the cat's body would be writhing with maggots. Life in death. It was how things were supposed be, but Fen pitied the corpse its coming defilement. He stood up, closing his eyes, then turned, opened his eyes, and resumed walking, with the cat preserved in his memory just as it was, deceased but undecayed.

Winter was coming.

Summer was gone, its blaze of heat barely remembered except occasionally, on days like today, when the sun was out and a south wind blew, and the air held an echo of aestival warmth. On days like today, you were reminded that the best of the year was not quite over and done with. But yes, all the same, irrefutably, winter was coming. The ember months had begun, and all over Down-bourne faces had taken on that vaguely resigned look, that shadow of weary apprehension. Winter was a miserable season. It was long, it was rainy and grey, it was, perhaps most heinously, boring. You slept a lot in winter. That was about the best that could be said for it. Short days and little to do to fill them: there wasn't much to get out of bed for. Keep the wood fire in the grate burning, keep the kerosene reservoirs in your lanterns topped up . . . And people died in winter. Old people, and the not-so-old as well.

But today, specifically today, there was no reason to think about any of that. Or rather, there was a reason to avoid thinking about any of that for a while.

Fen could hear the voices coming from the river's edge – an excited hubbub, now and then a shout, a laugh, a cheer, the odd *ooh* and *ahh*. Donald Bailey had brought him the news. 'Go and see for yourself, Fen,' he had said. 'It's not much but it's *something*.' And so Fen was going to see for himself, and he was not alone. Word had spread swiftly through town. He emerged from the waste ground to find at least a hundred people gathered on the riverbank near the footbridge, and dozens more converging on the spot. One man was the focal point of the crowd, and he was holding an object aloft for all to examine. It was not a large object. People at the periphery of the crowd had to crane their necks and squint in order to get a glimpse of it. But for all its lack of size, it generated an immense amount of amazement and joy.

Fen held back. Something stayed him, a brief flash of thought.

If only Moira were here.

He didn't often miss her, and when he did it was usually at the most unexpected of moments and for the most unlikely of reasons. He could be performing some quite mundane task – digging in the garden, tidying up at the school, quietly reading a book – and all at once she would stray into his thoughts. Any tangential association could summon her, any chance alignment of situation and memory, or, as now, she could appear in his mind simply because he would have liked her to be where he was, to see what he was seeing.

And then, invariably, he would start to wonder how she was keeping, what she was up to, how her new life was panning out . . .

I don't often think about him. Days go by and he'll not have entered my mind even once. And then, for no reason at all, I'll find myself saying to myself, *I wonder how he's getting on down there in Downbourne.*

You don't spend a dozen years of your life with someone and then just forget about them in an instant, do you? And you can't help but continue to remember fondly someone who did what Fen did, coming after me like that, an act both so misguided and so heroic that I'm still not sure whether to laugh about it or cry.

There again, he's in the past, he's a part of my life that's gone, and I'm determinedly living in the present now. There's plenty to keep me occupied here in the present. (And, as it happens, there's the future to bear in mind as well now.) So I'm glad that I remember Fen every so often, and glad, also, that I don't remember him *too* often.

The rebuilding work in the compound and on the approach road is almost finished. We've been able to repair more of the damage than I would have thought possible. There's nothing we can do about the houses the bombs totally flattened, of course. We don't have the equipment or the raw materials. But where we can we've mended broken windows, we've retiled caved-in roofs, we've resurrected collapsed ceilings, we've shored up sagging walls, often using bits and pieces salvaged from rubble nearby, so that the destroyed houses have played their part in restoring the damaged. And the boys, under my foremanship, have worked hard and worked well. A great number of them used to be in the construction trade before the Unlucky Gamble. Putting their old skills to use like this has made them unusually happy. Irrepressibly happy at times, but I don't really mind too much the wolf-whistling and the single entendres. Boys will be boys.

The rebuilding work outside the compound – the job of re-establishing trust and faith among the people of Lewisham – remains very much an ongoing process. It's going to take time. But Craig is out in the borough almost every day, trying his hardest, doing all he can, playing the diplomat, mending fences while I, here in the compound, mend walls.

He tires easily, but that's only to be expected. For a man who was blown out of his shoes by the blast from an International Community missile, he's bearing up remarkably well, all things considered. From time to time he complains about his ribs hurting, but that doesn't get him much sympathy from me. It's his own fault. He refused to stay in bed and allow them time to mend like I told him he should. He was the worst kind of invalid, up and about all the time, finding any excuse not to rest. He wouldn't listen to my advice, so if his bones haven't knitted properly, he has no one but himself to blame.

It was his burns that really worried me, but fortunately they've healed pretty well. The scarring's permanent, but I'm used to it and in certain lights it doesn't even show. A few patches of his skin are a little raised, a little shinier and smoother than the rest – that's all. It's unsightly but it's not gruesome.

Others weren't as lucky as him.

Lauren, for one. Neville's house took a direct hit. They found some of her later. Not much.

Neville himself.

I remember coming across his body. The immediate aftermath of the International Community attack is all a bit hazy for me, but I remember wandering along the approach road, stepping around Bulldogs, around Frantiks, some alive, some not, while smoke billowed up from the burning buildings on either side. I remember I was looking for Craig, although I don't know quite why because I was convinced he was dead, that the missile impacts had obliterated him. But I wandered anyway, through a muffled, ringing world, and everything was in black and white. That's my visual recollection of those minutes, everything for some reason in monochrome, as though, in shock, my eyesight had reverted to a more primitive mode of seeing. And I remember coming across Neville's body and thinking, *oh, there's Neville*, without surprise, as if it was just a matter of course that I should find him there in the roadway, curled in a foetal clench, with a huge gaping hole in his torso. His white skin, his grey innards, his black, black blood. His hopeless, staring eyes.

I want to feel that he got no more than he deserved. I want to feel that nemesis visited him in the form of a shard of shrapnel, that he received due comeuppance for all he did. And sometimes I do think that, although I remember that at the time I felt little about him one way or another. I felt little about any of the dead and the wounded and the unharmed around me. They were just things. Not people any more. Just objects that looked like they might once have been people, some of them moving, some lying still.

Then Craig came tottering towards me through the smoke pall, shoeless, one arm clamped around his chest, charred shreds of clothing and skin hanging off him, a great shambling sock-footed mess of a man. I spoke to him but he couldn't hear me properly; I couldn't even hear myself properly. I tried to find out from him how badly he was hurt, using signs and signals. He didn't understand. Then he caught sight of Neville, and for a long while he just stood there, swaying slightly, gazing down at his friend and betrayer. I couldn't make out what was going on in his face. Contempt and pity can often appear the same. Then, stiffly, keeping his upper body as rigid as he could, he knelt, and I thought he might be about to pray for Neville's soul – no reason why he should, no reason why he shouldn't – but instead he reached into Neville's mouth, and took hold of his Gold Tooth, and began twisting and tugging. The effort caused him agony, I could see, but he persevered. The muscles in his arm bunched and coiled. Still he pulled. He may well have screamed. Abruptly the tooth came free. He held it up between thumb and forefinger, studying it. Then he clasped it in his fist and, with a great deal of wincing and grimacing, got to his feet. And then together, with me supporting much of his weight, we made our way towards the compound entrance.

Days later, I asked him why. What did he want with the tooth?

His reply was simple. 'Just taking back what's mine, Moira.'

And he continues to take back what's his, reclaiming the borough, resecuring his territory and his right to run it. Peace has been brokered with the Frantik Posse. They've been no less devastated by the missile attack than we Bulldogs have. We're all a little shell shocked still. It's been a time for taking stock, for reassessment, for rapprochement.

Maybe the International Community has done us a good turn, who knows?

The thing about surviving something like that, having a close encounter with death, being offered a brief glimpse into hell – it gives you a renewed love of life. You want to hold on to it all. You don't want a single minute to slip by unused, uncherished. You live in the moment. You live *for* the moment.

Old clichés, but my God, I understand now how true they are.

So I exist in the present. I don't dwell on the past, not any more. And if I think of the future, it's only because nowadays I have to. I have no choice in the matter.

Because the last three mornings in a row, I've woken up feeling distinctly and familiarly unwell. I haven't thrown up, but only just. Some dry-heaving over the toilet bowl, the nausea slowly abating. I don't think Craig's heard. I don't think he's noticed anything yet.

But I'm going to have to tell him soon.

And it's his child, and so, like him, it'll be strong.

It will be born.

It will survive.

. . . and his thoughts would turn to the last time he saw her, as the van pulled out of the Bulldog compound, with him and Zoë squashed hip to hip in the passenger seat and that little fellow, Mushroom, driving. The van was the foremost in a convoy of three. Each had a cargo of Downbourne women, who sat wan and tired and silent but with relief evident in their faces nonetheless. There would be much for them to deal with when they got home, many difficult weeks and months ahead. But for now, simple happiness at being free. He remembered the van reaching the compound gate, and Moira being there to watch it on its way. Not a wave from her as the van passed. His eyes met hers, and had she raised her hand he would have reciprocated, but she did not. She stood unmoving and unmoved, and there was nothing in her gaze but solemn acknowledgement. This parting was necessary and hence should not be memorialised or sentimentalised. Here was where she belonged and where Fen did not. The van rolled on, and he watched her reflection recede in the wing-mirror, and he knew – and somehow he had always known – that this was how it would turn out. How it *had to* turn out. All that was taking place now was a confirmation, an affirmation. The mental distance which had manifested between them needed to be reinforced by a geographical distance. It was right and fitting. It was the only way.

It was the only way, and that was why he had subsequently done what he had done at the M25 checkpoint, when the guard cavilled over the bribe Mushroom presented to him.

'Just this?' the guard said, peering at the packets of disposable razors, before gesturing at the three vans. 'For all you lot?' He shook his head and sucked on his teeth. 'I don't know.'

'I forgot,' Fen said, reaching across in front of Mushroom. 'There's this as well.'

The guard took the item Fen was proffering him. He held it up, squinted at it, bit it with the side of his mouth, twirled it around, scrutinised it from every angle, and finally said, 'Yeah, all right,' and slipped it into a pocket. 'On your way then.'

'Was that what I think it was?' Mushroom said as they drew away from the checkpoint.

Fen nodded.

'Yours?'

'Moira's.'

'Oh,' said Mushroom. Then, 'Yeah.'

It was no great loss. The wedding band had served one purpose, years ago; now it had served another. You might even say that its existence had come full circle (and where better for that to happen than on an orbital motorway?). Fen surrendered it without regret, with just a feeling of satisfying aptness. All was concluded and done. Life could begin afresh.

'Mayor?'

Someone was talking to him. Fen snapped to, realising he had been lost in reverie.

'Hello there, Alan.'

Alan Greeley grinned at him, not a little quizzically. Holly-Anne was balanced on his shoulders, and Andrea was standing a short way off, cradling baby Nathan, who, with his stocky body and cuboid head, was a little homunculus replica of his father.

'Away with the fairies, eh?'

Fen gave a sheepish smile. 'Afraid so.'

'*Real* fairies?' asked Holly-Anne.

'Well, some of them were,' Fen said.

She looked behind him, on the off chance that he was telling the truth and some of the little elven folk were still in view, hovering nearby. Seeing none, she frowned, then giggled. 'You're silly.'

Fen stuck his tongue out. 'Exceptionally.'

'Have you seen it yet?' Greeley enquired. 'Reg's little miracle?'

'Not yet. You?'

'Not yet. There's so many people now, I'm not sure how we're going to get a decent look.'

'Well, perhaps I can help you there,' Fen said. 'Stick close.'

He set off towards the crowd, making sure the Greeleys were following. It was nice that he could be confident that the crowd would part for him if requested. He didn't expect it, any more than he expected to be addressed the way Greeley had addressed him, as mayor. If people wished to extend him that courtesy, then fine, but he didn't automatically think it his due. They could call him mayor if they liked or Fen if they liked. They could treat him with deference or as an equal. That was their prerogative. They, after all, had elected him.

But the crowd did part. He was permitted through, and the Greeley family also, to the epicentre of the attention.

A hush fell as he and Reginald Bailey greeted each other. Reginald was looking about as pleased as it was possible for a human being to look. With the kind of pride that comes only from utter vindication, he held out his prize for Fen to inspect.

Fen inspected.

Fen nodded.

Fen pronounced it a marvellous thing indeed.

'Perch,' Reginald said, in case Fen had not been able to identify the species (he hadn't).

Fen admired the green stripes, the bright red fins.

'Only a little 'un,' Reginald added. 'But still . . .'

But still, it was a fish. Not much bigger than the palm of a man's hand, but it was life from a river that was believed to contain none. Dead now, of course, thanks to Reginald plucking it from its native environment – but where there was one fish, there had to be others. All of a sudden the river was no longer a flow of dilute poison. All of a sudden, in its slow brown turbidity, all manner of possibility lurked.

'Tonight,' Fen said, raising his voice so that everyone could hear, 'we should have a celebration of some sort, I feel. To mark the occasion.'

There was no disagreement from the assembled Downbournians, and consequently that evening, the last truly clement evening of that year, an impromptu festival took place on the riverbank. Tables and chairs were set out. Cooking fires were lit. Food was roasted, alcohol imbibed.

And because it was a special occasion, Fen turned up dressed in what he would come to think of, from there on after, as his ceremonial garb.

It was the first time he had worn it, and he was expecting strange looks as he passed among the revellers, but received none. People simply glanced at him and smiled, as if it came as no surprise to them to see him in this guise. There was the odd double-take, but only because a few individuals didn't immediately recognise who it was they were looking at, all got up in those monochrome clothes (most of which Fen had had to borrow), skin and hair stained with vegetable dye (which, to his surprise, reeked vilely). For a brief, perturbing moment, before the truth dawned, they thought that Michael Hollingbury was among them again.

It wasn't Michael Hollingbury, of course. It was only their mayor, the head of the town council, a man lost and found, who had left without fuss and returned in triumph, bringing back with him wives and mothers and daughters and sisters whom the townsfolk had given up for dead. It was only Fen Morris, decked out in the manner befitting the incarnate spirit of Downbourne, top to toe in a myriad shades of green.

Acknowledgements

I'd like to thank Simon Spanton for providing me with research material and for performing yet another bang-up editing job; Jan Bailey for occupational therapy advice; Piers R. Connor at trainweb.org for information relating to railways (I have taken huge liberties with what is technically feasible, for which I beg his indulgence and that of all rail enthusiasts); Eric Brown for his help with the Indian stuff; Guy Stredwick for the M25 traffic jam; Michael Rowley for his continued championing of my work; Ariel for his sterling efforts with the website and for his music recommendations; Pete Crowther for the usual bouncy banter and badinage; Beak for our Filth Sessions; David Mathew and Anne Gay for asking intelligent questions; Andy Cox at *The Third Alternative* for his support and eclecticism; Oisin Murphy-Lawless for being 'deadly'; and Nicola Sinclair for being professionally lippy.

During the writing of *Untied Kingdom*, three people in particular helped keep me inspired and (mostly) sane:

Ian Miller – with pearls of Zen wisdom such as 'Bend like the young bamboo and hope there's enough spring left for a good fart';

Antony Harwood – unstinting in his encouragement right from the very start;

and Lou.

Love on ya!

For further biographical and bibliographical information about the author, please 'hit', 'log onto', 'visit', or otherwise gain access to:
www.jameslovegrove.com